Somewhere Beyond the Sea

Miranda Dickinson has always had a head full of stories. From an early age she dreamed of writing a book that would make the heady heights of Kingswinford Library and today she is a bestselling author. She began to write in earnest when a friend gave her The World's Slowest PC, and has subsequently written the bestselling novels *Fairytale of New York*, *Welcome to My World*, *It Started With a Kiss*, *When I Fall in Love*, *Take a Look at Me Now*, *I'll Take New York*, *A Parcel for Anna Browne* and *Searching for a Silver Lining*. Miranda lives with her husband Bob and daughter Flo in Dudley.

@wurdsmyth

MirandaDickinsonAuthor

www.miranda-dickinson.com

Also by Miranda Dickinson

Somewhere Beyond the Sea

Miranda Dickinson

PAN BOOKS

First published 2018 by Pan Books
an imprint of Pan Macmillan
20 New Wharf Road, London N1 9RR
Associated companies throughout the world
www.panmacmillan.com

ISBN 978-1-4472-7609-8

1 3 5 7 9 8 6 4 2

A CIP catalogue record for this book is available from the British Library.

Typeset in Sabon LT Std 11/15 pt by
Palimpsest Book Production Limited, Falkirk, Stirlingshire
Printed and bound by CPI Group (UK) Ltd, Croydon, CR0 4YY

For Mum
You're amazing and I love you
xxx

'I know nothing with any certainty, but the sight of the stars makes me dream.'

VINCENT VAN GOGH

Chapter One

Seren

It's still dark as I carefully pick my way down the sandy steps to the beach, the narrow beam from my torch the only guide for my feet. The rush of waves against rocks is deafening, and it's cold – the kind of cold that sneaks in between the layers of your clothing and seeps into your bones. My hands sting where they hold the torch and the small red tin bucket I've had ever since I was a kid. I should probably wear gloves this early in the year; the Cornish early spring wind is unforgiving against my skin. But I like the wildness, the rawness of it.

This is my special place and I adore it all year round.

Walking down to an empty beach before the sun is even up feels like the biggest adventure. And even though I make the journey almost every morning before work, I'm still thrilled by it. For a short time the beach belongs to me, before the surfers and dog-walkers and fellow beach-combers wake and venture down onto the clotted-cream sand. I am queen of all I survey – even if right now that

1

mostly consists of shadow and silhouette, with the faintest line of paler blue at the horizon breaking over the ink-black waves.

But I haven't just come here to admire the view. I'm hunting for magic.

There are three special beaches where the treasure I'm seeking can be found. Two of them are close to my home in St Ives, but this one – Gwithian Beach – lies at the opposite end of St Ives Bay. I can see it if I sit on the harbour wall, the tall tower of Godrevy Lighthouse marking its location at the end of the sweeping bay far in the distance. But the journey here – and the impossibly early start it requires – is absolutely worth it for what I find on this beach.

Seaglass.

Tiny pieces of multicoloured glass, worn smooth by waves and time, that are hidden among the shingle, seaweed and driftwood strewn across the sandy beaches. Ethereal, like snowy-white, palest pinks, turquoise and mint; or striking – startling cyan, dragon-green and brown – they are impossible to resist picking up. When my dad first showed me them, almost a lifetime ago, I thought mermaids had scattered treasure between the rocks for us to find. I still think it's spellbinding – and now I collect the pieces in my red tin bucket for the jewellery I make in my spare time. One day it will be my business, and I will conjure my own magic from the pieces of sea-treasure I've found on the beach. But my dream is on hold for now, so this is the best I can do.

I think I'm alone on Gwithian Beach. But my torch

2

beam catches something lying on the sand that challenges my assumption. At first I think I've found a particularly rich vein of seaglass, but as the light follows the line of glass pieces I see it's forming a shape.

Behind me, far out on the horizon, the first rays of sunlight begin to shine, and in the strengthening pink-gold light that slowly washes up the beach, I see the whole shape. It's a star – almost complete. Its fifth point is missing. I look up to scan the brightening beach, trying to see if the person who left this shape is still around. But Gwithian Beach is deserted.

It's beautiful. As I look closer I can see the care with which the starmaker has placed each tiny piece of seaglass. Why didn't they finish it? It seems strange to go to so much trouble and then leave it incomplete. Maybe they ran out of time here, or were disturbed. Or maybe . . . I can hardly believe I'm even thinking this, but what if they left it unfinished for someone else to take up the challenge?

What if they left it for me?

I look down into my bucket at the handfuls of glinting, sea-smoothed gems I've collected this morning and feel a smile break across my skin. It's too much of an invitation to ignore. I can't thank the maker of this gorgeous star, but maybe I can show my appreciation with my own treasure.

In the earliest light of the dawn, I kneel in the damp sand and carefully place my own line of seaglass pieces to make the final point . . .

Doing this takes almost all the time I'd allowed myself

to be here – my stolen hours before I have to return to the day and all the competing voices vying for my attention. It's emptied my bucket too, the finds I'd intended for my bracelets all nestled in the sand completing the star. But it's worth it. When I stand to admire my handiwork, my heart feels close to exploding. I don't even feel the bitter March cold any more. For a moment, here on the golden-light-kissed beach with the sparkling seaglass star, all is right with the world. Nothing can touch me and no fears darken my day. For the first time in weeks, I just breathe. And suddenly, I don't feel so alone – as though the person who left the star for me to discover is a friend I haven't met yet.

I take one last look at the star down on the beach as I walk back to my car, still amazed by the gift of finding it. And I smile all the way back to St Ives . . .

Chapter Two

Jack

If she ignores me one more time, I'm going to lose it.

Never underestimate the sheer bloody-mindedness of a seven-year-old on a school morning. Especially when she has a maths test and the beach is calling. 'Nessie Dixon, come on, please,' I say – *again*. I've lost count of the number of times I've repeated myself since I woke today.

My daughter continues her improvised interpretative dance piece around her small bedroom, pyjama top swinging around her neck like a superhero cape – as far as she's got in changing for school – and one trouser leg rolled up to the knee, which is the overnight fate of every pair of pyjama bottoms she's worn since the age of two. It would be endearing if I didn't have less than an hour to get her washed, dressed, fed and delivered to the small village school five miles away.

Mornings like these are the only time I wish Tash were here. My wife could do *that thing* with her voice where all games cease and order is restored. In the seven months since she died I've failed to master it. Sometimes it was just an '*Erm* . . .' in that tone. Remarkable. There are so many things I don't miss about Tash, mostly the yelling – but her '*erm*' ability is a gap I've yet to fill.

'Daaa-*deee*,' Nessie says, in that singsong way that makes me want to hug and yell at her simultaneously. 'It's your turn now.'

'No, ladybug, it's *your* turn to get ready for school.' I daren't look at my watch. I know it'll be bad news. 'Come on. Please?'

Nessie stops twirling and gives me a stare that could refreeze polar ice caps. 'You're no fun,' she states, hands on hips.

I'm inclined to agree.

On the way, Nessie chatters about the million-and-one things she has to do after school today. I half-expect to hear her mention 'taking over the world' as one of them.

'And can we go down to the beach again tonight? After tea?'

Like I could stop her if I even wanted to. 'Sure. *If* you eat all your tea.'

'I will. We need to finish the star.'

The star? For a moment the rush of the morning school run, plus the list of everything I have to do today, fogs my brain, and it takes me a while to work out what she means. Then I remember. Last night on the beach we collected a handful of seaglass. The storm in the early hours had raked a harvest of sea-worn treasure further up the beach than usual. Nessie and I enjoyed a happy half-hour of beachcombing, and then I suggested we make a shape in the sand with our haul. Behind the rocks, just up from the line of high tide. Nessie chose a star. So we set to work.

Unfortunately, our artistic ambition was hampered by our seaglass-gathering skills, so the star only had four of its five points. Nessie wanted to find more glass, but by then it was getting too dark to see, so I said we should leave it. Perhaps if I'd brought an extra jumper for her or insisted we wear coats we could've stayed longer. But it was freezing, and the last thing Ness needs is another cold. Not with her asthma.

I hated leading her away from our unfinished *magnum opus*. It's times like that I find hardest being a dad – when you have to be the grown-up and be sensible. I always feel a little like I'm betraying our true nature. Nessie understood, of course. But I still secretly hated it.

'It will still be there, won't it, Dad?'

'I don't see why not. There aren't many people on the beach this time of year.'

'I'm going to find the biggest bits and fill in the middle of the star, too.'

'We might not find as much as you think, Ness . . .'

'Er, we *will*. Because we are Super Mega Awesome Seaglass Finders.'

In that case, Nessie, we definitely will.

We make the school gates with three minutes to spare and I'm granted a swift air-kiss before she dashes off. Then, as she always does, Nessie stops in the middle of the playground, turns back and races into my arms for a huge hug.

'Secret sign,' she murmurs into my shoulder.

7

'Secret sign,' I reply, wanting to squeeze her forever.

Two and a half minutes to the bell. But I'll forgive her the thirty seconds we lost.

Chapter Three

Seren

It's quiet in the shop today. But then, most days it is.

I look around MacArthur's and feel the all-too-familiar sinking of my heart. So much of Dad is tied up in this place, and while I've repainted the walls and rearranged the furniture, it still feels like his fingerprints are everywhere. I expect him to walk in at any moment, frown and move a display table three inches to the right. Or dust something. Or grab my hand and perform an impromptu jig. Dad was a dreamer, and his tiny art and craft gallery in its tiny courtyard just off Fore Street was the business he'd always dreamed of.

But it was never meant to be *my* business. Nevertheless, here I am. It passed to Mum three months ago when Dad died, and she had no idea how to run it, so she asked me. The business is mine in every sense except the yearly rent, which Mum pays from Dad's now dwindling savings account, the tiny amount left in his business account long since used up. I'm determined to make the shop completely self-sufficient before we try to sell it on.

It's hard work. Long days that often stretch into long nights trying to make the accounts a little less horrific. Through it all, those tiny scraps of light-catching treasure I've discovered on my beachcombs each morning help me stay on the right side of terrified. Because after the shop stuff is done, that's the time my real passion can take over.

I take a small drawstring bag from the back pocket of my jeans and start laying out the seaglass pieces on the driftwood counter. Pale green, peridot, smoky grey and cobalt blue – a line of treasure that will soon be looped together with silver wire. It calms my mind, settles my soul.

Until the front door whips open like a gale has blown into the courtyard, the tiny brass bell above the door almost flying clean off its bracket.

'I brought you coffee. Large one, with an extra shot. You look like you need it.'

My best friend Aggie breezes into the shop like a strong southwesterly, making my only customer turn in surprise. She's on her break from the small coffee hut she owns just above Porthgwidden Beach, but she would appear to be in a hurry regardless of whether she was working or not. I love this blustery force of nature. When Agatha Keats arrives in your life, you *know* things are about to get interesting.

'Hey, you. How's business?'

'Brisk,' she grins, leaning against the counter and handing me a large takeaway cup of what I know is the best coffee in St Ives. 'But good. You?'

The only customer I've seen all morning has gone, the

10

brass bell still swinging over the door in his wake. 'Could be better.'

'It's a blip, Ser.'

'Long blip.'

'It'll pass. It's early in the season – not even Easter yet. Whole town's been quiet lately.'

'Except for your place.'

Aggie's silver charm bracelets jingle as she dismisses this. 'I serve legal addictive stimulants for a very reasonable price. People will forget me once their coffee's drunk. You provide art that lasts forever. You can't rush that.'

'I'd settle for the best coffee in town.'

'Which is why I brought you one.' She pats the white lid of the coffee cup. 'So it's not all bad, is it, bird?'

I have to smile. 'Maybe not.'

'No *maybe* about it. Drink up.' She looks down at the seaglass shapes. 'This your latest one?'

'Might be. Like it?'

She gives me a look like I've just asked if the sea is made of syrup. 'Like it? I love it! It's *gorgeous*. Just like *you*.'

'Thank you.'

'You're welcome.' She fiddles with the price label on the display of carved wooden shell-shaped keyrings on the counter. I have learned over the years that Aggie's fiddles always precede something she's embarrassed about.

She's inspecting the shells for a long time this morning, so I decide to rescue her. 'So why did you really come to see me?'

She doesn't even try to feign injury. 'Can't hide anything from you, can I?'

11

'No, you can't. Out with it.'

'I don't suppose you've seen Kieran today?'

I haven't. Which is odd, as Kieran Macklin is usually my first visitor of the morning. He's also the Third Amigo to Aggie and me, ever since our last year of secondary school. Whatever happens in life, and no matter where we've found ourselves, our bond remains solid as rock. Kieran's a photographer, known internationally for his gorgeous images of southwest Cornwall and locally for being the best source of gossip; but to us he'll always be the cheeky chap who crashed our drama club's Christmas party blind drunk and quoting Shakespeare badly. And although he has a legion of devoted fans who follow his work on Instagram and Facebook, Ag and I like to think we were the first Macklinites. 'Did he say he was over this way today?'

'Should be. He's doing a wall art commission for that new bar on Market Place – supposed to be overseeing its installation all week.'

'He could be there already?'

'Nope. I just passed it. No sign of life.'

'Have you called him?'

The charm bracelets jangle as she runs a hand through her bright red and bottle-blonde-streaked hair. 'Haven't had time. Busy-busy, you know.'

Aggie Keats acting strangely is not unusual, but it feels like she's being *too* dismissive this morning. 'If I see him, I'll tell him you were asking.'

'Right.' She's picking at a thread on her coat cuff now, and suddenly seems to have shrunk in height. This is not like her at all.

'Aggie?'

There's a long pause – and then the bomb drops. 'Kieran and me – we had a – *thing* – last night.'

'You and Kieran?'

'Yep.'

'What sort of a *thing*? A kiss thing? A something-more thing?'

She shuts her eyes as if the truth might escape from her lashes. 'A kiss thing. And a going-back-to-his thing. And a several times during the night thing . . .'

'*Wow*. Okay.' Kieran and Aggie are my oldest, dearest friends, and while there's always been a lot of inappropriate flirting between them, I'd assumed it was just what they did. This is a huge development – and I can't hide my shock.

'Yes. I *know*, don't give me that look!'

'What happened?'

'He kissed me. Right out the blue. We'd been on the balcony at Fred's, you know, like always; Buds and vapes and talking bollocks . . . And then – honestly, Ser, I don't know what happened. He just leaned in, then I was kissing him back, then I was back at his . . .' Her forehead drops to the counter and she groans. 'I don't know what I was thinkin'.'

'My life . . .'

'Yep.'

'When did you leave?'

'In the early hours. He was still sleepin'.'

'Did you leave a note?' I stare at her. 'Text him at least?'

'I just dashed to work. There wasn't time – I didn't know what to say . . .'

13

'Oh, *Ag*.'

'I'm a fool, aren't I? And now he hates me.'

'He doesn't hate you. Maybe he's just lying low.'

'Avoiding me.'

'Possibly. Was he – were you drunk?'

'That's the worst bit. Stone cold sober, both of us.' There's a flush of red above her eyebrows when she raises her head. 'He said he *loved me*.'

'Wow.'

'I know. I just don't know what to do with that. We've been friends all this time and he never said a word before. Has he ever told you about it?'

'No, nothing. Oh Ag. How do you feel?'

'I don't know. Confused. Frustrated. Terrified I just lost a friend.'

'But you must have felt the same last night?'

'I did. I *think* I did. What if I took advantage? Just got swept up in the suddenness and left my brain at the bar?'

She's pacing now, trying to make it look like she's browsing the shop. It isn't convincing.

'Don't worry. He might be shocked by it all like you are. He's probably gone off with his camera somewhere to clear his head.'

'Sophie and Martin are workin' today and they think I'm nuts. I've been a proper cloud-cadet all mornin'. I took an early lunch just to give the poor kids a break.' She shakes her head. 'I'm sorry to put it all on you, bird.'

'I'm glad you did. You can always talk to me.' I spread my hands wide to the emptiness of my shop. 'I mean, what else would I be doing?'

14

She narrows her eyes. 'You all right, Ser?'

'I'm fine. Why?'

'Somethin's different about you today. You had your hair done?'

'No. How am I different?'

Aggie shrugs. 'I dunno. Glowy. I haven't seen you lookin' glowy for months.'

I do feel brighter today. Finding the star on the beach this morning has made everything else feel easier, as if I've found a pocket of optimism I'd lost. I almost tell Aggie about the star. But I don't think I'm ready to share it with anyone yet. It's novel to have something that just belongs to me for a change, and it's probably a one-off; one of life's serendipities that sparkle up at you just when you need them.

All the same, as I've been working on my new bracelet this morning I've been wondering about it. I usually alternate between the beaches I visit, but I've already decided that tomorrow I will go back to Gwithian Beach. It's the furthest away from St Ives and will mean a painfully early start. But I want to see if the star is still there. Just for me. To keep the magic a little longer . . .

Chapter Four

Jack

'I'm sorry, Jack.'

I stare at the well-dressed, middle-aged man who, until thirty seconds ago, was my best customer. I've done regular building jobs for Charlie Smith for the last five years and was counting on his help again.

'Are you sure? I can do anything, you know. Gardening, handyman stuff . . .'

Charlie shifts position as though an awkward burden balances on his shoulders. 'I wish I could, mate. But the estate's hit financial problems and I'm having to lay off staff.'

And you're not even staff, his expression says. It's the truth: Charlie offered me a job a few years back, but contracts were easier to come by then and I thought I could do it on my own. Back when it wasn't just my wage keeping a roof over our heads. Things must be bad at the Tremorra Estate if Charlie's making staff redundancies. Most of the people who work across the historic house and its land have been there for years. 'I'm sorry to hear that. I didn't know.'

'It's tough for everyone right now. If I can streamline here we might be in a better position in six months, but nobody really knows.' His smile is kind, but a closed door. 'Listen, if I hear of anyone looking, you'll be the first name I give them, okay? I'm afraid that's the best I can do.'

My heart is in my boots as I drive away. I'd banked on Charlie having work for me. Early spring is traditionally the time he asks me to repair and rebuild bits of the crumbling estate, before the summer season fills his holiday cottages and books out the hall for expensive weddings. He's usually good for three or four weeks' work at least.

I could kick myself. I was so confident of this job that I haven't actively sought to fill my diary for the coming month. Now I have no work, and others will have snapped up any jobs going for the next few months. It's my own stupid fault.

As my aged Volvo bumps along the rutted country lane leading from Tremorra, a bright orange light begins to flash angrily on the dashboard. *Great.* Another mistake. The drive out here is a bit of a trek but I thought it was worth it. Now I'm low on fuel, I have hardly any money in my account and I'm miles away from the nearest garage. Can today get any better?

I reach Hayle on vapours and fervent prayer, fill up as much as I dare and wait in the garage kiosk queue, flicking my credit card nervously between my fingers. I'd promised myself not to put anything else on the plastic; the amount I owe is too scary to think about. But I have to make sure

I have money for Nessie's food and the cranky old electric meter that eats 50p pieces, so I daren't touch what's left in my account. As the cashier turns the card machine to me, I swallow my fear and put my faith in the gods of Visa to rescue me . . .

When my wife died, I thought it would be easy to carry on. Well, not *easy*, but possible. I hadn't banked on the financial mess she would leave behind, or the challenge of being a sole parent. If I had a salaried job it would be easier, but running my own business and trying to keep everything ticking over for Ness is so hard. I don't know what will happen if I can't find work. I'm not ruling out finding a job – or several jobs – to make ends meet. Dreams are the first thing you have to trade when reality kicks you.

The thing is, I want to believe I can make it work. I *can* do it, I just have to up my game. I won't let Nessie down. I'm all she has.

By the time I've collected Ness from school and we're driving home, I've promised myself I won't be defeated by this situation. Despite everything life has chucked our way over the past seven months, Nessie is as full of life and joy as ever. Being by the beach has only magnified her happiness. I know she misses her mum, but the freedom and space she feels in our current home have gone a long way to comfort her. My mate Jeb suggested we move into the small wooden chalet on the edge of his caravan park overlooking Gwithian Beach last November, when our house was repossessed. It was out of season and quiet, he said, so we wouldn't be in the way of paying guests. To be honest, I didn't expect it

18

to be as good as it's proved to be. What it lacks in design and furnishings it more than makes up for in character and Ness adores it. Now spring has arrived, I'm getting nervous. It's still early and Jeb's unlikely to need it back yet, but when the summer comes, who knows? He's a great mate and hasn't said anything yet, so I'm making a point of not mentioning it. Or thinking about it. Or worrying . . . Nessie is in a good place now, and I have to protect that. I just need to work out how on earth I can do it.

It's blustery when we get down to the beach after Nessie's changed out of her school uniform. We haven't waited for tea, my daughter being too excited to consider eating yet. She isn't the only one desperate to get down on the sand tonight. I need the wildness of it this evening, the wind blasting away all the other rubbish in my head. Out here, as the waves crash onto the beach and the last of the sea birds call on the night, I can believe that the day's problems are being washed away. I wish it were that easy. If only I could write it all down in the sand and wake tomorrow to find the ocean has smoothed away every worry, every concern, leaving nothing but a perfectly smooth, wide open shore.

Nessie is skipping ahead, the wind gusting her long dark hair in dancing ribbons high above her head. She loves the wildness of this place too, and when I remember to be thankful for the good stuff, this is one of the blessings I count. In our previous home she was cooped up in small, boxy rooms with only a postage stamp of a garden to run in. Here, while we don't have much in the way of space in the chalet, her backyard is the vastness of Gwithian Beach. Part of me wishes we could be here without the

19

shadow of money ever darkening our steps: just being happy and wild and free. But that's an illusion. Like going on holiday and believing you could move there permanently. In real life, it doesn't happen. Reality finds you, no matter how idyllic your surroundings. Unless I can secure our future, everything is uncertain.

I hate that. I hate that so much of this is out of my control. I like to be the one with solutions. But now it's all on me, and I'm floundering.

'*Daaa*-aaad!'

Nessie is over by the rocks near the weathered wooden steps that lead back up to Jeb's caravan park, waving like crazy. I jog over but I'm clearly not fast enough: by the time I arrive she is cross-armed and despairing of her old dad.

'I *said* hurry,' she admonishes me.

I can't help but smile. 'Sorry. What is it?'

Her smile seems to illuminate the growing dusk shadows beneath the rocks. 'Look! The mermaids came back!'

She's pointing at the star we left half-made yesterday.

Somebody has finished it.

I feel a shiver of excitement as I see its perfectly complete shape, a glistening white quartz pebble at its heart. All the concerns of the day finally blow away, as we crouch down to look at the mermaids' handiwork.

The mermaids. Another Jack Dixon story come back to bite me . . .

Since we've been in Jeb's chalet, I've made a point of bringing Nessie to the beach after school. When the evenings get lighter we'll come down later, but for now we

20

dash straight to the sand as soon as we get back. Nessie was still in her school uniform yesterday, and it was heavy with damp sand within minutes of reaching the beach.

'Let's do something different today,' she'd yelled over the sound of the waves.

'Like what?'

'Let's make a star! Out of the glass stuff! A big one!'

I had shown her seaglass on our first night at the beach, something I remember from school trips as a kid. Back then it was magical – I wanted Ness to experience that, too.

'It can't be too big,' I'd called back, looking at the darkening sky and the thin strips of sunset painting the underside of clouds across the bay. 'It'll be dark soon.'

Almost an hour later, with the torch from my iPhone our only working light, I'd finally persuaded Nessie that we should finish.

'But it isn't ready yet,' she protested, strands of damp hair blowing across her face.

'We can see if it's here tomorrow.'

Her big eyes mooned mournfully up at me. 'But what if it isn't?'

'We'll make another one. A bigger one.' She still wasn't convinced as I coaxed her away from the seaglass star, so for want of something else to say, I added, 'Who knows? Maybe the mermaids will see it and finish it for you.'

Ness has been obsessed with mermaids since she met the real St Ives Mermaid – a local lady who swims with a mermaid tail – at a friend's birthday swimming party. Mentioning mermaids last night was a throwaway line, just

21

something to distract Ness long enough to get her off the beach and home. But now, as we look at the completed star, I know exactly what she's thinking.

'It's the *mermaids*, Dad! They finished the star! Like *you* said . . .'

I don't know who did this, but I want to hug them. My little girl's eyes are bright in the evening light, enormous with delight. She is the most *Nessie* I've ever seen her be. And that is more of a gift than I could ever wish for.

'Wow, Ness,' I say, pulling her onto my knee as we gaze at the star together. 'You were right. The mermaids *did* come back.' Her hair smells of the sea as she snuggles into me.

'I knew they would. They know we're here now, Dad.' She pats my hand and a tiny wrinkle appears over the bridge of her nose. 'And – even if they aren't mermaids, even if it's someone else, we'll call them mermaids for now. Okay?'

It's such a hesitant, grown-up thing to say and I wish she didn't have to be on the cusp of reality. She's seven but soon she'll be eight – already kids in her class are starting to define what is and isn't acceptable to believe in. Pretty soon I'll get the Christmas question, which I'm dreading. I want to tell her magic is real and the worries of real life are transient, because that's what I wish was the truth. I hate that part of being her dad is preparing her for losing her dreams. 'For now we'll call them mermaids,' I say, giving her a squeeze. 'And for as long as you want to.'

Chapter Five

Seren

It's still dark when I leave home and head down the worn stone steps to the quiet street. There's a low grumble beside me, and I look down to see my dog Molly puffing along a few paces behind. She lifts her head and observes me with doggy puzzlement, her thick tail wagging despite her obvious misgivings. I don't always take her with me on my beachcombing walks, but this morning her soft head and huge eyes whipped up from her basket in the kitchen as soon as I passed. In Molly's world, that's volunteering.

'You can go back if it's too early,' I offer; but my dog has just caught the scent of salt on the air, and is now waddling ahead to our small garage where my car is waiting, just down the street.

It's strange, the smell of the sea. It sneaks up on you when you least expect it. Being so close to the ocean means it's easy to forget during the week. I think you become accustomed to it, like the picturesque harbour and the quaint streets. But turn a certain corner in town and it suddenly, magnificently reminds you it's there. I love that whoosh of salt and breeze straight from the waves. It's the best wake-up call – and has soothed more than a few hangovers, too, in my life. I'm not hung over this morning, but my head is aching from too much thinking and not enough sleep.

I wasn't going to go to Gwithian again this week – before I found the star yesterday. There are other beaches, much closer to home, that yield as much if not more sea-glass. The harbour arches in St Ives can be treasure troves in the right conditions, for example, and they are a mere five minutes' walk from my house. But I've been thinking about the star on Gwithian Beach since I completed it, and I need to know if it was the only one.

I have no real reason to suppose there are any more, but the child in me wants to believe there might be. Maybe I just want to relive the thrill of finding it yesterday. Its discovery made my whole day better.

'Magic is everywhere, Seren, if you look hard enough for it.'

Dad believed that if you really wanted to see magic, you'd find it.

I want to believe it too, now more than ever.

The cold wind hits me when I arrive at the small car park by Gwithian Beach, the door of my ageing Fiat 500 buffeted by a blast of icy, salt-tang breeze that almost blows it shut again. In the back seat, on her tatty blue-and-red-check travel rug, Molly cowers into the upholstery.

'Come on, lady,' I grin, reaching across the seat to coax

24

her out of the car's warmth. 'It'll be lovely when we get down there.'

Reluctantly, she huffs her way out onto the grass and sand of the car park and leans heavily against my legs, as much to find shelter from the bracing conditions as to show affection. I love her for even being here.

It's dark on the beach and a little warmer, too. I'm wearing the head-torch that I bought for evening cycling but have found much more useful for early-morning beachcombing. As we slowly follow its beam over the shadowy sand, I try to remember the exact location of the star I discovered yesterday. The beach looks so different in the pre-dawn conditions; and anyway, the excitement of finding the seaglass shape all but obliterated my memory of where it was. The first two spots I head for are empty, and I retrace my steps as Molly grumbles beside me. And then my torchlight falls on a cluster of rocks I think are familiar. I scramble over them and stop in my tracks.

The star has vanished.

But something else is in its place.

A new star, its glass shard lines glimmering in the torch beam. And one of its points is missing . . .

The construction of the new star is almost identical to yesterday's. Did they find the star I finished? Or had the sea or other beach visitors claimed it before the starmaker returned?

I want to believe they saw the first star completed and created a new one to see if I'd accept the invitation. It's a tiny gesture that feels enormous – as if the new star is an outstretched hand. Dare I take it?

I don't even have to answer my own question.

The game is on . . .

By the time I have completed the star, adding a mini-star of opaque and bright white seaglass in the centre, dawn has begun to break on the horizon. As the sun emerges, Gwithian becomes a palette of yellow and grey against black rocks and the shadowy grey-white tower of the lighthouse. It takes my breath away.

For a precious moment, Dad is standing next to me, the sand collecting in tiny comical piles on the scuffed toes of his old trainers. 'If today can produce a sunrise like that,' I imagine him say, breathing out the words as if he's savouring each one, 'just imagine what it can do for the rest of the day . . .'

Just imagine . . .

I hear the familiar *flack-flack-flack* as Molly shakes her damp coat dry. She licks her lips and blinks expectantly up at me.

'Okay, lady, let's go,' I say, reluctantly leaving my memory of Dad at the edge of the surf. My heart is racing, despite what waits for me back in St Ives. Today I found magic. That's all that matters.

Chapter Six

Jack

Work may be thin on the ground, but at least Jeb always has something to occupy me in the caravan park. He inherited it from his uncle years ago in quite a run-down state and has worked hard to modernise the static caravans, park shop and communal areas like the bar and the pool. But it's a task that never ends: as soon as one bit is brought up to scratch, another thing crumbles.

One of the walls enclosing the car park has seen better days, so he's asked me to rebuild the top section. In truth, I think he's got wind of my lack of work and has found something to keep me busy. He doesn't need to – he's already letting us live in his chalet rent-free – but today I'm glad of his generosity. Rebuilding this wall is earning me another seventy quid, which will go a long way towards keeping us warm and fed.

At two p.m. I'm halfway up the ladder with a load of bricks when my mobile rings. In a move somewhere between sliding and falling with style, I manage to get to the bottom and answer in time.

'Mr Dixon? It's Gloria Masters from St Piran's Primary. I'm afraid we've had a – *situation* – with Nessie . . .'

I'm at the school within twenty minutes. I can't remember how fast I drove, only how grateful I am to the startled tractor driver coming the other way for pulling up onto the grass verge to let me pass and not swearing at me. Now I'm sitting in reception, I can't even remember if I locked my car. None of it matters: Nessie needs me.

I've been dreading something like this happening since Tash died. Ness is normally so upbeat, so happy, but grief has the potential to ambush that. I'm running through the possibilities in my mind now, dismissing them in time with the relentless *tick-tick* of the clock over the window-shielded reception desk.

Did she miss a test?

No, we've been doing our best to keep on top of test schedules and the school have kindly texted me reminders. And doing well in all of her tests is a point of pride for Nessie.

Has she cheeked a teacher?

I'm not as certain of this one. Of course, it depends on your definition of 'cheek'. Some might call it being cheeky. I would argue it's one of Nessie's most endearing features. But she's a good kid: she wouldn't set out to be cheeky on purpose.

I don't think she would.

At least, I hope she wouldn't . . .

Did she get in a fight?

No, not Nessie. She just isn't the sort to use physical violence. I dismiss this possibility immediately. Not my Ness . . .

'Mr Dixon – Jack – thank you for coming in so quickly.' Gloria Masters gives me *that smile* from the doorway of her office. I've had a truckload of *that smile* from everyone I've met since Tash died. In Nessie's head teacher's case, it's a little more worrying. Is she feeling bad that I lost my wife, or bad that I lost my wife and now my little girl is in trouble?

'Where's Ness?' I ask before I'm even seated at her desk.

'She's with her teacher. She'll be along in a moment. I just wanted to have a word with you first.'

Uh-oh . . .

I nod dumbly back, wondering how many trying-not-to-be-scared parents have occupied my seat before.

'Nessie is a lovely girl, Mr Dixon. Very popular. Helpful and positive. Her fellow students and teachers are very fond of her . . .'

I agree with all of this, but none of it is making me feel easier about what might be coming next.

'Which is why I'm most concerned by her behaviour today.'

There it is. My heart drops to the floor.

'What happened?'

Gloria sighs. 'Your daughter was involved in a disagreement at lunchtime that became physical.'

I can feel every nerve in my body twisting on edge. 'Physical? How physical?'

'She kicked one of her classmates.'

29

'Excuse me? No. Not Ness.'

'I'm afraid so. Caused quite a bruise. Now, I've explained to the other child's parents that the situation is being dealt with.' She narrows her eyes and looks down the long sweep of her nose at me. 'So I am relying upon you, Mr Dixon, to address this issue with your daughter. I trust that we will not be seeing a repeat of this behaviour?'

'Of course not,' I say, more out of a need to get out of there than a genuine desire to comply. My mind is whirring. Why would Nessie kick anyone? She's the most happy-go-lucky, non-confrontational kid I know. Something must have happened to make her react like that.

The weasel-faced school secretary ushers Nessie in, and I resist the urge to sweep her up in my arms and take her away from it all. I need to know what happened if I have any hope of dealing with it.

'Nessie, I've called your father here to help us get to the bottom of what happened today,' Mrs Masters says, eyeballing me.

That's my cue. I kneel beside Nessie and try to get her to look at me.

'Nessie – Ness – I'm not going to shout at you,' I say, hoping to heaven that I won't. 'What happened?'

She is sullen; the spark extinguished from her core, her body slumped. 'I kicked Brandon Travers.'

Oh, man . . .

'Ness, you know better than that.' I can feel the eyes of the head teacher on me, and wish I didn't feel it was me under her judgement rather than my daughter. 'We *never* hit or kick anyone.'

'He deserved it,' she says, her chin high – and my late wife is instantly staring me down, daring me to argue back.

'Ness . . .'

'But he did, Dad. He said, "Nessie's got a dead mum." And he kept on saying it, even when I told him to stop. So I kicked him really hard. *Then* he stopped.'

In that moment, I'm immensely proud of my little girl. Physical violence aside, her reasons have become noble. How dare any child be allowed to emotionally kick a grieving schoolmate? Charged with righteous indignation, I look up at Mrs Masters and Weasel Features, who have fallen suspiciously silent.

'Were you aware of this?' I ask, my even tone masking thick accusation.

'The reason is beside the point . . .' Mrs Masters begins, but the squeak in her voice registers a direct hit.

'I disagree. Ness didn't lash out unprovoked. She was defending herself.'

'Brandon Travers has the bruise . . . His parents . . .'

I pull myself up to my full height, which thankfully is just enough to stare down at her. 'And do his parents condone his harassment of a recently bereaved child?' I let my stare travel slowly from head teacher to secretary, their reddening faces a reward. 'Perhaps if they understood the full details of this incident, they might take up the matter with their son.'

'Mr Dixon, Nessie needs to apologise . . .'

'And she will.' I glare at my daughter, who has just stuck out her bottom lip at me, ready for another battle. 'As soon as Brandon has apologised for his remarks.'

As we walk back to the car, heads uniformly high, I bump my arm against Nessie's. 'I think that went well.'

'I'm not sorry, Dad.'

'I know. But you need to say it, ladybird. However much you think he deserved it.'

'It *sucks*.'

I stop walking and stare at my daughter. 'Where on earth did you learn that?'

She shrugs. 'Uncle Jeb says it all the time.'

'Well – he shouldn't.'

'That's not the worst thing he says.'

'Ness . . .'

She's remorseless as she clambers into the back seat and fastens her belt. 'It isn't. Last week he said *bummer* . . .'

As we drive out of the school car park I make a note to chat to Jeb about his language. I've heard the full extent of his flowery vocabulary – the last thing I need is Ness repeating *that* at school.

She's quiet on the way home but still races to change into jeans, a thick hoodie and red-and-white spotted wellies to go to the beach. As we clamber down the wooden steps from the caravan park, I'm praying our mystery starmaker has been busy again. Nessie needs magic after the day she's had.

The wind drops the moment we're on the sand, and I can hear the thud of my heart in my head as I follow Ness. *Please let it be there*, I plead with Gwithian Beach. *Even if it's the last one . . .*

She's far ahead of me now, skirting the rocks and

splashing through patches of seawater pooling in the rippled sand. I see her slowing – looking down – and then . . .

'*Dad!*'

Thank you, whoever you are. For Nessie. And for me.

Chapter Seven

Seren

There's a buzz in town today. I feel it as I'm walking to Warren's Bakery to pick up scones for a meeting with a supplier this afternoon. People smile at me as we pass; some offer a pat on the back or an encouraging word. It's surreal, but I'm bolstered by it.

The first of what will be four crucial public meetings for St Ives takes place tonight. It's time for the town to decide what happens to a building entrusted to its care. These meetings mark the culmination of a campaign my dad began, ten years ago. Except the person leading it this evening will be me. Dad's sudden death three months ago changed everything in my life; not just because I lost someone I loved so much and inherited the business he left behind, but also because it meant I became the leader of a campaign to preserve our heritage.

'You go get that bleddy Bill Brotherson, girl,' the lady from the Cath Kidston shop says. 'Send him packin' back to Plymouth!'

34

'Thanks,' I say, my heart bumping over Fore Street's cobbles.

'He hasn't a leg to stand on,' the guy in Warren's Bakery grins as he hands me a bag of still-warm scones. 'We'll stop his fun, won't we? And those are on the house, Seren. Your dad'll be cheering you on from the hereafter tonight.'

I'm not a leader. Or even a public speaker. But when Dad died the committee told me I was their only choice for the job. I've researched the topic and I have my notes prepared – backed up by the years of campaigning Dad did before. So, while I'm incredibly nervous about the meeting tonight, I have no intention of backing out. We're trying to save a building of incredible importance to St Ives, and we're facing a developer who wants to tear it down. People like Bill Brotherson only want to destroy our history to make money for themselves; Dad wanted to preserve it for the future, for everyone. I know whose side I'm on.

But before I face that battle, another one awaits.

The supplier I'm meeting is late, which doesn't bode well. Recently MacArthur's has been losing artists who have had stock with us for years. Dad collected people – he was passionate about local artists and craftspeople, and he wanted to bring their work to a wider audience. The problem now is that our customer base has shrunk, and our artists are getting nervy. Some people have just withdrawn their stock, while others have been havering for a while.

Faye Jesson-Lee is one of Dad's longest-standing suppliers, but she's become increasingly distant since we lost him. When she finally arrives I've been staring at the scones for twenty minutes, wishing I hadn't bothered.

'I need my stock,' she says as soon as the door closes behind her. Talk about cutting to the chase . . .

'Can we discuss this? At least stay for a drink?' What I want to do is tell her she is rude, and remind her how my dad supported her work when none of the other galleries in St Ives would even consider it. But Dad would have tried to solve the problem first, so I'll do the same.

She wrinkles her nose and eventually deigns to sit. 'This doesn't mean I've changed my mind.'

Undaunted, I pour tea and hand her a scone she hasn't asked for. I'm determined to make her realise the impact of what she's doing, not let her grab her things and run. 'I'd just like to see if we can come to a better arrangement. You've been part of MacArthur's for many years, and Dad was always very fond of your work – I'd like to honour that if I can.'

Faye looks like she's just been slapped. 'I'm not saying I'm not grateful, Seren. Your father was most kind. But I can't keep my work where it isn't selling. And there are other galleries in the town who offer better rates.'

I've heard this before. It's not difficult for those businesses to offer a better deal when they aren't heavily in debt. They can also drop artists and craftspeople on a whim because demand is so great. I wonder if Faye has heard the same horror stories about them that I have. 'Of course you're free to take your work anywhere. We've never asked for exclusivity.'

'Everyone knows your shop is in trouble.'

'We're not . . .'

'That's not the word in the art community. Your father

was kind to many people. But frankly, his business should have passed with him. It's obvious you can't save it, any more than he could. I'm sorry, Seren, but if the shop closes I don't want it taking my work with it.' She puts her plate on the counter, the scone on it untouched.

In similar conversations I've had lately, this would be the point at which I'd start begging. But now I think about making the star on the beach this morning – of how I felt completely at peace with myself – and I just don't want to bow to anyone any more. Mum won't be happy, but if our artists want to leave, I'm not going to stand in their way. If they have so little faith in the shop my father built, and so little hope in my ability to save it, then I don't want them to be part of it any more.

'Fine. I'll fetch the paintings for you,' I say, rising from my seat. I turn my back on her shocked expression and start lifting her abstract canvasses off the wall, stacking them up on the counter. Then I fetch the five paintings we have in the stockroom and add them to the pile. Ignoring the gaping hole in the main display, where now only dust outlines remain of Faye Jesson-Lee's work, I fold my arms and wait, head high, as she scrabbles to pick them all up.

'And there's the money you owe me for sales,' she rushes, her cheeks flushing.

'I'm sorry, we haven't sold any of your paintings for months,' I reply, the steel in my voice an unfamiliar sound. 'You have your full inventory.'

No more. I won't be held over a barrel by anyone. Let them leave.

'Well, *really*, I . . .'

37

'Let me get the door for you.' I swing it open and stand, sentry-like, determined to see this woman off the premises. 'Goodbye, Faye.'

I don't move, don't flinch until she has hurried out of the shop, taking her paintings with her. Let her go. I'm done with pleading for people to stay. It's surprisingly easy to stand my ground, righteous indignation firing through my body. Only when I am certain she has gone do I slam the door and yell out my frustration, the echoes of it left ringing in the glass sculptures by the window.

By the time I get to St Ives Guildhall for the meeting, I'm more than ready for a fight. Even so, when I meet Aggie outside, my nerves are making an unwelcome return.

'Ready for this?' she asks.

'As I'll ever be. Is there a good crowd?' I try to peer around her to see inside the hall.

Aggie blows her last puff of vape smoke, and nods. 'Pretty big. Hearing Bill Brotherson was going to be here was the decider for a lot of people, I reckon.'

'Has he arrived yet?'

'Just. Cerrie's making him tea and trying her best to be nice.'

Of all the people on the Save the Parsonage committee, I'm glad my friend Cerrie Austin was the one to greet the developer. While I know she dislikes him, her nature is impeccably fair. Perhaps it's because she sees the child in everyone and responds to that with her teacher's approach. It's a devastatingly effective approach, too: I've seen her reduce bolshie adults to doe-eyed kids in minutes.

Inside, the committee and residents are mingling around the refreshment table, but already I can see the divide. It's in the way people stand, the surreptitious glances across the room, an unspoken sorting into 'us' and 'them'. I don't know whether to be heartened by this or a little scared. Most people I know don't want the Rectory Fields development to happen, but there are other people in St Ives who believe it would be good for the economy. As a shop owner, maybe I should be one of them.

But the parsonage was once home to Elinor Carne – a parson's wife, and one of the great unsung heroes of British astronomy. And although she's a stranger to many now, her memory all but gone, this incredible woman has been part of my life for the best part of ten years.

Dad was a keen amateur astronomer – hence my name, Seren, which is Welsh for 'star'. He built his own observatory, affectionately known as the Shedservatory, in our back garden when I was born, so I grew up learning to stargaze with him. The stars and the sea: a perfect combination that stole Dad's heart first, and then mine.

When Dad was working in Grandpa's pub, before I was born and before MacArthur's existed, he'd heard local stories of the vicar's wife who'd identified a star; but until a decade ago, he had never found any information about her. Then an elderly lady from Carbis Bay got in contact to share a bundle of journals she'd been left by her mother. Elinor Carne had been her great-great-aunt, and the books had been kept safe in their family for years. This lady was now the last surviving member of the Carne family. She'd heard of Dad's interest, and wanted to pass them on.

Reading Elinor's journals, Dad found out that she'd discovered a star long before the official sighting was recorded. So he had it verified with the British Astronomical Association, and then he began campaigning to have her recognised for her contribution to astronomy. It took him the best part of ten years, and there is still work to be done.

I remember the first time he opened the journals – at our kitchen table after dinner, each cloth-bound volume spilling out its contents across the knotted oak. Elinor's handwriting was elegant and controlled, the words adorning each page like miniature works of art. Her line drawings of the night sky, which she'd observed from a small observatory she'd built in the parsonage garden, were things of beauty. I remember sitting with Mum as Dad read each entry – and the sense of reverence as Elinor Carne's passion was given voice again, so many years after her death.

And it sounds improbable, but I felt as if she were speaking to me. She was a woman with enormous dreams, caught in a time and a position that demanded she deny them. Her discoveries should have placed her in the esteemed company of the great astronomers: William and Caroline Herschel, Mary Somerville, Isaac Newton and Pierre-Simon Laplace. But the scientific community ignored her because she was a woman and a lowly parson's wife. So instead she dedicated her life to the tiny rural parish in the hills above St Ives, supporting her husband and gazing at the skies whenever she could.

I think of Elinor now, as I walk into the packed hall. She pursued her dream in the only way she was able, but the discoveries and observations she made were far beyond anything she was expected by society to achieve.

I see Cerrie still talking to Bill Brotherson at the far end of the hall. If he sees the evil looks being aimed at him from the committee, he isn't acknowledging them. But then, he doesn't think he's doing anything wrong. It's easy to absolve your conscience when you believe you have a God-given right to do whatever you want.

He's here because he has to gain permission from the people of the town before any development can go ahead. The land on which the parsonage stands is under a moral covenant to belong to the people of St Ives for perpetuity – the town doesn't own the land, but it has a casting vote in what happens with it. Dad made this discovery when he requested the original land registry plans. Without this knowledge, Elinor's home and what remains of her original observatory could have been lost years ago. I'm so proud of Dad for that – it's a gift he has left to his beloved St Ives in order to protect the legacy of its most important resident.

Bill Brotherson doesn't care about Elinor Carne's legacy, or about my dad's work to preserve her memory and bring her the recognition she deserves. I've seen the property developments he's bankrolled across the southwest. He is no respecter of history; his horrible, box-like monstrosities strip beautiful buildings of their soul and repackage their heritage as crass selling points. All he cares about is maximising profit, not the devastation he leaves in his wake.

He's a bloated, over-tanned and under-exercised lump of a man with a ridiculous cavalier-style beard and an assumed swagger that makes him appear constantly constipated.

41

When he talks he has a permanent sneer, as if he is surrounded by an unpleasant odour. It would be comical, if he weren't so successful. Or powerful.

'Ah, Mr Brotherson; have you met Seren MacArthur?' Cerrie says, waving at me. I can sense her relief from across the room.

Brotherson nods. 'Miss MacArthur.'

'Mr Brotherson.'

He doesn't offer a handshake, and I wouldn't accept one anyway.

'You know, we could save everyone a whole heap of time if you and I could just reach an agreement over this.'

'It's not my decision to make. The covenant concerns the whole of the town.'

He nods again, but I notice a small flicker at the corner of one eye. Good. My dad wasn't a pushover, and I won't be either.

Lou Helmsworth is tapping on a mug with a teaspoon at the front of the room, and the crowd begins to hush.

'Ladies and gentlemen, thank you for bein' here,' he smiles. 'If you would like to take your seats, we'll make a start.'

The rows of brown plastic chairs begin to fill with people I've known my entire life. Familiar faces, neighbours, fellow business owners, former schoolmates – the great and the good of St Ives have convened for this meeting. I don't know how many will support Bill Brotherson, but right now it feels like the odds are in our favour.

I take my place at the row of trestle tables arranged on the small stage at the front of the hall, and watch as the developer wrestles himself into a seat at the opposite end. Lou sits in the middle, purportedly to act as a mediator, although I know full well he supports me.

Part of me wonders how I ended up as the spearhead of this campaign. I was always in favour of stopping the development, but it came as a shock when the committee voted me as leader after Dad died. It was simultaneously lovely and terrifying: honouring his memory, but putting me completely out of my comfort zone. I can give all the arguments in the world for why the development shouldn't go ahead; but saying them in front of the entire town and calling myself a campaign leader scares the living daylights out of me. I've always been more comfortable behind the scenes – that's one reason I worked as a graphic designer before the company that employed me folded last year. I could create beautiful campaigns with only occasional meetings with clients – never entire halls full of people. Gazing out at the assembled audience now, I wish myself back at Grafyx – and wonder again what would have happened if I'd accepted a job with my former colleague there, before Dad died. Had I done that, I'd be in Falmouth now, a world away from the expectant eyes of St Ives residents . . .

Lou is thanking everyone for coming and laying out ground rules for the forthcoming debate. There are five public meetings planned. It's supposed to allow everyone a chance to have their say. So tonight's meeting will be both sides presenting opening statements of their case to the town, the next will be a detailed presentation of the two proposals for the site, the third a chance for both sides to answer questions, and the fourth will be the final debate. The last meeting will be when St Ives votes. Lou's planned a week without one in between the third and fourth meetings to allow both sides as much time as possible for campaigning. He thinks it's a foregone conclusion already; I'm aware we need to work as if it isn't. We don't know how the town will vote, and people can change their minds at the eleventh hour. Whatever happens, I think this plan is fair. Everyone wants what's best for the town: this way, no rash decisions can be made. Time to think, time to talk. It's what Dad would have wanted, too.

Bill Brotherson speaks first, with Lou unveiling a large card-mounted artists' impression of the completed development while he talks. It's mostly glass and stone – impressive, if you like buildings that completely ignore their former lives. It wouldn't look out of place in London's Docklands, or on a swanky beachside estate like Sandbanks in Dorset. But on the hill above St Ives? I can't imagine it blending into the environment. Sympathetic development is not a term Bill Brotherson understands. This one looks a little less monstrous than his previous developments, I'll give him that. But the only nod to the parsonage's past or Elinor Carne's former observatory seems to be one line of coving stones salvaged from the east aspect. To anyone unfamiliar with the old building, these few stones wouldn't mean a thing.

The audience is being kind, for now at least, but I don't see many smiles directed at the millionaire developer as he gives his marketing spiel.

'Of course we will be sympathetic to the past,' he says, that half-smile of his flashing for a millisecond. 'Rectory Fields will have a section known as the Elinor Carne Wing.'

'That's big of ya,' says a voice from the crowd. And then I feel it – the deep rumble of dissent sounding around the room, like a storm approaching across the sea. It's small, but it's growing.

And Bill Brotherson has no idea of the tempest heading his way.

'Why not go all out, Bill? Name a parking space after her, an' all!' calls another voice, and a peppering of laughs follow.

'We are currently in talks with the council to formally name the approach road to the property "Elinor Carne Way".' Brotherson grins, thinking he has done well.

Oh dear . . .

'While you destroy everything she worked for?'

'What gives you the right to do that?'

'What's next? You giving all your swanky buyers Elinor Carne T-shirts to wear when they move in?'

He bats the heckles away like summer midges. 'We have consulted widely, and we are one hundred per cent convinced that our plans are the most appropriate for the area . . .'

'*How* widely?' Another resident stands in the hall.

Bill Brotherson's mouth flaps like a goldfish out of its bowl, and for the first time tonight I can see him flailing. 'I'm sorry?'

'Two interns and a digger driver, I'll bet!'

'Aye, an' the post-boy if he's lucky!'

Raucous laughter breaks out like the first cracks of thunder, and there it is: rebellion rising in the heart of St Ives.

'Ladies and gentlemen, *please*—' Lou is standing now,

slapping his hand on the trestle table to summon order. I see ripples in my water glass and it feels like a portent of approaching danger. 'Let's just listen to what Mr Brotherson came here to tell us. There will be an opportunity for questions and debate next time . . .'

'People like *him* don't care about what we think.' I recognise the woman pointing her finger at the developer. Sharon has run Wax-a-Daisy candle shop, a few doors down from MacArthur's, for the past ten years. She's one of the nicest people I know, but I've never seen her this angry before. She points at Bill Brotherson, who is staring back, clearly thrown by the hostility. 'You just waltz in, build your pig-ugly little buildings and hightail it out. Does he care what he leaves behind? Or what is lost?'

And then more people are shouting, more fingers jabbing towards the stage – and I can feel the floor shaking as chairs are pushed back and feet hit the floor . . .

'Well, that went well,' Aggie says, raising her half-drained cider bottle as everyone at the pub table laughs. We've been sitting here for almost an hour in stunned silence: it feels good to break the tension.

'I didn't expect *that* at the first meetin',' Lou says. The flush on his cheeks has yet to fade. After trying and failing to wrestle the meeting back to order, he had finally called time and sent everyone home.

'Nobody expected that.' I hope it reassures him. He'll be blaming himself for not maintaining civility. 'I had no idea feelings ran so deep.'

'It isn't just the parsonage,' Kieran says, downing the last of one pint and beginning a fresh one that's just been bought for him by a local who was at the meeting. 'Bill Brotherson hasn't exactly won many friends around here over the years. Tonight was their chance to say it to his face.'

'All the same, if this was the friendly introduction, I dread to think what the next four meetings will be like.' Lou nods his appreciation to me as I pat his arm. 'And you didn't even get the chance to speak, Seren. I'm so sorry.'

'There'll be time for that,' I say, secretly glad the meeting was ended before I presented our case. I've been staring at my notes all day, and was convinced I wouldn't be able to put into words what's in my heart. As it turned out, the vast majority of the town spoke for me. It's only a brief postponement, but at least I have a week now to plan my speech.

I've always been daunted by speaking in public. In conversation with small groups of friends I think I hold my own, but it's completely different when a roomful of eyes are trained on you. And even though I probably knew two-thirds of the people in the Guildhall tonight, I was still shaking at the thought of addressing them. It's where Dad and I differed: he was at his best with an audience. That's why he was the natural choice to lead the Save the Parsonage campaign. I, on the other hand, have all of his passion but none of his confidence in large crowds.

I *am* passionate about saving Elinor's home. That's why I'm determined to do the best job I can of leading the campaign. But having a little more time to prepare is a gift I wasn't expecting.

'Did you see his face?' Aggie says, her new bottle of

cider already half-empty. 'I don't think I've ever seen Brotherson terrified before. I wouldn't be surprised if he arrived with a bodyguard next week.'

'Judging by the mood tonight, he might need several. Anyone for another round?' Kieran stands.

The others accept, but I don't. When Kieran and Aggie protest – carefully avoiding each other's eyes, as they have been all evening – I raise my hands to defend myself. 'I have a couple of hours of accounts to do tonight. And I want to get the website in order.' The thought of it makes my heart sink. I set the website up for Dad six months ago, but he didn't really see the point of it, so most of the items listed are already sold. After Faye Jesson-Lee's departure today I spent the afternoon taking photos of the stock in the shop, using a makeshift mini-studio of a white sheet draped over one of the shelves and two anglepoise lamps. All a bit rough and ready, but I'm quite pleased with the result.

Aggie flings an arm around my shoulders and squeezes me into her generous bosom. 'Bird, do you ever give yourself a break? We're worried about you.'

'I'm fine,' I lie – because it's far easier than the alternative. 'I have my morning beach walks.' *And the stars*, I add to myself, enjoying the shiver of excitement it causes. *I have the seaglass stars . . .*

Chapter Eight

Jack

It's there.

I see it before Nessie this time, and I am surprised by the shot of joy it gives me. For the last three evenings we have found these stars, and already I can see the effect it's having on Ness. She's always looked forward to going to the beach after school but I don't think I've ever seen her as excited as she has been for these few days. I see it now as her face lights up, the thrill passing from her delighted smile to her legs, which kick into a sprint.

'Again!' she yells, her spotted wellies kicking up showers of sand and shale as she skirts the rocks. 'They did it again!'

Our mystery star-completer has added a line of shells from the tip of each of the star's points – they get gradually smaller, with tiny periwinkle shells at the ends, which makes the whole thing look as though it's sparkling. I don't know when they did their stuff, but finding those small shells must've been quite a task. It makes me appreciate the effort even more.

This afternoon as I was pitching for a building job (unsuccessfully, as it turned out), I found myself thinking about the beach stars. I'm way behind my daughter on this, I realise, but today was the first time I've been aware of it. I'd figured we might see a couple of completions at most before the other person grew tired of it. But it seems they are as daft as Ness and me. Which is a nice thing to find.

How the stars are completed doesn't matter, to be honest, although I appreciate the care and attention applied to them. It's more that finally, unexpectedly, we have something happening that is exactly what it seems: a little bit of joy just for the sake of it. We have no more control over the stars than we had over Tash's death, or losing our home, or having to live in temporary accommodation during the late winter and early spring. But where those factors have brought constant problems and worry, the seaglass stars are a gift.

'We have to make another one,' Nessie says, scooping the seaglass and shells into the Mickey Mouse bucket we found in the chalet. She's started to reuse the bits, then scour the beach for extra pieces, rather than try to build the whole star afresh – her idea, which I'm very proud of. If it were down to me, we'd still be spending hours each evening frantically gathering new materials. I love how Ness is changing our approach to make the best use of our time and maximise the fun of the task. Maybe she'll be a builder like me one day. Or an architect. When she's not busy fulfilling her superhero, cafe-owner and unicorn duties, that is . . .

Later that night, I tuck her into bed and am about to

close the door to the small box-room when she calls me back.

'Do you think they mind?'

'Who?'

'The mermaids. Do you think they mind having to finish our stars?'

I walk back into the room and sit on the edge of her bed. It creaks with a forty-year-old weariness. Like everything else in the chalet, it sounds dangerously close to collapse.

'Do you think they would carry on if they didn't find it fun?'

Nessie's nose wrinkles as she considers this. 'I s'pose not.'

'Well, there you go. Stop worrying. And go to sleep.'

'Okay. Thanks, Dad.'

I stroke her soft forehead and wish I could make this last forever for her. 'No problem. Sleep well, noodle.'

'You too, Big Noodle.'

Big Noodle. Where did she get that from? I smile as I gently close the door behind me, feeling my face fall as I see the stack of brown envelopes waiting for me on the sofa. End-of-month accounts – depressing in every way imaginable. I think of the dusty whisky bottles stashed in the sideboard, given as thank-you gifts to me from customers but never opened. I wish I could stomach the stuff. Tonight, strong spirits would definitely be an advantage . . .

Chapter Nine

Seren

Mum is in the kitchen when I get back from the shop today. She's sitting at the table drinking coffee from her favourite mug, the yellow-striped Cornishware one Dad bought her years ago. Dad's favourite blue-and-white striped mug now has a small white orchid growing in it on the kitchen window. Mum's best friend Lottie suggested it and the idea appealed to Mum – a new thing growing from an old one.

'Hi, Mum.' I kiss the top of her head. She smells like roses.

'Hi, sweetheart.'

I look down at the magazine spread out between her hands. 'Good read?'

'The usual. Hearts and flowers and country kitchens.' She smiles up at me with sleep-stolen eyes. 'My favourite. But I might pop down to the bookshop in Fore Street tomorrow and pick up something better to read. I fancy escaping into someone else's world for a bit.'

I know how she feels.

I make myself a drink and join her at the table, pushing my work bag underneath. The account books are in there for me to go through again later – I don't want her to see them yet.

'How was your day?' I ask.

'Pretty productive, actually. Jeanie at Porthminster Interiors is interested in buying some of my quilts.'

'Mum, that's fantastic! I hope you said yes?'

'I did. Haggled her up on the price, too.' She looks pleased with herself, and my heart swells with pride for her. She's coped with so much since we lost Dad. Most people would still be hiding away from the world, but not her. I think forward is the only direction she knows, so she's just carrying on, one foot in front of the other, one breath at a time. And I haven't seen her make any quilts for at least a year. She made a batch before that and was about to start taking them to craft fairs when Dad died. It put the brakes on everything and I wondered if she'd ever take the quilts out again after that. Time stops when you lose someone so full of life so suddenly. It's hard to get going again.

'How much?'

'She'll buy them for £100, sell them for £180. It's all online business these days, she says, then a few in the shop in high season when the well-off Home Counties lot come down. She wants three a month, so that'll help keep the wolf from the door, won't it?'

There's a scratch of Labrador paws on the slate tiles of the kitchen and Molly flops down over my feet.

'We're not talking about you, Moll,' I smile, reaching

down to tickle the warm velvet of her ear. 'Do you think you could do it, Mum?'

'It would keep me busy, that's for sure. But I already have seven made upstairs, so I'd have a head start.' She takes a slow sip of coffee and places her mug very deliberately down on the table. In our house, this is a sign of a serious conversation approaching. 'Now. How are you?'

'I'm okay.' My voice doesn't sound as enthusiastic as I want it to.

'And the shop?'

The account books are as heavy against my right leg as Molly's head is across my left foot. 'Bubbling along.'

She frowns. 'Seren May MacArthur . . .'

The steam from my mug is blown sideways by my sigh. 'It's tough going. We aren't at the point of no return, but we aren't fully solvent yet. I'm working on it.'

'I know you are. Oh, my brave girl . . .' She cups my chin with her hand. 'All this stress and pressure on you. I'm so sorry.'

'Don't apologise. It's not your fault.'

'Could we sell it as a going concern? No, hear me out, please. I'm wondering if we should just cut our losses?'

I didn't want to have this conversation, not now. She knows MacArthur's is in trouble, but what she doesn't know is how badly. Or that the problems started long before Dad died. He was such a dyed-in-the-wool optimist that I think he just kept on, believing the debt would right itself. Or stuck his head in the sand so he couldn't see the scary deficit towering above him.

'Nobody would buy the shop as it is. We don't have

enough of a sales record to be attractive to buyers. And we need to be working to reduce the debt so that we can sell and have a hope of covering what we owe. I'm sorry, Mum, but Dad was dealing with this for a lot longer than any of us realised.'

Her reaction is inevitable, but it breaks my heart. No widow should have to discover that her late partner was hiding secrets from her. It doesn't take anything away from who Dad was or what he meant to us, but the reality is cold and hard and impossible to dismiss. He was a lovely husband, a wonderful dad – but a struggling businessman. I pass her the box of tissues that has taken up residence on the kitchen table recently, then hold her hand and wait until she's had time to take the news in.

'I never thought that . . . He kept saying we were okay, but . . . oh, your dad was a sly one when he wanted to be.' She blows her nose. 'Right. So what's the plan?'

I watch tiny waves shudder across the top of my coffee as I move my mug, and feel the drag of dread at the edges of my heart. 'Keep going with the shop. Build up the online side of the business. And let the artists who want to leave us do so. I'd rather concentrate on what we can sell, rather than dashing after every supplier who wants to go. If we build something sustainable, we have to trust they'll be back.'

'But some of our suppliers have been with us for thirty years . . .' Mum sees my expression and holds her hand up. 'Okay, do what you think is best. Your dad would be so proud of you.'

*

55

Down on Porthmeor Beach that evening, taking Molly for her evening stroll, I gaze out at the layered pink sunset framing the chapel on the Island. *Would* Dad be proud of me? He never made any intimation that he expected me to inherit his business. If anything, he did everything he could to dissuade me from following in his footsteps. Would he be proud of me for struggling on with his mess?

I think about the star on Gwithian Beach, right around the coast. Has the other starmaker found it yet? Dad would have wholeheartedly approved of my newfound game. Which settles it: I'm going to Gwithian every morning until the stars stop appearing.

I'll start tomorrow.

Chapter Ten

Jack

'Da-*aad* . . .' Nessie singsongs, in the way she does when an Ask is coming.

Ever since she could first say my name, Nessie has wielded the Power of Cuteness. I've never worked out how she does it, but my daughter can make her eyes look about fifty times bigger when she wants something. She's doing it when she appears, wearing an irresistibly cheeky smile, one hand twirling around the end of a strand of dark hair. It's longer now than it has ever been and probably needs a cut, but she giggles when the sea breeze whips its curls around her face, so I can't ask her to trim it yet. As long as my little girl wants to tie her hair beneath her chin and laugh herself silly wiggling her 'beard', she doesn't have to change a thing.

'Wha-*aat*?' I sing back, chuckling when I see the hard Paddington stare she's aiming at me.

'Can we take a bottle from the sideboard when we go to the beach tonight?'

Whatever I thought Nessie was about to ask for, this wasn't it. The only bottles in the end cupboard of the old sideboard in our chalet are those dust-gathering thank-you gifts from previous customers. Truth is, I hate whisky. No matter what age or region it hails from, to me it always tastes like municipal toilet cleaning fluid smells. I realise it's heresy to admit this. But if someone gives me a bottle, it's a kind thought, so I can't refuse. And it's one of those things now where I've left it too late to say that actually beer would be nicer, and whisky gives me the worst migraines. So people think I *like* it. I've tried palming the bottles off on Dad, but he's a beer fan, too. Hence the unwanted stash in its dusty dumping ground.

'No.'

'You can't say no.'

I laugh at her brazenness. 'I think you'll find I can. We are not taking whisky to the beach.'

Balled fists slam onto my daughter's hips. 'Dad. We *have* to.'

'We don't have to do anything of the sort, Ness. You're not taking a bottle.'

'But Da-*aad*! We have to take *something*.'

'If you think you'll be thirsty I'll take a bottle of water.'

'We can't take water! The sea is *full* of water!'

Suddenly, my head hurts. How are you supposed to argue with a seven-year-old's logic in full, indignant flow? 'Nessie . . .'

Her shoulders rise and drop dramatically in the most overblown sigh she can manage. 'You just don't get it, *do* you?' All of a sudden, I see Tash in miniature. Always Jack's fault, even if he doesn't know what he's supposedly guilty of. Always Jack's lack of understanding, lack of empathy, lack of whatever attribute she'd decided I should have had that day . . .

No, wait. Stop it.

I shake off my irritation. This isn't Tash. It's Ness. My beautiful, brave, bloody annoying little girl who is growing up at an alarming rate. I take a breath, trying to will back some control.

'Ladybird, tell me what you want the whisky for.'

'For the *mermaids*, Dad.' She says it like it's the most obvious thing in the world. And with it is the tiniest glimpse of disappointment that I didn't understand immediately. So much of being a parent, I'm learning, is being reminded how often you fall short of the mark.

'To say thank you for the seaglass stars?'

She nods.

'Ah. Mermaids don't like whisky, Ness.'

The baby-blue eyes widen. With my superior mermaid knowledge, I'm back in the game. 'Don't they?'

'Nope. Gets them too squiffy and they end up swimming sideways. They get nasty tail-cramps and have to rest in sea caves until they're better.'

Any last scrap of frustration has vanished from my daughter's face and now she's hanging on my every word. '*Do* they?'

'Mm-hmm. So they miss out on all the sea parties and shipwreck discos and it makes them very sad.'

'They have *discos* on *shipwrecks*?'

'They do.' I rock at this! It was the thing that irritated

Tash the most about me – that I could happily talk non-sense and tell tales with no ulterior motive. But Nessie loves it. She's every bit her own person, but I like to think she gets her imagination from me.

'I don't want our mermaids to miss the discos. Or have hurty tails.' Deep in thought, she flops down on the creaking ancient G-Plan armchair, the bulge of its threadbare seat appearing beneath the frame. Jeb tried sitting there last week, and the rubber pad where springs should be finally gave up the ghost. It's held together now with figure-of-eight loops of brown string. I have no idea how long the repair will last.

'I tell you what mermaids *do* like,' I say, an idea popping into my mind.

'What?'

'Marshmallows.'

The magic word. Nessie gasps. 'But – that's my favourite too!'

I mirror her surprise. 'I *know*. Who'd have thought it?'

'Why do they like marshmallows?'

Why *do* they like marshmallows, Jack? I've peaked too early – now I'm scrabbling to find a plausible reply. 'Well . . . They float. In the sea. And the mermaids like that because they can eat them and swim at the same time. No sticky fingers, you see. And . . . Not that you should throw marshmallows into the sea,' I add quickly, picturing Nessie causing a minor maritime disaster by filling the bay with bobbing pink and white confectionery. 'What they love best is getting a few marshmallows in a little box, left

60

behind the rocks on the shore. So they can find them and take them back home.'

Did I sound convincing? I *think* she bought it . . .

Nessie jumps up, the chair breathing an audible sigh of relief. 'Then let's get some! Come *on*, Dad!'

I watch her race off into the wood-clad kitchen, and feel my heart swell. If only all problems could be that easy to solve for my girl. Life would be so much easier if all it took was a box of marshmallows hidden in the right place.

Our fellow starmaker has finished the star with such care that I almost stop Nessie taking it to bits. I've started to photograph the stars, to keep a visual record – because I know they could stop appearing as suddenly as they began. In future years I want Nessie to remember the kindness of strangers and the possibility of magic.

I watch my girl skipping around the beach, her joy infectious and unbridled. And suddenly I'm scared. I'm scared I won't be able to get us out of this mess. I'm scared of letting Nessie down. Jobs are thin on the ground, and I can't rely on the generosity of friends forever. I've been telling myself that I still have options, that there are many avenues I've not yet ventured down; but the stark truth is that unless something big comes along soon, we are in real trouble.

'Give me the box!' Nessie is by my side, her feet jigging an excited dance in the sand.

I remember I have the wooden box with the mermaids' marshmallows, and a note in the pocket of my hoodie. 'Sorry, Ness. There you go.'

With great care and reverence, Nessie puts the box at the centre of the new incomplete star. Then she stands back and closes her eyes. Her stillness is startling. I wait a while until I speak.

'What are you doing, ladybird?'

'*Shh!*'

'Sorry.'

Screwing up her eyes, she begins to whisper, her hands clasped together like a saint in prayer. I stand helpless and watch, not really sure what the proper response is. After another minute, she opens her eyes. 'Okay, that's done.'

'What is?'

Nessie rolls her eyes, because of course I should have known the answer. 'I asked Mum to tell the mermaids to come.'

My world tilts. It hadn't even occurred to me that Ness might be talking to Tash. I should have asked. I should have known. 'And what did Mum say?'

'Nothing.' She shrugs. 'I suppose she's busy.' I can't read her expression – it isn't sadness, more resignation.

'I bet she heard, though,' I offer, not sure whether she is looking for reassurance or not.

'It doesn't matter anyway. George at school says if you think it loud enough, the universe hears it.'

Is my seven-year-old daughter explaining cosmic ordering to me? 'And does the universe then tell the mermaids?'

'No, Dad. The mermaids aren't in the universe. They're in the *sea*.'

'Right. Sorry.' My brain hurts.

My daughter picks up her bucket and pats my arm with pity. 'Don't worry about it. Let's go home.'

I follow my extraordinary, surprising, brilliantly weird little girl away from the almost-dark beach to the warm lights of our chalet, and make a silent-loud thought of my own.

Don't let me let her down . . .

Chapter Eleven

Seren

Marshmallows?

I sit in my car to escape the driving rain and stare at the small wooden box I found on the beach with today's half-finished star. Inside are four marshmallows – two pink, two white – and a typed note:

For the mermaids xx

What is that supposed to mean? It's a sweet gesture, but what do marshmallows have to do with seaglass stars? And who are the mermaids?

There's a grumble from the back seat. I look around to see a familiar chocolate snout slide between the driver and passenger seats. If there's one thing Molly loves, it's marshmallows.

'Dream on,' I tell her. 'You only get these if you braved the beach this morning.'

Her eyes moon up at me.

'I'm sorry, Moll. You wimp out of a wet beach, you lose the treats.'

Rain pelts the windows of the car and drums like impatient fingers on the roof. Usually I wouldn't even venture to the closest beaches in weather like this, but the stars have changed that. I drove through the rain this morning without a moment's hesitation. I don't want to miss a day while this continues.

This morning's star was a seaglass outline filled with blue-purple mussel shells. Thankfully they had been pushed well down into the sand, so the rain hadn't dislodged them. As I've come to expect, the fifth point was unfinished, but today as well as completing it, I've added wispy strands of black seaweed around the outside of the star. When I left it on the beach, it looked like a sliver of black velvet sky had fallen around the star.

The note that was tucked inside the small wooden box is printed, so I have no clues that handwriting might provide. Does the other starmaker think they're making stars with mermaids?

Molly's nose nudges my elbow.

'Oh, go on then.'

She snaffles the sweet in one delighted chomp and her satisfied mumbling as she chews makes me laugh out loud. That feels good.

And then I realise: this gift represents a step up from the game we've been playing. It's the first attempt to communicate beyond the starmaking. And while it might be a little cryptic – and definitely unexpected – it shows me that the game means as much to them as it does to me.

That makes me smile.

They like what we're doing. It matters. And that means that even though we could be walking past one another as strangers every day, down here in this small corner of Gwithian Beach, we are friends. I like having friends who pursue magic. It feels like coming home.

The discovery of the marshmallows seems to have a sweetening effect on everything that morning. Four customers come into the shop, and two of them actually buy something. I have three more sales on the MacArthur's Etsy shop and one request for a commission, which I pass on to a delighted potter in one of the nicest phone calls I've made since Dad died.

After lunch, the bell above the door rings out and a familiar face enters. Liz is one of our newest artists and definitely one of our most positive. Her delicately layered paper-collage cards and framed pictures are gorgeous works of art inspired by the wildflowers, sea plants and birds of this coastline. They brighten the corner of the shop where they are displayed and I smile every time I see them.

'I brought you cake,' she beams, pulling a flowered tin from her embroidered boho handbag. This is always a welcome sight; Liz's baking skills are as well honed as her artistic ones. 'Salted caramel and white chocolate – it's a new recipe, so I thought I'd enlist your help as a beta-taster.'

'Sounds perfect,' I say, hurrying to find plates and mugs, our ageing kettle creaking and clicking as the water starts to boil.

'Now, I wanted to see you about the shop,' Liz says when cake and tea are served. My heart drops. It's been such an unusually good day that I don't want any bad news to spoil it. I think back to my spiky conversation with Faye Jesson-Lee, and the four similar conversations I've endured with artists over the phone since. *Please don't let this be another.*

'Things are tough at the moment,' I begin, but she holds up her hand to silence me.

'I know. That's why I wanted to come to see you.'

'We can't make anyone stay if they don't want to . . .'

'More fool them for leaving. We don't quit just because the sea gets a bit choppy, do we?' She smiles at my surprise. 'I have no intention of going anywhere, Seren. Your dad championed my art long before anyone else. I just wanted to reassure you that my work stays here, for as long as you want it.'

I am so stunned that I don't know what to say. Tears well and all I can do is stare back.

Liz takes my hand across the counter. 'My poor love, this must be so hard on you. How are you doing?'

'I'm getting through it,' I manage, wiping a tear that falls when I blink. 'But thank you for staying. Dad would have been so pleased.'

'I hope so. But I'm not doing it for him. I think your hard work should be rewarded. I've seen what you've done to keep this place running, and I think it's marvellous. And those in the art community who are saying it can't be done are idiots. I've told several of them this.'

I have to smile. Liz is the loveliest lady, but she would

be formidable as an opponent. 'Thank you. That means so much.'

'You just keep going, Seren. My grandma used to say that we are all like seeds: born with everything necessary to succeed already inside us. You can make this happen if you believe you can do it.'

When I leave the shop later on, I feel lighter than I have for a long time. Maybe Liz is right: regardless of how out of my control my situation has been, I have the potential to make it work.

As I walk back home, I remember the marshmallows from Gwithian Beach this morning. The box is still in my jacket pocket, one marshmallow of each colour remaining inside. I'm not sure I believe in fate, but finding this gift seems to have unlocked something positive today. Maybe I *can* do this. If enough people put their faith in the shop, like Liz has done, we might just survive. And the swell of support for the Save the Parsonage campaign after the first meeting suggests the town is behind Dad's cause, too.

Perhaps I just need to start believing it's all possible.

Chapter Twelve

Jack

There's a lot to be said for a hot mug of tea by a warm fire after a hard day's work. I relax in the old armchair next to the roaring fire in my brother Owen's farmhouse and inhale the wonderful smell of baking. I love the buzz of aching muscles after a day of work, and it's become a physical badge of honour since we had to move to Jeb's chalet. Every day I work is one day less to worry about.

Today a builder friend called me at short notice to cover him on a roofing job. He'd come down with a sickness bug but his customer was demanding the work be done, so he thought of me. It was good money, even if my back is now disgusted with me. Nessie had an inset day from school, so I'd been looking at a day not working, but thankfully Owen and my sister-in-law Sarah were able to have her so I could accept the job. She was overjoyed to be granted an unexpected visit to her beloved cousins Ellis, Arthur and Seth, and an extra home-cooked tea from Auntie Sarah.

I can hear Ness and the boys dashing about upstairs,

their laughter and thudding footsteps sounding through the floorboards in the two-hundred-year-old farmhouse. It's the kind of happy noise I remember from my childhood. I'm so glad Nessie gets to experience it.

My brother and his wife have been rocks to me since we lost Tash. I know Owen wishes he could do more, but to be honest, them occasionally having Nessie for tea after school and cooking us Sunday lunch every now and again is all we need. Their farmhouse between Helston and Liskeard is the kind of homely place I'd always imagined us living in eventually. The dream was to find an old building, renovate it with locally sourced materials and move in. Well, that was *my* dream. Tash saw things differently. She was aiming for the faceless, shapeless new-build mansion, all glass balconies, polished steel and sweeping stone floors, devoid of personality. It wouldn't have mattered to her if the materials had spent weeks at sea being shipped from China, rather than being hewn from the foundations of Cornwall. But it matters to me.

I think that's when I knew the damage between us was irreparable; when we had the biggest argument of our marriage over a dream home she'd seen on a television show. That was us in a nutshell. We never argued about the things that actually mattered, but all of the angst and frustration went into stupid, overblown arguments about proposed train lines, or soap opera stories, or decisions our friends were taking in their lives. Everything became about passing the blame on to other things. Before she died, I half-expected her to file for divorce on the grounds of 'irreconcilable tastes in wallpaper'.

The arguments had become bigger than we were, the cracks too wide to repair. And that's the worst thing, because while people assume I'm the devastated widower who tragically lost the love of his life, I know the truth.

The day she died, I was going to leave her.

I'd talked it through with Owen over beer late into the night, and he'd agreed to help me move out. I planned to take Nessie with me. The sad thing is, I don't think Tash would have fought me over that decision. I don't believe in making people saints when they die, and it helps to admit the truth to myself about Tash. She could be wonderful, kind, caring, but she also saw me – and by extension, Ness – as unnecessary limits placed upon her life. I wish it had been different – and I won't ever tell Nessie how she should remember her mum – but I have to remember how bad it was before.

I don't know whether or not to feel guilty that all this was going on. I do feel guilty for not challenging Tash about it more when she was alive. I sat it out, waiting for her maternal instinct to kick in. I don't know what I was expecting to happen, exactly. I think I just hoped things would change. But they didn't – and even with Ness as young as she was, I could see she was waiting for something her mum never gave her, too.

'Is Nessie okay?' Sarah, my sister-in-law, pulls yet another perfect pie from the Aga and frowns at me.

'She's great. She's doing really well.' I never know if this type of question is aimed more at me for not doing something I should be, rather than a genuine enquiry after

71

Nessie's wellbeing. I sound defensive, but I hope Sarah just assumes I'm tired.

'Good. You know, if you ever need time out, Jack, Nessie can always stay with us for a bit.'

'That's very kind. But we're okay.'

She returns to her baking as Owen strides in. He's much more like my dad than I am, in build and attitude and character. Being a farmer suits him, even if for years all he ever wanted to do was work in finance and live in a swanky flat in London. I don't know what happened to him five years ago, but it was enough to bring him home to Cornwall and completely overhaul his life. Meeting Sarah was a large part of that, I think. She fits the lifestyle perfectly and I can't imagine her as the corporate lawyer she once was. And neither of them is scared of the tough demands of running a farm while bringing up three kids. They are two of the hardest-working people I know.

'Hey, Stink,' my brother says, the mountain of a man becoming a five-year-old again.

I grin back. 'Hey, Reekie.'

Mr Reekie and Mr Stink were unlikely superheroes, but the characters we created for ourselves as kids were the biggest, baddest, coolest crime-fighting duo our primary-school playground had ever seen. All through our childhood, Reekie and Stink's exploits entertained us for hours. Mum despaired, but Dad always encouraged us. We didn't have much compared with our friends, but our imagination gave us secret riches.

'I was just saying to Jack we could take Nessie for a bit, if he needed us to,' Sarah says.

I catch the flicker of frustration in my brother's expression and suddenly realise my sister-in-law wasn't just making an off-the-cuff offer. 'Leave it, girl.'

'Should my ears have been burning?' I ask, my defences clicking into action.

'It's nothing like that . . .' Owen says.

'Okay, now I'm worried.'

'Don't be.'

'It's just that maybe Nessie would benefit from a bit more stability . . .' Sarah folds her arms.

'Stability? So you think I'm not giving her that?'

'Bruv, it isn't like that. But she could stay here for a bit. The boys would love it. We could move Seth out of the box-room into his brothers' bedroom and Nessie could have his bed. Sarah could get Ness over to school every day. You could carry on living at Jeb's chalet – good place for work and everything – and come and see Nessie whenever you could.'

'Wait – so you're not offering me bed and board, too? I'm supposed to live away from my daughter?'

'Stink, we don't have the room for both of you. But we could help ease the burden while you sort things. Easier to do that alone than with a kid in tow. We just thought it might give you a bit of breathing space . . .'

I eyeball him, my blood starting to singe my veins. 'How much breathing space are we talking about, exactly?'

Sarah has moved to Owen's side and I'm suddenly facing an unexpected battalion. 'Just a few weeks – maybe a couple of months – just until you're back on your feet.'

'*No.*'

'Jack . . .'

'I said no!'

'We're concerned.' Sarah says. And there it is. *That* look.

'We're *fine*.'

By the fire, Owen's sheepdog Floss growls in her sleep.

'But you aren't really, are you?' My sister-in-law has dropped any pretence of niceness now.

It's an ambush. My fingers whiten at the knuckles around my mug of tea. 'In what way?'

'Don't take it like that. Sarah and me . . .'

'And you, too?' I would've expected it of Sarah, who has spent most of her adult life fire-fighting for other people, spotting potential risks before they happen. But not my big brother. I want to get up and leave, but Nessie is upstairs playing with her cousins, and she's been looking forward to it all week. I lower my voice, the effort making every syllable shake. 'We are *fine*. We are coping. Better than that, actually. I'm pitching for jobs every day. It's only a matter of time before something comes up. The chalet is perfectly okay for us for now and Ness adores the beach.'

'But what security can you offer her at the moment?' Sarah holds up an oven-gloved hand to dismiss my brother's protest. 'No, come on, Jack, I want to know. It all sounds very noble, but what happens if the work doesn't arrive? Or if your mate at the caravan park suddenly wants his house back? Have you even thought about that?'

Okay, that's it. 'I don't have to listen to this. *Nessie!*'

Owen and Sarah rush to stop me, but I'm already on my way to the hall.

'Jack, sit down. Let's drop this, have dinner and . . .'

'I don't think you can drop it.' If I don't leave now I'll say something I can't take back. And I need my family, in the long run. Nessie needs them. I snatch our coats from the bottom of the stair banister. '*Nessie*, come on!'

'But *Daa-aad* . . .'

'Jack, don't go.'

'I said we're going, Ness. Come downstairs, please.'

'Oka-a-a-ay . . .' I can't blame her for being annoyed with me. I *am* being unreasonable. But I'm damned if I'm going to stay here and take this.

I stop as my brother's huge hand clamps onto my shoulder. 'No, wait. We need to forget this conversation ever happened. You're doing great, Jack. Really. Everyone thinks so.'

I stare at him, then at Sarah, who is red-faced and staring at the ceiling. 'Obviously not everyone. And for your information, Sarah, I think about that stuff all the time. Night and day. And it scares me so much I can hardly breathe. So the next time you think I'm being selfish, or not putting Ness first, just you remember that, okay?'

'Why are we going?' Nessie is standing forlornly at the top of the stairs. I really hope she didn't hear everything I just said.

'We're just – I think it's better if we go home now.'

'But Auntie Sarah's making pie.'

My fight is gone, but I don't want Owen and Sarah to know that. 'We'll have some next time.'

'Sunday,' Sarah says – and that's the closest to an apology she'll ever offer.

I force a smile. 'Sunday.'

'Take a pie with you,' she says, hurrying into the kitchen without waiting for an answer.

My daughter immediately brightens. 'Can we, Dad?'

I nod, wishing I didn't feel like a wretch as I hold her coat out for her to wriggle into.

I'm still shaking an hour later. From the kitchen I can see Nessie cross-legged on the floor watching television, her head on one side, blue light from the screen dancing across the soft waves of her dark hair. I shouldn't have taken her away. It wasn't Nessie's fault. Am I ever going to be able to shake off other people's well-meant comments? I feel like I'm constantly ready to fight these days. What others thought of me never used to matter. But now . . . Well, now I feel like a soldier on a never-ending patrol.

I can't believe they were discussing me. Or making plans about my life. Sarah, maybe – she hasn't been my biggest fan over the years, although I thought we'd turned a corner lately. But it's Owen's involvement that stings the most. He should know better than to plan to take someone's child away. Especially his own brother's. And while I'd like to think Sarah was the instigator, the look I saw in his eyes suggested otherwise. Have they mentioned it to Dad, too?

I know people talk. I get it. And it probably comes from a good place. But it doesn't feel like that when you're the one under scrutiny. I know things aren't great, but Nessie is my life and everything I'm doing is for her. How dare they suggest I'm not coping?

The money situation is the big issue here. I'm going to have to redouble my efforts and start leaning on anyone who might give me work. And I'll do it, whatever it takes.

'Dad, are you not so mad now?' Ness has arrived in the kitchen and is staring up at me with wide, ocean-blue eyes.

'Yeah. Sorry, ladybird.'

She shrugs. 'It's okay. Grown-ups get mad sometimes.'

I love her matter-of-factness. But a seven-year-old shouldn't have to know that, let alone see it in action.

'Hey,' I say, wanting to shelve the subject, 'why don't we take Auntie Sarah's pie and eat it on the beach?'

Delight illuminates my daughter's face. 'Can we? And eat it from the tin?'

I pull two teaspoons from the cutlery drawer and brandish them like broadswords. 'Let's do it!'

The beach is still this afternoon, the tide far out and the late afternoon sun making the tall tower of Godrevy Lighthouse glow like polished quartz. We find a couple of rocks with bum-shaped dents in them and commence our two-spooned attack on the pie. The childish part of me doesn't want to enjoy it as much as I do, still smarting about the comments from its maker. But my sister-in-law makes a mean apple pie and this one is every bit as warm, sweet and spicy with cinnamon as usual.

'In the summer we'll do this with ice cream from the park shop,' I say, instantly regretting even promising Nessie a summer here. Is it fair, when I don't know where we'll be yet?

Stuff it – even if we aren't here, we'll steal one of Sarah's pies and buy ice cream from Jeb's shop and come to

Gwithian Beach. Ness needs security and I'll give it to her, one way or another.

'Honeycomb? Or Confetti Cake?'

'Anything you like.' I can't promise the world, but I can damn well promise ice cream.

'I like it here, Dad.'

'Me too, Ness.'

'I like it with you. And the glass stars. And the mermaids.'

I think my heart might just give out right here on the beach. 'Good.'

Nessie licks her spoon and giggles as she picks pie-crust crumbs from her hair. Then she fixes me with a look. 'Why are you scared?'

Crap. She heard. At this point I could lie and pretend everything is all right. But she *heard* me. 'Because I need to find more work,' I say, loathing the necessity of sharing this problem with her. All she should be worried about is eating stolen pie on a beach and dreaming of summer ice cream. 'It's okay, though. I'll find some.'

'Are we poor now?'

Oh, *great*. 'No, we're not poor.' Heading that way, but not quite destitute yet.

The thinking-wrinkle appears above her nose. 'But we're not very rich.'

'That's true. But we have pie.'

She brightens a little. 'And you're not scared of pie.'

'Absolutely not.' I growl at the half-eaten pie and stab it with my spoon. 'Take that, pie!'

As she gleefully joins the game, I start to make a mental

78

list of people I should call later. Someone must have work they need doing, or know people who do. This is a hole I can get us out of. I just have to try harder.

Chapter Thirteen

Seren

The town is very quiet as I walk to work the next day. St Ives is such a different place in the winter and early spring, before the crowds descend. When it's busy it's fun and buzzing, but summers in St Ives can be a bit like spending days with a tantrum-throwing toddler. I love them, but they are constantly demanding. Some people leave the town during the six-week school holidays, when tourists can be especially testing. But not me. I love it in every light and shade, every sunburst and thundering storm.

I get that from my dad. He was twenty years old when he arrived in St Ives – 'blown in by the wind', as Mum used to say. She was working in my grandparents' pub when a ragtag band of musicians turned up. They had travelled down from Caerphilly, only to find their gig in another local inn had been unexpectedly cancelled and they were adrift with nowhere to play or sleep. My grandpa offered them board for the night in exchange for a gig. He'd harboured a lifelong hankering to play jazz instead of running a pub, and I think he saw in them the person he might have been. They agreed, the gig was played, and that was that. Dad saw Mum behind the bar and composed a song for her during the improvised set. She was smitten, as was he. Grandpa loved Dad instantly, and when Dad's band was heading home, he promised Mum he'd return. A month later he moved to St Ives. They never looked back.

That's another thing I love about this town: that my family's story is woven through the winding streets, nestled between the cobbles on Fore Street and set in stone in what became Mum and Dad's house. Literally, in fact: when they moved in, Dad carved a brick with their wedding date and initials and set it into the wall of the house. When I was born, he did the same. So long after we've all gone, our stories will be part of St Ives.

MacArthur's seems darker this morning when I unlock the door, as if shrouded in sea fog. There's definitely a shadow hanging over the place these days, but this morning it seems even more pronounced. The front door wedges half-open on the pile of brown envelopes strewn across the mat. I don't have to open them to know what they are.

How did you let it get into this state, Dad?

I know he won't answer, but as the final demands stack ever higher I really wish he'd find a way. His optimism was one of his best and brightest features, but you can't build a business on that. He thought people would see his vision for the shop. Unfortunately, it turns out that banks and mortgage companies, suppliers and utility companies are

81

singularly unromantic bodies. I know it was never Dad's intention to leave us with all of this – I have to keep reminding myself of it because I'm growing angrier as each day passes. Heart attacks are no respecter of personal circumstances. He couldn't have known it would end when it did. He probably expected to live into his nineties. But I just wish he'd planned ahead a little, sought the financial advice he was always supposedly getting round to asking for.

It's pointless going over this again. I have the same conversation with myself every morning as I walk to work and I'm never going to find any answers. It's my job to find solutions.

But this morning I'm tired. Last night I worked a shift at Becca's Bar, a few streets away from the harbour, a favourite haunt of St Ives folk. I've known Becca a long time – her stepdaughter Daisy was my classmate through school. She's a bit of a local legend, a tiny lady covered in rainbow-coloured tattoos who could break your arm if you cross her. Thankfully, she's as well known for her heart of gold as she is for her balls of steel, and she's always been lovely to me.

Even still, I was surprised when she offered me a job a month ago.

It's only a few evenings a week, but it brings in extra money that's so needed. It's a bit tricky fitting it in around all the after-hours shop work, trying to make my own jewellery and my early-morning trips to Gwithian; but what I lose in sleep, I gain in peace of mind.

I took a flask of extra-strong coffee with me to the beach

this morning, the drag of weariness heavy on my body. But it remained forgotten in my rucksack when I started working on the star. Today's star was made almost entirely of green seaglass – and it made me wonder if the other star-maker is saving the pieces from previous stars, to be able to choose colours like that. It would be highly unusual to find so much of a single colour during one visit to the beach. I like that they're finding new ways to be creative – the planning involved makes me believe they're committed to our starmaking. That makes me smile despite needing sleep. And I needed that today, more than before.

'Happy birthday, stargirl.'

I turn in my shop to see a bunch of yellow roses coming in through the door, closely followed by Kieran's welcome grin. The sight of him is impossibly lovely.

'I didn't think anyone would remember.' I wasn't sure I wanted to remember, it being my first without Dad and so close to losing him.

'How good a friend would I be if I forgot? I couldn't have my favourite beachcomber without blooms on such an auspicious day.' He looks down as his shoe scuffs the mountain of brown envelopes. 'Although I see you're a woman in demand already.'

'*Final* demand,' I grimace.

He chuckles and pulls me into a hug. 'Darling, being in any kind of demand is preferable to being invisible.' He plants a large kiss on the top of my head. 'Gorgeous woman. Shall I put the kettle on?'

As usual, he doesn't wait for my reply, and within minutes the tea is made and we are sitting in Dad's old mismatched armchairs at the back of the shop. Kieran has brought still-warm chocolate twists from the bakery opposite the Baptist church and is all birthday smiles, but I get the feeling he has another reason for visiting. A reason that might own a beachside coffee hut and be partial to huge hugs . . .

'These flowers are beautiful,' I say, loving the brightness of the blooms against the gloom of the shop. 'But I wonder if maybe someone else in St Ives would appreciate them more?'

He gives me a withering look but it's too late: I've rumbled him and he knows it. 'She wouldn't accept them.'

'She said that?' I know Aggie is still crushingly embarrassed about their unexpected night, but would she really turn down flowers?

'No, but . . .'

'So you haven't even tried.'

'What's the point? She'd think they were a guilt offering.'

'Or she might be happy you bought her roses.'

'It's complicated, Ser. What happened – it changed things. I don't know how to *be* with Aggie any more.'

I love him for confessing this. Usually Kieran remains stoically silent on his own feelings. In all the time we've been friends, I think he's only talked about matters of his heart three times. 'You really like her, don't you?'

'I don't know.' He claps a hand to his forehead and groans. 'It's hopeless.'

'No, it isn't. *Talk* to her. Work it out together.'

'Maybe. *If* you talk to your mum.'

I did not see that coming. 'This isn't about me. Don't change the subject.'

'But really it's the same thing, isn't it? We both want to move on with our lives but we're too scared to talk to the person who could make it happen.'

'I can't tell Mum I don't want the shop.' The space around us suddenly feels cramped and stifling. Both Kieran and Aggie have been saying this recently, but I can't do that to Mum. I'm all she has, and while she's making great strides, she's in no state to run the place. It's not in the best state of repair, and there are a thousand and one things I want to do with it before I'd ever let it go.

Besides, what would Dad say?

'I disagree.'

When you're so tired you can barely think, it's not the right time to be challenged about huge life questions. I just can't deal with this today.

'Can we talk about something else, Kieran, please?'

'Claiming birthday girl privilege, are we?' His smile is reproachful but I think he knows not to push this. 'Fair enough. *But* you are coming to The Hub with us for birthday dinner tonight and I won't take no for an answer.'

I love my friends and am touched they want to celebrate with me, so even though what I most want to do after work is curl up under a duvet and sleep, I drag myself back out into town after half an hour at home. I've drunk so much coffee, I'm vibrating. I just hope I can stay awake long enough to eat.

'To the birthday girl!' Aggie yells, raising her beer bottle, as my friends sitting around the semi-circular booth do the same.

I clink what I've promised myself is my only cider tonight against their bottles and we settle back for a good night.

And it *is* a good night, despite my weariness, and the final demands, and the worries that seem to grow every day. For a few precious hours I'm just Seren, not Seren-whose-business-is-on-the-rocks, or Seren-who-lost-her-dad. Old jokes, old stories and old memories flow around the table, taking us back to when all we had to worry about was having fun and finding our way in the world. I wish it could last forever . . .

Chapter Fourteen

Jack

The asking begins next morning. In between jobs I've promised Jeb I'll do and taking Nessie to school, I make calls from a long list I wrote in the early hours, my head too full of worries to sleep. One by one, lines of biro cancel them out, each stroke thicker and more frustrated than the last, leaving heavy indents on the other side of the paper. People I've known for years either flatly turn me down, or explain at length why now isn't the right time for them to be sharing work. Every excuse is valid, every apology sincere, but they might as well be throwing rocks at my head.

By midday, my hope is fading. By two p.m. I'm starting to panic. In my car outside Nessie's school at three fifteen I'm banging my head against the steering wheel, wishing I'd never started the damn list.

And then, just when I'm beginning to wonder if Sarah might be right about my prospects, there's a breakthrough. Dave Ellis, a builder from Padstow I worked with a few years back, returns my call and suggests we meet. He's visiting a job near St Ives next day, so I arrange to meet him for lunch in a pub in Lelant.

I have to be realistic, I tell myself as I leave my car in The Watermill's car park: it might be another dead end. But my pulse is racing as I enter the pub. Dave is waiting at the bar, a little greyer than the last time I saw him, but his booming laugh and huge grin haven't changed.

'Jack! Good to see you!' He slaps a hand against my back and almost sends me sailing across the bar. 'How's business?'

'Slow,' I say, resisting the urge to play down my situation. Today I need to look desperate. 'Don't suppose you've heard of anything kicking around?'

Dave grimaces, and I remember why his nickname when I worked for him was Bucky. *Enormous* front teeth. I make myself stop staring.

'Can't say I have, boy. Things bad since . . . ?' He doesn't say it, but I know what he means. Everyone knows by now. News like that travels fast in the local trades community. In a strange way we're family, even though we're all competing for the same jobs. I've had conversations about other colleagues' misfortunes over the years, so I know how it works.

'We lost the house.'

'No! Mate . . .'

I try to shrug the irritation from my prickling shoulders. 'Yeah. Hard times. So I need to get as much work as I can.'

Compassion graces his broad face for a moment. 'Then I'm buying your beer. No arguments. Let's sit down and see if we can't come up with some ideas.'

I'm grateful he's even prepared to talk about it, but I'm aware of every muscle tensing as we sit. I don't like asking for help. It grates against everything I am. But I'm learning how to, and right now I appreciate Dave's gesture more than I'd ever let on.

We huddle over beer by a small table near bookshelves stacked with the obligatory artful junk of the gastro pub. A strange blue pottery jug shaped like a monkey eyes me suspiciously between a table tennis bat that has seen better days and a faded copy of *Tom Brown's School Days*. It's a bit unnerving, so I look over Dave's shoulder to watch a beer delivery bloke struggling through the fire exit of the pub.

'Gotta say, Jack, you're not the only one askin' for jobs. There's more work than a few years ago, but the same people keep grabbin' it. I seen several blokes go out of business this year alone.' He takes a huge gulp of his pint, setting the glass down with a thump on the table. 'Don't mean we can't find you somethin', though, so don't you lose heart. Let's have a think . . .'

A couple at the bar are having a heavily whispered row and it catches my attention as Dave starts listing possibilities. I can see the two young bartenders giggling behind the optics as they watch the not-so-silent argument. A year ago that could have been Tash and me – except we'd passed the point of pub lunch dates by then, our relationship played out in a series of increasingly bitter WhatsApp exchanges. I hope the couple here can find a way back to one another, that it isn't already too late . . .

'. . . Wes Smith was lookin' a while back, I know, but

that might've gone already. Tom Harvey might be worth a call, I s'pose. But even Jim Derham was layin' blokes off, last I heard. And you know how flush for work he usually is. Is it foreman work you're after?'

I nod, but in truth I'll take anything.

He runs through a few more names, none of which sound promising, but I'll try them anyway. Then he leans across the table and, in a low voice, says, 'Failing that, there *is* Brotherson Developments.'

His tone mirrors my gut reaction. Images of horrid, bland buildings fill my mind. Bill Brotherson is to sensitive renovation what Joseph Stalin was to international relations. He buys up old and derelict buildings across the southwest and turns them into identikit, homogenised apartments – the kind my late wife lusted over. I imagine him playing a real-life game of Monopoly across Cornwall and Devon, plonking his faceless houses down all over the landscape like those nasty plastic green houses and red hotels.

'Is he looking?' I hate myself for even asking.

'He is. Now don't get me wrong, I'm not the man's biggest fan. Brotherson's a total git, but he's good for the money.' His bushy brows drop over his eyes. 'I could always mention your name to him, if you wanted?'

It's a heavily loaded question, the kind Gandalf might ask Frodo Baggins just before they enter an Orc-plagued forest: *In there? Are you* sure, *Frodo?* Working for Brotherson would be about the worst thing I could do professionally. Once you're linked with a man like that, you're labelled for life in the trade.

But it's better than bankruptcy.

I think of Nessie this morning, how she hugged me extra-tightly outside school, her concern for her failing father all too evident. I don't have a choice. This could be our best hope.

'Please – if you wouldn't mind,' I reply.

Over Dave's shoulder, the fire exit door slams.

Chapter Fifteen

Seren

With the next town meeting imminent, Lou and Aggie call a meeting of the Save the Parsonage committee after work. I close the shop at three p.m. and walk to Porthgwidden Beach, enjoying the brief spell of sunshine that has graced the afternoon. The sea sparkles where it catches the sun and peeks between the houses as I pass through Downalong. I take a longer route along Porthmeor Road and drop down the slipway onto Porthmeor Beach, pausing for a while to enjoy the view of its wide sweeping bay. Then I take the footpath that rises from the beach to the Island. With time to spare, I follow the footpath around the Island, watching blue surf breaking in white spray on black rocks down in the coves along the shoreline far below.

I love this walk – it's been my favourite route for as long as I can remember, the scene of countless summer strolls, rock-pooling expeditions, a spate of morning runs when I was on a health kick a few years back and even my first kiss, which happened on a bench near the chapel on the peak of the hill with a boy I've long since forgotten. I've laughed and cried here, watched dawns break and days end. I've whiled away hours, and escaped for precious stolen minutes.

The morning after we lost Dad – when I woke up for the first time in my life without him in the world – I ran here and yelled my pain and anger into the new day. The Island heard my anguish; Porthmeor caught my tears. I am linked to this land in every way possible and it will always be my sanctuary – the place I run to.

Today the sun smiles on the wind-buffeted grass, warming my back as I skirt the Island path. I hear the padding of shoes on the tarmac and look up to see a runner heading in my direction. He slows as he draws level with me, then pauses to take a drink from the water bottle he's carrying.

'Lovely day,' he smiles, rubbing sweat from his forehead with the back of his hand. He's an older man, his thinning hair white against the tan of his skin, but his frame is athletic and he looks in the peak of health. His summer-blue eyes twinkle like the sun shimmering on the sea around us. I think I've seen him before, but I can't place where. That happens all the time in St Ives – so many people make frequent return visits to the town that familiar faces can come from anywhere in the world.

'It is,' I say. 'Having a good run?'

'The best, thank you. This place just begs you to be out in it, doesn't it?' He smiles again and presses a button on his digital watch. 'Doing my best times right now, too. You having a nice walk?'

'I am.'

'Lovely. Nice to see you again.' With a last flash of his smile, he is off, sprinting like a man half his age.

I watch him until he disappears around the curve of the path, inexplicably cheered by the meeting. This place creates a positivity that you end up sharing with everyone, whether you know them or not. People in love with St Ives have a strong common bond – it's like meeting family.

Lou and Aggie are deep in conversation when I arrive at the coffee hut. They look so serious that I want to giggle, biting my tongue as they look up to see me.

'I went for a walk,' I explain, glancing at the clock. I'm only five minutes late, but my friends have clearly started without me.

Lou nods. 'Well, you're here now. Take a seat, girl, you look exhausted. Have you been sleepin' much?'

'No more than usual.'

'You need your sleep, Seren. There's a battle to fight.'

Several battles, actually, I reply in my head, but I don't say it out loud. Lou is a sweetheart and is just voicing concern for my wellbeing. He bustles about, getting Aggie to make me a large coffee and grabbing a cushion from one of the chairs by the entrance.

'Bleddy Nora, Lou, let her be. Anyone would think she was pregnant, the way you're fussin'.'

'I'm just protectin' our greatest asset,' Lou retorts, shooting a quick glance at me. 'She *isn't* – is she?'

'No, Lou, I'm not pregnant,' I say quickly, before the evil glint in my friend's eye is allowed to wreak havoc.

'Not that it wouldn't be okay if you were . . . I mean,

what you choose to do or – erm – *not* do is completely your business . . .'

Aggie's snort of laughter bounces off the tiled floor and fills the coffee hut. 'Oh give over, Lou. When do you think Seren has the chance to even think about sex, let alone be bothered to find anyone to have a go with?'

'Well, I wasn't implyin' . . .' He flushes red. 'I didn't mean . . .'

I have to smile. Lou is famous for backing himself into verbal corners and it never stops being amusing to watch, but someone has to rescue him before he digs a hole he can't clamber out of. 'Relax, mate. I'm missing three key factors in that department.'

'Which are?'

'Time. Energy. And opportunity.'

Thankfully, he sees the joke. 'Ah! Ha ha! Good one.' Saved from further embarrassment, he gratefully resumes his seat.

'Drink that, lovely.' Aggie pushes a huge, bowl-sized cup of dark, smoky coffee towards me and joins us at the table.

'Cheers. So what's the reason for the meeting?'

Lou's features beam into a smile. 'Strategy, girl. We've got Brotherson on the hop, and we need to keep our advantage.'

'The whole town is behind you,' Aggie says. 'Those who matter, at any rate. If it carries on we might not need four meetings for everyone to decide.'

Lou raps his fingers on the table as if trying to pin down his thoughts. 'I say we keep goin'. Stoke up the fury against Brotherson Developments. Keepin' order, mind. I don't want a brawl like last time. Just enough anger to scare Bill Brotherson back to his swanky offices in Plymouth.'

There's a knock on the coffee hut door and Kieran and Cerrie walk in, too busy doling out hugs to Aggie and me to see Lou's pointed stare at his watch.

'What have we missed?' Kieran swings into the seat next to me. 'World domination? Unleashing the hounds of hell on Bill Brotherson?'

Lou sniffs. 'I might've known you'd be the one mockin' our victory, Mr Macklin.'

'Always happy to oblige, Lou. When are you planning on distributing the Brotherson voodoo dolls and pins?'

I glare at him to stop, but where teasing Lou is concerned, Kieran knows no boundaries.

'That's quite enough from you, Captain Flippant!'

Seeing Lou's neck begin to flush an angry red, I decide to step in. 'So what's the plan for the next meeting, Ag?'

'Both sides face questions from the floor and respond to those raised last time,' Aggie intones, as if reading Lou's notes from memory.

'Nice that *someone's* bothered to read my meeting minutes,' Lou says. 'Thank you, Agatha.'

'Happy to oblige, Louis. Although seeing as last time ended in a punch-up, what happens on Wednesday night is anyone's guess.'

Kieran snorts, and I see Cerrie dig him in the ribs with her elbow. 'I say we take the higher ground,' she suggests, ever the cool head of reason in our meetings. 'Brotherson knows we have history and the heritage of this town on our side. We would save the site for the town and wider public. He just wants to make money from it and move on. The only way he operates is by discrediting his enemies. So we refuse to be drawn into a dirty fight.'

'Good point.' I think about how flustered the developer was at the first meeting when faced with an angry crowd. 'Do you think he'll even turn up?'

'Has to, if he wants to win this. Can't wriggle his way out of it, can he?'

Kieran nods. 'We have him over a barrel. I honestly think we can win this. And with Seren leading us in Mark MacArthur's name, we have the best chance of success.'

In Mark MacArthur's name. So much of my life has become underscored with that phrase. Running the shop, looking after Mum, leading the campaign . . . I'm proud to carry on the work Dad started, but it's a heavy burden, too. If we can win this campaign and save Elinor Carne's home from destruction, it will be a sweet victory indeed – proof that my father was right to champion her cause. And at least in this I'm not on my own.

I look around the table at the team and my heart swells. Together, we can make this happen. We can defeat Bill Brotherson and win.

My phone has been vibrating like a disgruntled wasp in my jacket pocket all through the meeting. When it ends and I step out into the early evening, I find four missed calls, all from Mum. Walking home, I call her back. I'll be seeing her in ten minutes' time, but she might want something picking up for tea, so I ought to check.

She answers after the first ring. 'Oh Seren, thank goodness.'

'Are you okay?'

I can hear her gasps of breath on the line. 'I've – been so – *worried* . . .'

'Mum, slow down. Tell me what's happened.'

'A letter's come. From the bank.'

I stop walking and lean against the stone wall of the Island car park. 'A letter? It's probably a circular, Mum. We get them all the time.'

'It isn't. I know it isn't.'

Mum's been prone to panics like this in recent weeks. Last week she was convinced her debit card had been stolen, only for us to find it at the bottom of her handbag instead of its usual place in her purse. Things outside of her control scare her – understandably, given Dad's sudden passing.

'Are you coming home? Where have you been? I need you to sort this, Seren.'

I take a breath and answer as calmly and quietly as possible. 'I've been at the campaign meeting. I went straight there after work. I'll be home soon.'

'How soon?'

All of a sudden, I don't want to hurry home. I've had a good day, and I'm starting to believe we can win this vote for the town, for Elinor Carne and most importantly, for Dad. The glow inside is made even brighter by the secret seaglass stars I've been making every morning, and the realisation that there is so much more in the world for me than just being Dad's substitute.

'I have a couple of errands to run. And then I'll be home. I just need a bit of time, Mum . . .' I've already started walking back towards the town.

'I opened it,' she blurts out, a soft whimper following it. 'I'm sorry. I knew it had to be bad for them to send this to our house, not the shop.'

'How bad?'

'The bank manager is calling us to a meeting, in two weeks' time. Seren, they want us to bring the account books in. This is bad news.'

I can't think about this now. I don't want the responsibility. I want to hang on to the optimism I've found within for as long as I can. 'Put it on the shelf and forget about it. I'll be home soon, I promise.'

I end the call and walk quickly back into Downalong. I need somewhere I can be quiet with my thoughts. And I know the perfect place.

At the land side of Smeaton's Pier, one arm of St Ives' harbour that houses a proud white metal lighthouse, there's a shelter overlooking the town beach. At night during the summer this is the local kids' hangout of choice. It's a little more sheltered than the sea wall, but still wild enough to feel like you're on the edge of the world. Even out of season some kids meet here, judging by the cheekily stashed cider cans under the bench where I'm now sitting.

I love the sea in early spring. It's slate-green, with white-headed waves breaking across fudge-coloured sands that seem to glow even on the dankest, dreariest days. The rocks and wooden posts stand out jet-black and stoic against the sea. But the light that for years has called artists to St Ives still makes everything shine as if lit from within.

From here I can see the sweep of the bay, its rich cream sands stretching around the headland to the gleaming white tower of Godrevy Lighthouse far in the distance. The sea beneath its rocky island home is a thin streak of ice blue on the horizon, the glow of the setting sun behind it.

I think about Gwithian Beach – and the box of marshmallows for the mermaids – and I feel warm inside, despite the cold wind numbing my face and hands and the threat of what awaits me at home biting at my nerves. What is the other starmaker doing now, I wonder? Are they on the beach opposite the lighthouse, snuggled down against the prevailing wind, thinking of me?

I hope they are.

I don't know anything about the other person, but we are connected like St Ives to the bay that follows the headland to Gwithian Beach. We are part of the St Ives Bay story. Mystery has shrouded this coastline for centuries. You feel it as you walk through the fishing villages and towns, or follow ancient footsteps around the cliff paths and across the beaches. This area is rich in stories of adventure, of love found and lost, of smugglers and soldiers and magicians. It sings from the sands and echoes across the cliffs. I feel privileged to be at the beginning of a new story here – the Gwithian Beach stars – and even though I don't know how long it will last, I want so much to take my place in it.

I'll go home soon, face the contents of the letter with Mum and prepare for the next battle. But for now, I sit and I think of the starmaker – and hold on to the feeling of completeness it gives me.

Chapter Sixteen

Jack

The challenge of making a new star every day has meant us collecting and reusing pieces of seaglass in every colour we can find. Currently Nessie has a bucket almost full of the stuff, but it can be hard to find enough pieces of the colours she wants for each star.

One night I wake inexplicably at four a.m. It's the kind of jumping-to-attention, wide-awake sensation that makes returning to sleep impossible. Resigned to an early rise, I get up, make a pot of tea and look around the still-dark interior of the chalet. I don't want to put the TV on for fear of waking Ness, and my eyes ache too much to consider reading. With two hours to kill before our day officially begins, I look around for something to occupy myself. Having so much time with nothing to do is dangerous for me – too much opportunity for worries and thoughts to fill my mind.

On my second mug of tea, I spot Nessie's seaglass bucket beneath the coat rack by the front door. I remember her frustration as she rifled through it yesterday evening on the beach.

'There isn't enough blue. It's all too jumbly, Dad!'

Right. Time to sort the pieces out, so she can find the colours she needs more easily.

Last week I found two old cat-feeding trays under the sink, presumably left by a previous resident. Each tray has four compartments, each with their own hinged lids that no longer close. They must have once been operated by clockwork timers to open at set times when the owner was out, but all that remains on the lids are the circles where the dials once were. I fetch them out now and give them a soak in warm soapy water to remove the few remaining crusts of ancient cat food. When they are dried and on the table, they look almost as good as new. Fetching Nessie's bucket, I settle myself at the table and start to sort the pieces into separate colours. Seven compartments for sea-glass, one for the smooth pieces of pottery we've found when beachcombing.

It's a strangely calming activity and even though my body could have done with a few more hours' sleep, my mind relaxes into the steady rhythm of it. The seaglass pieces are cool and smooth in my fingers. As they pass from the bucket through my hands to the sorting trays I remember all the seaglass stars we have made and found completed on the beach. Because I don't know who has been finishing our stars, I can't escape the magic of it. Not having all the answers means I don't have to look for them. That is so refreshing. Every other consideration in my life feels like it has to be quantified, explored, put into priority order, obsessed over. This isn't something I can control – and that is a true gift.

By five thirty a.m., the bucket is empty and a rainbow of glittering glass fills the trays. I'm tempted to wake Nessie to show her, but the magic might be lost in her annoyance at being woken too early. Making a new mug of tea, I pull on my hooded sweatshirt and quietly step outside onto the chalet's veranda.

From the salt-aged wooden steps I can see out over the wide sweep of Gwithian Towans towards St Ives far to the left, and Godrevy Lighthouse's white tower just beginning to catch the gold of the sunrise to the right. The slowly emerging sun shimmers across the sea and the sky above it is unnaturally blue, the hue you see above the clouds from an aeroplane. Against the dark shadow of the rows of static caravan roofs and undulating dunes, the light glows. Watching it makes me hopeful, and I realise I've only just begun to feel that again since we've made the stars on the beach.

Is our starmaker down there now? Are they completing the pale blue and white glass star we made last night? Knowing they might be close makes me smile, despite everything else that lies in store today. A friend, on the beach we love, thinking of us. In this moment, I have the sunrise, the sea and the promise of our star-completing friend close to our home. For now, everything is good.

The phone call later that morning came out of the blue and now, two days later, I still can't quite believe it. After months of trying to make ends meet and unsuccessfully quoting for building jobs, suddenly there's a job offer. It feels too good to be true. It might yet be.

I'm sitting in the vast reception area of Brotherson Developments, feeling like thirteen-year-old me waiting outside the head teacher's office. Mr Harrison put the fear of God into me as a kid, and often for good reason. Usually it was my own fault, although towards the end of my school years I became my teachers' default scapegoat in any punishable situations. I wasn't a bad kid, just very energetic – and more inspired by the fun my friends were having than by the subjects I was supposed to be learning. I pulled it back eventually, when it mattered. But fun was always more appealing.

My palms are clammy and I wish the chair were more comfortable. Somewhere in the UK I'm convinced there is a manufacturer of office reception chairs specifically designed to make visitors uncomfortable. It's probably a selling point – to give the business owner the upper hand. You're never at your best when one half of your bum is numb . . .

Always flippant, Jack. Always the joker . . .

I can hear Tash's disapproval even now. If she were still alive I would have had a stern pep talk this morning about 'not letting my sense of humour ruin a great opportunity'. It was one of a growing list of things we differed on. I have to hand it to her, though: she was the perfect professional when she needed to be. I used to watch her working the room at her gallery events – it was like observing a finely tuned machine. She would have loved a meeting like this. I, on the other hand, would much rather chat over a pint at the local pub. I feel straitjacketed in a suit.

But Bill Brotherson is the kind of customer you don't say no to. He's the leading developer in the southwest, and a formidable force. If I'm completely honest, I think his developments could be more attractive, and make more use of the phenomenal local building materials all around us. But as *he* called *me*, perhaps I won't mention that to him today.

I've tried my best not to think about what this could mean for Ness and me, but it's hard not to. Brotherson Developments is a multimillion-pound operation. If they offer me a building contract, it could change everything. Tash would be telling me to pull my head out of the clouds, but I can't help it. This is the biggest thing to happen to my business in years. It might just save us.

'Mr Dixon?'

This is it. Or it could be. Either way, *don't stuff it up, Jack . . .*

Bill Brotherson is sitting behind a desk so vast it makes him look like a kid at a dining table. He's what my brother Owen would call an 'overcompensator' – surrounding himself with magnificence to make up for his lack of height. You're *supposed* to be impressed by his office, everything within it yells. The too-plush carpet that would be more at home in a five-star hotel bedroom than an office; the over-sized canvasses on the walls with artfully shot images of the developer poring over plans in a pristine hard hat; the lighting that all seems to be pointed at the man behind the desk. It's all part of the theatre of being a business mogul.

And it's *terrifying*.

But I smile, and try not to mind that he doesn't even get

up from his seat to greet me. My dad would *hate* that. *'Bleddy ideas above his station. Manners cost nothin', do they?'*

'Jack,' Brotherson says, pronouncing my name with far too many vowels: *Ja-a-ack*. 'Appreciate you popping over.'

Gwithian to Plymouth was one hell of a pop, I think. Stuck in traffic and praying my satnav was lying about my estimated arrival time . . . Thank heaven for Owen and Sarah offering to pick Nessie up from school. Heaven knows when I'll be home.

'Bill,' I venture, extending my hand, which thankfully he deigns to shake.

'Sit. Sit. Would you like coffee?'

I've had so much coffee while I was waiting in reception I'm practically floating. Forty-five minutes is a long time to inhale caffeine. 'No, thanks.'

'Sorry to keep you waiting. You know how it is in business, Jack. Always on call, a million and one jobs demanding your attention.'

I laugh and nod. *I wish*. I can't remember the last time I had more than one job at once, let alone a million and one.

'So, like I said on the phone, I wanted to chat about a contract. Local to you, actually. Outskirts of St Ives.'

'Oh?'

'It's a derelict Georgian building with potential for eight two-bed executive apartments. Views down into St Ives Bay. Great location. I need a construction manager to co-ordinate it. Be my eyes and ears on the site, make my very expensive architect plans work in the real world.

106

Standard stuff, oversight, day-to-day, managing a build team I'll supply. Interested?'

Daft question. But there's one thing that doesn't make sense. 'I am. But I'm a builder primarily, Bill. What made you decide to ask me?' Tash could be yelling at me now, but I want to know. If this job offer is as good as it sounds, I don't want to be in any doubt about it.

Brotherson chuckles and leans back in his black leather and chrome executive chair, which protests a little. 'I like you, Jack. You think like I do. I saw the development in Fowey you worked on a few years back. Good materials, seemed to have general support from the community. I think you could bring those qualities to this build. As construction manager, you'd be the link between Brotherson Developments and the community. You know your stuff. And word is, you care about what you do. I like that.'

The Fowey development was five years ago, which feels like a lifetime. I think Tash had hoped we'd move there when it was done – she was never particularly fond of our new-build semi in Penzance. We couldn't have afforded it, though, even back then, and despite that project making me a good amount of money I always felt her disappointment clouding the achievement. Nevertheless, I was proud of that one. It was much smaller than the development Brotherson is proposing, and I did a lot of the work myself, bringing in a small team of guys I used for the next few years but had to let go when Tash died. We decided to use local stone and source fixtures and fittings from Cornish suppliers wherever possible. It was a key selling point and on the few occasions I've been in the area since, I've always visited it. To prove to myself it happened.

I did that . . .

The chance to do it again would be too good to miss. Not to mention the money it could bring in, which is the main reason I came here today.

I take a deep breath. 'What kind of figures are we talking?'

Brotherson observes me for just a moment longer than is comfortable, then pulls a gold-plated fountain pen from a glass cube on the desk and scribbles a figure on a piece of headed notepaper. It pivots under his thick finger as he turns it to face me.

The numbers swim in my vision.

'I'll do it,' I say, for once not caring if I sound desperate. I *am* desperate. And the amount Bill Brotherson has just written down would provide for Nessie and me for a year or more.

This is the break I've been praying for. And I can hardly breathe.

Chapter Seventeen

Seren

The Guildhall is packed when I arrive, even though the meeting doesn't start for another forty minutes. Lou is looking worried already, his fears not helped by recent jokes about people bringing popcorn to watch the continuing grudge match between Brotherson Developments and the residents of St Ives.

'Best thing to watch on a Wednesday night for ages.' Fred Philips from Poldark Pasties grins as he takes his seat beside me. 'You should sell tickets, Seren. Make a fortune, you would.'

I grin back, but I'm nervous. I know many people in the room support me, but tonight is the first time I'll be speaking as leader of the campaign. I've carried my notes for the speech with me all week, going over them at the shop, on the beach, in the shelter on Smeaton's Pier during my lunch break and in my room, late into the night. I'm pretty sure I've gone over it in my sleep, too. I want to get it right – not just for me, but for everyone on the committee as well. And Dad. Especially Dad.

Elinor Carne is a woman forgotten by history. Her contribution to British astronomy was so important, and yet for many years it was ignored. We want to promote the work she did and ensure she will be remembered in St Ives, not just today but for countless generations to come . . .

I hope I won't sound pompous. Or fluff my lines. The words I've written in Dad's old stargazing notebook don't seem big enough to contain all the admiration I have for Elinor. I wish I could plug the microphone straight into my heart and let it speak for me. Most people aren't objecting to the development because of her, I know. It's more of a protest at developers like Bill Brotherson riding roughshod over our heritage, destroying historic buildings with his horrible designs. But Elinor Carne has inspired me so much; I just want the town to feel it too. Maybe if they feel they're fighting for her memory, not just bricks and mortar, they will be more likely to vote against the development. Maybe then we'll have a hope of winning.

I have a beautiful pen-and-ink print on my bedroom wall by the artist Charlie Bowater. It's called *The Old Astronomer* – and I bought it because it made me think of Elinor Carne. In it she's reaching up to touch a star in the sky. No photographs or drawings survive of our astronomer, so I like to think of her as the woman in the drawing. Reaching beyond the expectations and conventions of her time, daring to be something more. She inspires me to do the same, to keep reaching, to keep ignoring everything that would hold me back, eyes always focused on my dreams.

110

I watch the hall filling up, feel the anticipation like static buzzing around me. I should probably find my friends and talk to them, but I feel like all the words I have for tonight are contained within the notebook: I don't have any left to make conversation. Besides, every row of seats filled fuels the nerves within me. Everyone will be watching me tonight. Everyone will make up their minds based upon what I say.

I look at my notes again and my heart hits the floor. Why did I ever think I could do this?

'Coffee?'

I jump and look up. There's a man standing next to me by the refreshment table, holding up a polystyrene cup. He's tall, with dark wavy hair and a peppering of a beard across his jaw. He's wearing a bottle-green hoodie with a white T-shirt beneath and blue jeans. His boots are a little scuffed. I didn't hear him arrive and it takes me a moment to realise he's talking to me. 'Sorry – um . . .'

'Or tea? I think there's both.' He gives a rueful smile. 'I sound like an idiot. Sorry. I'm new here.'

'Oh.' I must look like a goldfish to him. Gathering myself together, I manage to return his smile. 'Forgive me. Tea would be lovely, thanks.'

Relief floods his expression and he busies himself with the crotchety old tea urn, laughing when the plastic spoon bends, Uri Geller-style, as he tries to remove the tea bag. 'I'm not doing well, am I? Um . . . Milk? Sugar?'

Not wanting to prolong the awkward business, I reach out and rescue my cup. 'I'll sort that. Thanks.' Remembering my manners, I tuck Dad's notebook under one arm and offer my hand. 'I'm Seren, by the way.'

111

'Jack.' He looks at the rapidly filling rows of chairs. 'This place is packed.'

'It is. I wasn't expecting such a good turnout.'

'Bit daunting, actually.' He has a nice smile, I think. And what Mum would call an 'open face'. Trustworthy. I don't think he'd be good at keeping secrets.

Why did I just think that?

'Weren't you at the last meeting?' I ask, ignoring the train of thought that's threatening to carry me away.

'Unfortunately not. But I heard about it.'

I grin. 'I think half of Cornwall heard about it, judging by the crowd tonight.'

'Actually, I . . .'

But I don't hear what Jack says next because a loud thump from the stage summons our attention. Lou taps the already dented microphone one more time and raises his hand.

'Ladies and gentlemen, if you could take your seats, please. We'll be startin' shortly. Thank you. Before we begin, however, I want to reiterate the ground rules for this meetin' and those that will follow. I don't want a repeat of last week and I don't think anyone else does, either.'

There is a loud snigger from somewhere in the hall, met by a chorus of shushes.

Lou rolls his eyes. 'Cheers for that. Now, it is imperative that we allow both sides of the debate sufficient time to make their cases. Last week – well, I'm guessin' most of you are well aware of what happened last week, so all I'll say is *please*, let's show some decency to both speakers tonight. I'm making time for questions in the last part of the meetin', so if there's somethin' you'd like to say you'll get your chance then.'

The room has hushed. I clutch Dad's notebook as the time to make my speech approaches.

'Good. So, I would like you all to welcome our spokespeople for each side of this town debate. For the Save the Parsonage campaign, Miss Seren MacArthur, and representin' Brotherson Developments, Rectory Fields' project manager, Mr Jack Dixon.'

I'm halfway to the stage when I hear Jack's name and turn to see him following me. He looks as shocked as I feel . . .

I was expecting Bill Brotherson to be opposite me at the debating table tonight. In my mind I've played out the exchange all week – how I would state my case and stand against his objections. I've tried to picture myself as a valiant knight, facing an angry, red-faced dragon, fighting the good fight for Elinor Carne's honour. It made me believe we could win.

I wasn't expecting Jack Dixon.

How didn't I realise he was on the opposing side?

As we take our seats I stare over at him. He appears to have lost the ability to make eye contact with me. I could kick myself. Why didn't I guess the stranger was linked to Brotherson?

I wish I hadn't liked his smile now.

Lou is continuing the introductions, mentioning that from now on Jack will be the official representative of Brotherson Developments; he will be the one tearing down the remaining physical evidence of Elinor Carne's home and constructing a Brotherson monstrosity in its place. Part of me isn't surprised that Bill Brotherson chickened out of facing us all again. It's the sort of cowardly, toe-rag action you'd expect of a man who doesn't like his little kingdom being challenged. Send someone more innocuous, someone with a sincere smile and professional charm, to do his dirty work, so he gets his way without getting his hands mucky. Ugh. And to think I thought Jack Dixon was on *our* side . . .

'. . . the leader of the Save the Parsonage campaign will now address the room,' Lou says, and suddenly I feel the blood drain from my face. This is it: the moment I've been dreading all week. Packing away my anger, I rise shakily to my feet. The faded leather of Dad's old notebook feels warm and reassuring under my fingers and I shut my eyes for a moment, imagining the vastness of his hand closing around mine, like it used to do when I was little. It didn't matter what scary monsters I thought I faced back then; if my dad was holding my hand, I was a superhero . . .

'I represent the people of St Ives,' I begin, deliberately slowing myself down and letting the words breathe out of me. 'And we are opposed to the Rectory Fields development on the former Bethel Parsonage site. It is our intention to preserve the parsonage to honour its most eminent inhabitant, a woman who made significant advances in the field of astronomy during her time as a parson's wife in the 1800s.'

Lou and Aggie are smiling at me. Jack Dixon has taken a sudden deep interest in the empty sheet of paper on the table in front of him. I lift my chin and feel every righteous bone in my body strengthening.

'Elinor Carne is a woman forgotten by history. Her contribution to British astronomy was so important, and yet for many years it was ignored. We want to promote the work she did and ensure she will be remembered in St Ives, not just today but for countless generations to come . . .'

Chapter Eighteen

Jack

I'm such a fool.

I didn't realise Seren MacArthur was on *their* side. I wondered why she was a bit strange when I offered her a coffee. She probably thinks I was trying to persuade her to defect. Which is stupid, considering she's their bloody leader. If I was hoping to prepare the ground for a reasoned compromise, I've stuffed up any chance of that now. The thing was, I thought I was prepared. I thought I knew all my arguments. But the moment the floor opened for questions, I came unstuck. And Seren MacArthur was on my case immediately. I'm annoyed but I can't blame her: if the tables had been turned, I would have pushed my advantage, too.

'Are you saying the development would be better for the community than saving Elinor Carne's home?' she asked me, when I tried to explain how many local suppliers we hoped to use for Rectory Fields.

'Well, no – um – what I meant was . . .'

'Because, honestly, if your employer believes that he's more deluded than we thought.'

'I think Mr Brotherson . . .'

'And furthermore, it proves the contempt he has for *this* community that he thinks we can be so easily bought off . . .'

The cheers. The groundswell of support for every point she made and the rumble of laughter whenever I tried to argue back. It wasn't just embarrassing. It was *mortifying*.

Idiot!

I catch sight of my reflection in the windows of Harbour Fish & Chips as I walk past, collar pulled up against the cold wind coming off the sea. Man, I look pale. Like I haven't slept in a year. This could be because I haven't – or not slept well, at any rate. Not like I used to. My chin has stubble that refuses to yield to any razor and my clothes still look like I nicked them from a bloke two sizes bigger, which doesn't help my overall appearance. People think I look like this because I'm grieving for Tash, but in reality I'm not. I'm in shock about the mess she left us with. I lie awake most nights terrified about how close to the abyss Nessie and I are. Right now, we're okay, but if life kicks us one more time it could nudge us straight over the edge.

No wonder Seren MacArthur looked shocked. She probably thinks a half-bearded ghost at the refreshment table pounced on her tonight.

I stop outside the darkened lifeboat station at the end of Wharf Road. Why do I care what she thinks of me? And *why* do I keep thinking about her?

Jeb reckons I'm attracted to cryptic women. 'Like them

bleddy awful crosswords only clever dicks like. They don't make sense to anyone else.' He's probably right. Thing is, I can't work out why Seren doesn't want this development to go ahead. She owns a business in town, the kind that needs the type of people Rectory Fields will bring in. Local people don't want artisan crafts, or not regularly enough to sustain a small shop like hers, at any rate. And when you consider the months when tourist trade could make a difference, it isn't enough to keep a business going all year round. The others on the opposing side I can understand – most of them over sixty, and all the sort who love getting behind a local campaign. Seren stands out among them for being so young.

And confident.

And pretty.

Really pretty – like forget-what-you-were-saying pretty . . .

Oh no.

Not now, Jack. Are you *insane*?

An angry flush prickles my face as I shake off whatever ridiculous, completely ill-advised thought my head was just entertaining and stomp my way up the hill to the station car park. It's high time I went home.

Nessie is asleep when I get back, Dad fast asleep too in front of the television. He's good for looking after her at short notice and I think secretly he was pleased I asked. It's been tricky since Tash died. I know he wants to help but we haven't always had the easiest of relationships, and asking doesn't come naturally to either of us. He's been a good support but I've been wary of asking too often, not wanting to shake the equilibrium we've found in recent months. And then there's his social life with his partner, Pru, which puts mine to shame. Even when I've wanted to ask him, he hasn't always been available. But tonight his diary was free and Ness was delighted that her grandad was coming to look after her.

Beside him where he dozes in the sagging armchair is a pile of my daughter's things – books, paper and felt-tip pens, lengths of ribbon and her collection of Spider-Man figures – an indicator of the kind of evening they've had. Nessie would have run him ragged as ever, but I imagine Grandad Dave loved every exhausting minute.

I wait just a moment before I wake him, watching my old man sleep, mouth open, white curly head resting back against his rolled-up jumper. I remember many nights as a kid with Dad sleeping in the armchair in the tiny bedroom I shared with my brother back in Padstow, where we grew up. For months after my mother left home Owen and I wanted Dad close, terrified he would pack his things and disappear in the middle of the night, too. Mum was an alcoholic and suffered from clinical depression, but we didn't know that back then. Dad hid the worst of it from us, only revealing the truth when we reached our late teens. All we knew was that one day our mother was at home, being Mum, and the next there was an empty space where she'd once been. Dad never told us where she'd gone, or why, only that she wasn't coming back. He took all of our hurt and anger and tears without question, letting it all run its course. Strong, stoic and dependable. He stayed the same when everything else fell apart. Being a father now, I understand that all-encompassing urge to protect your kid from the ugliness of the world. It wasn't easy for him. Often the only way he could coax us to sleep was by dragging an armchair into our already cramped bunk-bedroom and staying with us. Dad's not a man who finds declarations of love easy, but that gesture was all the reassurance of his love that we needed.

Tonight a shadow of that old fear passes over me. But I'm not scared of losing him any more. What happened tonight is what's stirring up eddies inside me.

I gently pat his shoulder and he grumbles awake, blinking away sleep as he sits up.

'Alright, son. How was it?'

'Interesting.' I don't want to relive it, not yet. Not until I've worked out what I feel about it. 'It's late – you should be getting home.'

'How late?'

'Past eleven. Sorry, it took me a while.'

He struggles free of the armchair's jealous clutches and stiffly finds his feet. 'No problem. Wednesdays are Pru's book club nights, so she won't be home till gone midnight. More studyin' labels of wine bottles than debatin' book plots, if you get what I mean.'

Dad's partner has been the making of him, transforming the last four years of his life. He jokes about her, but she really is the love of his life. But she's yet to convert him to the delights of her book group, so midweek they have a night apart. 'Give her our love, eh?'

'I will. Listen, do you still want a hand with that roof tomorrow? I've a free lunchtime if you need me.'

'That would be great, thanks.'

'Good one. Night-night, Jackboy.' He clamps a hand to my shoulder and kisses my forehead, the way he always has.

I stand on the veranda to wave him off, the feeling of unease returning as the red rear lights of his old Land Rover slip away from view. Despite the debacle of the question-and-answer session, I think I was well received. I wasn't pelted from the stage with rotten fruit, which Bill Brotherson had joked might happen, but I could have done so much better. I *will* do better next time. I have to, if I have a hope of winning this contract for Brotherson and the construction manager job that comes with it for me. All of this is fixable, except one thing: the discovery of my opponent in the debate. It shouldn't matter who is leading the other campaign when there is so much at stake for me financially. But it does.

She thinks I'm the enemy. She couldn't even look at me.

In the dark, with the rumble of the sea in the distance, I realise what I'm up against. It isn't the town I most have to convince, although that's a considerably tall order. It's Seren MacArthur.

Chapter Nineteen

Seren

My head is a mess when I get home, unable to process what happened tonight. I need to think, to put out the pieces of the evening's events one by one, like I do the seaglass pieces for my jewellery, to try to make sense of it all.

There's only one place I can do that.

Mum's at her drama group and won't be home for a while yet. I take a thermal mug of tea and a blanket and head out to the dark garden, followed by the skittering sound of Molly's paws on the stepping stones in the damp lawn behind me. At the end of the path, looking out down the hill to the harbour far below, the small wooden building stands, as rickety and reassuring as ever. I have made this journey countless times since Dad built his project at the bottom of the garden but it never stops feeling special, even with its architect gone.

I unlock the door with the huge key that usually hangs on a hook by the back door of the house, and instantly the smell hits me. Warm wood, old carpet, brass polish and the faintest hint of lavender from the ancient bunch hung high in the rafters. At the centre, a ladder to a small mezzanine that as a child I'd imagine was Heidi's bedroom; above that, a double window; and, shrouded under a cover made by Mum years ago from an old pink Dralon sofa cover, Dad's pride and joy: Clarabell, his telescope.

Dad did many wonderful things in his life, but the Shedservatory is perhaps his finest achievement. His own observatory looking up to the night skies above St Ives, but so much more than a place to gaze at the heavens. This was *our* place. When the world below got too much, or too confusing, this is where I would come, to hang out with constellations, planets and my dad. We'd slide open the double hatch window in its roof and huddle on deckchairs beneath the stars, wrapped up in blankets and old duvets, drinking hot chocolate from Dad's old thermos flask, putting the world to rights.

Dad was out here most nights, but he never minded company. I think he enjoyed it as much as me. Mum would stay indoors, 'like a sensible person', laughing as she watched us from the warmth and light of the living room. All of the most important decisions and discussions about my life have happened here, on the creaky mezzanine floor of the Shedservatory. It was here I told Dad I'd been accepted to Plymouth University – and that even though it was the closest university to home, I wanted to move into halls and live there while I studied. After I graduated, I snuggled up beside him under the old blue wool blanket and told him I wanted to travel for a year; the stars were my witness when I returned with news that I was moving to Falmouth to work at a graphic design agency; and then last year I admitted I'd been made redundant, and he invited me to move back home.

There was another conversation here two weeks before he died, when I told him a former colleague had offered me another job and a fresh start, and Dad urged me to accept. But I don't like to think about that conversation. Or about why I decided not to take the job. Because that was the beginning of the end – and I never knew how close I was to losing him.

Leaving Molly in the old crate filled with blankets on the ground floor, I climb the ladder and push back the hatch windows. They're stiff after the rain today, so it takes both hands to do it, but the scent of pine fills my nostrils as the windows finally creak open. Clouds in the inky black sky are starting to part in places, the twinkle of brave stars pushing through. I sit on the bench Dad made to finally retire the threadbare deckchairs last year and breathe in the view. Pinned to the ledge below the hatch is Dad's old star wheel. Carefully, I rotate the inner disc to the correct date and find the constellations above me tonight. There are swanky apps for this now and I do have one on my phone, but using the battered old cardboard discs is infinitely more magical. It's the difference between using a GPRS tracker and tracing your route on a real paper map. Dad showed me how to do this when the star wheel was new and my hands much smaller as I turned its disc.

Orion is directly overhead tonight, although I can only make out two of the stars of his belt through the moonlit clouds. Ursa Minor is somewhere to the right; beyond that the Plough, the Pole Star and Cassiopeia. Orion was always my favourite – the stars marking his bow and arrow always looked more like outstretched arms to me. But I love all of the constellations. They are faithful, ancient friends, ever-present and forever beautiful. They have been there for millions of years before I existed and will be there for millions more after I've gone, the length of my life not even a flash of light to them. Everything is put into context when you consider that. It helps, when problems seem insurmountable. To my friends in the sky, they don't even exist.

Molly's snores are drifting up through the space and I smile, remembering Dad's comedy disdain for her canine sleep noises. 'That dog's snoring makes a Force Ten gale sound quiet,' he would say, the loving gaze he sent Molly's way betraying his true feelings. Molly was meant to be my dog, but she was really always his. She'd come to the shop with him every day, as she does most days now with me, curling up in her basket beneath the driftwood counter. She loves being there with me, but every so often I get the feeling she's a little disappointed when Dad doesn't appear. I know how she feels. I still expect him to arrive any moment, blowing on his fingers and telling me how cold the walk over the garden was. Sitting in the open hatch, with the old wool blanket that still smells a little of him wrapped around my shoulders, I can almost feel Dad by my side. 'Bustle up, young 'un,' he'd say in his comical half-Welsh, half-Cornish accent, squeezing onto the small bench seat next to me. And everything would be okay.

I wish he were here now. He would know what to do.

This was meant to be a simple fight, good versus bad; the people who love St Ives' heritage against the developer who wants to destroy it. A fight we could win.

It wasn't supposed to include Jack Dixon.

The crowd seemed to warm to him, too, their heckles during the question-and-answer session relatively good-natured compared with what they'd thrown at Brotherson last time. At the end I saw several groups of people shaking his hand. Maybe they were being kind, but what happens if they respected what he said? His presentation before the Q&A seemed professional and well rehearsed and he came across as affable, despite the monster that sent him. The crowd might have found his bumbling amusing; but what happens if they listened to him and liked what they heard? And what if next time he makes no mistakes?

Worst of all, I can't believe I liked him before I realised who he was . . .

We have a fight on our hands. It began the moment Jack Dixon walked onto that stage. And suddenly, victory isn't the foregone conclusion I thought it was any more.

I look up at Orion, but he has hidden behind a thick bank of cloud.

What do I do now?

Chapter Twenty

Jack

Following a restless night and a desperate morning dash to St Piran's Primary after Nessie and I both oversleep, I am feeling far from my best. Seren MacArthur aside, was my first round in the St Ives debate convincing? Before I stuffed up the Q&A I think I did quite well. People listened. I said everything I'd intended to and nobody shot me down in flames. I told them how much the development will respect the memory of the astronomer. I said we were committed to using locally sourced materials and local manpower, where possible. I told them that the people the development will bring into the area would be good financially for St Ives. I reiterated how committed Brotherson Developments are to making a development that both honours the past and looks to the future.

But was it enough?

I'm still mulling this over at lunchtime while I foot a ladder and question my bright idea to ask Dad to help me.

Since he retired he's been like a dog with an unreachable itch. It's best to keep him busy to keep him out of trouble.

I'm still thinking about how I could have presented myself better last night at the meeting. I should have prepared more. But how was I to know what awaited me? Brotherson had made it sound no scarier than a couple of busybodies who might ask a few awkward questions. He said it was a done deal. But then he would have said that, wouldn't he? He wanted me to take the job because he didn't want to face the town. What worries me is that he doesn't come across as someone easily scared – so how bad must the previous meeting have been to make him avoid going back?

Dad's now heard the whole sorry tale, and is on a rant about my hopefully soon-to-be client.

'What's Bill Brotherson mucking about over, eh? He's promised you the job – why isn't he letting you get on with it?'

'Because I have to convince the town first. Or at least, try to.'

'Wish you'd done better last night, then?'

I grimace at the memory of Seren MacArthur's stare. 'Yes.'

On the top of his ladder, my dad tuts. To be precise, it's a cross between a clicked tongue and a mechanic's intake of breath before he delivers bad news about your car, but for Dad it's shorthand for everything from mild irritation to abject insult. 'Bleddy rich do-gooders. It's all very well getting put out about someone else's building when you're cosy in your million-pound house. Where are the poor, hardworking, normal folks supposed to live, huh? That lot don't give a monkey's!'

I could reply that the people living in the finished Rectory Fields development are highly unlikely to be poor. But I don't. For now it's quite endearing to have him fired up on my behalf. 'They care about their town. And their questions were good. They mean well, Dad.'

Dad's universal sound of disapproval floats down again. '*Meaning well* won't get you back on your feet. *Meaning well* won't pay your bills. Your problem is you're too sentimental, son. What has that ever got you, hmm?' He jabs the hammer towards me. 'That's why you're doing odd jobs in this craphole instead of building the houses you want to.'

Not true, technically. I'm doing odd jobs here in return for free accommodation for Nessie and me. Because we couldn't keep up mortgage payments to stay in our house on just my wage after Tash died. She didn't have life insurance – of course she didn't. Who thinks they're likely to die from a cerebral aneurysm at thirty-three? Tash thought she was invincible and had most of the southwest believing it, too. Just shows how wrong you can be.

'We're lucky to be here,' I say, squinting at the sun. 'Jeb's been good to us.'

That's an understatement. I'm thoroughly indebted to Jeb for rescuing us. It's still a mystery why he offered, but then there's a lot mysterious about Jeb. His real name is Tony, for example. Nobody knows why they call him Jeb. They just do.

'Dunno what Jeb was thinking, bringing you and Ness here. Damp, wind-battered. T'aint no place for a kiddie.'

'Ness loves it here,' I say, resisting the urge to add, *and you didn't want us living with you*. There wouldn't have been sufficient room with him and Pru, of course, not in Dad's small Victorian terraced house with its already cramped space. And although he'd made it clear he'd support us in any way he could, I knew his house was off-limits. They've been great in other ways, which is really all that matters. I just think Dad having to cope with me and Ness under his roof would have brought back memories of life looking after Owen and me post-Mum, and I don't think his heart could have taken it. So it was an unspoken agreement from the outset when we knew we had to give up our house. Dad would be there for us, as long as we weren't *there* with him.

It doesn't stop him having an opinion on our living accommodation, though.

'Yeah, well, kids are happy anywhere there's a beach, aren't they? It's just when they're *almost forty* you'd hope they'd change their expectations.'

Almost forty? Cheek. I'm thirty-six. Hardly on the precipice of forty yet. But I don't rise to the bait. I need Dad on side this morning. Besides, the beach has suddenly become magical for me again. I half-consider mentioning the mysterious seaglass stars to Dad, but quickly think better of it. Dad's idea of magic is when he wins on the fruit machine in the Harbour Arcade. Anyway, it feels good to have a secret that's just for Nessie and me. So much of our lives have become public property since Tash died. It's nice to know something everyone else doesn't. And I have to admit, looking for the stars on the beach each evening has given my days a bit of a spark. Heaven knows I need that right now.

'You know me, Dad. Always a big kid.'

That tut floats out from the chalet roof again. 'Just like your old man then, eh? Right pair we are.'

I smile.

Chapter Twenty-one

Seren

It's so deserted at the shop this morning that by eleven a.m., I've had enough. I scribble a 'Back in 20 minutes' sign and stick it to the door. The spring air billows fresh around me as I walk onto the harbour front and up through the higgledy-piggledy backstreets of Downalong. Skirting the Island car park, I head down to Porthgwidden Beach. I need to be in good company and if there happens to be excellent coffee too, so much the better.

Pots of fresh Cornish daffodils adorn the small wooden tables and line the bar of Aggie's coffee hut this morning. The salt-heavy breeze from the beach is making their sunny petals dance in their small glass milk-bottle vases. People buzz in and out, a group of regulars relaxing near the counter. And in the middle of them, my best friend holds court.

Aggie is full of the meeting last night. The whole town is talking about it, apparently – or at least, the percentage that have already visited her to buy coffee this morning.

'It was such a one-horse race, you wouldn't believe it,'

she is telling the gathered regulars. 'Seren, hi! I was just sayin' how good the meeting was. And you were magnificent, as ever.' She reaches over the weathered oak counter to pat my cheek like I'm a small child. 'Wasn't she, Jude?'

The guy who runs the surf school grins at me from a nearby table. 'Totally nailed it, Ser. All the lads said so. You should be on telly.'

'No fear. I was so nervous.'

'You didn't show it. Put that minion of Brotherson's right in his place.'

I've been worried that Jack was liked by the crowd at the meeting and that we might have lost ground, so it's reassuring to know other people saw it differently. Despite the unease I still feel about fighting Jack Dixon instead of Brotherson, I must admit that watching him struggle to answer questions last night made me feel like our side had scored a point. Even if a part of me felt sorry for him. He obviously had no idea of the storm he was sailing into. Poor bloke.

But actually, maybe he should have been better prepared. This issue is too important and there's too much at stake to wander into a debate without all the necessary facts. I've planned for this for weeks: I was hoping my opponent might do the same. And if Bill Brotherson chose to send Jack into that situation without preparing him for it, well, that isn't my problem. Maybe it just confirms what half the town already knows about the developer. He's a rat, and he doesn't care about anyone or anything but making money.

'Tenner says there'll be a different Brotherson rep next

133

week,' Aggie grins. 'He'll just keep sendin' them in and Seren will smack them all down like a gladiator! Destroy! Destroy!' She whips the counter with a tea towel, making everyone laugh. A large part of the joy of visiting the coffee hut is the floorshow when Aggie's on form.

I love her confidence in me, but the mental image isn't all that appealing. I'm a little taken aback by how it makes me feel. I don't want to destroy anyone: I just don't want Brotherson to get his way.

'We have right on our side,' I say, inadvertently sounding like I should be wearing a cape and Lycra tights. 'Brotherson can say what he likes, but we have a right to protect our heritage. Elinor's legacy is too important to let go.'

'You said that last night. When you were being magnificent. Keep on like that and we'll send Bill Brotherson and his cronies packin' for good!'

I give a bow, slightly embarrassed. 'Let's hope, eh?'

'I'll say one thing for Brotherson's minions, though. The one last night was a *lot* easier on the eye than his master. We should encourage more of that.'

I laugh with Aggie, then wonder if her comment might have been aimed at me. Until I knew who he was I might have agreed with her. But if Jack Dixon chooses to work with Brotherson, his smiles mean nothing.

'Did you hear what Maggie from the Post Office said about him, though?' A lady with a sea-soaked Springer spaniel has joined us, and lowers her voice as another group of customers move off to find a table.

'Who? Brotherson?'

'No, that lad representing him last night.'

The prospect of gossip draws our heads together like moths to a lantern. 'What about him?'

'Lost his wife.'

'She left him?'

'She *died*.'

And just like that, the air is snatched from my sails.

'When?'

I've asked the question before I can think better of it. I shouldn't think of Jack Dixon as anything other than the enemy. But nobody deserves to lose someone they love.

'Seven or eight months ago. Dreadful business. She died at work, apparently. Fell and hit her head, dropped dead an hour after. Only young as well – early thirties or so? Left him on his own with a little 'un. Maggie reckons they lost their house too after the mum died.'

Aggie's shoulders droop and she glances at me. 'Oh, now that's awful.'

'How old's his kid?'

'Dunno. Young, though.'

'Poor bloke,' Jude says. 'My mate Ned lost his missus last year, twins to bring up and only summer work guaranteed. It's been hard for him.'

The cafe noise hushes to just the distant roar of waves and cries of gulls on Porthgwidden Beach beyond. After a while, Aggie's cough brings us back.

'Thing is, though, he's still workin' for Brotherson, isn't he? I mean, tragic for him and his missus of course, but he's still leadin' the opposition. This changes nothin', does it? Ain't that right, Ser?'

135

'Yes,' I say, wishing I felt more certain. 'Yes, nothing changes.'

I think about this all day. It's hard not to when there's so little else at work to distract me. I try everything – doing the week's accounts, making some difficult phone calls I've been putting off, even completely taking the main displays to bits and rebuilding them in the hope of attracting more custom. But the revelation sticks in my mind and won't budge.

I wish Jack hadn't lost his wife, crazy as it sounds. I wish I didn't know about it. Because it changes things. I've tried to hate him, to see him as Bill Brotherson with a different face. But he lost his wife. He's probably going through exactly what I am, although worse, because he *chose* her. I'm so grateful that I got to be Dad's daughter, but Jack chose to marry his wife out of everyone in the world. To find someone you love that much and then lose them must be unbearable. And while it's hard to be left with a business to keep alive, it's nothing compared with safeguarding a child's life.

Grief isn't a point-scoring game, I know, but I feel like I've just lost ground. I just hope last night's meeting scared Jack Dixon away, and that next week there'll be a brand new Brotherson Developments rep facing the debate – someone faceless, without a story to hook me with. Aggie and Jude seemed to think that the likeliest outcome, so that's what I'll wish for, too. We have to win this fight – and if I'm going to lead the winning campaign, I have to refocus.

Chapter Twenty-Two

Jack

There are days here when it's like the weather is playing chicken with you. It throws everything at your head and dares you to cave first. Visitors to Cornwall always talk about the superb quality of the light and how even being caught in the rain here has a charm of its own. And yes, the light is lovely and the landscape beneath the storm breathtaking. But when you live here all the time and have been solidly rained on for a week, it's pretty much just wet.

Our clothes are draped over every available surface in our temporary home and the chalet smells of damp things making everything else damp. Part of the problem is that neither of us is prepared to give up our evening beach visits, so we've been making seaglass stars despite the relentless rain. I've been trying to dry our wet clothes during the day while Nessie's at school, so that the evenings are free from extra moisture in the air, which might affect her asthma. But seven days' worth of laundry is more than this faithful old place can easily contain.

There are the *sounds*, too – the ominous *drip-drip* of water invading our space somewhere. I've patched this roof roughly once every fortnight since we've been at Gwithian, and still the water is finding ways in. There's an ancient chipped enamel teapot catching drips at one end of the small kitchen, and a huge steel saucepan doing the same in the bathroom. But until the rain decides to give me a break, I can't get up on the roof to tackle the source of the leaks.

I couldn't work even if I had any jobs today – the rain is just too hard to do any building work at all – but staying inside is driving me insane. Leaving the damp palace of our current residence, I brave the downpour and dash to my car.

Unsurprisingly, I am the only driver on the road over the hills, save for a disgruntled farmer parked up in his tractor. I pass him at the brow of one of the hills and we are both surprised to see each other. He shares a sympathetic shrug with me over the red top of his newspaper in the fogged-up cab of the tractor.

I've been thinking about Rectory Fields since the town meeting and it's high time I paid the site a visit. I had so little notice when Brotherson gave me the job that I wasn't able to physically see the site before the town meeting – and while I've studied the initial plans in detail, I need to see it for myself. I don't think you can get a sense of a building – new or ancient – until you stand beside it. Photographs only tell you so much; there is no substitute for being there.

I know the plans focus on what Brotherson wants to

build. But I believe the raw materials are important. To give a building life and a heart that will mean something to the people who make it their home, you have to know where you're coming from. Unless you understand the land on which a building rests and get a true sense of its former life, you can't see its potential.

I learned this early in life and it's always served me well. Dad took Owen and me to Tintagel when we were little. I couldn't have been more than five or six years old, but I can still feel the energy of the place when I remember our visit. The wildness of Tintagel Castle's ruins clinging to the cliff, that some say was King Arthur's fabled Camelot, reached by a scary-looking bridge and steps carved into the storm-battered rock. It felt like you were a great adventurer just reaching the site. On the day we visited the angry clouds above and the wind-churned sea lashing the shore far below added to the feeling of an epic journey. I'm not particularly spiritual, but the story of that site *hummed* through the ground. I could almost hear the people who had lived there before and worshipped in the small church, now only a ruin; the subliminal bass of footsteps, the distant rhythms of speech. If you built any-thing on that site you would have to honour what the land told you, or else the building would have no soul.

I park on the patch of hardstanding that is all that remains of an entrance road to the parsonage and listen to the heavy drumming of raindrops on the roof of my car. It isn't the best weather for viewing a site, but it doesn't matter. I stare through the slowly misting windscreen at the dark bones of the building, its edges and lines blurring and morphing through streaming rainwater running over the glass.

It's a bleak place, especially in a storm. What hardships would its former occupants have willingly faced in order to serve the people here? I try to imagine living in this place, blown by winds roaming across the hills, lashed by rain, frozen by winter's chill, with only candlelight and little heat from small fireplaces to ward off the cold. People were made of sterner stuff back then. I consider it a hardship having crotchety old storage heaters, no WiFi and not enough space to dry washing in the chalet; I can't imagine surviving in a place like this.

But I can't learn anything from the comfort of my car. I pull on waterproofs, stuff a folded envelope into one pocket with a biro and head out into the diagonal rain.

The remaining stones of the main parsonage building are scratched and marked by time, but solidly constructed. Leaning close, I walk slowly around the perimeter, making a note of usable materials where I find them. There's more than I'd expected. When I find pockets of shelter around the walls I scribble notes on the damp envelope. Brotherson dismissed my question about how much of the building fabric we could salvage. He didn't think we'd find any. Has he even visited this site, I wonder?

I pace out the footprint of the building, imagining Brotherson's expensive architect plans overlaying the parsonage's remains. So much of building is interpretation: taking an architect's vision and making it work in real life. You have to work with what you have as a starting point, I think. Two hundred years ago, this building was made by people who understood the land upon which it stood. They knew what would work best in these conditions and built the parsonage accordingly. What would be the point of demolishing everything and starting a new building without trying to learn from its previous structure?

It's a job, I remind myself before the romantic in me is swept away by this broken old structure crying out to be saved. It shouldn't matter to me what happens here, only that the site is made safe and viable again.

It's not even my project yet – not until we win the St Ives town vote. But it's too late: I already care about this place.

And I know exactly why it matters to me. I walked into that meeting completely unprepared – many of the questions I was bombarded by would have been easy to answer if I'd done my homework. I might have been still in shock that Brotherson had chosen me for the job, but I won't make the same mistake again. I have to know what I'm talking about, or Seren and her team might as well claim victory now.

I swear I caught her smiling when I couldn't answer the town's questions. I can't hand victory to my opponents like that. Next time I talk to them, I'm going to be fully prepared.

I pat the rutted stone wall and look up to the skeleton of burned and gnarled wooden struts that once formed the roof. Since it fell out of use it's been victim to several arson attacks and the abuse has scarred the parsonage past the point of salvation. It's sad that somewhere used by so many people should fall at the hands of a few brainless vandals. No windows remain; the original heavy oak door is long gone, replaced by an ugly grey metal security panel. DANGER and DO NOT ENTER site signs have been plastered over it and several sections are cordoned off with red-and-white hazard tape, the ends of which rise and fly in the wind.

I can make something of this, I tell myself. I'm excited, despite the dreary, sad shell of a building beside me – and the rain finding its way into my waterproofs and soaking through the last dry set of clothes I own. There is potential here. I just need the people of St Ives to put their faith in me to make it happen.

Chapter Twenty-Three

Seren

'Seren? Sweetheart, are you awake?'

I should reply, invite Mum in and talk like she wants us to. I know I should. But instead I hold my breath, waiting for her soft footsteps to fade, the creak on the penultimate step of the attic stairs and the gentle click of the door at the bottom. At least she thinks I'm asleep, not hiding in my room pretending not to hear her.

Today at the shop felt like the longest yet. The meeting with the bank is preying on my mind and it was all I could think of. This awful weather hasn't helped, either. It's rained every day and there haven't been any breaks, meaning Fore Street has been pretty much deserted all week. And if there's nobody wandering there, the courtyard doesn't stand a chance of seeing any custom. I braved the accounts book at three p.m., but gave up two hours later when I'd singularly failed to make them look any healthier.

I'm so tired of trying to make this work. And I know Mum needs me and it's probably selfish to want it, but I wish I had my own life back. If it weren't for my jewellery and starmaking trips to Gwithian every morning, I don't think I'd recognise myself any more.

At least I still have the seaglass stars. I have to say I admire my fellow starmaker's commitment. Most people would have given up as soon as the weather worsened. My friend on the beach is a cut above. I just wish they weren't a stranger. I would love a friend who doesn't know everything else about me right now.

I breathe out, feeling the knots in my shoulders protest. It isn't that I don't love Mum – I do, so much – but sometimes I just need a moment, the smallest pinch of time, for me. Since we lost Dad, there are so few minutes in each day that I can truly claim as my own. My beachcombing walks every morning used to be my time, but now even these are crowded with thoughts and worries and contingencies for the day ahead. In the shop I'm bombarded by memories of Dad and the threatening voices of all the bills he left behind. At home, I've become Mum's counsellor, her nearest sounding post for the worries she's hoarded like piles of pebbles throughout the day. All of it is my responsibility and I do it because I love Mum and I want to sort out Dad's business. But I miss the *before* days – when worry wasn't constantly snapping at my heels. When it was just me; my hopes and my dreams and my lazily wasted minutes. Back before the graphic design agency folded, I had a good life in Falmouth. I'd built it steadily over five years – a great place to live, good friends, occasional fun weekends back with Aggie, Kieran and Cerrie, but always returning to my own life for Monday mornings. I felt like I had an identity, a purpose, dreams and ambitions within reach. I'd make enough money to start up my own studio and gradually decrease my days at Grafyx until I could make my jewellery business pay full-time. And for most of the time there had been Karl, the guy I thought would be around for a lot longer than he ended up being. I still wonder if us breaking up started the rot that eventually took my job, my lovely rented home with its view of the harbour and the life I'd so carefully constructed.

It doesn't do any good going over the past. What's happened has happened: I'm here now, for better or worse. I just have to work harder to see the positives.

The bracelet I'm making this evening is twisted silver with palest pink and sea-green glass beads. It's the most complex design I've attempted, but I love how it's gradually appearing in my hands. It's beautiful, and I wonder about the person who will one day wear it. Will they be chasing after their dreams like the tiny glass jewels, or be caught up in the twists and folds of life like the silver wire that holds them? Perhaps they'll buy this bracelet to inspire them to aim higher, or to remind them of the simple beauty of the sea. Maybe a lover will buy it for them. Could it be a promise? A proposal? An unrequited dream?

I smile, the sensation travelling like a wave across my face. Guessing who the eventual owner might be is my favourite game when I'm making my jewellery. One of the unexpected joys of selling my work online is that I don't know who will buy it. Strangers from across the world could discover my jewellery on Etsy and something I have made from my heart will connect with theirs. Even though we've never met. There's something intensely romantic and magical about that.

Instantly, I think of the other seaglass starmaker. Although we're strangers, we're connected by the stars. There's a kind of romance being played out between us – and that feels special. I don't know how long it will last, but then who knows that in any kind of romance when it first begins? You don't analyse the future too much; all that matters is you and the other person in that moment. It's part of the magic. You just jump in.

There are so many things in my life that are chained by the heavy weight of future worries. This is different, and it's exactly what I've been searching for. It's a chance to live in the moment and forget what lies ahead.

I want to find my fellow starmaker and thank them, but part of me wants this to go on forever. The *not* knowing is almost more magical than the knowing . . .

Chapter Twenty-Four

Jack

By day, I am a jobbing builder grabbing scraps of work where I can find it. By night, I am fast becoming an expert in the Bethel Parsonage site. I've made countless visits between jobs while Nessie is at school, written more notes than I have for any other job, even visited the local county records office in Truro to view the original building's plans. I feel like the site is getting into my blood, with each step I pace around its perimeter fixing plans in my mind. I need to know the site in intricate detail if I'm going to fully realise the building that will one day stand there.

It's past midnight and Nessie has been in bed for hours. The small dining table is buried beneath a sea of paper – notes, copies of plans, maps I've made of the existing site and list upon list of materials, both new and repurposed. Every muscle in my body aches, but I'm buzzing. This is the kind of project I've been waiting for and I'm determined not to blow my chance.

It's only two days until the next town meeting, and

there is no way I'm going into it as ill-prepared as last time. It's just me leading the charge for Rectory Fields, so I have to cover all my bases. Seren and her campaign team will have put the hours in, I'm sure. It helps that she has more people on her team to spread the workload, I guess; but all of their plans are useless if Seren can't communicate what they know to the people at the meeting. So when it comes down to it, it's her versus me. On that count, we're equal.

I'm still smarting from the last time we met and even though I've tried to see Seren as the enemy, I can't quite make the label fit. The only way I'm going to be able to face her again is to think of what's at stake for me. If I see the Save the Parsonage campaign as a group trying to prevent Nessie having stability and a proper home, it's enough to rouse the warrior in me. They seem nice enough people, but the consequence of them winning could mean financial peril for me and my little girl.

That's how I'll face them at Wednesday's meeting: ready to do battle for the life Ness and I need. Seren and her team can think what they like of me: I can't lose this fight.

The rainbow trays of seaglass by the front door catch my eye as I look up from my research. We're getting low on blue, I notice. Ness and I need to go on a blue-hunting mission after school. She'll love that, just as she loves the trays. I regularly catch her crouching beside them, gently patting the glass pieces. I like that seaglass has become part of our lives, as much as the chalet or the beach. I'm tempted to sneak seaglass into the Rectory Fields development somewhere, but I'm not sure I could get that past

Brotherson. Maybe that's the next challenge, if the development wins the St Ives vote . . .

I imagine Tash's horror at me suggesting seaglass-related subterfuge. She would have loved me working for Bill Brotherson, but would be constantly reminding me not to stuff it up.

'You get carried away.'

'No, I don't.'

'Yes, you do. Keep your mind on the job, Jack. Don't try to have fun with it.'

'Can't I do both?'

'No. That's your problem. You don't take anything seriously . . .'

There's plenty I'm taking seriously now, I think, stretching my aching back against the dining chair.

I wonder if there will ever be a time I can think of Tash without hearing her disappointment, her judgement. People tell me about stages of grief: I seem to have stopped at 'angry'. But then, I'd felt that way for a long time before I lost Tash. The sad truth is, I can't remember the good times. Perhaps their memory will return when enough time has passed. I hope they do, for Nessie's sake. Tash is still her mum, no matter what.

That's why I'm taking every opportunity to build happy memories for Ness now. Post-Tash. I want her to remember our time at Gwithian as one of the happiest in her life. I don't want money worries or fear for the future to cloud that. So while I watch the scarily dwindling funds in my bank account and renew my prayers that Jeb won't ask for his chalet back before the summer, I only want Nessie

149

to be concerned with dashing down to the beach to make our stars, choosing which ice cream she wants to eat or twirling around the chalet until she's too dizzy to stand.

Her freedom – her right to a childhood free of worry – *that's* what I will fight for on Wednesday night. People can think whatever they like of Bill Brotherson: when I take to the stage at the Guildhall before the people of St Ives, I'm going to prove I am the best person to take Bethel Parsonage to the next phase of its life.

Chapter Twenty-Five

Seren

Becca's Bar is packed this evening. It's a local wedding – a guy from the lifeboat crew and his bride who works in the ice cream shop on the harbour front that stays open every month except February. Everyone is happy and I'm surrounded by smiles. It's a good place to be.

I'm tired, but glad of the constant work tonight. The worst shifts are those where customers trickle in and the large antique station clock over the bar draws my eye every five minutes. This evening I barely have time to share knowing looks with my fellow bartenders, Garvey and Shep. They call me 'Mum', which is bit disconcerting, but it's meant sweetly. I suppose all thirty-one-year-olds seem old to twenty-year-olds. Garvey quit university six months ago and Becca took pity on him, like she did most of the rest of her staff. She's what Aggie calls a 'rescuer'. She collects people and helps where she can. Shep is a bricklayer by day, but he's working evenings here to save money to go travelling. I reckon he'll find his heart in some lovely place on the other side of the world and never leave it. They are both what Dad would have called 'strapping lads' – easily over six feet – and they dwarf me by comparison. But they are lovely guys and very protective of me, even though I haven't worked here for long.

'Groom'll be lucky to be standing by last orders,' Shep says, nudging alongside me to pull a pint of cider. 'Look at him, poor beggar!'

In the middle of the packed bar Yestin Carmichael is slow-dancing to Feeder, one arm raised, his half-drunk pint of beer sloshing above his head. His best man and ushers aren't faring much better, the four of them shuffling to the song, arms slung about each other's shoulders, heads nodding at the bar's whitewashed floorboards.

I look across the dancing, smiling crowd of guests to find the bride. The new Mrs Carmichael is surrounded by her girlfriends, singing loudly. 'I don't think Joely's going to mind,' I say.

'I dated her once.' Garvey reaches between Shep and me to flip the top off two bottles of Tribute on the bottle-opener screwed to the bar.

Shep and I exchange amused grins.

'You didn't.'

'Last year. January time? She came to see my band play at the Blue Mariner and we ended up snogging. She was pretty good at snogging, from what I recall.' He winks at us and disappears back to the other end of the bar, where arms are reaching out waving money at him. In the bar, the song ends to a huge cheer.

'Bollocks did he date her,' Shep scoffs.

I hand the pint to a waiting customer and shine my brightest smile when he tells me to keep the change. Another reason I like busy shifts . . . 'You don't think so?'

'Nah. Talkin' out of his bum as usual. Joely's got too much taste.'

I look back at Joely Carmichael's new husband, who now has his wedding tie around his head and is rocking out to Dire Straits' 'Brothers in Arms'. There's someone for everyone, they reckon.

'Is this a good night or what?' Aggie arrives at the bar, not minding that she's pushed aside a bloke who's been waiting for a while. She's flushed from dancing and is wiggling her empty glass at me. 'Pop another one in there, will you, bird? I'm gaspin'!'

'Oi, wait your turn,' says the man next to her – clearly not one of the locals.

Aggie turns to him slowly, her smile as intimidating as a gangster's knuckleduster. 'What's that? You're buyin' my drink? Aw, sweetheart, cider, thanks. What a gent. Ain't he a gent, Ser?'

The man is so blindsided by her front that he just nods numbly and accepts her thanks as if it was his noble idea after all. She's dreadful, but I love her. Aggie is the kind of person who refuses to accept obstacles, no matter what size. I love her unshakeable innate sense of belief and I aspire to be like her.

Working here has another major advantage besides the money: I never feel alone at Becca's. At the shop it's often just me – Molly being not big on conversation whenever she accompanies me. I can sometimes go a whole day

153

without seeing another person. That kind of isolation chips away at your soul after a while.

Today, even Molly deserted me. She refused to leave her basket in the kitchen, chin glumly resting on her favourite toy – a grubby bunny she found on the beach with Dad years ago and guards jealously with her big chocolate paws. She's had days like this since Dad died. All we can do is make sure her food and fresh water are close by and leave her until she's ready to plod into the living room to see us. Mum was happy to stay with her. I can't blame Molly for taking time out. There are days I wish I could, too.

But the new star I found on Gwithian Beach this morning has warmed my heart all day. Today's star was tiny but made almost entirely of blue – pale blue and deep blue, with slivers of blue-grey slate and blue-green seaweed threaded through the lines so that it appeared to be growing out of the glass pieces. Every star has been different so far, some with just seaglass, some featuring shards of found pottery and driftwood. And that's the challenge for me each day: to find similar pieces to complete the last one or two points of the star. And I know anyone else would think me mad for thinking this, but it feels like my unknown beach friend is encouraging me to indulge in my passion, to stretch myself, to see what more I am capable of. It's been such a long time since anyone did that.

'Oi! *Oi!* Pack it in!' A shout beside me grabs my attention, and I look up from the pint I'm pulling to see Garvey vaulting over the bar towards a couple of ushers who are throwing drunken punches above each other's heads. Shep

154

is hot on his heels and together they manage to pull the sparring guests apart. There's a brief ripple of applause and I look up at the station clock, grabbing the bell pull to ring it.

'Last orders, please!'

The drama is forgotten in the rush to the bar.

When the last of the guests have finally been coaxed out onto the street, Shep bolts the door and we all breathe a collective sigh of relief. At least everyone left as friends – some more so than others, judging by the newly paired-up couples blowing us kisses on the way out.

After we complete all the end-of-the-night jobs I join my bar colleagues on the step at the back of Becca's. It's at the top of a narrow paved alley that winds its way steeply down to the harbour and is the best view from the bar, although only those lucky enough to work here actually get to see it. Tonight the sky is clear and I can see the edge of the Plough twinkling over the harbour as the new moon lights the returning tide. For my first few shifts at Becca's I would hurry home as soon as it was over, but Shep persuaded me to stay for a drink one evening and now it's something I look forward to. It's a chance to delay my return to all the paperwork waiting for me at home. I like that all I have to do for the next thirty minutes is chat and watch the sliver of St Ives harbour shimmering in the moonlight.

'So, you ready for the town meeting tomorrow?' Garvey asks, bumping his elbow against my arm.

'As ready as I'll ever be.'

'We've lined up some questions for Brotherson's lackey,' Shep grins, the moonlight painting his cigarette smoke as he breathes it out into the night. 'Like to see him charm his way out of those.'

Aggie and Kieran have intimated something similar. I'm anticipating an ambush being set for tomorrow night. 'I think he'll have a lot of tough questions to answer.'

'You know me and the lads will help with restoring the place, Mum,' Shep offers. 'When you have the money to do it.'

'That's great. Thank you.' I'm touched by his offer, but the truth is that I haven't really thought beyond winning the campaign. There's a basic plan to eventually restore the entire parsonage and turn it into the Elinor Carne Museum, but that could be years ahead. For the time being we will fundraise and aim to erect a temporary exhibition as soon as possible, rebuilding Elinor's original small wooden observatory from plans Dad and Lou discovered in the county archives. I don't know how much that will cost or how many hours it will entail yet. I'm guessing Dad had plans of his own, probably far more detailed and considered than ours. But he died before he could share them with anybody. I didn't think about the future of the parsonage when I agreed to take Dad's place as leader; the priority was just winning the right to save Elinor's home. But now I can see what an enormous task this is going to be if we win the town vote. With everything else going on, how will I be able to do that, too?

I catch myself and think of Aggie, bare-facedly braving out whatever challenge she faces. I'll find a way to do it, if we win. Taking a long sip of cider, I bask in the smiles of Garvey and Shep and correct myself.

When we win . . .

Chapter Twenty-Six

Jack

I arrive at Brotherson Developments a little before eleven a.m. This is it: D-Day for my presentation. After I spoke with him about my site visit, Bill Brotherson suggested I run my presentation past him before delivering it to the town meeting this evening.

I haven't revised this hard since college and my brain is stuffed with every bit of information I could cram into it. I've carried notes on index cards in my back pocket, the fridge in the chalet is covered in a rainbow of sticky notes – much to Nessie's delight – and I think Dad may disown me if he has to listen to my Rectory Fields pitch one more time. It's been the first thing I've looked at when I wake and the last thing I read before I sleep. In the small space between late bedtimes and early risings I'm pretty sure I've dreamed of it, too.

But it's the only way I'm going to convince people to back the development. If I'm not convinced, I can't expect them to be.

Now all I need to do is convince Bill Brotherson . . .

Cassandra, his PA, gives me a sympathetic smile as soon as I enter Brotherson's spacious office suite. So much for the cool and calm air I'd hoped to arrive with.

'Hi, Jack. Don't worry, you'll be great.'

'Thanks.'

She lowers her voice. 'And if you need a shot of Rescue Remedy before you go in, I've a bottle in my bag.'

I decline, wishing I was better at concealing my nerves.

Brotherson beckons me into his office and I throw back my most confident smile. I can do this.

'Good to see you, Jack. So, you ready?'

'I am.'

Am I?

'Excellent. We'll head to the conference room. Give your laptop to Cassandra and she'll set it up on the big screen. We'll grab coffee on the way.'

A conference room? I thought I'd be talking Brotherson through my presentation in the comfort of his office. But it appears he wants the full floorshow. Rocket-fuel-strong coffee in hand, we enter an oval room that wouldn't look out of place in a James Bond villain's lair. Blinds close at the switch of a remote, a huge white screen descending in sync as the ceiling spots fade. I almost expect steel shutters to slam closed and trap me inside, or a trap door to swing open in the floor revealing a waiting shark tank if Brotherson doesn't like my performance.

I have to calm down. In eight hours' time I have to present this for real, and compared with the crowd gathered for the meeting, Bill Brotherson will be a walk in the park.

159

He settles himself in a chair at the far end of the room and I'm instantly reminded of my primary school teachers who always pretended to be 'the little old lady at the back with her hearing aid switched off' to encourage us all to speak up. The smile I have to hide helps. I take a breath, picture my notes and begin.

I try to gauge his reaction as I run through my presentation. The PowerPoint slides I spent ages preparing flood the screen behind me and it's all I can do not to just stare dumbly at the supersized graphs and graphics. Brotherson wears an odd grin that appears to be the default setting for his face. It comes across as a little insincere, but I know from what he's told me how much he wants to build this development. Best to ignore it and stick to the facts: as a derelict building in need of complete renovation, the site is unworkable. As Rectory Fields it will go on into the future, its heritage preserved for generations to come. The development will be sensitive to its local environment, using materials and skilled labour from the area to marry the structure to the land, setting a precedent for future building developments across the southwest. Rectory Fields will represent a new direction for Brotherson developments – working with and for the local community to create buildings that benefit everyone . . .

'Good.'

'There's more . . .'

Brotherson nods. 'And it'll be good. You're the man for this job, Jack, no doubting that at all.'

I wait for him to continue, but I'm left in awkward silence facing his strange grin. He makes no move and I can't think of what to say, my much-practised flow being cut mid-performance. I'm aware my smile has become inane as my embarrassment blooms. He seems happy; but if he has heard enough halfway in, will the townspeople at the meeting follow suit?

'So – anything you'd like to add?'

Brotherson leans back in his executive chair at the foot of the table. 'Like I said, you've got everything I'm looking for. Sell them this development, Jack. I don't care how you do it, but make Rectory Fields look good. Once we get their yes, the real fun can begin.'

Many possibilities of what Bill Brotherson considers 'fun' run through my head on my journey home, and none of them particularly fill me with hope. I should just trust his response and get on with the job he's given me. But presenting a convincing argument tonight is going to be a tall order.

By the time I arrive back in Gwithian, my palms are sweating.

An hour later, on the beach with Nessie, who had the joy of being collected from school by Dad and Pru today, nerves are getting the better of me.

'Have you got a cough?' Nessie asks, crouching over the third completed point of our star.

'No.'

'Then why do you keep going *ahem-ahem*?' She mimics clearing her throat, which is something I've been told I do when I'm on edge. I didn't even realise I was making a sound.

I flop down in the cold sand beside her. 'I'm a bit nervous about tonight.'

'Doing your assembly?'

The closest analogy I could offer Ness when I explained about the town meeting last week was likening it to her class assembly, in which she recently had a leading role. 'Yes, that.'

She gives me a side-look, the breeze from the sea sending strands of hair dancing across her cheek. 'I was scared when I had to do my speech, too. Not as scared as Joshua Levens, though. His bum kept trumping all the way through his words.'

I love how my daughter can floor me with one line. It's good to laugh, my shoulders shaking the tension of the last few hours away. 'Oh dear. Poor Josh.'

Nessie beams, having just earned major Making Dad Laugh points. 'So you'll be fine as long as you don't do any trumps.'

Now there is a maxim I can live my life by.

It's only when I park in St Ives and start walking towards the Guildhall that I realise Nessie has stuffed my jacket pockets with handfuls of hopeful seaglass. Mermaid treasure for luck. Magic in my pockets. I love her so much. And that reminds me *why* I'm doing this.

When we can move out of Jeb's chalet into a more permanent home, I can give Nessie the bedroom she secretly dreams of – a fairy-light-crowned bed and furniture she has chosen, soft carpet beneath her feet and pictures of hearts and stars and her beloved superheroes adorning the walls. I can provide the space she needs to grow and the

162

security we lost when Tash died. All I have to do tonight is keep Nessie and our future at the forefront of my mind.

And remember not to trump.

Chapter Twenty-Seven

Seren

I keep thinking about what Aggie told me about Jack. Losing his wife, then his home; left alone to look after his little girl. I don't know if he has family nearby to help, or if anyone from his former life stuck around after his wife's death. It shouldn't change a thing: Jack Dixon still works for Bill Brotherson; he will be the one tearing down Elinor Carne's home if the town votes for Rectory Fields. But we share a common experience – and that changes things. Losing someone you love changes everything. So he can't just be the bad guy in my head.

Nevertheless, spirits are high as we gather for the town meeting. Tonight we present our ideas for the parsonage site. We're suggesting the site be restored eventually, but that some kind of visitor centre is built as soon as possible, so that we can tell Elinor's story to local people and capitalise on the crowds of tourists due to descend on the town in the summer. Her own observatory that she built behind the parsonage is all but gone; just a single line of stones marking its footprint remains. But maybe some of it can be rebuilt, in wood at first – which we know from her journals, and what Dad and Lou discovered in the county archives, is what the earliest incarnation of the observatory was made of – and stone later. Lou and Dad founded the Elinor Carne Foundation a few weeks before he died, and since then Lou's hard work to recruit local businesses across southwest Cornwall as donors has raised almost £10,000. So our plans aren't pie in the sky. But nobody is under any illusion about the task ahead – *if* we get the vote.

I've decided to tag-team our presentation with Aggie this evening, so that we cover all aspects of our proposal. She knows more about the logistics required to make our plans happen, while I'm Elinor Carne's champion, having read her journals and learned about her life from the research Dad did. I'm grateful that the responsibility doesn't just rest on my shoulders tonight. I'm conflicted by the news about Jack and I can't afford to give my doubts any ground.

I find myself looking for him as soon as the doors open and people start to wander in. Last time he disappeared as soon as the meeting was over, even though he'd been friendly when we first met. But neither of us had realised who the other was then. He probably won't want to talk to me. And I probably shouldn't talk to him. But I feel I ought to . . .

'Jack.' Lou is walking towards the entrance, hand out-stretched, and I see Jack Dixon accepting it. 'Do you need any help setting anything up?'

'Yeah, please. I've got a presentation on this to show?' He lifts a laptop from under his arm.

'No problem. Step this way, son . . .'

As they walk to the front of the hall, Jack looks across and catches my eye. He gives a slight smile and turns away.

I suppose that's an improvement on last time.

I'm glad we present first. The crowd is hugely supportive again and their questions are sensible and well informed. I leave the stage exchanging satisfied smiles with Aggie, who is flushed from the experience but was a total star up there. Jack going second was Kieran's idea: to give us the chance to really listen to what Brotherson Developments are proposing without being preoccupied with what we were going to say. So after a coffee break and Lou reconvening the meeting, Jack Dixon takes the stage.

'You will have heard many rumours about what Brotherson Developments is proposing for the former parsonage site. What I want to do tonight is present what I intend to do there, as the development's construction manager. I believe in protecting our heritage, in preserving beautiful, ancient buildings for future generations to enjoy.'

There's a ripple of disquiet around the hall and Kieran nudges me.

'This should be interesting.'

But Jack doesn't seem concerned by the bubbling dissent. 'I'm guessing you didn't expect to hear that from me. Fair enough. I realise that in the past Brotherson Developments hasn't been known for sympathetic renovation, but this is the approach Mr Brotherson and I agree is best. We understand the heritage of the site. And, with respect, the Rectory Fields development will preserve the former parsonage far more quickly than a project that has to wait for sufficient funds to be raised.'

Another ripple of reaction crosses the floor.

Jack gives a slight shrug. 'I mean no disrespect to our opponents. If you've visited the site you'll know it's in a bad state. The observatory is gone; the fabric of the main building is water-damaged and it's structurally unsafe. To restore any of the structures will require most of them being rebuilt from the ground up. But our plans for the Rectory Fields development will take the best of the current buildings and make them better.'

I glance at my friends. Kieran is still grinning about the disquiet in the hall, Aggie looks like she wants to punch Jack, Cerrie and Lou are deep in whispered conversation. No worried glances, no visible panicking. So far, so good.

'Let me show you what I mean.'

The lights go off as Jack's video presentation begins. After the usual Brotherson Developments CAD-rendered overview (which Bill Brotherson tried to show at the first meeting) a series of PowerPoint slides appear. They show impressive-looking buildings with grass-covered roofs, old stone meeting glass walls, architectural details incorporated into new structures. They are the kind of buildings you see on TV programmes like *Grand Designs* and *Restoration Man*. I can hear whispering behind me, the creak of plastic chairs as people lean forward to listen.

'I believe in using the same materials that old buildings like the parsonage were built from to make something new. I don't want a faceless development on this site. In fact, as long as the build is mine, I'll make sure it isn't. A building should look to the future but never ignore its past. What I want to do is honour the parsonage and all the people it has served over the years – including the astronomer – by using locally sourced materials and labour. I want this to be a truly Cornish development, acknowledging its history and making it fit for the future.'

'He played the Cornish card,' Aggie half-whispers, eyes wide. 'I can't believe he did that.'

The air around us seems to move as Jack continues his presentation. The Save the Parsonage team shift uncomfortably beside me. But I can't stop looking at Jack. I don't want to be impressed by what he's saying, but I am. He really cares about this build. It's a complete surprise to discover he actually believes in what he's proposing. It radiates out of him, animating his movements and fuelling his words. Dad used to say that passionate people can make you passionate about anything, and this is like watching his theory in action. Jack lights up when he talks about building, the same way Dad used to when he spoke about watching the stars.

The applause he receives at the end of his presentation is decidedly warmer and it's clear I'm not the only one who's been impressed. Lou's smile is tight as he closes the meeting, and there's a pervading shadow over the Save the Parsonage team as we gather at the front of the hall.

'He's just a nice guy,' Kieran offers. 'That's bound to impress people. But it's still Brotherson's money. He still gets the casting vote.'

'We need to regroup,' Lou says, turning on an Oscar-worthy smile as a group of locals congratulate him on their way out. 'We can't let this bloke win.'

I should be right in the middle of their planning, but my attention is drawn to Jack Dixon making his way towards the exit. I came here this evening intending to talk to him after the meeting. And even though I still don't know exactly what I'll say, I excuse myself from my friends' conversation and follow him out.

Chapter Twenty-Eight

Jack

I *think* that went well.

People are pleasant enough as I leave the Guildhall. They listened well to my presentation – but I saw Lou and the Save the Parsonage team huddling at the front of the stage and a number of people congratulating them. They have the ear of the town, it would appear, helped by the fact that they all live in St Ives. Even though I'm only around the coast in Gwithian, I might as well be from another planet. And Brotherson is practically at the other side of the universe in Plymouth. Round here, proximity matters.

Dad's at the chalet babysitting Ness and he's planning to stay the night on the crotchety old sofa bed, so I have a little time before I need to be back. My back is damp from where I sweated on the stage, so fresh air is what I need now.

The tide is just beginning to fill the harbour again as I walk along the front, the boats nearest Smeaton's Pier already afloat, while those towards the town watch enviously, still beached and leaning into the sand.

I didn't get a drink earlier and my throat is dry from speaking, so I make for the fish and chip restaurant on the harbour front that does a mean takeaway tea, even at nine o'clock at night. I'm about to walk in when I hear my name.

'Jack!'

Seren MacArthur is sprinting towards me along Harbour Road. After the look she gave me earlier, I'm not sure if this is a good thing.

I raise my hand. 'Hey.'

She's a little out of breath as she reaches me. 'Sorry, I just wanted a word.'

'I was about to get a hot drink. Would you like one?' I'm not sure why I offer, but given that she hasn't launched an attack on me yet, I figure it's a good idea.

'I'd love one, thanks.'

We walk into Harbour Fish and Chips and stand awkwardly side by side as we wait to be served. I'm struck by the thought that this is like the most embarrassing first date, but then I check myself. If I end up giggling she'll definitely think I'm strange. But it's more surreal than it should be. We haven't really spoken before and now we're being very British, queuing in silence for tea.

We share self-conscious smiles.

Man, this is weird . . .

We don't speak again until we're outside.

'Shall we walk a bit?' Seren asks, and I agree because I don't know how else to respond. I follow her to the end of the harbour wall, past the lifeboat station, and we sit

171

on a bench at the end looking back towards the lights of the town.

'This is good tea,' she says.

'Mm, it is.'

'Well done on the presentation.'

I observe her. It's a genuine compliment. I wasn't expecting that. 'Thank you. Yours, too.'

She nods and blows steam from her paper cup.

'I guess it's strange being on opposing sides,' I say, wanting to reassure myself as much as her. 'It's such an emotive subject. The moral covenant, I mean. I don't know how people will decide.'

She doesn't reply.

The need to fill the silence is overwhelming. I press on. 'The thing is, I think . . .'

'I didn't know,' she says, so suddenly I almost spill my tea. 'About your wife.'

'Oh.' Now I'm the one lost for words.

'I'm sorry.' She closes her eyes and exhales. I watch silver swirls of her breath snaking up into the night sky. 'Why do people always say sorry when they hear someone's died? I'll never understand that. Unless they hired a hitman, what do they have to apologise for?'

I get the impression her question isn't one she expects me to answer. But then everything becomes clear – I see that sadness of hers wash across her face again, and I understand. 'Have you . . . ? Did you lose someone too?'

'My dad.' Her voice cracks as she says it.

'When?'

'Three months ago.'

'Wow. I'm sorry.' I catch the flicker of a smallest smile as I hold up my hands. 'And I don't know any hitmen.'

'Glad to hear it.' She swirls the tea around in her paper cup and takes another sip. 'Grief is the *worst*, isn't it? It's so insipid and cruel. I hate that it's stolen the part of my life where Dad used to be. People keep telling me time is the great healer, but how can it be, when you've loved someone your entire life?'

I stare at her, my grief completely eclipsed by hers. Because she *has* grief: brutal, raw, visceral loss gnawing her soul to shreds. Seren isn't just grieving; she *is* grief. And I realise – that's what people think I'm going through, isn't it? Seren's kind of grief. Or maybe they see me functioning, moving on as best I can, and think I'm in denial. Am I in denial? I don't think so, but what do I know? Answers haven't been straightforward since Tash died.

'I'm not sure healing is what matters,' I say slowly, picking my words like seaglass from between beach pebbles. 'I think you keep shifting direction until you can move forward.'

'I don't feel I'm moving forward. I'm just treading water to stop myself drowning.'

Finally, we agree.

'Me too.' I glance at her, wonder if it's worth the risk. I haven't told anyone how I really feel, not in a long time. Even Dad and Owen and Sarah have had edited versions of the truth. Seren MacArthur is on the opposing side in the battle for my livelihood. There are a hundred reasons why I shouldn't give her anything she can use as ammunition. And yet she's just bared a piece of her soul to me, when she had all the same reasons not to. Surely that means something?

I can see tiny rolling crests of white against the inky black waves of the water filling the harbour. If clouds weren't shielding the moon, each one would sparkle against the shadows. My mum used to say the white crests were the spray from nocturnal mermaids' tails, flipping up the dark water. Thinking of mermaids makes me return to Nessie, to our new evening game with seaglass shapes and the handfuls of it currently residing in my pockets. Sometimes all you have to do is accept that you don't know everything. Magic happens that way.

'I wish I could feel like that,' I say, surprised to feel my eyes prickle with saltwater. She is staring at me, but I keep my focus resolutely on the mermaid-tail wakes in the bay. 'People think I do. They think I'm devastated and only carrying on for Nessie.' I realise this is the first time I've mentioned her. I should stop. I should pull back and just be sympathetic. But it's already too late. 'I have a daughter,' I say. 'She's seven and she's going to take over the world.'

'That must be hard. Looking after her on your own.' Her voice is almost lost in the night breeze.

'It is and it isn't. The thing is, my marriage died long before Tash did.' I baulk at my words. They sound cruel – I'd expect anyone else hearing them to be shocked. But Seren doesn't flinch. That's new. 'I mean, I tried for so many years to make Tash happy, but the fact is she blamed me. For bringing her to Cornwall, for her falling pregnant with Ness. And then she blamed Ness by inference, which I couldn't stand. It's sad that she died before she had a chance to realise what a mistake she was making. And it's sad that Nessie had to lose her mum when she was six years old. But I can't feel devastated by her loss. Not for me, anyway.'

She is quiet for a while and I instantly regret my confession. Saying that stuff to someone so raw with her own loss is irresponsible. I must sound like the most heartless man in the world.

'I'm sorry,' I say, feeling like stinking seaweed wrapped beneath a trawler. 'That wasn't . . . Forget I said anything.'

'I don't know how that must feel.' She's turned her head back to the sea. 'Although I understand the anger. A little of it. Not for my dad, but for all the stuff he left behind.'

'Your business?'

'*His* business.' The emphasis carries a world on its shoulders.

'Right. Like you find yourself in a life you didn't plan for?'

She nods. 'Like waking up in someone else's existence.'

'It's hard.'

'Hmm.'

'But we carry on. Because what choice do we have?'

'Struggle on. Hope that the cracks don't show.'

How can someone so confident, so ready to fight for what she believes in, think she appears weak? 'If it helps, you don't look like you're struggling. You look—'

I stop myself. Because what I want to say would be far more than I'm ready to admit. She's still on the opposing side. She could still deliver the fatal blow to the project. We are worlds apart.

'It's getting late,' she says, standing. 'Thanks for the tea.'

I struggle to my feet, not sure if I've just been saved or missed the chance to change everything. 'Sure. You're welcome.'

'I'll see you a week on Wednesday? Next round of the fight?' She smiles.

'Of course.'

The other side of the divide, across a table that might as well be an ocean that separates us . . .

I watch her walk away. And nothing is certain any more.

Chapter Twenty-Nine

Seren

'We have to do something about Jack Dixon.'

Around the table at Aggie's cafe, every head nods. I wondered why Aggie and Lou had called an extraordinary meeting of the Save the Parsonage committee – now I know.

War-planning aside, I love being at Aggie's place after it closes to the public. Over the years we've enjoyed great gatherings here, from birthday parties to summer evening music nights, supper clubs and even an autumn wedding, when all the evening guests spilled onto the beach wrapped in blankets against the night chill. But the times I've loved best have always been just a few close friends chatting and laughing together into the small hours, illuminated by candle lanterns on the tables and festooned fairy lights twinkling from the wooden ceiling.

I needed to be here tonight, among friends, even if the conversation is more serious than usual. It's too quiet at home; there are too many concerns yelling for my attention.

Here, at least for a couple of hours, I only have to think about the people sitting with me around the salt-bleached wooden table.

And, it transpires, Jack Dixon.

'He did too well at the meetin'.' Lou says, his usually smooth bald head furrowed by a frown. 'Everyone is talkin' about him. And *not* in a bad way.'

'We still have support,' Cerrie argues. Though she'd hate me for noticing, she's always a schoolteacher, even off duty. Her tone is even and reassuring, as though soothing a fretting child. 'You'll see. People around here care about their history.'

'Why did Brotherson have to go and find someone nicer than himself? It just isn't fair.'

Sharon from the candle shop rolls her eyes. She's the most recent addition to the committee but by far the most fervent supporter. It's great to have her here, even if I suspect Lou is a little intimidated by her. 'Oh for heaven's sake, Lou, the man's not daft. He bombed spectacularly at the first meeting. I don't blame him for wimping out of the others.'

'He ran scared.' Kieran returns from behind the counter, where he's been making coffee in the espresso machine. I notice Aggie didn't stop him – usually she's so territorial about her cafe equipment. She'd run her business for three years before she'd even let me behind the counter – and I'm her best friend. Kieran hands a cup to Aggie so tentatively it's like he's approaching an unexploded bomb, and she gives a self-conscious nod. Are they ever going to sort this situation out? 'Plus, Brotherson's a businessman. If you find that you're a deal-breaker, you delegate to someone more palatable. He wants to win.'

'I don't understand why someone like Jack Dixon wants to work for Brotherson.'

They all look at me. I'm not sorry I said that. It's what I've been asking myself since I heard Jack's presentation – and our conversation on the harbour wall afterwards. I can't square *that* Jack with a cynical Brotherson minion.

'Money, Seren. It's always about that.'

'Is it, though, Ag? I mean, if he's as passionate about sympathetic renovation and locally sourced materials as he says, why align himself with someone who never gives either a second thought?'

Aggie gives me a look that says *Why does it matter to you?* – but at least she doesn't voice it. 'I still think he needs the money. Let's face it, we all do.'

I can't argue there. 'Is there anything we can do to counter him?'

Lou wipes cappuccino foam from his moustache. 'We have to step up the campaign. Focus all attention back on the organ grinder, not the monkey. Brotherson is a git and everyone knows it. So we remind them who's really behind Rectory Fields. An' make bleddy sure nobody buys Jack Dixon's velvet words.'

Kieran nearly chokes on coffee. 'Would you listen to yourself? "Velvet words" . . . You been reading too many Poldark novels again, have you?'

'Oh, you can laugh, Kieran, but I tell you, that man's a threat. We had this vote in the bag until young twinkle-eyes showed up.'

179

'"Young twinkle-eyes"!' The candle lanterns clink together as Kieran's laughter rocks the table. 'You're insane.'

'Glad I'm amusin' you,' Lou huffs.

'We could run stories in the *Western Morning News*,' Sharon suggests. 'Make it all about our proud town standing up to the big, bad developer. There's a journalist from the paper comes into my shop all the time. I could ask her.'

'Great,' Lou notes down her suggestion, glaring again at Kieran, who is still giggling. 'Any more?'

'Poster campaign,' Aggie says. '*SAVE THE PARSONAGE!* I'll get some made and we'll ask every shop owner in St Ives to display them in their windows.'

'*Posters* . . . Excellent.'

'Local TV?'

'Sharon, my love, you are on fire this evenin'. *TV*. Good. I'll invite crews from *BBC Spotlight* and *West Country Tonight* down, shout 'em lunch at The Hub. That ought to do it. More?'

'Flyers. Get the locals involved. I'll ask Mitchell Jakes if his scout troop could give them out on the streets at the weekend.'

'Great, Aggie, great. This is good, folks. Rampin' up the grass-roots support.' Lou's smile fades. 'Got anythin' sensible to add, boy?'

Kieran, wiping tears from his eyes, shakes his head. 'Probably not.'

'And Seren? You've been very quiet.'

Have I? I'm weary from a long day, and my thoughts have strayed to Gwithian Beach and what I might find there tomorrow. I used to daydream all the time as a child – I

180

was forever being told off about it. But when you live within a minute's walk of the sea and you have a dad who gazes at stars and delights in dreaming up awesome, inspiring stories to tell you, it's impossible not to be tempted away from reality.

I've been thinking about leaving something else along with the completed star for the other starmaker to find – a return gift for the little marshmallow box. The stars have meant so much to me: I just want to let them know. While I was on the beach this morning I found a small blue glass bottle, almost intact. There's one chip on the rim of its neck, but the sea has smoothed it over time. It's the perfect size to slip a note inside.

At first, I thought about just leaving a note in the bottle in the middle of the seaglass star. But words alone don't seem adequate to convey everything the stars have meant to me. It doesn't seem reward enough for all the effort the starmaker has gone to on my behalf. After all, they have made most of each star: I've just completed them.

And then I had the idea.

I'm going to make them a seaglass bracelet. But a better, bolder, more intricate design than I've ever attempted before. When I've found the seaglass stars on Gwithian Beach, it's as if the best version of me has responded. I want to make something that represents the person I want to be – the future I want for myself. I haven't lost my dream of making seaglass jewellery for a living, but before I found the Gwithian stars, that dream was hidden beneath all the responsibility I've inherited. Finding the stars has brought

181

my dream back out into the sunlight – and I want to thank the starmaker for that.

I remember the sweetly odd little note I received with the box of marshmallows two weeks ago – *For the mermaids* – and it suddenly strikes me as a perfect reply. What if the Gwithian Beach mermaids sent a present in return?

An ancient term for seaglass is 'mermaids' tears'. So what if Gwithian's mermaids took their tears of joy and crafted them into a bracelet?

All day I've been dreaming of the colours, the design and the construction of the mermaids' gift. Gold wire instead of silver, with pearlescent 'soap-bubble' beads in between to look like sea spray caught in sunlight and a silver star-shaped charm at the centre of the circle . . .

'Seren?'

Lou is rapping the bowl of a teaspoon on the table impatiently. I've forgotten the question – Aggie's sly grin doesn't help me remember, either.

'Yes?'

'Do you have anything to add? As the *figurehead* of this campaign?

'"The figurehead!" . . .'

'Drink your coffee and button it, Kieran!'

'Yes, Lou. Sorry, Lou.'

I scramble my wayward thoughts together. 'I think you need to focus on Elinor Carne, not the building.'

'Meanin' . . . ?'

'If we ask people to save a site that – let's face it – is pretty run-down and uninspiring, not everyone will understand the importance. But if we focus on Elinor and the injustice she faced for years, I think people will relate to that. She worked so hard all her life but was denied the recognition she deserved because she was a woman. She was a pioneer born at the wrong time, a victim of the society she lived in. Look at the great female pioneers of astronomy: Mary Somerville, Caroline Herschel – only two names we are aware of, yet both faced years of being referred to as male astronomers' *helpers*.'

'So we're going the feminist route?'

I sigh. 'No, Lou, we're going the *human* route. Everyone knows what injustice feels like, on some level or another. Everyone has been passed over in favour of someone else, or had to watch another person take credit for their work. It's a universal thing. If we link that with Elinor's struggle – and the ongoing campaign to have her contribution officially recognised – I think people will see it as a chance to redress the balance.'

My friends observe me in silence. Even Kieran has stopped laughing.

'You should come to my school,' Cerrie says. 'Talk to the children in my class. I think they would love Elinor's story – and if they tell their parents . . . We could make it a whole-school campaign.'

'Now *that* is *brilliant*. Would you do it, Seren?'

I don't even have to think about it. 'Yes, I'd love to. When?'

Cerrie grins. 'Next week. Before the town meeting.'

Chapter Thirty

Jack

It's Thursday morning. I'm at the site again and thankfully the sun has decided to shine on me. I need to think: I've found peace by this old parsonage in recent days. I take off my jacket and lay it over a jumble of old stones a little way from the main building, flopping down to enjoy the sun on my face.

Owen sent me a text earlier. I heard the ringtone as I was driving Nessie to school. When I reached the parsonage site, I read it:

Hey Stink. How'd it go last night?

How *did* it go? I'm still not sure.

I was confident enough when I left the Guildhall, but what happened next clouded everything. I didn't sleep much last night, my conversation with Seren replaying over and over in my mind. She was so honest, when she had no need to be. It won't help her cause with the campaign, but

I got the impression she left her role as leader of it at the Guildhall door. She sought me out. I still don't know why, or how I should feel about it. I only know something changed last night. We're on opposing sides, but outside of the debate we've moved closer.

I look around the ancient stones kissed by the sun this morning and I wonder what happens now. The future of this site is our main concern – it has to be. But it turns out the two people leading the fight for its possible futures have more in common than we thought.

As for the meeting, I'm proud I didn't let myself down this time. I thought of Nessie as I addressed the town; of the life I hope to make for us, if this project goes ahead. The seaglass in my pocket helped. I told her that this morning as we dashed to get ready for school.

'Of course it helped you,' Nessie replied. 'It was magic.'

'It was magic because you put it there. Thanks, noodle.'

'*You're* a noodle! So, did you win?'

'I won't know that for a bit.'

She wrinkled her nose. 'Why?'

'Because it's an important decision that the town has to make. They need time to hear both sides to make the right choice.'

'But *you're* the right choice, Dad. Everybody knows that.'

I wish they did. And I wish they all had Nessie's confidence in me.

I may have changed a few minds last night, but there's more to be done. I find the roll of plans in my jacket pocket and spread them out on the grass at my feet. As I

185

do so, a handful of Nessie's good-luck seaglass tumbles out. Smiling, I stoop to pick the pieces up, watching the sun dance around them in my palm. Nessie calls them 'sun jewels' in the daytime, holding them up one by one to see how the light hits them.

Wait a second . . .

I hold a piece of pale green glass up to the light, then look down at the plans. The design for the side of the building closest to me currently adds two extra storeys, crowned with a gently sloping roof I've proposed we cover in sedum and grass. Looking at the shell of the parsonage, I imagine how the new walls will rise from the old. The materials list has the top storey clad in dark wood; but I'm not sure it will work. Part of the beauty of the original building is its pale stone. In the warm sunlight, it almost glows. Wood cladding will absorb the light and spoil the effect. I take a pencil from my back pocket and write a note on the plan. Then I stand and begin to walk the perimeter of the building, paying attention to where the light falls and where the shadows rest. It's completely different in some parts from how I'd remembered and I'd be willing to bet Brotherson's architect hasn't spent a sunny few hours watching the light travel across the site, either.

Suddenly, I'm excited again. If we get this right, it could totally transform Rectory Fields. We can work with the path of the light through the day to maximise its effect within the building. More light will mean a better living experience for the people who live here. I'd hoped we would utilise the best materials the local area could offer, but I'd forgotten Cornwall's most famous commodity.

Light has summoned artists here for years; it's inspired countless authors and poets, photographers and crafts-people. Part of the beauty of this place is its unique light – we'd be crazy not to play to its strengths.

It will mean submitting a verification order to the archi-tect up in Plymouth, so I'll have to talk to Brotherson and get him to okay it; but I'm so convinced this will make Rectory Fields a truly special development.

An hour later, the plan is covered in my handwriting and my mind is alive with possibilities. I don't wait for an invitation: I call Brotherson's office and ask to meet him.

If we're celebrating Cornwall's light in the development, it might sway some voters. I don't know if it will make a difference, but I have to try. I have Nessie's good-luck gift from last night to thank for finding it. Maybe she was right – perhaps the seaglass is magic after all.

Chapter Thirty-One

Seren

'Let me get this straight – you do this for *fun*?'

'What, sit in one place for hours on end to catch sight of an incredible natural phenomenon?' I grin at Kieran and hand him a steaming thermos mug. 'Yes, I do.'

'You strange, strange woman.'

'Oh, and it's so different from your job because . . . ?'

'Listen, I don't sit in elevated sheds for hours on end staring at the sky,' he argues back. 'When I do landscape shoots, I choose locations with a hope of a warm fire nearby. Or, preferably, in countries where the night temperature won't chill your martini.'

I know he's hamming it up to amuse me, and that his photographic assignments often require him to visit pretty remote places. But the performance is appreciated. 'You've photographed stars before, though?'

He is holding the hot chocolate like it's about to save his life. 'Yeah. Out in Canada, a few years back. My mate in Ontario specialises in long-exposure time-lapse composites.

I asked him to show me how to capture star trails, so we went up to the mountains to shoot the Perseid meteor shower. But I just helped him set it up – I haven't done a solo shoot before.'

'So tonight is a new experience for both of us?'

'It is. Not least in my discovering how long I can sit on this shed bench and still retain feeling in my legs . . .'

'Oh, stop moaning. This was your idea, remember?'

He can't deny that. When he visited MacArthur's yesterday afternoon we began talking about how I was going to enthuse a bunch of primary-school kids about astronomy. And, specifically, about Elinor Carne.

'Words are okay,' he said, 'but kids love visuals. I did a talk at Cerrie's school last year and I'd planned to talk a bit about how I get my shots, but pretty quickly the kids' eyes started glazing over. It was like the worst job interview I've ever had. I was *terrified*. Just to survive I started to share my favourite photos from around the world, telling them the story behind each one, and the response was incredible. So you can tell them Elinor Carne's story, but if you want them to really connect with it you need to bring them into her world. Show them why Elinor was so passionate about the stars. I mean, you're the best person to understand that and share it, aren't you?'

I immediately thought about the amazing star-trail photographs that cause such a stir in the astronomy forums I'm a member of. Several times I've been rendered speechless by the otherworldly arcs being drawn across the night sky, as the camera maps the path of each star.

189

Having a resident camera expert on the spot, I asked him to help me.

It's taken almost an hour to set up the bank of cameras on their curved tripods on the flat part of the roof below the hatch window – but now we're huddled on the hatch bench, hearing the rhythmic click of the timer between each simultaneous shutter movement. I'm glad we brought supplies. It's not very cold by Shedservatory standards, but sitting in one place for hours is going to get pretty chilly, especially in the small hours of the night. Plenty of time to chat, though . . .

'Still seems weird not seeing your dad around town,' Kieran says, nodding at a battered old photo of him I've drawing-pinned to the hatch frame beside the ancient star wheel. In it he has an arm slung protectively over his telescope, Clarabell, and is grinning like an Olympic champion. A mate of his who worked for the *Western Morning News* took the picture, and Dad was very proud of being the first local amateur astronomer to appear on the front page for eighty years.

'It is weird.'

He nods. Nothing else is needed. We sit in silence for a while, two shutter rounds firing and the distant singing of a confused songbird serenading a streetlight beside its nest the only other sounds around us. The sea is little more than a white-noise rumble from here, but if I tune my ears into it I can catch it.

'The town looks good tonight.'

'It does.'

'I love how the lights on the other side of the bay look

like stars,' he says, pointing out of the hatch to the hill opposite ours. 'Ever noticed that? They twinkle.' A tiny cluster of wrinkles pools at his brow. 'And if you ever tell anyone I said that, I'll deny it.'

'Don't worry, it goes no further than here.' I pat the smooth larch lap shed frame to reassure him. 'Anyway, just blame the Shedservatory. It makes you lyrical.'

I haven't made the link between St Ives' nightscape and the constellations before. I've always been too intent on looking up. I wonder if Dad ever noticed it? And what about Elinor Carne? The lights were different in her day, but did she view St Ives from the hills and see the stars in the streets mirroring those in the firmament? How much did her role as a parson's wife and servant of the tiny hilltop parish tether her to the ground? Did she look to the stars as an escape from hardship on earth?

I smile to myself, having thus proved my point about the Shedservatory's lyric-inducing qualities.

'I reckon in the next meeting we just blow Jack Dixon out of the water for good. Fix him, win the vote and move on.'

I'm startled by the sudden venom coming from my friend's mouth. It doesn't suit him, and yet at the same time I'm surprised by my own gut reaction – of wanting to protect Jack instead of go in for the kill. Because we could – *I* could. We needn't wait for the final consultation meeting. From everything I've heard and seen around St Ives this week, Jack and Brotherson are still very much in second place. We could call forward the vote and finish this now. I hear the rumblings of impatience in the streets and shops, distant for now, like the faint rumble of the sea from our shed-top perch. Most of the people I've talked to want the parsonage saved, the matter closed once and for all.

But I don't want Brotherson to take Jack Dixon down with him. Jack is a nice guy. Misguided in his choice of employer, certainly, but I can't believe he is hell-bent on wreaking havoc for the town. I suddenly realise a truth more uncomfortable than the Shedservatory's bench seat: I *like* Jack. Something no leader of the opposing side to his development should ever admit. Something I shouldn't even consider.

I glance at Kieran – the revelation is so loud in my ears I half-expect him to have heard it, too – but he's too busy trying to wrap himself bodily around his thermal mug to have noticed anything. Relieved not to have been found out, I look up at the stars. But my eyes keep being dragged back to the twinkling land-stars on the opposite side of the bay. Which does Jack regard the most? Is he dreaming of higher things, or only those he can build on the land?

Chapter Thirty-Two

Jack

I'm fixing yet another broken fence on the caravan park's perimeter when I'm interrupted by a familiar voice.

'Alright, Jack?'

'Hey, Jeb. How are you?'

Jeb sniffs and clicks the stud in his tongue between his teeth. 'In a bit of bother, truth be told.'

I wrench the old nails out of the splintered panel. 'What's up?'

'Promised Wenna I'd pick up the dress she ordered from her favourite shop in St Ives today, but the jeep's broke.'

'Ah.' Any story that includes Jeb's inimitable, mermaid-haired fiancée being denied what she wants is never going to have a happy ending. 'Not good.'

'She's not happy, I'll tell you that.'

'I'll bet.'

'Trev at the garage says he can't get parts till next week. I reckon that jeep's for the scrapheap. Thing is, we've got Chrissy Michaels' wedding tomorrow and Wenna wanted the dress for then . . .' It's almost endearing seeing the tattooed, pierced hulk of a man trying *not* to ask for a favour.

I drop the hammer into my toolbox and decide to rescue him. 'Did you want a lift, mate?'

Jeb's smile is brighter than a lighthouse lantern's bulb. 'Would you? I know you're busy with this blasted fence.'

'It's secure enough for now. What makes these holes, Jeb? Is it kids, do you think?'

'Could be rogue badgers for all I know. The wildlife's vicious round here . . .'

Once in St Ives, my very grateful friend heads off to Ebb and Flow on the harbour front to collect Wenna's parcel while I take the opportunity to grab a few essentials for home. We're out of washing detergent and loo roll, tea-bags and tinfoil – things the chalet seems to eat. I stop by Boots to get a bottle of the bubble bath Nessie really likes, and the cheapest shampoo I can find for me.

The lady behind the till smiles as she takes my basket. 'You're the builder bloke, aren't you?'

I'm not sure how to react, considering I haven't paid for my shopping yet and Nessie *really* needs that bubble bath. If I say yes and she's supporting the opposition, I might be kicked out of the shop empty-handed. I've been nervous about coming to St Ives after my presentation at the town meeting. Not because of what I said – I believe in all of it – but because of whom I now represent. I'm not used to being the spokesman for somebody else, and it's taking some getting used to.

She's scanned the items now. All I have to do is pay. Can

I wait until then to answer her question? She smiles at me again. Ah, well . . .

'Yes, I am. Construction manager, actually. Hi.'

'Thought you did well Wednesday night. Changed a lot of folks' minds, I reckon.'

'Really?' I should ask that again, in a far lower tone.

'I was sitting with my friend Sandra, right, and she said she'd trust you to build her house. And Sandra don't trust most folk.'

'Does she need a house building?' I ask, ever the optimist.

'Not right now. But she'll *definitely* bear you in mind.' She gives me a startlingly suggestive wink as she hands me my change.

And it continues, as I walk along Fore Street, past the bookshop, clothes shops and the art gallery, the deli with its picture-perfect display of fruit and veg, and Sky's Diner with its pile of fresh pasties in the window. In the children's clothing shop with its giant Peter Rabbit toy, a bloke changing the window display gives me a thumbs-up; a lady stops outside the Poppy Treffry shop to wish me all the best. I'd expected accusing looks and a town determined to fight the Big Bad Developer, but I get the sense that the decision is far from made.

I'm heading to the Post Office at the end of Fore Street to buy Nessie a new sketchpad and the watercolour pencils she's lusted after since our last visit, when I see an A-board sign resting on the cobbles.

MACARTHUR'S
~ local art and crafts ~

195

MacArthur's – Seren MacArthur's shop. I peer up the alleyway to the small courtyard, clutching my carrier bags for security. Why do I feel nervous? It isn't like I'm doing anything wrong. *Come in and browse!*, the sign invites me. I notice the paint is beginning to flake around its edges. The hinges are rusted, and a screw is working loose at one end. It seems tired, almost resigned. Looking up the alley, I can see the shop sign painted in identical colours – sea-green with a rambling pink wild rose edging the name, which is painted in white, looping text. It reminds me of the Romany caravan art Dad used to have in his shed, all that remained of a distant relative's traditional horse-drawn home. Like those panels, the sign has seen better days. I can't see the shop's window from where I'm standing, but I wonder what 'local art and crafts' MacArthur's sells. It looks so different from the polished galleries that litter the town. Does Seren paint? I don't know anything about her, other than that she opposes Rectory Fields, owns this shop and recently lost her father. That seems wrong, somehow. Like I should know my opponent better.

People jostle past, Fore Street bustling as ever despite it being early in the season. But there's a strange stillness in the courtyard, as if it's frozen in time beyond the arched entrance, no more than a realistic painting. It's oddly quiet, considering the famous street it borders. Do people go in there at all?

Maybe I should just walk in? Say hello?

No, Jack. Don't be daft. What would I say? I can hardly claim to be 'just passing', when it's a closed courtyard.

And St Ives isn't where I live, so I can't pretend I just happened to be here, even if I did.

But I remember what Seren said – about Tash, and her dad – after the meeting. She looked so lost when she described her grief. And I was worse than useless. I should have said more, responded better. She just threw me with her honesty. It ended on a strange note, and I want to let her know she didn't tell me too much. Since we lost Tash I've sometimes worried that I've been too honest when people have asked me about her. When you're living something twenty-four hours a day, seven days a week, it's easy to forget it isn't the constant commentary to other people's lives. She might be embarrassed, or wishing she'd never said anything . . .

Stuff it. I'm going in.

A bump to my shoulder shifts my attention back to the street.

'Excuse me, mate.' A tall, blond bloke in a sharp suit holds up his hand to apologise. He looks like a footballer, or maybe a millionaire. Two women walking past giggle like teenagers when he smiles in their direction.

'Sorry.'

'No worries. Hey, good presentation the other night.'

I start to thank him, but he's already walking up the alley to the courtyard – straight into Seren's shop.

'Hey, babe . . .' he calls as he disappears inside.

Well, one thing's for certain. Seren MacArthur isn't worrying about *me*.

*

197

This evening's star has a bright green heart. I found a pile of spring-green glass under a rock by the path to the top of the dunes – the relatively recent remains of an old cider bottle, by the looks of it – and have used the pieces to carefully fill the middle of the star. Nessie is impressed, but then I am in her good books because I arrived home with her favourite bubble bath, the sketchbook and pencils *and* a tub of highly prized Moomaid of Zennor ice cream as a treat. For tonight, at least, I am the Greatest Dad in the World.

'It looks so good,' Nessie says, hands on hips as she stands back to view our evening's work. 'We should do blue tomorrow night. Or pink . . .'

'It depends on what the mermaids leave for us,' I say.

'Pink please, mermaids!' Ness yells.

I love her enthusiasm and how she never once questions whether the star will be complete in the morning. I'm learning to trust the stars will be there – and I'm starting to depend on it. As we were gathering seaglass tonight, I thought about how much has changed since we made the first star. I now have a firm offer of a job that could potentially secure our immediate future and beyond. In her fifth month there, Nessie is settling in at school (barring the bully-kicking incident, which neither of us refers to); and my experience in St Ives today has made me dare to believe that Rectory Fields could win the town's vote.

Tash used to mock me for seeking signs, but I've always done it. I'm not superstitious – not in terms of avoiding black cats or walking under ladders – but I have always looked for things to pin my hope on. We had so little of that before we made the first star that I was starting to think our downward spiral couldn't be reversed.

The stars changed that.

And even if they are just a fun game we're enjoying with a stranger who needs it too, as far as I'm concerned each star is a talisman for Ness and me. A promise of better things and brighter days. I look forward to making them and finding each one complete the next evening. I don't know if the person who finishes each star realises what they mean to us. I hope they do. In any case, the stars they help us create have heralded a new season for my girl and me. I feel it every time we walk on Gwithian Beach: magic at work . . .

'Dad, look!'

Nessie's face is washed in a deep pink-gold light as I follow her pointing finger to the sunset exploding colour across the horizon and over the waves to the beach where we stand. A blood-red sun dips in the electric blue strip where sea meets sky; fiery orange and pink arc above it. The clouds beyond are edged in gold and even the sound of the sea seems to hush in respect. The glowing light warms everything around us – the sand and the rocks, our faces and bodies – making the new, almost-made star sparkle at our feet. Tash once said I'd never see the magic I believed I'd find. She was wrong.

Things are changing for Nessie and me. Here is where the good stuff begins.

Chapter Thirty-Three

Seren

'Hey, babe . . .'

I look up from the counter and grin. 'Alright, *'ansum?*'

This has been our patter of choice since school and we see no reason to change it now. It's good to have something so familiar today, with all the new thoughts of Jack still swirling around my head.

'Looking beautiful as ever, star girl.' Kieran plants a kiss on my cheek. 'And smelling good, too. Has the kettle boiled recently?'

He's shameless, but luckily for Kieran it still amuses me. 'I made a fresh pot of coffee about ten minutes ago,' I reply, pointing at the still untouched jug on the coffee machine. I fully intended to enjoy it as soon as it was brewed, but the bracelet I'm working on refused to let me leave it, even for a minute. I haven't been this excited by one of my designs before and I'm loving the rush. 'What's with the suit? I haven't seen you wear one for – it must be years.'

'Ross Marchant's wedding, 2010,' he says, filling two

mugs with coffee and bringing one to me. 'Not this suit, I hasten to add. We all got drunk on sloe gin and crashed out at mine for two days straight, remember?'

I have a very distant memory of an epically painful hangover and laughing ourselves breathless at Kieran's post-drunken attempts to make porridge for ten people. 'I haven't touched sloe gin since.'

Kieran chuckles. 'Me neither.'

'So why wear a suit today? Planning to get drunk again?'

'No fear! Actually, I had a meeting with a journalist from the *Telegraph* this morning.'

'Kieran, that's amazing!'

'Pretty cool, huh? Came about completely by accident, too. Guy's an old friend from art college who's down here on holiday, and he suggested we meet up. His girlfriend was there, too. Who happens to be the paper's picture editor. She's looking for a photographer for their travel section. Six-month contract, plus ongoing projects. Quite an opportunity. So I thought I'd better scrub up.'

'I don't suppose Aggie's seen you looking like this, has she?' I imagine my best friend being tipped completely over the edge by that particular sight.

'I don't suppose you'd like to change the subject, would you?'

'Ooh, touchy.'

'Shush, you.'

'Haven't you two sorted this out yet? Come on, what are you waiting for? You like her, she likes you . . .'

'I've just applied for a job that will take me overseas *a lot* . . .'

I fix him with a stare. 'Clever. How to run away from your problems.'

'You call it running away, I call it professional development.' He shakes his head as I start to reply. 'No, please don't say anything. I *know*, okay? I'll sort it – in my own time.'

I can't push him any more. 'Fine. I just want you to be happy.'

'Cheers. So, what are you working on?'

The bracelet – I'd forgotten it was there. Instinctively I flatten my hands over the pieces. 'Nothing. Just messing about with bits . . .'

Too late. His mug meets the counter with a *thunk* and he gently prises my hands away. 'Don't be shy, just show me . . . My life, Seren, this is . . .'

'It's nothing, really . . .'

I hear his intake of breath as he takes in my work. 'Geddon, girl, this is *astounding*. Where did you learn to do this?'

'Nowhere. I just designed it myself.'

He's still holding my hands as he looks up at me. 'Why aren't you selling these in the shop? You'd make a fortune.'

'No.'

'Are you crazy? It's stunning! Tourists would go mad for that.'

I pull my hands away from his and scoop the half-made bracelet into a velvet bag. 'It's not for sale.'

'Why?'

How can I ever explain it to him? *I'm making a gift from the mermaids for a stranger I've been making seaglass stars on the beach with* . . . Nobody knows about this one small part of my life. Kieran knows most things about me, Aggie even more – but this is too special to share. Because however much they love me, it will end up being picked over and pulled apart, like everything else in my life. And I don't want to share it.

'It isn't what the shop sells.'

'Maybe that's why the shop is struggling to make money.'

'I can't sell these here.'

'Why, Ser? It's not like your dad's going to object . . .' He clamps a hand to his mouth. 'I'm sorry. That came out wrong.'

It's so hard to explain. MacArthur's is a shrine to everything Dad believed in. I don't want my jewellery to jostle for position with everyone else's things. And I know that's completely irrational, but it's my decision. My jewellery represents the only thing that's still mine. I lost my job and my home in Falmouth, the possibility of a new start last Christmas when I passed up the chance of a new job because Dad wasn't well – and now I have *his* business, *his* campaign to run, and I'm living in *his* house because I can't afford to live anywhere else. If I sold my bracelets here, it would feel like I'd surrendered that part of me, too. 'This isn't my shop. It's Dad's. I just want my business to be separate for now, that's all.'

'But that bracelet—'

'– isn't for sale. Anywhere. It's not my usual style, just an experiment.'

Kieran observes me for a while. 'So, who's it for?'

I can't escape this conversation without answering him. 'A friend.'

'Right.' He nods slowly and returns to drinking his coffee. I think he's got the message. My heart is thudding, though. Why do I feel as if I've been caught out? And why does making this gift for the starmaker feel like such a risk?

Next morning I arrive at Gwithian an hour earlier than usual. I want to give myself enough time to complete the star, leave my gift and be off the beach as soon as I can. Today of all days, I don't want to be found.

I finished the bracelet in the early hours, taking time to attach each element. It was like a meditation on the last three weeks. I don't know if the other starmaker will feel my thanks for all they have done, but I willed my gratitude into every piece of seaglass.

It's in my pocket now, with the blue glass bottle, its note already carefully written and rolled up inside, capped with a cover of silver foil secured with a tiny green rubber band to keep out the moisture. I've wrapped the bracelet in tissue paper the colour of cowslips, slipped it into a turquoise velvet drawstring bag, then wound blue bubble wrap around the whole package and fastened it with loops of brown string. I'm hoping it will be protected from the elements as much as possible, and I'm relieved to be greeted by a dry morning with a gentle westerly breeze.

Molly plods beside me as I scour the beach for glass. Her sand-covered tail bumps against my leg as I crouch to lay each piece in place, as I have done every morning for the past three weeks. She knows to wait now, flopping down in the sand beside me.

Until the moment when I complete the star and place the package carefully at its heart, with the blue glass bottle and message beside it, I can't quite believe I'll be able to leave my precious creation on the beach. But as soon as it is in place, it no longer belongs to me. The stars were a gift. This is mine.

'Come on, lady,' I say to Molly, my voice catching. Because suddenly it means the world to be doing this, and I don't want to do anything that might make it stop. 'Let's go home.'

When I get back to my car Molly curls up on the back seat, while I sit and watch the dawn breaking over Gwithian Beach. My hands are shaking in my lap and I don't know whether to laugh or cry. This is it, the next step up of the game. Until now our creations have been fleeting: lasting long enough for the other starmaker to see, but ultimately destined to return to the beach. But now there's a lasting reminder. Will they accept it?

For the first time I feel like I've left a part of me on the beach in the middle of the seaglass star. My hopes and dreams are woven into that bracelet. I've never shared these with anyone before. Mum doesn't know the extent of my dream; neither did Dad. They assumed my beach-combing trips were a hobby, and even when I started my Etsy shop, they thought it was a nice way to make a little pocket money. I'm a graphic designer by training and trade, so they assumed that profession would eventually call me back. Computers, technology, not ancient craft skills . . . Even I wasn't sure I could make a business out of it. So I've kept it secret. And I *like* the secrecy of it. After Dad died, having something only I knew about was a lifeline. Everything gets knocked when you lose someone you love. Your confidence, your life, your plans for the future that now have to be different from what you'd imagined because that person can't be part of it . . . I have harboured my dream in secret, a precious treasure just for me. But finding the seaglass stars has made me dare to share it with someone else.

So the bracelet waits, surrounded by the newest star.

Today, everything changes. Will there be a new star waiting for me tomorrow morning? Or will my gift scare them away? All I can do is wait.

Chapter Thirty-Four

Jack

We almost missed it.

Now we're sitting together on the creaky old sofa in the chalet and neither of us can quite believe it.

'Is this because of the marshmallows?' Nessie asks, her question not much more than breath.

Is it? It's one heck of a leap from sweets to *this*.

'I don't know. Maybe?'

And we so nearly didn't see it. The small blue bubble-wrapped package was only just visible in a pile of seaweed the lunchtime storm must have dragged up the beach. We had to clear strands off the star to be able to see the finished shape. I thought the package was just a bit of rubbish dropped by a careless visitor – we don't get much on Gwithian Beach, so when something is discarded in the sand it's noticeable. Thank goodness Nessie decided to investigate.

The blue glass bottle with its printed note is exciting enough. But within a small velvet pouch we discovered the most amazing piece of jewellery I've ever seen. It's – I can't even find words worthy to describe it.

We were so shocked we almost forgot to make the new star. I'm grateful I found presence of mind enough to realise in time. How would that have looked to the starmaker if our response to their incredible gift was no star at all? It took every ounce of our combined resolve to dismantle the current one and rearrange the seaglass into a new design, a multicoloured explosion of random pieces that made me think of stained-glass windows. Nessie couldn't have found the patience to choose an alternating pattern this evening. Neither could I. By the time we'd finished, my daughter was so overexcited that all her words deserted her. She could only communicate with furious nods, her eyes ablaze and her smile wide. I've never seen Nessie sprint for home as fast as she did this evening, not even stopping to gaze up at the bats circling the top of the cliff steps, which would usually command her attention.

She's shaking a little beside me now. She's always done this when her excitement levels reach bursting point. Her feet tap repeatedly on the rag-rug in front of the sofa – if we were standing up she'd be dancing like the Irish dancers in *Riverdance*.

'Dad?'

'Yes?'

'Can I try it on?'

'Do it.'

It's too big for her wrist, but the seaglass and gold wire glow against Nessie's pale skin. There are beads in it, too, that look like bubbles of sea foam in the sun, and a silver star charm in the centre of the bracelet. It's the perfect mix of found objects and new materials, and its construction is astounding.

I've always been drawn to projects that use the fabric of the land to create something new. There is such beauty in found natural objects. If Brotherson and his architect agree, I want us to pursue this ethos in as many aspects as possible of the Rectory Fields build. Our local environment is too rich in natural materials to even consider looking elsewhere. I believe a building should come from the land – its environment should inform its character.

Whoever made the bracelet understands that.

And their gift makes me feel like they understand me, too. *Us.* Nessie and me.

As I watch Nessie inspecting each seaglass element, I am struck by the strangest feeling of not being alone, of being connected again. We've been out on our own for months – and years before that. I was alone in my marriage until Ness came along, then alone as her parent even when Tash was alive. I'd wonder what she would have made of this discovery, but I already know the answer. For someone who dealt daily in art, she had no concept of the act of creation. To her, the work she hung in the gallery was no more than a price tag, a net worth.

This bracelet would be difficult to put a price on. It's too beautiful to be reduced to pounds and pence.

And the starmaker made it for us.

I unroll the message from the bottle again.

To the starmaker, with love from the mermaids of Gwithian xx

Like the message we left with the marshmallows, the words have been printed, so there is no indication of the starmaker's identity here. But the person is obviously an artist – we already know that from the many ways they have completed our beach stars.

'It's so lovely,' my daughter breathes, her cheeks flushed by surprise and joy. 'Can we keep it?'

I hug her to me. 'They made it for us.'

'I'm going to take such good care of it, Dad. And you have to as well.'

'I promise.'

'Wait till I tell Flo about this at school on Monday. She's going to be so surprised!'

Nessie launches into an excited monologue about all the mermaid stories she and her school friend have shared lately, as my mind begins to stray. We should make something in return – now that the game of stars has taken a large leap forward. A thank-you note wouldn't be anywhere near enough.

I think about it all night, any chance of sleep lost to the thrill of the evening's discovery. Possibilities crowd my mind as I lie in bed staring up at the wood-clad ceiling. But I don't mind. I have waited too long for the return of inspiration. Sleep can wait: I feel more alive than I have for months.

Chapter Thirty-Five

Seren

I wake an hour before my alarm is set to go off, but there's no chance of going back to sleep. My first thought is of the other starmaker and how they will have reacted to the gift I left. Last night I dreamed of visiting Gwithian but finding no star at all. I hope it isn't a portent of things to come.

I'm nervous about what I'll find – or not find – on the beach, but one thing's for certain: I did the right thing. We needed to move forward, as sure as the tides rise and fall. It was time to show the starmaker what their work has meant to me. What it *still* means to me.

I catch sight of my pale reflection in the stainless-steel kettle as it boils noisily, and wish I looked as confident on the outside as I feel on the inside. It's early, though; I'm tired, and the lack of sleep from my tossing and turning last night is all too evident.

I go through the motions of preparing my flask of coffee, filling a bottle of water for Molly, fetching her rug

I washed and dried last night to take my mind off what might be happening on Gwithian Beach, and packing what I need for my beachcombing. Every step is deliberately slow and methodical, fighting the urge to grab whatever I can as fast as possible and bolt out of the house. I slow my breathing, noticing every cold intake of air and warm exhale, like I learned in the yoga class that runs during the summer above Porthmeor Beach Cafe.

Focus, Seren. Breathe. I repeat it as a mantra, imagining Dad's amusement at my battle. I remember him telling me off during one childhood visit to Flambards theme park, which I'd begged him and Mum to take me to for months. When I got there the excitement was so great I dashed from one attraction to the next, and after an hour was completely overwrought. I remember Dad leading me gently to a bench, getting me to take deep breaths and then advising me to take my time.

'Slow down, stargirl. *Breathe.* You've got to take the time to see things – take them in, enjoy every bit. Hurrying misses the magic.'

Okay, Dad. I'm slowing down . . .

Molly is keen to accompany me this morning despite the early start. She barely gives me time to spread her blanket over the back seat of my car before she clambers in, then spends the entire journey with her nose pressed to the rear passenger window, watching the darkened fields whizzing past. We drive through Hayle and out onto the road that winds along St Ives Bay, the first glow of the breaking day just visible where the dark sky meets the ocean. I'm getting more nervous as we near Gwithian. What if they hated the bracelet? What if it scared them away?

All I want to do now is go down onto the sand and find out for myself what's waiting there for me. Or what *isn't*.

I scramble down the steps to the beach, but when I reach the bottom I stop. Molly crashes into the back of my legs and grumbles loudly.

'Sorry,' I say, my heartbeat pounding in my ears. I'm scared to look, to go over to the spot where our seaglass stars are always made, in case it's empty. I don't want this game to end yet, or to do anything to stop it. If the other starmaker didn't like the gift – or thought it a step too far – it might all be over.

Molly bumps her head against my calves and looks up as if to ask what I'm doing.

What *am* I doing?

This is ridiculous. There's only one way to find out whether my fears are unfounded or not. And it isn't by hovering on the bottom step, too scared to visit the beach.

'Let's just go and see,' I say, but Molly is already padding across the sand towards the rocks.

I clamber over them, almost falling when the toe of my boot catches the top of one of the jagged boulders. I reach out and find a handhold on the next rock, bringing myself to a stop that jars my shoulder but prevents a head-dive to the stones. But by then, it doesn't matter. I see the sand beyond – and the place where every star has been made – and my heart leaps ten feet into the air.

There's a new star!

Molly's ears lift in shock when I yell, but I can't help

myself. I'm just so relieved that the starmaker wasn't scared away by my gift. As my dog pads away to investigate the early-morning beach smells, I kneel down beside the incomplete star to take a closer look. It's the same outline shape as all of the previous stars, but the seaglass filling it isn't as carefully placed as the others. There are no patterns, no alternating colours, just a tumble of seaglass of all shapes, sizes and hues. It's beautiful, in a new way, but I feel a slight dip of disappointment. It feels rushed, somehow.

I stand up and rub my shoulder where it stings from my almost-fall. I don't know why the new star doesn't thrill me. I should just be relieved that it's there at all. The salt air stings my throat as I breathe it in and I shake the sand from my coat sleeve, annoyed with myself. Having a new star is a gift, as much as the others were. Maybe I built this morning up too much. I'd been so terrified that the game would be over that perhaps my expectations of finding I was wrong were too high. Did I expect the starmaker to thank me for the bracelet? Leave a note, or some acknowledgement that they had received it?

Perhaps.

But the new star is here. Isn't that enough?

I set about gathering handfuls of seaglass to complete the star. The game is continuing, so I have to follow suit. I fill in the fifth point to match the other four: showers of multicoloured seaglass falling into place, finding their own order.

When it's done, I call Molly to my side and turn my back on the star. I won't be disappointed in this, I decide.

I just can't let the game I've loved so much be allowed even a glimpse of the dismay that's clouded every other aspect of my life. This is still my beautiful secret, my own gift. The starmaker hasn't abandoned me, like I'd feared. I need to stop expecting anything more than I find on the beach every morning and just enjoy the ride.

Chapter Thirty-Six

Jack

In the small hours it comes to me: the perfect response. Pulling a jumper on, I venture out of bed and click on the kitchen light. I find sheets of paper and Nessie's drawing pencils on top of the old sideboard and start to sketch out plans.

What time will our starmaker be on the beach today? It's too early now, I think, but I wonder if they are making their way to Gwithian even now. It's strange to think our lives run in parallel, when if we met in the street we'd be no more than strangers.

I'm so glad we remembered to make the star in all the surprise and thrill of finding the mermaid bracelet. If they were to arrive on the beach this morning and find no star, what would they think of us? Part of me wishes I'd already planned what to make for them, so that they could discover it this morning. But they took time to craft the gift they left for us; to rush something in return would be a mistake.

Daylight is beginning to seep through the gaps in the living-room curtains by the time my design is complete. Nessie will be up soon – I want her to see this before the craziness of our Sunday begins. We've errands to run, a few odd jobs to do for Jeb, and then I have to get Ness over to Owen and Sarah's for one p.m. so she can go with them and the boys to a water park near Newquay. I want her to know what I'm going to spend the afternoon making for the mermaids.

It's almost nine a.m. when she wakes, and the first thing she wants to do is check the seaglass bracelet is still there.

'It might have been a dream, Dad,' she says, hurrying to the mantelpiece where we put the bracelet last night. 'It wasn't! It's still here!'

'I told you it would be. Come and see what I've been working on . . .'

'Dad, I've been thinking.' She's standing in the middle of the living room, hands on her hips and her most serious expression – a comical combination with her one-leg-up, one-leg-down pyjamas and wild morning hair.

'Yes, ladybird?'

'We absolutely have to make something for the mermaids. To say thank you. And not just marshmallows this time.'

'I think you're right. That's what I've been planning.' I hold up the sheet of paper. 'Want to see?'

Her stance forgotten, she races to my side and perches on the arm of the old sofa as I show her the plans I've drawn and redrawn since two thirty a.m.

'Can you make this?'

'I think so. We'll need to find all the bits on the beach, and then I'll work out a way of constructing it.'

'Then we have to start right away!' She leaps from the sofa and begins pulling on her wellies over her pyjamas.

'Ness – wait – you need to get dressed and have breakfast, and we've jobs to do before we go to Uncle Owen and Auntie Sarah's . . .'

'I can't wait for all of *that*,' my daughter retorts from halfway inside a hoodie. 'We have to go now!'

I should insist and play the Dad card, but I love Nessie's passion. Errands can wait, and the work for Jeb can be done any time. A morning beachcombing for building materials would be good for both of us. 'Okay, but I'm making us toast to eat on the beach. And put your jeans on over your PJs – and your coat, too. It's chilly out there this morning.'

I'm buzzing as we head down the steps to the beach. I've been thinking for hours about how we could thank our fellow starmaker, and this is the perfect opportunity. They've been busy already – we find our star from last night perfectly completed with multicoloured seaglass, a length of sea-frayed blue acrylic rope looping around it and small, flat pieces of driftwood placed like weatherboarding around its perimeter. With Nessie's permission I carefully remove these, along with some of the shells we used to fill the star's centre yesterday. Now all we need is moss and something to bind all the elements together.

Later that afternoon, I lay out all the pieces and a few tools I've brought in from my car on a small table outside the chalet in what passes as our garden. It feels like the beginning of something special and I'm relishing the challenge of building it. I carefully cut the driftwood pieces to the right size, taking care not to waste anything, winding moss and brown string around them to form a frame. Then I take a mix of cement and beach sand and start to fill in the structure, adding tiny scraps of mussel shell as I go. The iridescent mother-of-pearl shell inlays look magical against the buff-coloured mortar and grey driftwood. Suitably fitting for any mermaid worth her salt.

As I work, I wonder who will find this on the beach tomorrow morning. Will they be expecting a gift? And will this tiny structure mean as much to them as their gift has to Nessie and me? I hope it will. I've thought about them a great deal recently. Their kindness is one thing; but it's their creativity that really blows me away. It takes a special kind of person to see the possibility in a half-finished star and commit to completing them time and again. And then to offer something as unique and special as the bracelet, with no expectation of anything in return – well, that's nothing short of extraordinary, as far as I'm concerned.

When my brother drops Nessie home just before six p.m. she is all ready to go straight to the beach, protesting loudly when I insist she eats tea first.

'But Dad! We have to make the present for the mermaids!'

'Relax, kid, I've already made it.'

'You have? Where is it? Can I see? Oh Dad, I want to see it. Can I? Please, please, please?'

I take the tiny gift from my pocket where it's been hiding, awaiting her return. 'Here.'

Her blue eyes widen and she gives a little squeal. 'It's perfect! They're going to love it! We need to take it to the beach right now. Have you done a note, too?'

'I thought you should decide what we'll write,' I reply, loving her reaction. 'So how about you grab the laptop, and I'll sort tea?'

My plan rumbled, Nessie gives a loud tut Grandad Dave would be proud of. 'Okay then. But I'm not having pudding till after the beach, and you can't make me. This is just too important.'

It is important, I realise as I'm dishing stew out into two bowls. This game means more to me than anything I've done since we lost Tash. So we type and print our message, slip it into the blue glass bottle and head down to Gwithian Beach for the next chapter in the star game.

Chapter Thirty-Seven

Seren

I can hardly breathe.

I'd come to the beach today determined to love whatever I found, being so disgusted with my reaction to the multicoloured star yesterday morning. All day I sat in MacArthur's feeling like the most selfish woman in the world. Last night I dreamed of sitting next to Dad in the Shedservatory and enduring a lecture about my attitude. I resolved to do better, to slow down like Dad had told me and delight in every tiny detail.

The new star was waiting for me this morning as they have been every morning. It's beautiful – delicate shades of pale green and white with a flower of grey-blue mussel shells in the middle. But that isn't why I'm staring at it, incapable of moving. It's because of what else lay at its heart, now resting softly in my palm.

A note, rolled into the blue glass bottle I sent my own note in. And a package, not much bigger than the one I left for the starmaker with the bracelet. I want to open both now, but the light is only just appearing and I have a star to complete. So I put them in my pocket and set to work. Knowing they are there makes my hands work faster, and within thirty minutes I've placed the last piece of seaglass at the star's heart. Smiling at our latest collaboration, I head back up to the car park, followed by a huffing, puffing dog.

In the warmth of my car, with Molly contentedly eating a dog biscuit, I take out the note and the package, placing them carefully on the passenger seat.

I read the note first. It's typed, in a curling script font:

The bracelet is beautiful. Thank you.
Here's a gift to show how much your stars mean.
Thank you for being a friend x

The package is wrapped in cellophane with brown paper underneath. Bubble-wrap forms the next layer down, and a crumpled square of red tissue paper below that. When I unwrap it, I can't believe my eyes.

It's a house. A tiny, round-sided house that fits in the palm of my hand. Its walls are constructed from small vertical panels of driftwood, with a stick-framed door and window and a layered driftwood roof covered with moss. It's beautifully made and the detail on it is breathtaking. Silver stars are woven into the moss, and the windows are filled with pieces of pearlescent shell that shimmer like soap bubbles in the dawn light.

I'm still smiling when I open the shop, the sight of the gorgeous gift on the counter beside me sustaining me through the slow trickle of customers. The meeting with the bank is scarily close now, and I'm not ready. Mum is jittery and we've already had several arguments over it. She thinks we should put the shop on the market now, before I meet the bank manager, but I know we aren't a good enough prospect to sell yet. We argue on the phone at lunchtime and again when I get home. She won't back down and neither will I. So she leaves for her book group and I retreat to my room, where I lie on my bed gazing at the tiny driftwood house, glad I have one friend in the world who knows nothing about my shop or my dad. The person who made this only knows me as their friend who completes the seaglass stars and made them a bracelet. This house will be a sign that I can be something different from the person everyone expects me to be: not a shop owner, daughter or campaign leader. Just *me*.

At least I have a week without a town meeting to contend with, which feels like a blessing in the midst of all the tension and worry around me. I'm going to make the most of it, I decide; focus on the meeting with the bank and try not to think about the conversations buzzing around the town as St Ives decides the fate of Bethel Parsonage.

Mum still isn't back at ten p.m., so I grab some blankets and head down the garden to the Shedservatory, my beautiful driftwood house safely stored in the pocket of my coat.

Tonight the stars are the brightest they have been all year. It's a cold night, and I can see my breath as I gaze up through the Shedservatory's hatch. Ursa Major is twinkling at me as if she's trying to grab my attention; Venus is bright and the Pole Star shimmering. I don't need Clara-bell to see the major constellations. Since we lost Dad I don't always use her. My earliest memories are of just staring up at the jewelled sky snuggled up next to him, thinking he must be the cleverest man in the world as he pointed out each constellation.

He was equally able to point out the shapes and seasons of my life – and I think that's what I miss most. I would pour out my heart to him up here for hours as he watched the sky, and then he'd be able to sum it all up in one wise statement. He knew when I was unhappy at college before I did; after I'd spent months feeling alone and adrift but not knowing why. Without his, 'Well, it's that course, isn't it? You need to find one that fits,' I would never have ditched psychology and sought out the graphic course that introduced me to a love of design, which later led to me discovering jewellery making. Dad's utter confidence in me made the difference. He never once doubted my ability to succeed.

My eyes naturally drift to Orion, and I wonder what Dad would really think of me trying to keep MacArthur's afloat. I won't admit it to anyone, not even Aggie and Kieran, but I am harbouring the smallest, quietest doubt that he wouldn't be happy. Not that I had a choice. Well, I *did* – but when the alternative was seeing my mum strug-gle and lose her livelihood, what real choice did I have? Mum's doing what she can to make money and get by, but she couldn't have run the shop alone, and Dad's prefer-ence for keeping a (now dwindling) savings account rather than paying into a pension left her no option but to try

224

and keep it going. I think Dad would be ashamed of the financial mess he left; I know he would. But what's done is done. I just have to make the best of it, don't I?

There's a scratching sound at the base of the mezzanine ladder, and I look down to see expectant doggy eyes. I have dog biscuits in my pocket and Molly misses nothing food-related. Shrugging the woollen blankets off my shoulders, I climb down to deliver the desired treat in person. I kneel beside her and she automatically flops her heavy chin on my shoulder, as she's done ever since she was a puppy. Her breath is loud and warm against my ear and she makes the slightest whimper. This was also *her* favourite place with Dad.

'I know, lady. I miss him too.'

Molly turns her head a little and licks my ear, which makes me laugh.

'Ugh, get off,' I say, but I'm glad of the gesture.

She's shivering a little and so am I. Reluctantly, I go back to close the hatch and replace Clarabell's pink Dralon cover.

'Night-night,' I whisper. In the stillness, I imagine Dad's spirit filling the space. I breathe it in . . .

The moment is swiftly broken by the steady thump of Labrador tail against the Shedservatory door. It's time to go back to the house, apologise to Mum and work out for myself what I'm going to do.

Chapter Thirty-Eight

Jack

'Light?'

'Yes.'

'We're selling Rectory Fields based on its *light*?' Brotherson sits back in his expensive desk chair and lifts his eyes from the verification order I've brought him to stare at a point somewhere over my head. 'But don't all buildings have to have light?'

I smile. 'They do, but not all of them are built to harness the natural light of their surroundings. Rectory Fields can be different.'

'Explain.'

'We're already pledging to acknowledge the heritage of the site with our building,' I say, playing out the same conversation I'd had with Dad and Owen when I knew the meeting with Brotherson had been confirmed. 'We're using as much of the original stone as we can salvage, and giving a nod to the parsonage's former life by installing a replica altar window in the entrance lobby. But what will make that stone and the window truly special is the light that falls on them.'

Brotherson blinks. 'Nah, you've lost me. This is why I pay Rory at Wilton & Partners to come up with all that architect gobbledegook for me.'

'Rory's plans are great, but I think he's missed this. I walked around the site this week, on a sunny day, and the way the sunlight painted the building was wonderful. If we remove the dark wood cladding from the design and draw attention to the stone on the top storey, it will make the building shine in the right conditions. And the interiors can be used to harness that light throughout the day, too.' I slide my notes across the desk to him.

'This is impressive. So you've been camping out there, have you? Checking up on the sun and shadows?'

'I've been visiting the site in different conditions, trying to plan how it will work in all weathers. I believe you have to understand the land in order to make it work best. The people who built the parsonage understood that: I just want to follow their lead.'

Now Brotherson is interested. He pats a hand on the plans. 'And this'll pacify that lot down in St Ives, won't it? Gives us the perfect comeback to their argument that they're the only ones capable of caring for the site.'

I hadn't thought of that, but it's true. It would certainly allay fears that the Big Bad Developer is just going to stick a building there without respecting the land around it. 'They won't have a monopoly on being the best trustees for the place. In fact, I reckon we'd be able to make *better* use of the site because we're building something that makes the most of the environment. A patched-up old ruin with piecemeal renovations wouldn't serve the land better.'

'See, I knew you were my man for the job! Good work, Jack. I'll take this back to Rory and get him to look at it again. Might bring you in for a meeting with him when we're ready to start, too. Get all of us singing from the same hymn sheet.' He claps his hands and rubs them together. 'I like it. This'll have the St Ives mob eating out of the palms of our hands next week!'

I drive home pleased with myself. At least Brotherson listened to me. It's one small change, but if the architect agrees it will be my own stamp on the building. I like the step up from the building work I've done to construction manager – it feels like a bigger nod to my skills. Something else has started, too, since my visits to the old site: I've started to imagine I could do more one day. Since I made the driftwood house for our starmaker, I've been thinking about what I'd do with the site if I had free rein. My dream was always to build my own houses, from design to build to completion. For the last few years I'd felt it drift further and further from view, but in my quiet moments lately, after Nessie goes to bed and before she wakes next morning, I've dared to consider it again. The driftwood house felt like a down payment on that dream – and now I wonder if it might be possible after all.

Has the starmaker discovered their gift yet? I know it will be the first thing Nessie wants to know when she races down to the beach this evening. I want to know, too. I hope it means as much to them as it has done to me.

With Brotherson on my side and the thrill of leaving the driftwood house on the beach, I feel a renewed confidence about our future. I plan to go into St Ives tomorrow and buy some things for the chalet, to make it feel more like a proper home. Nessie and I deserve a bit of indulgence, I think. Until the St Ives vote, Brotherson is paying me for my contribution – a warm glow in my bank account that hasn't been there for a very long time. I probably should be guarding every penny, but a little treat for Ness and me is justified, I think. I'm going to see it as an investment in the future I hope to secure when Rectory Fields is approved by the town. I feel positive today, as if the sea is changing in my favour at last. Smiling to myself, I relax in my seat and enjoy the ride home.

Chapter Thirty-Nine

Seren

It's only a short walk to my bank in the High Street from MacArthur's, but I notice every step. I spent last night going over the books and hoping I might find a secret stash of money somewhere that will buy us time. If it's there, it eluded me. I wish I felt less dread at the prospect of meeting the bank manager today, but I'm determined to show a brave face. There are some positives, however small. Business in the Etsy shop is beginning to pick up in the new financial year, and we had five orders this week alone. That is what I'll say to Mr Trevelyan this morning, my best smile firmly fixed. I just hope he believes me. Or takes pity on me. Honestly, I'll settle for either.

My shifts at Becca's Bar are helping our finances too, if not my sleep. Working most nights till midnight, sorting out the shop's accounts and getting up early every morning to drive to Gwithian is taking its toll on my body – and that's not even counting running the shop every day, together with all the work I'm doing on the Save the Parsonage campaign. I'm trying not to think about all of it at once. If I did, I might crumble like sand . . .

'Seren!'

I look up and smile – too late to realise who just called my name.

'Oh. Hello.'

Jack Dixon chuckles, and I wish a tidal wave would wash me out to sea. 'Sorry, didn't mean to startle you.' He nods at the armful of books I'm carrying. 'Busy day?'

'Meeting with the bank manager.'

He pulls a face. 'Ouch – business going well?'

'Good.' I road-test my confident smile for the meeting, but it doesn't quite fit. 'Yours?'

'Also good. I hope.' He folds his arms across his blue T-shirt. *DIXON CONSTRUCTION* is embroidered on the faded marine blue. There's a stray thread dangling from the 'X' and the material looks like it has been washed many times. 'I have another meeting with Mr Brotherson the day after tomorrow, so . . . Ah. I probably shouldn't tell you that.'

'You don't need my permission.'

'Well, *technically* I do.'

I have to smile. That was a good comeback. 'Hope it goes well.'

'Yours, too. Bank managers scare me.' He smiles and I expect him to say something else, but he gives a self-conscious laugh, raises his hand and continues on his way.

I resist turning back to watch him walk down the hill towards St Ia's church. He has every right to be in St Ives this morning, but why pick the very same time to walk

231

down the High Street as I'm walking up? I'm still trying to get my head around the last meeting, when I found myself impressed by what he said, even though it's essentially against everything I'm fighting for. I suppose he's just a nice bloke caught in a bad situation, but it would be so much easier if I could just hate him.

I'm still reeling from seeing Jack as I sit in the too-green waiting area of my bank. The black horse above the door looks like it's making a bid for freedom, and I wish I could hop on its back and gallop off into the sunset. When I do dream these days, it's always about running away. Packing my car at night and driving through pitch-dark country lanes, climbing from the harbour wall onto a waiting boat and slipping out to sea, or running to my favourite spot on the hills overlooking St Ives and taking off like a bird, my feet finding the lift of the air as they leave the land . . .

'Miss MacArthur?' A middle-aged lady in a grey suit is walking across the green carpet towards me.

'Hello,' I say, standing quickly and catching an accounts book that's about to drop from the pile in my arms.

'I'm Margaret Lowrie, Small Business Development Manager. I'm seeing you with Mr Trevelyan today.'

Great, two of them to convince. But at least Margaret has a kind smile. The last time I saw John Trevelyan, he didn't smile once.

'Are we waiting for Mrs MacArthur?' Margaret asks, looking expectantly towards the door.

I don't tell her that Mum hardly slept last night, or that she burst into tears this morning when she came down for breakfast and it took me twenty minutes to calm her down.

It's just all too much for her; I totally understand. She's scared MacArthur's will be snatched from us just like Dad was – taken against our will by something completely outside of our control. She thought she'd be able to sit with me in John Trevelyan's office today, but Fear had other ideas. Margaret Lowrie doesn't need to know any of that, though.

'Unfortunately not. My mum's not very well. She sends her apologies.'

Margaret's smile isn't quite as sympathetic as I'd hoped.

It's bad news as soon as the account books are open across the bank manager's desk. There's a strong smell of furniture polish and new carpet that seems to swell as I watch them nodding silently. The pleasantries only last a minute, and then it's straight to business. I feel like I'm being judged and I'm scared I'll be found wanting. I know it's bad. I've tried for weeks to make our situation look better, but deep down I know we're in trouble. I think Dad knew it long before he died, and I wonder how much it contributed to the heart attack that killed him.

A flash of memory passes unheralded across my mind. Jack Dixon's smile – and that odd laugh he did before he left. Why am I thinking of that now? Surely he was a portent of the doom awaiting me inside the bank this morning, not a friend meeting a friend in the sunny High Street. If I believed in signs, of course. Which I don't.

But the thing is, he *felt* almost like a friend . . .

'It's deeply concerning,' Margaret Lowrie says, and I almost agree with her until I remember she's pointing at the accounts as she's speaking. Any hope her friendly smile might have given me before has been well and truly stubbed out within five minutes of entering the meeting room. By comparison, John Trevelyan is practically a sweetheart. They stare at me, and I notice that both of them have rather beaklike noses. Maybe they're related. Or perhaps all bank managers resemble birds of prey.

'We're doing everything we can,' I reply. 'And the online shop is starting to see real business . . .'

'. . . Where your physical shop is struggling,' John Trevelyan says.

'Yes, it has been quiet in the shop. But it's early in the season, and . . .'

'If I had a pound for every time I heard that line from small business owners in this town,' Margaret singsongs, and I dig my fingernails into my palm instead of letting her attitude get to me. 'Having the sea on your doorstop doesn't make you immune to insolvency.'

I keep my chin high, even more determined not to let them see their words are wounding me. 'It's hard, running a business here. We have to work with the custom as it comes in. But we're doing everything we can. And when the season starts properly, I'm confident the shop will start to turn around.'

'Miss MacArthur, I feel it would be wrong of me to give you false hope. We are very close to foreclosing on your loans.' There isn't even a hint of compassion in John Trevelyan's statement.

'But it's early in the season,' I say again, as if repeating it will elicit a different reaction. But my financial judges are like the stone gargoyles guarding St Ia's doors.

'And yet your business will fail,' he says, tapping the

books on the desk. 'It *will* fail, Miss MacArthur. My best advice to you is to strongly consider selling the property. With prices in the town what they are at the moment, it's your best hope of repaying the debt. It might even leave you and your mother with a nest egg, if the right buyer is found. MacArthur's is in an enviable location. I'm confident a buyer could be found quickly.'

'And if we choose to carry on?' My question is out almost before I realise I've said it. Maybe it's their gleeful dismissal of everything we've been trying to do, or the smug expressions on their beaky faces, but I'm not ready to admit defeat yet. Mum doesn't want us to sell yet. I promised her I would make enough to clear some of our debts before we even considered selling. I think of Dad's hard work to keep MacArthur's going, before any of us knew the trouble he was in, and I suddenly want to make one final push before we think of selling. I have nothing to lose by asking – and maybe it will prove to the bank how committed we are to turning MacArthur's around. I imagine Dad sitting beside me in the chair they'd put out for Mum today, and I take a deep breath. 'Give me six months and if the business still hasn't improved, I'll sell.'

'Two months.'

'Four. *Please.*'

'Miss MacArthur, this isn't an exercise in bargaining. We are giving you two months from today to make your business profitable again. Margaret and I will meet you at the end of this time and make the final decision. That's the best I can do. I'm sorry.'

Chapter Forty

Jack

'Do you think they liked the house, Dad?' Nessie is mid-way through selecting seaglass for our new star when she pauses to ask me the question.

'I'm sure they did. They finished a lovely star for us yesterday.'

'Hmm.' The thought-wrinkle plays above her nose. 'If it was *me*, I'd have said thank you.'

I must admit, I've wondered this myself. But in a way the driftwood house was a thank you for the seaglass bracelet, so perhaps they consider we're even. Since we left it on the beach I've realised how important it was to me to get it right. That house represents the kind of buildings I would love to make. And I don't know why it matters to me to win the approval of a complete stranger, but it does. Maybe if they like it, others will too.

I've started sketching again. It's at least three years since I last picked up a pencil, but making the house reignited a spark and now buildings fill my mind, like they used to when I first decided what I wanted to do for a living. After I bumped into Seren yesterday I went to the Post Office and while waiting in the queue to buy stamps and envelopes, I saw the sketchpads. Before I could think better of it I'd bought one, along with a pack of pencils. I've got them in my car, under the seat, so I can sketch whenever I get a moment. It feels like an indulgence, especially when Nessie has a pot full of coloured pencils and lots of sketching paper in the house; but these ones are just for me.

I was fifteen when I decided I wanted to build. I'd seen Dad do bits of building work around our house and sometimes he'd let me help. Then my uncle Paul gave me a week of work experience on his building site. But what sealed it was a trip from school to see a field centre that had been built near Plymouth. An award-winning architect had designed it using only materials sourced within a fifty-mile radius. It seemed to have risen from the ground fully formed, both brand new and ancient. I fell in love with it and decided that was what I wanted to do. My initial plans to study architecture were scuppered by less than impressive GCSE results, but I soon realised that it was the building of those structures that fascinated me. I didn't want to sit in an office, miles away from a site, planning projects I would never get my hands on. I wanted to be the one raising walls from the earth and putting my own stamp on the landscape. So every college notebook was covered with doodles of fanciful glass, stone and wood constructions, working ancient architectural details into futuristic designs. I built small-scale models at home and submitted them for college projects and filled my childhood bedroom with ever more intricate building plans, Blu-tacked to the wall.

Even when I started working on sites where my own designs never came into play, I loved learning my trade – and I discovered I had a real flair for building. But my designs were always my hobby. I have a box of notebooks at the chalet full of them, a decade or more of plans and dreams sealed in dusty cardboard.

Tash thought them an indulgence, of course. The box of notebooks was gradually shunted out of the house to the darkest recesses of the garage. If we'd owned a garden big enough for a shed, they would most likely have been relegated there instead, but our lack of square footage proved their salvation. When Ness was born I didn't have time to design anything, much preferring to spend time with the most amazing thing I've ever made. But one of her first toys was a set of building blocks. And as she grew, our primary-coloured constructions grew ever more ambitious. I thought I'd left my sketches in the parcel of time known as 'my life before dadhood'. But making the driftwood house has inspired me to start dreaming again.

I know Brotherson has the final say. I fully expect my suggestions to be slowly amalgamated into a much more conventional building. But I'm daring to believe this job might open doors to one day making the buildings that live in my sketchbooks. If I can gain his trust – and prove that my ideas will work – who knows what might be possible?

'What do you think?' Nessie is standing beside me, her knees two ovals of damp sand from where she's been kneeling. The star is lovely – completely her own design this time. Using the rainbow trays, she has laid lines of alternating blue, white and green glass to form the star, its fifth point left unfinished as usual.

'It's gorgeous.'

'I made it up myself,' she says, proudly. 'I drew it in my book, just like you've been doing.'

At that moment I am the proudest dad in the world. And anything is possible . . .

Chapter Forty-One

Seren

Driving out to St Piran's Primary School, I don't feel the slightest qualms about closing the shop for the day. It's freeing, actually – a brief respite from everything tied to Dad's business. I feel like I've been granted a stay of execution after yesterday's meeting with the bank. We can't make any money to ease the debt today, but at least we can't fall any further behind.

Besides, I've been looking forward to meeting Cerrie's class. Kieran gave me the finished pictures from our night photographing the sky. They are stunning. Arcs of pure white and gold in concentric half-circles emblazoned across the night sky, with the light-studded silhouette of St Ives below. It's magic captured on photo paper. Added to this, he made me a composite video, slowly merging all the shots together until they produce the final image. When I watched it on my laptop last night I burst into tears. I think about the effect it will have on Cerrie's class, how it could spark a passion that lasts for life – like it did in me when I first went stargazing with Dad. Whatever happens with the town vote, what I do today could create a legacy that outlives me.

That's worth leaving the shop for.

St Piran's Primary reception has the unmistakable scent of school that takes me right back to childhood in St Ives. Cleaning products, paper, the faint scent of already-cooking lunch, and dust, although there isn't a speck to be seen around me. There are some places where the smell is always the same, no matter how old you are or how much time has passed since you first experienced it. The green headiness of a florist's shop; a seaweed-and-salt beach after a storm; the warm wood and dust of the Shed-servatory; newsprint and sugar in a newsagent's shop; the scent of your childhood home. And school, with its too-warm entrances and floor-polish corridors. I breathe it in, excited and nervous in equal measure. Speaking in public isn't something I find easy, even with all my recent experience in the Save the Parsonage campaign. But today I'm sharing my passion, and that makes it feel easier. I can talk about stars and Elinor Carne forever and my audience are, reportedly, very excited to hear me talk to them.

'Seren, hi!' Cerrie is hurrying through the squeaky door to the main school building, red-faced and a little out of breath after the sprint from her classroom. Her hazel eyes twinkle under a fringe of shaggy blonde mane and she swoops down to give me a huge hug. 'Sorry I'm late. We had a bit of drama in registration this morning.'

'Is everything okay?'

'Oh, fine. Seven-year-olds are purveyors of the finest

dramas. It'll all be forgotten when they meet you.' She grins. 'So, how are you feeling?'

'Good. Excited.'

'They are so chuffed about having a visitor.'

'The receptionist told me.'

'Parents and teachers are excited too, actually. There's a lot of support for the campaign here.' She pats my shoulder as we start to walk to her classroom. 'So you're among friends.'

The classroom is large and open-plan with small blue tables arranged in the centre, each one surrounded by six red plastic chairs. All over the walls various displays have been made: rainbows of colourful paintings and jolly-looking bubble letters. One of the wall display boards is empty, but has been covered in indigo paper.

'That's going to be our Elinor Carne wall,' Cerrie grins. 'We're painting constellations after your talk.' She casts her gaze around the room and frowns. 'Ah. The drama continues.'

In the corner a dark-haired girl is sniffling in the arms of a classroom assistant, who is wiping her nose with a tissue. The poor little thing looks distraught and I notice several of her classmates are staring at the spectacle, half in solidarity, half in amusement. School can be vicious when you're a child – I still remember the push-pull of classroom politics.

'Is she okay?'

Cerrie rolls her eyes. 'She will be. She's upset because I confiscated something she brought in this morning. Honestly, you wouldn't believe some of the things these kids

242

bring to school. Listen, take a seat and I'll get them all ready. Right, Class 4, I need you all sitting in the story corner please, quick as you can. And remember – walk nicely . . .'

I sit at a small desk and watch the children file from their seats, eyes wide as they walk past me. Some of them take 'walking nicely' very seriously, all puffed-out chests and swinging straight arms. The girl who has been crying passes me, hand in hand with the classroom assistant, and offers a shy, red-rimmed-eyed smile. A little boy with a shock of curly black hair pauses to show me a sticker on his chest.

'It says WELL DONE on it,' he proudly informs me. 'Because I did good reading.'

'That's great,' I reply.

'Joshua Levens, hurry up, please,' Cerrie calls, her tone suggesting this isn't the first time she's said those words. Joshua beams a front-tooth-missing grin and hurries to join his classmates.

Surrounded by a sea of seated little heads, Cerrie raises a hand, wriggling her fingers in the air. One by one the children follow suit, until all the chatter and fidgeting has ceased.

'Brilliant, put your hands down. Now, you might have noticed that we have a visitor this morning. She's going to talk to us about stars.' There is a flutter of excitement from the class. 'Before we start, what do we do when we listen to someone?'

'Ears on! Lips shut!' the children chorus.

'Exactly.' She looks over at me and beckons. 'So let's give Miss MacArthur a big Class 4 welcome, shall we?'

To the patter of small hands, I walk to Cerrie's side. Thirty expectant faces beam up at me. 'Thank you for having me today, Class 4. And thanks to Miss Austin for inviting me. I'm going to tell you about stars today, and a very special lady who helped us to understand them a long time ago . . .'

While I talk, Cerrie is setting up the projector with my laptop. When the time arrives to show the kids Kieran's video, I take a breath before giving her a nod.

'All the stars move across the sky, but they do it very slowly, so we can only see where they end up each night. But if we take lots of photographs all through the night and then speed them up, we can see where they move to. I think it's a bit magical. Would you like to see it, too?'

Thirty vehement nods follow, and the classroom assistant turns the lights off. The screen behind me lights up, and I kneel down on the floor beside the children as the star trail composite plays. I can't resist sneaking a look at my audience as they watch. Across the room I see that same wonder I felt as a child, played out across sixty widening eyes. I see little mouths fall open, little chests quickening their breath. And I am right back in the Shedservatory next to Dad, the same age as the kids in Cerrie's class, feeling my own chin drop as the shapes of the constellations began to appear above us.

'Elinor Carne never saw what you're seeing now,' I say, as the composite starts to loop again. 'But she fell in love with watching the stars. She made her own little observatory in the back garden of her home, high on the hills above St Ives. And she watched every night, when everyone

244

else had gone to bed. She kept a diary of everything she saw – and one night when she was looking through her telescope, she saw a star nobody had ever seen before. When she told some other astronomers about it, they didn't believe her. Then a few years later, a man called William in Plymouth saw the same star and everyone listened to him. So for many years, everyone thought William discovered the star. But a few years ago, Elinor's diaries were found and the truth came out. She had written about the star on the night she first saw it – the date was much earlier than William's discovery.'

The video ends and the lights are switched back on. I stand and smile at the class. 'So the story has a happy ending, in a way. But Elinor never realised that people would one day believe her. In her time people didn't think women and girls were very important, and they didn't think they could be good at science.'

'Girls can do science stuff,' a girl with blonde plaits retorts. 'Everyone knows that.'

Several children around her nod their agreement.

'Of course they can. But when Elinor was alive, a long time ago, people didn't know that.'

'That's sad.' The girl who was upset earlier has her hand in the air but is talking anyway. 'Nobody should be able to say you can't do something, if you really want to do it.' I wonder if this might be slyly aimed at Cerrie for confiscating her property, but her young face is full of earnest concern. 'We need to tell everyone about Ellie.'

The children around her join in with loud suggestions and for a moment I can't keep up with all of their voices.

'What Miss MacArthur wants to do is to save Elinor's old house, so that lots more people can find out about her,' Cerrie says, causing all heads to turn to the back of the room. 'Do you think that would be good?'

There's an immediate chorus of *yes*es and I have to bite my lip to stop myself crying. It's impossible not to be moved by their unbridled enthusiasm. Cerrie asks for questions, and all the faces turn back to me. For the next ten minutes I'm bombarded by excited enquiries and as I answer I see Cerrie giving me a thumbs-up. Finally, she moves to stand beside me.

'Okay, Class 4, Miss MacArthur has asked me if I think you could paint us some wonderful star constellation pictures. I said my class are the best painters in St Piran's school. What do you think?'

An hour later, Cerrie walks me back to reception, laughing as she picks dried poster-paint splatters from her forearm. 'I'm not sure who was painted more, me or the stars!'

'That was so much fun. Although toothbrushes, poster paint and excited seven-year-olds is a pretty dangerous combination.' I'm sure I have tiny beads of white in my hair from the art session, but I don't care. This has been the best experience and I'm so glad I did it.

'You were a hit. Fancy doing this every week?'

'It was fun, but I think I might need counselling if I had to do it regularly.' I smile. 'I have no idea how you do it for a job.'

'Are you joking? I get to be a rock star five days a week. Older kids get wise to you, but my seven-year-olds are still just about at the magic stage where everything is amazing. Like you. They're so fired up about Elinor Carne. Especially Nessie.' She sees my confusion and rescues me. 'The girl who was upset when you first came in, and then led the charge to remember Elinor.'

I think of the dark-haired girl and how she'd visibly changed as I'd talked to the class. 'She certainly rallied to Elinor's cause. I thought she was awesome.'

'She is. And probably the most important person in the class to win over. Come on, I'll walk you to your car.' She holds the front door open for me and we head outside.

The sun has broken through the morning cloud and a brave blue sky smiles down on us. 'Why is Nessie important to win over?'

Cerrie leans against my car. 'Because her father is the one trying to destroy the parsonage.'

'Bill Brotherson is her dad?' I can't believe someone so repulsive could create such a sweet child.

'No, you idiot! Her dad is Jack Dixon.'

What?

And then I remember the conversation I had with Jack, after the last meeting. He told me he had a daughter – did he mention her name? I had the briefest recollection of hearing of a Nessie before when Cerrie said her name, but I didn't make the connection. How did I miss it?

I let it sink in. 'No . . .' And then, when I realise Cerrie's master plan all along, '*No!*'

She gives a shrug, clearly pleased with herself. 'I mean, I love all my kids but I thought *certain* kids might be particularly useful to your campaign. Nessie's a champion against injustice in Class 4. Any time there's a dispute or somebody is wrongfully blamed for something, Nessie Dixon is the one fighting their corner. And you saw how horrified she was by Elinor's experience. Maybe she'll tell her dad . . .'

I'm about to celebrate this absolutely genius master-stroke when my memory pulls me up. 'Then Nessie lost her mum recently?'

My friend's smile vanishes. 'Yeah. That was awful. She started at St Piran's not long after it happened. We had a staff briefing before she joined us. Such a horrible way to die, too.'

I don't want to know, really I don't. But I can't stop myself from asking. 'What happened?'

'Total freak accident. She fell off a ladder at work, seemed fine, but two hours later said she had a headache and keeled over. Aneurysm, apparently. But she was so young and no time to prepare, or say goodbye to her kid. It breaks your heart.'

'Does Nessie often get upset?' The thought of the bright-eyed girl having to deal with such a life-changing event is impossible for me to comprehend. Bad enough that I lost my dad after thirty-one years, but to have it happen at such a young age is unthinkable.

'Oh, you mean this morning? No, that hardly happens at all. I expected it to, but she's a pretty resilient kid.' She digs in her pocket for something. 'This is what the tears were over earlier. Said the mermaids gave it to her, and it was too special to leave at home. I mean, honestly, the imagination of my kids . . .' She pulls her hand from her pocket and opens her fingers to reveal a bracelet made of gold-wired drops of pale green and pink seaglass.

I can hardly breathe. I remember each twist of wire, each carefully chosen sea gem from my work box, finding the antique clasp that fitted the combination perfectly – my excitement as the bracelet slowly took shape in my hands. And the risk it felt to make it, take it to Gwithian Beach and leave it at the heart of the latest star I'd completed.

Cerrie nods. 'Gorgeous, huh? I mean, you should think of doing something like this. I know yours have silver wire, but the gold works so well against the seaglass colours . . .'

I don't remember driving home.

When I pull up outside Mum's house, I sit in the car for a long time. Is Nessie Dixon the other person I've been creating stars with across Gwithian Beach? She couldn't just have found the bracelet, because the note in the blue glass bottle thanked me for it. But could a seven-year-old have made something as intricate as the seaglass stars? I find it hard to believe a child that age could achieve such precision, however artistic she might be. And what about the little moss-and-driftwood house they left in return for the bracelet?

Oh *no* . . .

A *house*. From builder Jack Dixon's daughter . . .

I reach into the glove compartment and pull out the tiny house that has travelled like a talisman with me for the last few days, that has represented everything hopeful in my life. It's beautifully made from found materials . . .

I close my eyes and picture Jack addressing the last public meeting, the one where I found myself warming to his vision for the old parsonage because of how he talked about building something lasting from the land upon which it stands. Like Rectory Fields. Like *this* tiny house in my hands . . .

Is Jack my secret starmaker?

Chapter Forty-Two

Jack

'It's really great you could help with this,' my brother says as I help him lug a great lump of rock onto his tractor's trailer.

We're shifting old granite chunks from the corner of a fallow field he's clearing for a daffodil crop next year. I came as soon as Ness went to school and I'll be back there in less than an hour. Owen's offered to pay me for my time. I declined, naturally. Family jobs are free. Even if the money would have been useful . . .

'No problem,' I puff, wishing my back wasn't complaining as much as it is. The last thing I need is an injury if Rectory Fields gets the go-ahead. I think of my meeting with Brotherson tomorrow – where I'll find out the architect's response to my proposed change on the building – and hope I'll be upright enough to look capable. 'What are your plans for this lot?'

My brother gives me a look that suggests he's bracing

for a lecture. 'I hadn't planned anything. Probably just lob them down the hillside or something.'

'Great plan.'

'Ha ha, Stink! Your face.' He reaches across the corner of the trailer and ruffles my hair with his grubby gloves – something that never fails to wind me up. Owen's winning move in every childhood argument was to play the big brother card: a pat on the head, a chuck under the chin, or the dreaded patronising hair-ruffle. Which is annoying enough when you're six, but downright unfair thirty years later. 'If you can use 'em, you can have 'em. Not sure Jeb will be too happy with this little lot piled up by the chalet, though.'

'Cheap shot.'

'Sorry.'

'I might need them if this job comes off. Can you hold them for me?'

'Sure.' Owen chucks his gloves into the back of the trailer and claps the dust from his hands. 'Do you reckon Brotherson will let you, though? I don't see a lot of local stone in his builds.'

'True, but he hasn't had a build managed by me yet.' I hope I sound this confident tomorrow. 'Besides, this development's a bit different from his usual projects with the moral covenant. I think it merits a more sensitive approach.'

For a few seconds, my brother looks impressed. Then, it's business as usual. 'Get you, being all master-buildery. Anyone would think you know what you're talking about.'

He pulls two bottles of water from the tractor cab and throws one at me. I'm grateful for it, the growl of my stomach giving away the gnawing hunger I've been battling all day. I didn't have time for breakfast this morning as I was too busy dealing with a Mexican standoff with my daughter because she wanted to take that seaglass bracelet to school and I wouldn't let her. By the time I managed to get her into the car we were already running late. It's a good job the teacher out on playground duty this morning is sympathetic to us. He held the line for five minutes before taking the kids inside, much to the grumbles of the other parents as we dashed in. And then I came to the farm and said I'd eaten already because it was easier than having to sit in the kitchen with my sister-in-law. Chicken, I know. But it's survival. Better to have her at arm's length, but still officially be talking, than the alternative.

'Cheers,' I say, hoping to cover up my stomach's performance. But it grumbles again, louder this time.

'Blimmin' Nora, Jack, you need a decent meal. Let's go back to the house and Sarah can . . .'

'I'm good, thanks.'

I replied too quickly. He's sussed me in seconds. 'She *said* she was sorry.'

'I know she did. And I've accepted her apology.'

'But you won't eat her food.'

'It isn't like that.'

'Isn't it? Looks that way from where I'm standing. She just wanted to help, Jack.'

'By taking my kid . . .'

He swears and looks up at the threatening rainclouds, as if they might help him. 'Come and have some food and stop being so precious. You're in a tough spot, I get that.

Trust me, Jack, we all get it. So if the only thing we can do to help you right now is feed you, then bloody well suck up your pride and let us. A free meal is a gift, not a defeat.'

I wish *that* conversation had never happened. But I can't forget it. And I've tried, believe me. Something changed when Sarah suggested taking Nessie. She crossed a line. What's worse is that despite her apology, I still think she and Owen might bring it up again. I can't shake the feeling that they still think they were right to offer to take Ness. However much I want to put it behind me, I can't for now. 'Just give me time, yeah? I need to get my head around everything else first.'

I don't like disappointing Owen. He's been my hero for as long as I could toddle after him and he always will be. And Sarah is a good person, I know that. She's good for him and a great auntie for Ness. But she still disagrees with me and I don't have the energy to address that yet. I can live with her disapproval for the time being.

Nevertheless, I'm now parked outside Nessie's school with a basket of home-baked supplies on the passenger seat that Owen fetched from the farmhouse kitchen. I'm secretly grateful that he didn't push me more. And hidden in the bottom of the basket I've just found £100 in a sandwich bag, so it seems my brother was determined to provide for our monetary needs as well as our dietary ones.

Nessie is first out of the school, but I see her stop midway to the gates and turn back. Her teacher appears and I watch my daughter slope back to her. Miss Austin seems nice enough, from what I've seen and what Nessie's told me, but the conversation they are having seems to be serious. Ness hangs her head and nods slowly, then takes something from Miss Austin's outstretched hand and shoves it quickly in her coat pocket. What's been going on there?

As soon as she sees me, Nessie turns on her thousand-kilowatt smile and skips to my side as though nothing has happened. *Now* I'm worried . . .

'Dad!' she yells, running into my arms for a hug and holding onto my back a bit longer than usual.

I kiss the warmth of the top of her head. 'Hey you.'

Ness risks a look over her shoulder then grins at me. 'Let's go.'

Miss Austin has disappeared from the school entrance and I note the relief in my daughter. I want to ask her what happened straight away, but then I remember Auntie Sarah's baked goods bonanza waiting in the car and decide to leave it a while. After our all-out war before school this morning, I half-expected the silent treatment on the way home, so a smiling daughter is a much better discovery after a hard day. We'll talk about whatever it was later.

'. . . And Ellie found the star and she told people but the people thought she was just a silly girl and they didn't listen and she had to go away and not be a scientist even though she wanted to be one and . . .' My daughter pauses long enough to draw breath and take another bite of Sarah's Cornish pasty, flakes of pastry cascading down her school jumper as she continues. 'And it's just wrong, don't you think?'

I'm lost, to be honest. All I've managed to get from the

255

deluge of crumb-filled information flooding from the back seat of the car is that Nessie's school had a visitor today and a girl called Ellie couldn't be a scientist. I try to remember if one of the stash of school letters behind the weird-looking cuckoo clock on the mantelpiece in the chalet mentioned a visitor, but I can't recall seeing one. It could be hibernating in the murky depths of Nessie's school bag, of course, in which case it's lost forever . . .

'And it's just not fair,' Ness concludes.

'What isn't?'

'People telling people they can't do things, when they really want to.'

'O-*kay* . . .'

'Because if you really want to do something with all of your heart you should just do it.'

'Absolutely.'

'Like *you*, Dad.'

'Like me what?'

'You absolutely always wanted to build things. So that's what you do. And nobody can tell you that you shouldn't be a builder. Just because *they* think you shouldn't be.'

'Well, no. Obviously not . . .'

'But the thing is, Dad, at least you're a *boy*.'

I'm pretty sure there isn't a chapter in the parenting books I couldn't bring myself to read about navigating this kind of conversation. 'Why should that make a difference?'

'Because at least people don't think you shouldn't be a builder just because you have a willy.'

'*Ness!*'

'That's what Flo's mum says.'

'I don't care what – where on earth did you learn about . . . ?' Too late, I see the traffic light ahead changing to red and I slam on the brakes.

Ness fixes me with a look from the back seat. 'Flo's mum says that some people only let boys have important jobs because they have a willy and not a . . .'

'Okay, I get the picture.' I check her reaction in the rear-view mirror. 'You know that isn't right, though, don't you? Boys and girls can do whatever jobs they like.'

'I know *that*. But Ellie's people weren't as clever as us and they didn't know. So William got to name the star even though Ellie found it first.'

I'm still confused when we get home and Nessie dashes inside to change to go down on the beach. I'm hoping the act of making a new star will distract her long enough for me to make sense of this conversation.

As I wait on the small wooden veranda that runs the length of the chalet, I look out across the caravan park to the dunes beyond. With everything that's happened today, I've been looking forward to our evening starmaking. It's a relief to have something simple and positive to do. I've noticed I sleep better when we've been on the beach. It's calming finding the seaglass pieces and laying them out one by one. As if every other concern of the day dulls for a while. And it's become *our* thing – something only Ness and I share. A new thing, not something she once used to do with Tash. I like how it unites us.

The impending meeting with Brotherson can wait. Money worries can wait. The situation with Sarah and

Owen can wait, too. For the next couple of hours, all that matters is being with my girl, seeking tiny pieces of smooth glass to almost-make a star on a wide, empty beach.

Chapter Forty-Three

Seren

I've been thinking about this for hours. There's no way around it – Nessie Dixon has the seaglass bracelet I made, and I have the house made by someone who understands building. Like her father. There are too many coincidences for it to be a mistake. But if it's true, what happens now?

I like Jack, I really do. But until the vote happens, he's the enemy. The opposition. I have to look him in the eyes at the next meeting a week today and imagine Bill Brotherson sneering back at me. Because if I allow myself to see Jack Dixon there . . .

I can't ignore this now. I have to know.

Mum's out for the day walking Molly with a friend, so she won't miss me. And the shop won't reopen until tomorrow. If I don't go back there, this will drive me insane.

I head back around the coast road to Gwithian, not letting myself think better of it. I don't even know when the other starmaker goes to the beach – I may already be too late. But I'm banking on their visit being after school, if it is Jack and Nessie together. I don't think the seaglass stars could be made in the dark, and I'm at the beach so early in the mornings that they *have* to have been created the day before.

I reach Gwithian Beach a little before four p.m. and sit in my car watching the gulls weave and wheel over the dunes. Part of me wants to stay here, to feel safe, to try to calm the squall of questions in my head. But unless I venture outside, I'll never know for sure.

I pull on my oversized hoodie and beanie hat, drawing the cord tight to keep the wind from my neck. I have Molly's old travel rug with me and it catches the wind as I climb the dune a safe distance from the main path down to the beach, lifting like a sail at my side. When I reach the part of the cliff above where we make the stars, I spread Molly's rug over the hummocky grass as best I can in the strengthening breeze and half-kneel, half-crouch to watch.

The beach is deserted save for a few stalking seagulls who walk so close to the edge of the sea that they look like reluctant paddlers. White and grey clouds whip past overhead and the sea is a pure green. On any other day I would be down there, soaking in the view. But this afternoon I'm suddenly a stranger again, spying on Gwithian Beach from a distance, as though I have something to hide.

I wait for an hour, until my body is starting to feel numb and the wind on top of the cliff has chilled my face and hands. They aren't coming. Or it could be hours until they arrive.

Suddenly there's a rush of energy and noise to my right and I scramble to my feet, ready to defend myself. A ball of brown and white fur careers into me, knocking the breath from my lungs, and I stumble a little, stopped only from a tumble towards the cliff edge by a strong hand grabbing my elbow, hauling me back.

'Are you okay?' a man's voice asks.

I cough to bring the breath back and slowly dare to look up.

It isn't Jack.

But for a split-second, I thought it was.

'I'm fine, thanks.'

The older man shakes his head. 'I'm so sorry, miss. My dog – he likes meeting new people.'

The liver-and-white cocker spaniel knocks its head against my knee. My hand is shaking when I reach down to stroke its fur.

'Hello,' I manage, forcing a smile. But I feel sick.

What am I doing?

The man apologises again and, when he is certain that I'm okay, ushers his dog away to the cliff path. I sit back heavily on the rug and rub my eyes. Why did I think this was a good idea? And what difference does it make if Jack Dixon is the other starmaker? It just means I have more in common with him than I thought. He doesn't know who I am. I doubt it would alter his position on the Rectory Fields development even if he did.

The stars have nothing to do with the campaign. We can both carry on doing what we were doing before without knowing the truth about each other. We don't need to know all of it, do we?

So I could walk away now, forget about Nessie and the

bracelet and the tiny beachcombed house. I could go back to playing the game every morning. It would still be magical, wouldn't it?

I look back to the beach. It's still empty. Time to go home. I stand and shake the sand from Molly's blanket. It doesn't matter who made the stars, I tell myself. I can carry on not knowing.

'*Da-a-a-ad!* Look!'

And just like that, there she is. Nessie Dixon – the girl from Cerrie's class with the wild dark hair and boundless energy. She is right by the seaglass star I finished this morning, jumping like a grasshopper and waving her arms as though a plane is about to swoop down and land on Gwithian Beach at her command.

I crouch down in the grass because I have to see *him* follow his daughter. I already know the truth – I knew the moment Cerrie showed me my seaglass bracelet. But I want to see Jack standing by the star, to make it real.

'Dad! Come *on*!'

I hold my breath. I know that this moment could change everything.

'Okay, okay, here I am.'

Jack Dixon is on Gwithian Beach. With his daughter. We are linked by the seaglass stars, and now I know who has been making me smile every morning for the last three weeks. And he is the one person it *shouldn't* be.

'Hurry up! *Run!*'

'I'm not running, Ness.'

'You're just too slow.'

Jack reaches Nessie's side and gives her a playful nudge. 'And you're a noodle.'

'*You're* a noodle!'

I watch him grab his giggling girl and swing her up over his shoulder, dramatically stomping towards the rolling surf, his laughter and her delighted screams merging with the waves and the wind and the gulls wheeling above them. Tears sting my eyes. And suddenly, I can't stop staring at them together. Because it's the kind of carefree fun that every kid should share with their father. I was lucky enough to have that, but I know so many friends who never did. I wish I could bottle this picture and hand it out to everyone. Joy defined.

But it isn't me and my dad down there, splashing about in the sea. It's Jack Dixon and his daughter. And the one thing I thought was my simple pleasure isn't any more. Nothing can ever be the same.

Chapter Forty-Four

Jack

It's just possible that I went too far trying to out-man my brother shifting those boulders yesterday. Either that, or Brotherson Developments have installed concrete sofas in reception since my last visit. Nessie noticed my creakiness at breakfast as I hobbled around the chalet getting our things ready.

'Why are you walking like a robot, Dad?'

'I'm not.'

'Yes, you are. Dadbot! Dadbot alert! *Beepbopbeepbop . . .*'

This amused her all the way to school, and my last view of my daughter after I kissed her goodbye was of her robot-walking across the playground, giggling her small head off.

Charming.

I just hope Bill Brotherson's powers of observation aren't as sharp as Nessie's this morning. We may not have the go-ahead from the St Ives community for Rectory Fields yet, but I want to look ready to start work if we do.

No. *When* we do.

My internal critic kicks in again. Owen hauled me up over it yesterday – I didn't even realise I was saying it.

'You've got to watch how you talk about the job,' he said as we puffed our way back to the tractor, rocks in, arms. 'Sarah picks on me for that all the time. *When, not if. When, not if* . . . In her trade you can't let the other side see a moment of uncertainty. Same with you. Brotherson gave you the job. And you'll do a damn fine job. So talk like you mean it.'

I like that he believes in me. He could so easily take the side of the townspeople, tell me to find my own developments and not side with the devil himself. Owen is not shy when it comes to telling me what he thinks, even if it might not be what I want to hear. But he knows what's at stake. It's good to have allies.

'Jack, Bill will see you now,' Cassandra the PA smiles. It's scary how quickly we've moved from Mr Dixon and Mr Brotherson to just Jack and Bill. I remember Owen's words and correct myself. Not scary. *Impressive.*

Thankfully Cassandra's gaze returns immediately to her screen, so my jerky, awkward rise from the sofa has no witness. And Bill Brotherson is too engrossed in the revised architect plans spread across his vast desk to notice my Nessie-defined *Dadbot* walk into his office, either.

Impressive, Jack. *Impressive* . . .

'*Jaaack*, good to see you! Take a seat.'

I've made it most of the way unnoticed to the white leather chair opposite him, so it's only a single step and a shift of my body weight to my right foot to make it safely to the seat. I'm pretty sure I hid my wince, too. It's going well so far.

'Coffee?'

'Please.'

He doesn't bother with the intercom, strolling past me to the door and asking Cassandra to do the honours. I envy him his effortless sashay as he returns to his chair.

'Rory liked your proposed changes. Visited the site last week and agrees with you. So good call on that. You can tell the next town meeting about the change. Sweet-talk them all the way to the ballot box.'

'I'll do my best.'

'I know you will, boy. I hear from a colleague that you did well at the last meeting. No crap, just laid out your stall and let the beggars decide.'

'Thank you.'

'Bloody rabble, that lot. Glad it was you facing the firing squad this time.'

I can smile a little easier now my back doesn't hate me as much as it did. 'I think we're making good progress. Certainly the questions I fielded were intelligent and insightful. I think when they understand how sympathetic this project will be to the local environment, a lot of people will be reassured.'

'Yeah. Pander to the bastards a bit. Good.'

Not exactly what I was saying, but okay . . . 'Be upfront and honest with them, yes.'

Brotherson stretches back and his expensive chair gives the most elegant of creaks in gentle protest. 'Excellent. How many more stints in the lion pit do we have to survive?'

'One more meeting for discussion, then the one with the vote.'

'Good. I've got people on the ground ready to go when we get the Yes.'

You see, Jack? Positive thinking. 'Talking of that, is there anything else you want me to do before the vote? Schedules? Lists of material suppliers?'

I know we have no green light yet, but I want to be immersed in the project before any earth is broken. It's how I work best, lining up everything I need well in advance so that the job goes smoothly. And, in the case of Brotherson Developments, I want to ensure my vision is the one that makes it from the plans to the site. Considering how much I need this job to be a success, this is maybe a bit presumptuous. But I believe in the building I can make of the old parsonage – and if I can translate that to the build, then I think the people we're trying to convince to vote for it will believe in the project, too.

'Do what you need to get us to the start line. My guys will approve it from here. So sympathetic is the way to go, yeah?'

'I think so.'

His brow knots for a while, as if he's tasting the unfamiliar word and deciding whether he likes its strange flavour. He's interrupted by Cassandra bringing coffee and in an instant he is back to full Brotherson.

It hurts to lean forward to take my corporate mug. By the time it's safely in my hands the pain is making me feel too bilious to enjoy it.

'So, how's your kid?'

I wasn't expecting that question. 'She's good, thanks.'

'I've got three myself. That I know of, anyway.' He gives a nicotine-grated snigger as his thick fingers spin a clear acrylic photo block around on the desk to face me. It's like a Russian doll family of Brothersons: shrinking in stature but not attitude from the eldest, who I guess to be in his mid-teens, to the middle son, who might be a year or two older than Nessie, and a mini-Brotherson who can't be older than eighteen months.

'They look like fun.'

'Can't complain. Wonders of a nanny, eh? Can't complain about *her* either.'

There's a photograph of Nessie in my wallet, battered a little and a few years old now. It's one of my favourite pictures of her, taken by the quayside in Fowey. She's sitting on a beach towel and has a book in her hands that, until I asked her to smile for the camera, she was comically engrossed in. She is giving me the widest, most enthusiastic grin, her eyes almost disappearing behind her rising cheekbones. I feel like apologising to her photograph for even having her in the same room as Brotherson after a comment like that.

'I reckon we'll start work on Rectory Fields the day after the vote,' he continues, oblivious to my discomfort. 'Get the team ready and go in.'

I nod, not really knowing what else to say.

'And you'll win hearts and minds, Jack, I know you will. The opposition are nothing more than a few do-gooders and a girl who's continuing her dead dad's meddling like it's some bloody righteous crusade.'

'Do you mean Seren MacArthur?' I'm surprised by the edge to my question. Whatever our differences, she doesn't deserve to be characterised like that.

'Mark MacArthur was bad enough, stalking the council records for any way he could stop me. But his girl's worse. What does she care about the place?'

'She seems to care a lot. From what she said at the meeting.'

'Clever words, that. Emotional blackmail. Girl should be busy mourning her old man, not fighting his battles. Anyway, if what I hear about that shop of hers is true she'll soon have more important things to concern herself with.' He gives a sickly smirk as he swigs the last of his coffee.

'What about her shop?'

'On its uppers, en't it? Pal of mine at the golf club reckons she'll be out of business within two months.'

Two hours later I'm parked at Marazion, looking across a grey-blue sea to the hulk of the Mount rising like a fortress from the mist. I can't believe I didn't realise what was going on.

The other day, when I saw her in St Ives, I had no idea. She wasn't curt with me because I annoyed her. She was going to the bank because her business is in trouble. She was preoccupied with her own fight.

And there was me, bounding up to her like an idiot gazelle, making small talk badly, when she probably wanted to tell me to sod off.

There's more: Brotherson said it's her father's business she's trying to run. Inheriting his livelihood and the

269

campaign he started – that's a tall order for anyone. And where would you ever have any time for yourself in that situation? I think back to our conversation after the last meeting and it makes sense. To be grieving and trying to keep a business open must be taking its toll.

I should have said more. Or crossed the road, left her alone and not said anything. But since when did I ever choose the sensible option?

When she spoke about the old astronomer lady at the meeting I was impressed, I'll admit. But I didn't realise what it really meant to her. Finally, I understand.

We're both fighting for other people: me for Nessie and our future, Seren for her dad and his legacy. Neither of us deserves to lose. But one will walk away from the vote in two weeks' time denied our chance to fight for the people we love the most. It's completely unfair – and yet, here we are.

So, what now?

Chapter Forty-Five

Seren

The bunting flaps in the breeze within the courtyard all the way out to Fore Street and it's as if my hopes of saving the shop are carried on the small squares of rainbow fabric. This is the third special event I've put on since John Trevelyan's ultimatum, and I need it to work. The first – an evening preview with wine, advertised in the local paper and on flyers posted in friends' businesses – was only attended by Cerrie, her new boyfriend Tom, Kieran, Aggie and Mum. The second, an online sale event on our website, garnered three sales amounting to £150. We have to do better to have a hope of surviving. *I* have to do better.

I've spent hours getting MacArthur's ready for our Cream Tea event, and now I'm waiting by the open door. We've been blessed with good weather today. That's a relief. It's early in the season so we need all the help Mother Nature can give us to woo people out into the streets. She's outdone herself this morning: warm, bright sunshine, a little hazy over the sea but the kind of day that makes St

Ives sparkle. Mum will be here soon with back-up supplies of cream and scones for the crowds she's certain will flock into our little business.

I'm not so sure. I wish I were. I want to believe my own assertion at the bank meeting – that we can survive, that I can make it work. But we've been open for an hour and nobody has even ducked into the courtyard.

It's almost two p.m. when footsteps on the courtyard cobbles make my head snap up from the bracelet I've been making. A young man smiles in the doorway, a laptop nestled under one arm.

'Hey, is it okay to look inside?'

'Of course. Welcome!' I rush, wishing I didn't sound so desperate. Thankfully my sole customer doesn't turn on his heels and head for the hills.

'I'm Lee, by the way. Your stuff is awesome,' he grins, looking at the paintings on the walls. 'Do you paint it?'

'No, we show other artists' work. My mum paints – that one is hers,' I say, pointing to a landscape of Cape Cornwall painted in soft sweeps of watercolour. It's an old painting, one that I persuaded Mum to put in the shop for sale instead of hiding beneath dustsheets in the spare bedroom she used to use as a studio. Truth is, she hasn't painted since Dad died. She makes quilts, sometimes embroiders scenes or crochets – things she can do curled in her favourite armchair in the living room, instead of in the stark whiteness of the studio. I don't know if she'll ever want to paint again. It was always so tied up with Dad and the shop. It's still so early, of course. Maybe when more time has passed without Dad she'll feel inspired again.

'It's gorgeous.' His eyes sparkle when he smiles. 'When I get my book published and can write full-time I'd love to buy something like this.'

'You're a writer?'

He pats the laptop. 'Trying to be – no, I *am*. I decided to be positive about it. I have a good feeling about the story I'm writing at the moment, actually. St Ives just makes you want to write, don't you think?'

I've never thought about the town like that, but Cornwall is founded on stories so it makes sense. I wish he had money, though, and it's a harsh admission. Small talk is lovely and having anyone in the shop is a blessing, but it doesn't do anything to pull MacArthur's back from the brink.

'Do you mind if I take a photo of your mum's painting? I can pin it on my wall to show what I'm aiming for. One day I'll buy the real thing.'

So I watch while Lee takes photos of Mum's work, trying not to notice the plate of scones for the crowds that never came going stale on the counter.

And all the time, John Trevelyan's words haunt me: *Your business* will *fail, Miss MacArthur . . .*

I don't want to accept defeat, but I'm fresh out of ideas.

Luckily, my best friend has sent me the perfect text message, just when I needed it:

Maidens for beer?

It's a one-line text we send out as a call to arms. Or more precisely, a call to our favourite place on a hill overlooking the town. The Maidens is where we've gone since our teenage years when we need to think, or chat, or just

273

be away from the town. Aggie coined the phrase on the day we left secondary school and back then it *was* beer on the menu, amongst other more questionable spirits. It stuck and remains our code word for escape, regardless of what we're drinking. We don't need a reason to visit, but there usually is one. Tonight I have a feeling both of us need time away from our troubles in the town.

'Man, I needed this.' Aggie clinks her cider bottle against mine and takes a swig. I follow suit, safe in the knowledge that my head won't hurt in the morning like hers will. It was my turn to drive here tonight, so it's non-alcoholic bottles for me.

This is our place: as much mine and Aggie's as the Shed-servatory was mine and Dad's. This spot on the high hill overlooking St Ives has been our favourite since we were sixteen and non-alcoholic pear cider was definitely not in our rucksacks as we scrambled up the grass bank from the road. We come here in all weathers: wrapped up like fleece-swathed mummies in winter, and with hoodies over our shorts in summer. There's something about sitting hidden from view with the town at your feet that gives you perspective. Tonight the lights of St Ives are beginning to shimmer across the bay as the sunset paints the sky brilliant pink beneath wispy grey clouds.

'So how's Kieran?' I ask, seeing her grimace reflected in her cider bottle.

'If it's possible to ignore someone while still havin' a conversation with them, that pretty much covers it.' She shakes her head. 'I dunno, Ser. I mean, we're talkin' but *not* talkin'. He came to the hut today and stood by the bar while I was servin'. Chatted to me the whole time about nothing special, then he went. Am I supposed to take that as a sign?'

'A sign he wants to talk to you but doesn't know what to say?'

'Who knows? Thing is, I ain't a mind reader. I don't have the energy to decipher everythin' he says. Or *doesn't* say. It's bleddy annoyin', I know that.'

This has been going on for so long that I honestly don't know what to suggest – other than honesty. Which I know will be the last thing she wants to hear. 'Aggie, just ask him. Straight out.'

She stares at me like I've just suggested she cut off her arm. 'I can't.'

'Why?'

'I don't expect you to understand. It's *Kieran*, not some lad I've had a one-night stand with who doesn't matter. I know what I could lose if he decides it was a mistake. Once we go down that road, I could lose him if it goes wrong.'

'Or you could miss out on the biggest love of your life.'

She gives an uncomfortable nod. 'True.'

'How will you find out unless you try? Just ask him what he wants, Ag. All this dancing around each other is only making you both miserable. At least then you'd know for certain where you stand one way or another.'

'Yeah, well, maybe I don't want to know. Maybe I'm not ready for that. Don't worry, bird, I'm just lettin' off steam. You don't need to think about this with all you've got goin' on.'

I settle back on the grass and hear the sudden beat of

bat wings overhead. They fly out from the trees that edge The Maidens site when the sun dips below the sea and it's one of the signs that the nights are getting warmer. I love this place. Tonight I need the peace it's always brought me. Jack Dixon is on my mind and I can't seem to shake him. I thought about him today as I waited for customers to appear, and I've been thinking about him since I discovered he was making the stars with me. Something changed when I saw him and his daughter on Gwithian Beach. I think it's been growing for a while, hidden behind every other concern, but seeing him with Nessie and putting the pieces of the puzzle together has brought it out in the open. It isn't love – at least, not like I've ever experienced it. But I feel like a door has opened to the possibility.

The Maidens is an apt place for matters of the heart. Not just our many conversations and confessions about love over the years: the very stones are supposed to signify love and longing. Legend has it that three sisters wept on this hillside for their sweethearts lost at sea – and even though they knew they wouldn't return, they refused to leave in case the boat returned to harbour. Their tears gradually turned them to stone to forever keep watch for their lovers' return and they became the three standing stones behind Aggie and me. Cheery. And while they were actually put up in the 1930s by an entrepreneurial landowner who wanted a suitably mystical story for his visiting guests, genuine Cornish legends are full of stories like that – heartbreak, lost love, murder and ghosts. So many stories have been told in this place through history that you can almost hear them murmuring up from the ground beneath you.

Dad was a great collector of Cornish legends. He'd share them with his mates at the pub and swap them for even grislier, doom-laden tales. Several times a year he'd go to storytelling nights and recite his stories as if he was a born-and-bred Cornishman, not a Welshman in cunning disguise. 'I'm a sheep in wolf's clothing,' he'd often joke. He'd learned Welsh legends as a kid and saw great parallels between Wales and Cornwall. Maybe that's why he felt so at home here.

'How's it goin' at Becca's?' Aggie asks, stumping her empty bottle in a tuft of wild grass and taking two more from her bag. 'Never figured you as the barmaid type.'

'Neither did I, but it's fun. Tiring, though.'

'I'll bet.' She hands me another bottle, even though I haven't finished my first yet. 'Bar work and shop work. If you can survive workin' in them you can work bleddy anywhere. Ninja trainin', it is, especially at Christmas or high season.'

'Most of the regulars aren't bad. One or two are a bit set in their ways and can be rude, but I can handle them. Besides, Becca's never far away and no-one crosses her.'

'I'll bet. Becca Tomlinson's hard as rock. I saw her break a bloke's nose once,' Aggie grins.

'When?'

'Christmas party, a few years back. The guy was bein' mouthy, then he picked a fight with one of the surfers that come into my place. Becca was between them quick as winkin' and when the chap tried to push her out of the way, she grabbed his shoulders, yanked his head down and head-butted him!'

The thought of barely-five-feet-tall Becca doing that is scary and impressive in equal measure. She's brilliant – a total powerhouse of energy and positivity – but I wouldn't want to be on the wrong side of her. I'm still grateful she offered me bar work when she found out how much the shop was struggling.

'T'aint much, but it might just keep your head above water,' she said, then hugged me like a wrestler. That's the good thing about the local community in St Ives – everyone looks out for each other. It's hard to make a living out of season, so you do what you have to and help those who need it. If I'm ever in a position to offer work to someone, I won't hesitate.

'And what about the shop?'

I turn to her, grateful that she is the one person I don't have to pretend with. She *knows* I'm not fine. 'It's bad, Ag. I'm out of ideas.'

'Didn't you have anyone to the cream tea event?'

'One lovely bloke, but he couldn't afford to buy anything. And two more artists withdrew their stock yesterday. I keep thinking about what the bank manager said . . .'

Aggie snorts. 'John Trevelyan is a knob.'

'He's going to foreclose on us.'

'So he's a powerful knob with no sense of decency.' Kindness replaces the mischief in her eyes. 'If anyone can turn that business around, it's you. I believe that.'

'I think he might be right.' Saying the words aloud feels

like a betrayal, even the other side of the hill from Dad's shop. 'I think we might be best to sell.'

'Won't that put you and your mum in a bad way?'

'No worse than we're in already. We wouldn't have to find running costs. Maybe we should take the hit.'

Her eyes narrow as she looks at me. 'Do you want it to fail? No, before you tell me I'm off the mark, ask yourself this: would it be easier for you if the shop closed?'

Of course it would. But that wouldn't make it right. 'I don't know.'

'What we need,' says Aggie, raising her bottle as if lecturing the universe, 'is somethin' excitin' to happen. Somethin' magical.'

And right then, I almost tell her about the seaglass stars on Gwithian Beach. And the tiny driftwood, glass and moss house that right now is cradled in my left hand safely in the pocket of my hoodie. I don't know what stops me, but the words refuse to leave my lips. Under the cloud of foreclosure that hangs over MacArthur's and me, this is my sole beacon of light. I want to keep it just for me, while I try to decide what to do about Jack. Do I tell him the truth about the seaglass stars? Do I tell him I know he made them with me?

I can't decide. Not yet. There's too much at stake.

So instead I just agree with my best friend's wish for magic and drink my cider, pretending it's full of alcohol that will wash the cares of the day away, as the lights of St Ives glitter beneath my feet.

Chapter Forty-Six

Jack

It's only when Nessie's teacher Miss Austin sends a letter home explaining the school's intention to support the Save the Parsonage campaign that I realise who the class visitor was, and the identity of 'Ellie'. Ness has been banging on about poor Ellie and the silly men who didn't listen to her for days. She's fired up about it, which I love, but it helps that I know who she's referring to.

And it turns out that the 'Miss Carter' Ness said visited the class is far from a stranger. Seren MacArthur is responsible for my daughter's sudden passion for stargazers. I'm not sure how to feel about that yet.

I'm annoyed by the school's stance on the campaign, especially as the vast proportion of children at St Piran's don't live in St Ives. And it's our livelihood that's at stake. The letter details a whole programme of events both in school and with the local community, centred round Elinor Carne and her importance to the local area. Nessie is excited about it for now, but I'm worried all this attention on the St Ives vote for Rectory Fields could single her out if things turn nasty.

I think about it all night and call the head, Mrs Masters, to talk about it. To my surprise she asks me to meet her in school to address my concerns.

Which is why I'm here now, sitting outside the head teacher's office like a naughty kid. The difference is that this time I've done nothing wrong. I wasn't angry with the school until I arrived, but then a throwaway comment made by the school secretary annoyed me. And as I wait, I feel anger firing up like a furnace inside my chest.

'Bill Brotherson must be fun to work for.'

That's all she said. But she said it with *that look* – the one that says, *you're wrong, you're the enemy . . .*

Stay calm, Jack.

I'm overreacting, I know. She was probably attempting to make small talk. But I feel I have just cause to be annoyed by the school's attitude to the town vote.

Mrs Masters has apparently forgotten my last visit and the way Ness and I swept magnificently out after the kicking incident. She is as perfectly pleasant when she welcomes me into her office as she was six months ago when I came with Nessie to apply to the school. I was out of my depth with everything, and finding a new school for Ness seemed such an insurmountable task. But Mrs Masters helped sort everything. It's good to know she's sympathetic to our situation, but I need to make her understand that my choice of employer is a key part of safeguarding our ongoing life, too.

'Mr Dixon, thank you for coming in. I thought it best we discuss this in person.'

'Me too.'

She settles herself behind her desk and I already get the impression she isn't going to listen to me. 'So, about the project.'

'The project?' Is that how they're justifying their complete partisanship?

Deep breath, Jack. She hasn't declared war on you. Yet . . .

'The Elinor Carne project.'

'Right.'

'At St Piran's we are keen that our children understand and connect with their heritage. Elinor Carne was an important figure, not just locally but nationally and internationally since her findings have come to light. The increased publicity surrounding the campaign is bringing her story to public attention: we would be wrong to miss the opportunity to share Elinor's story with the children. Miss MacArthur so inspired Nessie's class that we want to capitalise on their enthusiasm for Elinor Carne's story. So you see, we're not taking sides in the campaign, just teaching the children their local history.'

'Then why choose the weeks prior to the St Ives vote to focus on her, if you aren't expecting the kids to take sides?'

'Protecting her legacy to Cornwall is important.'

'I agree. But there are ways of doing it that don't entail preserving a derelict building.'

Her nails are painted the colour of tin and they rap on

the desk like the drum of approaching rain. 'It seems the best place to start, given that it was her home.'

Hers is the kind of opinion formed by long, gossipy conversations with friends over wine: all shared offence and no facts. 'Have you actually visited the parsonage? There's so little left standing that in order to save it you would need to rebuild it. Effectively build something new on the site.'

'This isn't personal, Mr Dixon.'

'Maybe not to you.'

'It's a history project . . .'

I've heard enough. 'No, it isn't. With respect, it's a blatant attempt to take sides. And it would be bad enough if nobody in the school were involved with the opposite side of the argument. But somebody is. My daughter. Who, may I remind you, is still grieving for her mother.'

'Miss Austin tells me Nessie was very taken with Elinor's story.' Is she smiling? Is she seriously amused by this?

'And what happens when the children – who are so inspired and motivated by your not-at-all-discriminatory project – discover that Nessie's dad wants to rip down Elinor Carne's home? Don't you think that might put her in an impossible position?'

'I assure you that won't happen.'

Her smile grates like fingernails down a blackboard, and it's all I can do not to shout.

'Do you remember what it was like being seven at school, Mrs Masters? Because I do. If your friends turn against you it's the loneliest place in the world. I don't want Nessie to face that when she's done nothing wrong. I've worked hard to provide a safe, steady environment for my daughter. I thought St Piran's supported me in that. Nessie's been making great progress at your school and seems really settled and happy. But this could make her a target in her class – and in the school as a whole.'

'I understand your concerns, Mr Dixon, but equally we cannot stop an entire project just for the sake of one child. Or parent.'

That's it. I've tried to be nice, but it stops now. 'I need this job. If I win the contract it will give us financial stability for the rest of this year. We're in temporary accommodation, as you know, and I'm keen to change that. What you are doing is deliberately jeopardising my chances of providing a solid future for my child.'

'I think that's a little unfair . . .'

'No, it isn't. Have you even looked at the plans for Rectory Fields? Or come to any of the public meetings where I've explained the kind of sympathetic development I intend to create? No, I didn't think so.'

'Mr Dixon . . .'

'And what happens when my daughter discovers her father is the one trying to stop people remembering this woman, hmm? Have you considered that?' This is my real fear. Right now Nessie and me are in a good place. I'm all she has and she loves me, but if this came between us? I don't want to think how hard that could be. 'She wouldn't understand. She wouldn't trust me. Have you any idea how hard it is to bring up a child on your own?'

She has no answer for that. Despite her repeated

assurances, I stand. 'Reconsider your project. Or I will complain to the education authority on the grounds of your unfairly targeting an emotionally vulnerable child.'

An hour later, I'm still seething. Jeb raises his hand as he passes the chalet but heads over when he sees my expression.

'Alright, matey?'

'Not really.'

'Need a beer? Just had a delivery at the park bar.'

It's a sweet gesture, but I decline. 'Bit early for me, Jeb.'

'Fair 'nough. So, wasson?'

His bushy brows lift as I recount my morning battle.

'Upshot is that they're standing by their decision but focusing on the history rather than the campaign.'

'Bleddy unfair if you ask me. Your poor nipper. You tell Nessie from me that her Uncle Jeb'll sort out anyone who tries to pick on her. Tell her I know jiu-jitsu.'

My bearded, tattooed and many-pierced friend doesn't strike me as a martial arts devotee, but you don't question Jeb. It's entirely possible he trained in Japan with a martial arts master before he became a caravan park owner in southwest Cornwall.

'Wasson with this historic bird then?'

I pick at a splinter on the weatherbeaten veranda rail. 'Elinor Carne, parson's wife and amateur astronomer. Discovered a star or something. They got the leader of the campaign to save the parsonage to come and speak to the kids at school about her, and now she's all Nessie talks about.'

Not just anyone from the Save the Parsonage campaign.

Seren MacArthur. As my fury at the school has raged, something else has been building in my mind. Why did Seren have to get involved? I can't get over that she chose to come to my daughter's school, miles from St Ives, to talk about Elinor Carne. I've seen Nessie's teacher, Miss Austin, at the town meetings, sitting with Seren. Miss Austin knows I'm Nessie's dad. So, whose idea was it for Seren to visit? I like Seren. I've felt sorry for her, losing her dad and trying to save his business. I was impressed by her passion for Bethel Parsonage and touched by her compassion towards me when we talked about losing people we loved. But did she use me? Did she know she was going to meet my girl at the school?

The question sits like hot ash in the pit of my stomach, burning me as I turn over the facts.

'Used to like a bit of stargazin' myself, way back when,' Jeb says, oblivious to my inner battle. 'Thinkin' about it, I got an old telescope Ness can have if you fancy.'

'Have you?'

Jeb sniffs and strokes his ginger beard into a thoughtful point. 'Yep. 'Ad it when I were a young 'un. Thought I'd be an astronaut if I used it often enough. Fat lot of good it did me, eh? Mind you, I'm not sure them aliens would understand me in a first-contact situation. "Wasson boys? We come in peace an' that."' When he laughs I swear the chalet shakes.

'There's still time, you know. You could be NASA's secret weapon.'

'Nah, not bothered now. I reckon there's more extraterrestrials visit this place every summer than I'd ever find up there.'

'You might be right. What am I going to do, Jeb? Nessie's so excited about this woman, and sooner or later she's going to find out I'm the one who wants to build on her former home. I don't want to disappoint her and I don't want her schoolfriends to pick on her for it, either.'

'Well, do you know anything about the lady?'

'Not much.'

Jeb clamps a matey hand on my shoulder. 'Then don't you think you should find out?'

Jeb's workshop is less a place of work and more a museum to long-forgotten, broken things. As a kid I would've loved it here with all its strange half-objects. It reminds me of the junkyards Dad used to take Owen and me to on long summer weekends, often on the hunt for just the right bit to fix something that had broken at home. Dad's answer to everything has always been to try to mend it himself, however unprepossessing the result. I'm pretty sure Jeb inherited this dust-laden treasure trove from an earlier hoarder – some of the objects look as if they've been resident here for longer than their owner has been alive.

''Scuse the mess,' Jeb calls over his shoulder, stepping gingerly over upended boxes and rusting hulks of metal. 'It's some *ummin* in here.'

I love the Cornish slang Jeb uses, but even though I've been born and bred in Cornwall there are a lot of phrases I don't understand. Dad uses the odd word here and there, so those are the ones I know. And anyway, I'm still not

287

completely sure if all Jeb's turns of phrase are genuinely Cornish or uniquely Jeb. 'Ummin?'

He looks over his shoulder. '*Filthy*, my good man,' he enunciates in almost-perfect Eton English. 'An utter tip, if you will.' It's long been a joke between us that he thinks I'm too posh to call myself a Cornishman.

'I'll remember that.'

'You won't, but it's all right. Now I know I put it somewhere . . .'

After much clunking and worryingly destructive-sounding noises, Jeb emerges triumphant from the junk, holding a roll of faded tarpaulin aloft like a dusty green Excalibur. 'Got it! *Geddon!*'

Out in the much fresher air of his front garden, we unwrap the tarp to reveal an old wooden telescope. It's seen better days, much like the caravan park around us, but Jeb assures me it still works.

'I reckon your Ness'll love this,' he beams. 'Let us show you how to work it . . .'

By the time I pick Nessie up from school I'm so excited about her seeing the telescope that the fisticuffs with her head teacher have almost been forgotten. It's only when I see Mrs Masters briefly appear in the playground, looking anxious, that I remember. Well, let her worry. It's her problem, not mine.

It's all I can do to keep the surprise a secret on the drive home, which seems to take forever as several tractors slide into the rush-hour traffic to wend their weary way home.

When Nessie dashes towards the chalet from my car I finally give in.

'Hey, listen, before you go and change, I have something for you.'

She observes me with a withering look only a seven-year-old can perform. 'But the star, Dad. We have to get it made. I want to do the best one ever tonight. For *Ellie*. And the clouds are getting darker over the beach.'

She has a point, but this can't wait. 'It'll only take a couple of minutes. Ten at most. I promise.'

'O-*kaa-a-a-ay*,' she replies, plodding back to me.

Jeb has set up the telescope in the corner of the tiny patch of grass that passes as a back garden. And bless him, he's found an old dog show rosette from his Aladdin's cave of junk and has enthusiastically gaffer-taped it to one side.

Nessie stops dead when she sees it.

'What do you think?'

'What is it?'

'It's a telescope. For looking at the stars tonight.'

'Who's it for?' Her voice squeaks a little, a good sign.

'It's for you – if you want it. Uncle Jeb had it when he was little.'

And then she is screeching and jumping up and down and happy-dancing around the telescope, and talking at a million miles an hour, and hugging herself. Moments like these are what I've started to live for. I saw it when we first found the completed star on the beach, and it's so good to see it again now. I always want to make my girl this happy.

'A telescope!' she yells, dislodging a shiver of chattering starlings from the hedge. 'Is it really mine? Can I keep it? Oh *Dad*, it's just like Ellie's!'

'Her name was *Elinor*,' I say, this time with the conviction that comes from a frantic half-hour Google search on my mobile phone before I picked her up from school. Jeb was right – I need to know who this woman was and why she matters to everyone, especially Nessie. Maybe it will help me address concerns when they are raised, either in the meeting or – thanks to Miss Austin, Mrs Masters and Seren MacArthur – at the school gates.

Seren. Any way I look at it, she was part of the ambush on Ness.

I don't want to believe it. But what other explanation is there?

At best I hope she didn't know who Nessie was when she agreed to visit Cerrie Austin's class, but realistically that's unlikely. What kind of person uses a seven-year-old child to score a point? Well, Tash for one – many times when she wanted to win an argument, because she knew I'd always back down when she'd threaten to bring Ness into a row.

What annoys me most is that I'd hoped Seren was different . . .

I can't think about this now. Nessie is recounting the story of *her Ellie* again for me, her eyes bright with excitement. She's *shining*. And for once I want to forget about everything else except sharing my daughter's joy.

Chapter Forty-Seven

Seren

What will I say to Jack Dixon when I see him? Do I tell him I'm the other starmaker yet? Or test the water and see how he is? I don't know how he'd react, and part of me wants to stay silent because I want the stars to continue. They've come to mean so much to me, become such an important part of my life that I'm just not ready to let them go yet. Even though I know the secret.

Will knowing make the experience different? Take away the magic? Enhance it? I don't know.

Would Jack want to know he's making stars with me? He's difficult to read, and it doesn't help that I've tried my hardest *not* to read him since our first meeting. Aside from the feelings I have for him that I'm scared to investigate, I know how much is at stake. He's a conundrum: one minute friendly, the next Brotherson's mouthpiece. Our conversation about his late wife and my dad seemed to shift the ground beneath us. And now I know he is the kind soul leaving half-finished seaglass stars on Gwithian Beach, it's muddied the waters even more. When I saw him on the way to the bank he seemed happy to see me, as if he was greeting a friend rather than an opponent. At least, that's what I thought. Or was that me looking for an ally when I felt alone?

I can't tell him I watched him and his daughter on the beach, either, because how scary and deranged would that make me appear?

I look down at the half-finished seaglass bracelet in my hands and wish I didn't feel so conflicted. I've taken to bringing the jewellery I'm making into the shop lately, partly to give me something to fill the days and partly to provide a spectacle for any customers who might wander in. When Dad was alive I only occasionally sneaked my creations in, hiding them as soon as he appeared; even now, I'm looking over my shoulder in case he emerges from the back room and catches me.

Last night I went to the Shedservatory to watch the sky and even though a thick layer of cloud hung stubbornly over St Ives, I watched it anyway. Wishing Dad was there. Like the clouded sky above me, I have no point of reference for this situation, no map of how to proceed. Dad would have known what to do.

I like Jack. Really like him. And knowing he has been making stars with me on Gwithian Beach has only added to that. But he's the one person I shouldn't want to like me back. If I let him win – if I surrender everything I've worked for with the campaign – then what do I have?

I had a revelation of sorts last night, bundled up on the observation bench in the Shedservatory. It was finally time to be honest with myself. I want to win this for Dad. Not for me, or the shop, or even the town. That's the truth. Dad was so passionate about honouring Elinor and getting proper recognition for her work. I'm passionate about it, too. But now I wonder if the passion is really my own, or just a determination that my dad won't be forgotten.

I suspect it's the latter.

Seeing Jack with Nessie on Gwithian Beach changed things. Knowing who he really is and getting that glimpse into his life has challenged all my preconceptions about a man choosing to work for Brotherson Developments. I thought he was just trying to make money for himself. But now I don't think he is, however much he tells the public meetings he's passionate about the development. I imagine Jack is thinking of his little girl when he's selling his soul to Brotherson. And it isn't my problem, but now I know they made the stars with me, it feels like it should be.

While I was watching the clouds roll overhead from the hatch window last night I wondered for the first time if I could let him win. My financial situation won't be changed one bit if the parsonage is saved; neither will the shop's fortunes turn around. I have to be realistic about that. But Jack's whole world could change if he wins the vote.

What would Dad do? If it wasn't Elinor Carne's home and just an old derelict building with a bit of St Ives history attached to it? If he knew the stakes for someone like Jack Dixon, doing the best he can for his kid? I know Dad struggled to make ends meet when I was a child, but I never went without. Mum told me a while ago that he'd once worked four jobs just to keep the roof over our heads; that he'd bartered garden work with the lady who owned the school uniform supply shop to make sure I had a blazer that fitted me for my first term at secondary school. Dad understood the sacrifices he needed to make to look after his daughter. I suspect Jack understands it, too.

I can't let Jack win. I just can't. Even if it means I lose the chance of getting to know him. But can I stand to watch him lose?

By the time the meeting begins I'm a bag of nerves. I didn't see Jack when I arrived; it's only when I take my seat at the table on the stage that I see him walking towards me. His head is high, but he seems to look straight through me when our eyes meet. I've imagined everything, I tell myself, forcing my eyes to the notes in front of me. Tonight is the last chance to convince St Ives before the vote next week. I have to concentrate on doing what I came here to do.

Lou is already welcoming the crowd, which is considerable again. Cerrie and several teachers from her school are near the front on my side of the hall. I can see her encouraging smile and it gives me hope. People care about Elinor Carne – they will stand for her when the time comes. I just have to state our case again.

Aggie and Kieran stand at the back of the hall, keeping a close eye on proceedings with surreptitious glances at each other. It's surely only a matter of time before they admit they are in love. For now, they are locked in a careful waltz around each other, close enough to mean something but still with an arm's length between them.

'Jack . . . and Seren . . .' I look up as I hear my name and smile quickly when the room applauds. I have to focus and be clear. And *not* think about Jack Dixon and his daughter.

He goes first, repeating what he said at the last meeting and addressing some concerns that were raised in the question-and-answer section last time. He seems different, as if his body has been reinforced with steel. But I didn't know about the stars at the last meeting, so perhaps that's what I'm seeing now. Is this the real Jack Dixon? This absolutely matters to him. It isn't just his own livelihood he's fighting for.

And then it's my turn. I try to counter what Jack's said about the development, but it's as if my legs are wading through slow-setting concrete. I don't see alarm on the faces of my friends, so I know what I'm feeling is just within me. But I'm suddenly weary – *so* tired of everything. I'm tired of fighting, tired of living a life that was Dad's before, exhausted from trying to keep all the aspects of my life spinning like manic plates in a circus ring. I'm tired of smiling, of pretending that I can do any of this. I love Elinor Carne. I'm passionate that she shouldn't be forgotten by history as she was in life. But what if saving the parsonage site isn't the way to do it?

As I talk about preserving her memory and providing a place where generations can learn about her, I find myself thinking of Cerrie's class this week. Thirty children who left the classroom excited about astronomy and determined to follow Elinor's example. Would they have been this excited visiting a ruin of a building on the wind-battered moor?

Are their parents anywhere near as invested in Elinor's legacy after three weeks of campaigning as those kids were after ninety minutes of learning about her?

I put down my notes and smile at the assembled townspeople. 'You've heard so much from both sides. Thank you for listening. But now it's up to you. It isn't just about preserving history, although it's important for future generations to learn about Elinor Carne's contribution. But livelihoods are at stake.' I swallow a ball of sudden emotion.

Not just Jack's, but mine.

I can feel Jack Dixon's stare but I daren't look over.

'Please think carefully about your vote. We have a history but we also have the future. It's up to us all to decide what that will look like.'

There's silence as I retake my seat and then the applause begins like a raincloud breaking late over the sea. I finally risk a glance to the other side of the table, but Jack's chair is empty.

Shaken, I head to the exit, the atmosphere inside the Guildhall stifling. I don't know what happened in there but I'm glad the campaign is nearly over. People congratulate me on my way to the door and I smile in return without stopping to chat. I need to be away from this place.

The evening sky is a deep, dark blue with a half-moon that paints an undulating path over the waves in the harbour. I keep walking, not wanting to go back. Aggie and the others will understand – she'd said I looked tired when I arrived this evening. I'd hoped to see Jack, but the street outside was empty. I walk as far as I can on the harbour wall, then stop to look out to sea. The stone of the wall is

cold beneath my fingers as I lean against it. I close my eyes
and take in the sounds of the harbour at night: the clink
of ropes against metal masts, the slap of waves against the
bobbing hulls of moored boats, and the scraps of voices
and shots of laughter drifting across the dark water. This
place is my heartbeat, woven into my skin and bones, St
Ives infusing every nerve, every blood vessel, every muscle
with its light and life. I thought I'd left it behind me when
I moved to Falmouth, but lately I've realised just how much
I need this town. It's where I moor myself, where I reconnect. Taking away all other concerns, my love for St Ives is
as immovable as the rock upon which it stands.

Whatever happens, I'll be okay if I can be here.

'That was some speech.'

I jump, open my eyes. Jack Dixon is standing next to
me. I recognise the hooded jacket he wears from that
evening I watched him and Nessie on the beach.

'Thanks.'

'Did you mean any of it?' It's a question with a dia-
mond cutting edge.

'Yes, I did.' Then why do I sound so uncertain?

His eyes are full of the sea as he looks past me to the
darkening horizon. 'I thought you did.' It doesn't seem to
be a compliment.

Have I offended him? I can't tell, but this Jack Dixon is
a world away from the one who met me by the bank. 'I'm
sorry, is that a problem?'

He stares at me. 'That depends.'

'On what?'

'On how far you'd be prepared to go to secure the result you want in the vote next week.'

'I'm sorry, I don't understand.' Suddenly this isn't the friendly conversation I thought we'd be having.

He faces me and I see a whole world of questions in his stare. 'I don't know what to believe about you, Seren. I thought you were a decent human being. But now I'm not sure.'

'Excuse me?'

'Just answer me one question: did you know my daughter was in Cerrie Austin's class when you came to talk to them?'

Finally, it all makes sense. He thinks I set Nessie up. He actually believes me capable of using a child to win the vote. 'Absolutely not! Cerrie didn't tell me until I was leaving.'

'And would you still have done it had you known before?'

'No. *No*, I wouldn't. What do you take me for?' Now I'm angry. I'm angry that I thought Jack Dixon might be a friend in different circumstances. I'm angry that I've even thought of him at all. In that moment I decide: I won't tell him about the seaglass stars. He doesn't deserve to know.

'The whole school is supporting *your* campaign,' he says, no gentler than his last accusation.

'I didn't ask them to. And it isn't just my campaign,' I hit back. 'You think I have influence over the people of St Ives? Do you think if I did my primary concern would be saving a derelict parsonage? If I had the power you seem to think I have, don't you think I'd be saving my business?'

I let this hang in the air and see a battle break out over his face. Clearly he still wants a fight, but he wasn't expecting that shot.

'Is your business in trouble?' His question is almost drowned out by the sound of the lifeboat patrolling the bay.

'What do you think?' I'm tired and I'm cold and I don't need to be accused of this on top of everything else. Tears aren't far away, and I need to leave before he sees it. 'Goodnight.'

'Seren, wait . . .'

'It's late, and I'm tired.'

'I'm scared they'll make her life a misery. That they'll blame her instead of me . . .' The words tumble out of him.

'Who?'

'The kids at St Piran's. The school is going to fire them up about Elinor Carne and when they realise who Nessie is, she'll be their target.'

'And that's my fault?'

'Yes. No . . . Partly. I've seen how your visit affected Ness. She believes in Elinor Carne. Your old astronomer is all I've heard about since you visited St Piran's. If other kids in the class react the same way and tell their parents, what hope do I have of protecting my girl from the fall-out?'

How is any of this my fault? And why do I feel like Jack is expecting me to solve his problem? 'You should talk to the school, then. They have a duty of care to your daughter.'

'And you don't bear any responsibility for influencing the school?'

'You know what, Jack? I'm not the punch bag you're looking for. Take it up with Cerrie – Miss Austin. And for what it's worth, I think your daughter is great. I think she'll follow her heart no matter what anyone thinks. Maybe you should give her more credit instead of expecting problems.'

I've said too much. I don't want to be here and I'm done with talking. I walk past him but I can hear his steps behind me.

'Hang on, what right do you have to tell me about my kid?'

'None at all. Just as you have no right to tell me what to do with my life. But next week the vote happens and then we can forget about each other.'

I don't look back but I don't hear him following me. I've burned every bridge, destroyed any chance of knowing him as a friend rather than an enemy.

And my heart is broken.

Chapter Forty-Eight

Jack

Her business is dying. Brotherson said so, and she just confirmed it. She's lost her dad, is still fighting his battles and looks exhausted. And I just accused her of plotting against Ness.

Bloody hell, Jack.

I watch her hurry away from me and as she heads up the hill from the harbour I see the heavy shaking of her shoulders. I should go after her but I know I've scuppered any chance of being heard. The damage has been done – it would be cruel to risk any more. I sit on one of the benches lining the harbour wall and knock my head back against the cold, damp stone.

Idiot.

My mother used to say you shouldn't stamp on anyone because you don't know what battles they are facing. And she knew that better than any of us. For years I hated her for walking out on Dad and leaving him looking after Owen and me, but maybe she had a point. Her demons were too much to keep her playing happy families. Maybe she thought we'd be better off without her. As it turned out, we probably were. Apart from the odd birthday card when Owen and I were younger, she broke all contact. I found out she died a few years ago and it felt like I was mourning a ghost, a shadow from my past, rather than the mum I should have known. I'll never understand it, but it was her decision to make.

I shouldn't have hit out at Seren. What she said at the end of the meeting threw me. I couldn't see past her visit kick-starting Nessie's school's campaign and I thought she was being hypocritical. But was she offering balance? When she mentioned livelihoods was she not just referring to her own?

The problem isn't that she visited the school. Or that Ness is so taken with Elinor Carne. The problem is that I've started to care about her. The hurt and betrayal I've felt has nothing to do with dented pride, or fears for my daughter. Seren's been in my thoughts for a while and now I know why.

Finally I can see it for what it was, five minutes too late to prevent a huge mistake. Why couldn't I see past my own anger? Why couldn't I have recognised the truth? I've just become so used to fighting everyone and everything that I couldn't see someone who was trying to help – someone offering to be a friend. Because I think that's what Seren MacArthur was doing . . .

The town is eerily quiet as I walk back to the station car park. The crowds from the meeting have melted into the night and I am suddenly aware of my steps as they echo in the empty streets. I feel I've been judged and found wanting – and this time, it *is* my fault.

The morning brings Owen, Sarah and the boys, who are taking Nessie to Paradise Park for the day to make the most of the Easter holidays, while I meet the trades who will be working on Rectory Fields if we get the green light. I make polite conversation with my sister-in-law as Nessie dashes around the chalet with her cousins. I don't want to add any more people to the *Offended by Jack Dixon* list today. I'm grateful to Owen and Sarah for treating my daughter to a day out.

'You sure we can't tempt you to skive work and come with us?' Owen asks, munching a hot cross bun from the stash Sarah insisted on bringing. 'The JungleBarn slides rock.'

'Sorry. I need to be a grown-up today,' I grin back.

'Rubbish. Being a grown-up sucks.'

I smile over his shoulder. 'Nessie, make sure Uncle Owen behaves himself today, okay?'

Nessie pats her uncle's arm. 'You'll be safe with me, Uncle Owen.'

'Cheers, Ness.'

'We should get going,' Sarah says apologetically, checking her watch.

'Yep.' Owen takes a swig of my tea and scoops his car keys from the table. 'Come on, troops! Let's go play!'

Nessie flings her arms around me as I bundle her rucksack and coat to my brother. 'Cheers for this, Reekie.'

'Pleasure, Stink.' The Owen Dixon Hair Ruffle ensues. 'Don't work too hard. You look *rough*, man.'

I feel rough. I didn't sleep well after my showdown with Seren last night and woke this morning feeling like a total git. I've considered going to her shop in St Ives and apologising, but she'd be right to slam the door in my face. And what would I say, anyway?

I've well and truly screwed up there. Best to leave it now.

The group of trades Bill Brotherson has assembled to work on Rectory Fields is impressive. It isn't often a build team agrees to work on a project before it gets the green light, but Brotherson's paying a healthy retainer to secure all our services in anticipation of a Yes vote. We meet in the conference room of a chain hotel on the outskirts of Truro, and as each one goes over their plans for the apartments I can see the development taking shape in my mind. None of them bats an eyelid about my involvement as construction manager, either, which is a relief. I haven't worked with any of the guys but they are all highly rated within the business. When Brotherson said he wanted the best of the best to work on this, he wasn't joking. Most of them have worked on many Brotherson builds and they know his processes inside out. They're highly skilled and it feels good to be counted among them.

This will be the first site of this size I've managed and it's eighteen months since I worked on anything comparable. I'm up for the challenge and excited about the potential. Brotherson has promised free rein on specifications for the team, but we'll see. In my experience plans are always unlimited until the build begins and reality sets in. Still, it's the best starting point I could've hoped for and we leave the meeting with smiles all round.

They were all keen to know how last night's meeting went, so I told them what I knew. Truth is, I didn't stay long enough at the end of it to gauge the reaction of the crowd after our closing arguments. I wasn't heckled out of the Guildhall, but neither was I hailed a hero. It's going to be a close call and I don't think anyone can guess what the outcome will be. Next time we meet, neither Seren nor I will have to say anything: it's the turn of the town to decide. Are they more likely to vote for the development or against it? It's impossible to say. In a week's time a winner will emerge and all guesswork will be academic. I thought we did enough, but what do I know?

As I drive back towards home, I can't stop thinking about Seren. The way she looked at me last night – like I'd shape-shifted into a slug at her feet. I wish I could take back what I said to her. In the bright light of day it's sickeningly obvious that I was in the wrong.

I can't imagine what she's going through. I overheard Lou before the meeting saying how hard Seren's having to work and how they are all concerned about her. He was talking to Aggie from the beach cafe on Porthgwidden Beach and I don't think he knew I was in earshot. They seem to love her, so at least she has friends. But she looked so hurt last night and so tired. Why didn't I see it before I engaged my gob?

I pull into a roadside caravan cafe and try to eat a bacon sandwich, but the weight of my mistake sits like concrete in my stomach. I have to put this right. But how?

Chapter Forty-Nine

Seren

I shouldn't have yelled at Jack. He's as much a slave to his circumstances as I am to mine. But he accused me of using his daughter, and that was totally out of order. I was right to defend myself.

Nevertheless, I can't stop thinking about the look in his eyes when he voiced his fears for Nessie at school. It must be terrifying, seeing potential dangers everywhere for your child but having to let them go out into the world anyway. I'm not sure how I would cope with that. And I can see his point: if Cerrie's school makes an issue of the campaign and pits themselves against Brotherson, then Nessie is separated from her classmates by default. That isn't my problem to solve, but still it doesn't seem fair.

The thought I had during the meeting has been playing on my mind, too: that perhaps location isn't key to preserving Elinor Carne's memory. Lou has put together an initial breakdown of costs to do basic renovations on the parsonage. He showed it to us before the meeting and it was *scary*. I don't know how we'll ever raise that kind of money – and that would just be the beginning. We could be fundraising for years before we're even able to start work on the site. The building is already in a bad way – it's structurally unsafe and a target for local vandals. How much worse will it be by the time we raise the money to save it? Will there be any of it left to save?

Maybe it's because I'm so tired of fighting Dad's battles, but I'm really wondering if this fight is worth the energy. What do I get out of winning next week's vote? A victory for Elinor Carne perhaps, but the reality of that is signing myself up for so much more work. Maybe years of fund-raising. More debates, more fights, more and more of my life claimed by the ongoing campaign. If I'm honest I don't even know if this is the best way to honour Elinor. If we have so long to wait until her former home is restored, how does that get the word out about her? I want Elinor to be recognised and remembered, but am I willing to sac-rifice so much of my future to see it happen?

But what happens if we lose? If Jack wins? He isn't doing this job for himself; he's doing it to provide for his little girl. If we lost the vote and Brotherson Developments won, he could secure their future and the problems he fears with the school would be solved.

If Jack wins . . .

I need to think. This itch about the vote refuses to go away, which makes me think I should pay attention to it. But could I risk everything my friends and I have cam-paigned for? And what alternative could I offer them?

I leave the shop at four p.m. and walk up past Porthmeor

Beach, taking the cliff path around the headland. When I reach the highest point, I sit down and gaze out to sea.

Think, Seren. There has to be a way to make this happen.

There's a storm coming.

I can feel it.

In the air, in the subtle change of the breeze.

Over the sea, washes of grey cloud are beginning to bleed like watercolour strokes. I can see the rain approaching, sheets of leaden bullets heading for shore.

The breeze turns and suddenly it's the rush of air that precedes the rain, like the rush of wind before an underground train appears. I love this moment: when you can see what's coming and there's no way to stop it. I like the certainty. The brief warning. It's like a knowing nod from nature herself: *get ready, here we go* . . . The rush is energising, vital, real. I love knowing it's going to happen, and yet the thrill of not knowing quite *when*.

Sitting in the wild grass on the edge of the cliff, I wait, hugging my knees to my chin, feeling the wind lift my hair to make it dance around my face as my jacket hood billows behind my head.

Life should be like this, I think, as the waves of grey cloud rush across the sea towards me. *Constantly anticipating something happening, loving the thrill of waiting for it to arrive.* And in that moment, I understand. *This* is how I want my life to feel. Expectant, confident that something exciting will happen if I just wait for it.

If we win the vote, I can kiss this feeling goodbye. It will get buried beneath more layers of responsibility, more demands on my time. I can't compartmentalise my happiness any more. All I want is to feel on the edge of possibility. I have to make this happen. This should be *my* choice . . .

I close my eyes to keep my tears within.

And the rain starts to fall.

Chapter Fifty

Jack

There's a problem at the site.

The first I heard about it was this morning when Bill Brotherson's PA called me.

'So sorry to call at such short notice, Jack, but Bill was very insistent you meet him today. He's going over to the site at lunchtime. Is there any chance you could meet him there?'

Silly question. When your potential employer demands an urgent meeting, you don't hang about. Thankfully providence is on my side today: it's Nessie's night for tea with Owen and Sarah, and she's spending the day with my father beforehand. He'll drop her at Owen's farm so if the meeting is a long one I won't have to worry about getting her there. Gathering all my notes and plans, I drive over to the parsonage and arrive just as Brotherson's chauffeur-driven Jaguar appears on the approach road.

'Nice day for it, Jack.' Clive, Brotherson's chauffeur, gives me a wink as he gets out of the car and walks around to open his employer's door. Even Brotherson's employees I've never met before seem to be on first-name terms with me.

'I hope so,' I say, glad of the cloud-dappled sun being blown across the site. I wait for Bill to emerge, quickly stepping forward to shake his hand. He doesn't look happy.

'Hi, Bill.'

'Jack. Appreciate you coming.' He jams a blue Brotherson Developments hard hat on his head and hands his shoes to Clive as he pulls on a very new-looking pair of green Hunter wellingtons. Then he nods at me and we walk through the rusted gate and up the overgrown path to Bethel Parsonage.

'Cassandra said there was a problem?'

'Potentially. We did initial tests on the ground and some of the results are inconclusive. Geophys scans suggest a crack right across the foundations of the main building, travelling east to west.'

That is bad news. Or it could be. 'Would there be any way of shoring it up?'

'Nah. Best solution would be to flatten the site, dig everything out and start again.' He squints up at me. 'I know this isn't what you wanted to hear.'

I think on my feet. The news should utterly depress me, but, surprisingly, it doesn't. I've been questioning this build since my row with Seren and this seems to confirm my gut feeling. 'There are ways round it. If we can salvage the original stones and incorporate them into a new design, I don't see a conflict with our sustainable development goal.

It might mean working in extra time to take the building down brick by brick, but ultimately I think it'll be worth it.'

'Expensive, though.'

'But worth it in the final product.'

Brotherson shrugs. 'I reckon you're right.' He shoves his hands in the trouser pockets of his bespoke-tailored suit. 'Listen, Jack, I want us to win that vote. I want this site to be a success.'

'I know. I'm trying my hardest.'

'Oh, don't worry, I'll see you right, boy. I believe you'll win it, but I don't want you worrying if that rabble goes rogue and votes against us. Ways and means, Jack. Ways and means.'

I stare at him, not sure what to make of this. Is he offering me a job regardless of the vote's outcome? 'I really want this job, Bill.'

'I know you do, son. I appreciate what you've done for this project. Never had anyone go the extra mile the way you have. Light and sustainable development and all. Your cost-cutting plans are bloody genius, too. I like you, kid. More to the point, *people* like you. The construction team wants to work with you. Even those bods at the town meeting didn't rip your head off. You're an asset to my company.'

This wasn't what I thought he'd say. It's a massive compliment – and more than that, it's the security I've worked so hard to gain. 'Thank you.'

'You're a good man, Jack Dixon. We need more of you in construction. Now, I still believe we can win this vote on Wednesday night. But if it doesn't happen or we have to take the fight further, I have several other projects nearing agreement I'd like to set you working on in the meantime. That's if you're interested?'

'Yes, of course,' I rush to reply. 'Absolutely.'

It's like pieces of a puzzle are clicking into place. I sit in my car long after Brotherson has departed, mulling it over. I keep thinking about Seren – about everything she has lost and what is at stake if we win the vote. She was exhausted when we argued, the fight I'd seen in her gone. It wasn't right: she seemed to have so much life when I first saw her speak. What would happen if Brotherson lost the vote and her campaign won? Would it give her a boost? Help her see the old astronomer recognised and fulfil her father's wish? If her business folds, could the campaign to restore the parsonage take its place?

I hate that I yelled at her. I want to do something to redress the balance. Brotherson said I have a job regardless of what happens on Wednesday night – which means I can support Ness and me, my primary concern in all of this.

Could I help Seren's side win?

It's a long shot, but I have to try. A win for the opposition will make things easier for Ness, too. Less chance of her being singled out by her classmates. Everyone wins. I hope . . .

There's still time to pull back, albeit not much. With Brotherson's assurance of work beyond the St Ives decision, I can start influencing the vote Seren's way.

Seren MacArthur. How has she got under my skin so quickly? That's the real reason for the uncertainty I've felt recently. I've been so angry with myself for lashing out at her because, the truth is, I like her. I've wanted to pretend it isn't happening, but there's no mistake. I'm falling for her. It started the first time we met – and that's never happened to me before. Even with Tash, who I'd wanted so much to be the love of my life, I hovered around the decision for months before I finally let her in.

It's crazy. But the more I think of how things are working out, the more I wonder if it might be possible. With the vote decided, we will no longer be on opposing sides. There will be nothing in the way of us being friends – and maybe more.

I'll get Brotherson to firm up his offer of work first, so I know I'm covered. And then I'll start talking to people . . .

Chapter Fifty-One

Seren

I've made up my mind. I'm going to help Jack win.

It isn't being disrespectful to Dad – it's making the most of the opportunity we have. It isn't backing down on honouring Elinor Carne, either – we don't need the actual site of her observatory to make sure she is remembered. We can campaign for a new observatory, buy a piece of land in the hills nearby eventually and establish a centre for astronomy. We could partner with a university for further study, publish Elinor's journals online, maybe put together project days we can take around local schools. Start small, build up. In that way it's exactly what Dad would have done. He started his shop as a stall at a craft fair, bringing together his favourite artists to share with the town. From that humble beginning, MacArthur's was founded. And even though that part of the story is coming to an end, it doesn't erase anything he achieved.

I'm moving on, too. Taking the decision to sell has shifted the weight off my shoulders. I'm even daring to think about what I want my life to look like. Maybe a new campaign to have a permanent centre in Elinor's name might be part of that.

Could Jack be part of it, too?

I could be mistaken, or reading too much into our fledgling friendship, but I wonder if it could develop if the barrier of the Rectory Fields vote isn't there. He doesn't know I make the stars with him – would that be the final piece to bring us together?

I'm going to do everything I can to find out. I'm going to try to convince people to vote for Rectory Fields – and show them that saving the parsonage isn't the only way to honour Elinor. Then I'll tell Jack I'm the starmaker, when he wins. It's a risk, and it puts everything I thought I cared about on the line; but I've risked more indirectly with Jack on Gwithian Beach than I have with anyone else. I have to know.

I have less than a week to swing the vote. So I set to work.

When I pick up bread for home I talk to the guys in Warren's Bakery about the cost of renovating the parsonage, letting the smallest hint of doubt into my voice. As I leave, I see them deep in conversation.

Maggie in the Post Office tells me her niece enjoyed my talk at Cerrie's school, so I mention how the children responded to Elinor Carne's story – and that maybe we don't need a physical site to spread the word about her. Her parting words are, 'Well, if we lose the vote maybe you, Lou and the committee can put your energy into doing school visits. Start with the next generation and

316

build from there. I know several teachers who would sign up like a shot . . .'

I don't say anything to Kieran, Aggie or Lou. They would rumble me in an instant: I would rather we work together *after* losing the vote than me try to persuade them to ditch the campaign. But there is one person on the Save the Parsonage committee who I think might be a sympathetic ear.

If I'm going to convince anyone, I should start with Sharon. She's been a fantastic supporter of everything we've done, but she is also the voice of reason on the committee. People listen to her. So I make an excuse to visit her at her gorgeous candle shop, to make my play.

After the usual catch-up on town gossip, I casually make my opening gambit. 'You know, I've been thinking about what we do if we win the vote.'

'About time someone did. I've kept saying this to Lou and Aggie, but they can't see past beating Bill Brotherson.'

'I just think we need to consider what lies ahead. How much it's going to cost; the best use of our money and time.'

Sharon leans against one end of a display bench. 'And?'

I shrug, suddenly self-conscious. 'Maybe the parsonage site isn't the best place, I don't know.'

She blinks. 'You're not serious?'

Too obvious. I try a different approach. 'I mean, it's a bit out of the way if we wanted a centre that visitors could easily find. And there really isn't enough of the existing building left to renovate. We would have to build something new, whether it was there or somewhere else. So I'm

317

wondering if it might be better to find a more central location – to bring Elinor's story to as many people as possible.'

'In town?'

'Maybe. Think of the thousands of visitors that flock here
every year. If only a fraction of them caught the magic of
Elinor's story and took what they learned home, wouldn't
that have an amazing impact? When I talked to Cerrie's class
about Elinor every single one of them was excited. They all
wanted to do something to make sure she was remembered.
If thirty excited seven-year-olds in a rural school classroom
can have that reaction, imagine what we could achieve with
countless visitors from all over the world.'

As I lay out the reasons to support this plan, I feel my
own resolve strengthening. It absolutely makes sense – and
not only because Jack and Nessie's lives will be better for
a yes to Rectory Fields.

'I suppose so. I hadn't thought of it that way.' Her scrutiny of me is discomfiting. 'Are you okay?'

'I'm fine.' I smile as easily as I can. 'Bit tired, you know.'

'Aren't we all? I'm regretting not taking a month off in
February now. Next chance I'll have for a holiday is the
week after October half-term.' She reaches up to a shelf
and hands me a silver tin. 'There you go, on the house.'

'You don't have to do that,' I say, but Sharon's having
none of it. I lift the lid. The candle is beautiful – a swirl of
sea-green, white and Cornish blue with a sprinkling of iridescent glitter set into the wax. Its scent reminds me of
summer cliff-top walks with the smell of salt and lush sea
plants. 'That's so lovely.'

'It's one of my new candles – "Desire Path" – sea breeze,

318

rain and sage. Light it whenever you need inspiration. Or just to help you relax.'

'Thank you. You're very kind.'

She puts her arm around my shoulder and gives it a squeeze. 'And you're doing a great job. You just follow your heart, Seren. Don't worry about what anyone else thinks. You have a right to vote with your heart as much as anyone else in this town.'

Does she suspect what I'm doing? The moment passes, and nothing in the rest of our conversation suggests Sharon has rumbled my plan. I make a mental note to be more careful next time . . .

Chapter Fifty-Two

Jack

The town vote is tonight. I am surprisingly nervous – and not because I'm scared we won't win. I'm worried we will.

All week, I've been sowing seeds of doubt when I've spoken to people I think might be voting for me. It's actually been quite a freeing experience. Now I know mine and Nessie's future doesn't rest on Rectory Fields, it's been fun to talk about it. I've mentioned how strong I think the Save the Parsonage campaign is, how much support I'm seeing for them. I've even not flinched when parents at the school gate have questioned Brotherson's plans for the development. A shrug and a pair of crossed fingers have spoken more in reply than any heartfelt defence I might have launched before.

Is it enough? There's no way to tell. But with each new conversation I'm more convinced I'm doing the right thing. Nessie is still obsessed with Elinor Carne and using the telescope in our back garden. She's started a 'stargazing book' and is faithfully recording her sightings every evening

– even if at the moment most of them read, 'Lots of cloud'. I plan to take her to a real observatory if I can find one in the holidays. If Seren wins and the Elinor Carne Foundation reconstructs her observatory, it will quickly become my daughter's favourite place.

I remember what Seren said about Ness last week. I'm still shocked she could see so much in my daughter during one meeting. Perhaps I should give Ness more credit. Her growing passion for stargazing has endeared her to her schoolmates, making her the least likely to be picked on for the time being. Kids are notoriously fickle, but she's won her class over for now. She's done that by herself and I'm proud of her. All I ever want for my girl is for her to be able to be herself with no fear of anyone else's opinion.

Brotherson has been making noises about his latest acquisition on a site a few miles from the parsonage, and I've been out to see it at his request. He's serious about keeping me on and that means so much. Regardless of what happens at the vote tonight, Ness and I are sorted. I like stability. I've missed it.

I arrive in St Ives an hour early and meet the caretaker opening up the Guildhall for the meeting.

'You all ready for tonight?' he asks, swinging open the old doors and securing them with a cast-iron wedge.

'I think so.'

'It's been a good battle, I reckon.' Eric Losely grins, revealing several missing teeth. 'You did good, boy. Have to say, I'm probably votin' for Seren's lot, though. No offence to you. Gotta protect our heritage, ain't we?'

'That's why it's so important the people of St Ives have

a say,' I reply, encouraged that I've witnessed one definite vote for Seren. 'You know what's best for the town.'

'A sportin' response, sir,' Eric says, offering his crinkled-skin hand for me to shake. 'Let's just hope your employer is as benevolent.'

People begin arriving twenty minutes later and I stand at the back of the hall watching the seats filling up. Nobody is going to miss this tonight. Nerves worry my stomach as I try to guess who will vote for Seren, and who will vote for me. I give up after a few minutes: it's impossible to call.

And then I see her, walking into the hall. She's looking for someone, scanning the room over the tops of heads. Man, she's beautiful. Her hair is loose this evening, a slightly wavy chestnut cascade that rests between her shoulder blades. She's wearing a sea-green tunic over dark blue jeans, a jade scarf around her neck. If Nessie saw her, she might think a mermaid had just wandered into the Guildhall.

I'm probably staring. I don't care. Until our eyes meet and she offers a shy wave.

I want her to win. I want to give her this gift. But there's nothing more I can do. What happens next is down to the crowd filling the room, washing in like a rapid tide.

All I can do now is make my closing arguments. And wait.

Chapter Fifty-Three

Seren

'You've heard from both sides of this debate, but now the future of the site is in your hands. Regardless of who wins, we are honourin' a one-hundred-and-eighty-year-old moral covenant, which entrusted Bethel Parsonage to the people of St Ives. We have been trusted as guardians of this land. Let's take that responsibility seriously. Thank you to both speakers – to Seren and to Jack – for a respectful, intelligent debate, and to all of you for comin' each week to hear the arguments.'

A wave of warm applause washes around the hall.

I watch Lou and try to stop my hands from shaking. Everything I've secretly worked for this week is about to be put on the line. I glance across at Jack, who offers me a smile. It's so different from the last look he gave me after our argument, and I wonder if the days since have given us both time to reconsider our words.

'All that remains is for me to invite our two speakers to make any closin' statements they wish to offer.'

He offers the microphone to Jack, who invites me to speak first. This is my last chance to influence the vote and I'm suddenly nervous. I haven't prepared anything but I need to say the right thing. Taking a deep breath, I start speaking and hope my heart provides the words.

'My dad believed in small beginnings leading to mighty change. This campaign began with a few local stories passed down through generations and a bundle of old journals. And now, look how many people know about Elinor Carne as a result. As a town we've achieved so much over the past six weeks. I think all I want to say now is that we have options, no matter which way the vote goes tonight. Think of the future you want to see and the people you can affect with your decision. Then vote with your heart. Thank you.'

I take my seat shakily as applause thunders around the room. I've done all I can do – now it's out of my hands.

Jack takes centre stage and the hall becomes silent.

'I know much has been said on this stage and the debate has carried out into the town, too. I'd just like to thank you all for being open to hear both sides. I'll echo what Seren said –' He glances at me. My heart jumps. 'You know what you most want to happen. This town was built on people's hopes, from fishermen to artists, builders to shopkeepers. There's a proud history of looking to the future while protecting the past. Vote for what you think is right for this site. Thanks.'

Jack takes the seat next to me as Lou rises to start the voting process and I'm surprised when he leans over, his voice low.

'Not sure I can watch this bit. Shall we await our fate outside?'

I don't even have to think about it. 'Let's go.'

Groups of volunteers are handing out ballot papers and pens to the crowd, while Lou places a large black metal box on the stage with great ceremony. Jack and I skirt around the perimeter of the Guildhall and duck out through the entrance doors. I glance at my friends, but they are all too busy to notice. Good.

My heart is hammering as we sit on the steps in front of the Guildhall. Jack gives a nervous cough and I look up to see a few stars peeking through ghostly grey clouds over us.

'Well, that was intense,' Jack says.

'It was. It *is*.' I look at the warm light spilling from the entrance across the flagstone path. 'How do you think it'll go?'

'Your guess is as good as mine. Look, Seren, I owe you an apology for what I said last time . . .'

I look back at him, noticing how the light catches the contours of his face. 'Don't. I shouldn't have said anything about your daughter.'

'Yes, you should. And I was an idiot. You were right, anyway. Ness has been holding her own at school and there haven't been any problems. I was just—'

'Scared,' I finish for him. 'I know. This whole thing is scary.'

'Tell me about it. This has been the longest and most demanding job interview of my life.'

'It's felt like that at times, hasn't it?' I breathe out slowly to calm my nerves. 'I'll be glad when it's over.'

325

'Will you? I thought this was the first step on a long journey for you?'

I feel the full force of his stare and wish I hadn't been so candid. 'It is – not just for me, but the committee too. Lou's established the Elinor Carne Foundation, so after the vote the fundraising can begin.'

'I reckon it will be easy to get people involved. Hearing you speak about your old astronomer was inspirational. If it helps, my daughter is still buzzing after your visit to her class.'

'Is she?' This makes me inexplicably happy. The experience of talking to the children was the first time I'd dared to believe that we could tell Elinor's story anywhere. Being on a windswept hilltop might add some romanticism to the story, but Elinor's struggle is impressive without it. 'That's great to hear.'

'She's relentless. Made me research Elinor Carne, and we even have a telescope set up in our back garden now.'

'Brilliant.' Cerrie will be delighted to hear that: her master plan bearing fruit. We share smiles. 'I started stargazing because of my dad. He built a little observatory in our back garden.'

'Wow – I didn't know that.'

'It's a big shed, really. With a hatch that opens in the roof. It's very rough and ready but it's where I learned to love stars.' I stop myself, the mention of stars too scarily close to what I know about Jack and Nessie and Gwithian Beach. 'Does your daughter have a star wheel?'

'A what?'

'It shows you which stars are above your head at any

time in the year. You can get one for a couple of quid or . . .' I remember the app on my phone and pull it out of my back pocket. 'Hang on, I'll show you.'

'Ah now, phone stuff I understand.'

As I launch the app, Jack shuffles along the step, so that our shoulders are almost touching. The night around us stills.

I raise my phone and tilt the screen over our heads so he can see. 'It's cloudy tonight so it would be difficult to know where the stars are in relation to us. But with this you can find out exactly where they sit in the sky. You see?'

The screen fills with constellations that pivot as I move the phone across the sky.

Beside me, Jack takes a breath. 'Wow.'

I think of sitting next to Dad holding the star wheel over our heads like this, and my growing wonder as he pointed out each of the constellations. It was the most magical discovery, like seeing my first rainbow or swirling frost patterns on windows – only better, because the stars moved through the sky instead of being fixed, so the magic renewed each time. There was always something new to see, no matter when in the year you gazed up. 'So that's the Plough, then look up from the top star on the side without the handle and that's Polaris, or the Pole Star . . . That star doesn't appear to move but the others do around it, so from there you can work out where every other constellation is. That's Orion, Taurus, Gemini, Cancer, Leo and then Virgo is over there. And that brighter star is actually Jupiter.'

I risk a look at Jack and find him much closer to me

than I expect. His features are washed blue by the light from the screen and his expression is almost identical to his daughter's when I saw her watch the star trail video. I see wonder fill his eyes and in that moment I feel completely connected to him. *Now* he understands. It's a beautiful thing to see someone experience the awe you've known all your life. I know I'm staring, but I can't help it.

Without warning, his gaze slips from the screen to meet mine and I hear his breathing stop, just for a second.

'Thank you,' he says quietly.

'What for?'

'For – *this* . . .'

And then I see him – *really* see him – not as an opponent or a secret starmaker on a beach, but for who he is and who he could be. Jack Dixon has blocked the stars and filled my vision. Reflected in the dark pools of his eyes I see myself.

And then I am falling, tumbling forward, not caring where I land . . .

Chapter Fifty-Four

Jack

'*There* you are!'

Seren pulls back sharply as I turn to see Lou Helmsworth in the doorway, arms folded, frowning at us.

'What on earth are you doin' out here?'

'We didn't want to influence the vote,' Seren calls back, the beginnings of mischief playing on her lips. 'It's up to the town to decide.'

Thank goodness one of us is thinking quickly. I'm still reeling from what we almost did . . .

Lou considers Seren's words. 'Fair enough. And you don't need anythin'? Or any company?' His feet dance on the flagstones, revealing his impatience to see what's happening in the Guildhall.

'We're fine, thanks,' Seren replies. 'You can be our eyes and ears in there, Lou.'

'Yes. Good point. Right then, I'll just be . . .' The end of his sentence is lost as he hurries back inside.

The intensity between us has passed, but I can hear

Seren's voice shake as she laughs. I'm shaken too. What-ever else I thought might happen tonight, kissing Seren MacArthur was never part of the plan. But if Lou hadn't appeared, I don't think I could have stopped myself.

We don't have long until the result of the vote is announced. If I've done what I set out to do, Seren is close to victory. And then – who knows? Maybe I'll ask her for coffee. Do people even do that nowadays? It's a long time since I asked anyone but Tash out for anything.

I can't think about that now. I just want to enjoy this time before the town decides our fate. I get the feeling Seren does too. So, carefully avoiding the subject of what just happened, we talk about anything and everything, enjoying the freedom that the end of the campaign has given us. There's still the result to come, but until then we can just be two people passing the time in the heart of St Ives.

Nearly an hour later, there's the deep rumble of an announcement from the stage and the few people from the audience who are milling about outside the Guildhall stub out their cigarettes, empty the dregs of their coffee cups and file back inside.

We stand and turn towards the open door. Seren rubs her hands together. Nerves ball up in my stomach.

'So, this is it,' she says.

'Here we are. At last. Are you nervous?'

Amusement fills her eyes. 'Terrified. You?'

'The same.'

We've worked hard to get here. I know as soon as we set foot inside the hall, everything will change. I start to follow her up the path.

'Seren – wait.'

'What is it?'

'I just wanted to say, whatever happens in there, I hope we can still be friends?' I offer my hand in a ridiculously formal gesture, instantly regretting it.

'I hope we can, too,' she smiles.

Then, instead of taking my hand, she hugs me.

It's completely unexpected and it blows me away.

As soon as it began, it ends, before I have the chance to pull her closer or say the really profound thing you're supposed to say when a beautiful woman hugs you.

Totally thrown, I trail dumbly after her into the Guild-hall.

There's a noticeable buzz in the room, all eyes on Seren and me as we make our way up onto the stage with Lou and Agatha. The ballot box has gone, with two piles of folded white paper sheets in wire baskets on the front of the stage. From my seat, it's impossible to see which is the biggest, although I think the Save the Parsonage pile might contain a shade more.

Lou thumps the microphone, adding another dent to its poor metal head. I can almost hear it breathe a sigh of relief that this is the last time it will have to endure the Lou Helmsworth treatment.

'All right, ladies and gentlemen, hush if you will. Thank you. The votes are in and we have the result. I don't know what it is, so I'll invite Nick Boleyn from the St Ives RNLI squad – our independent adjudicator – to bring the result.'

A tanned smiling beast of a man strides to the front of the stage and accepts the microphone from Lou.

This is it.

Seren is watching and I can see her holding her breath like I am. I want to offer her one last smile before we hear the result, but her attention is taken by the man with the envelope. On this stage we have become opponents again, divided by a single question:

Which proposal do you approve for the Bethel Parsonage site?
A: Save the Parsonage campaign (Elinor Carne Foundation)
B: Brotherson Developments (Rectory Fields)

'All votes have been independently counted and verified. As adjudicator I can announce that the people of St Ives vote to approve . . .'

Lou's face is bright red. The members of Seren's committee are on the edge of their seats. The only supporter I have for my side is me; and I am crossing everything for defeat.

'. . . Brotherson Developments for Rectory Fields.'

There is a pause before the hall explodes with applause.

No, no, *no* – it's all wrong! They were supposed to vote for Seren, for her father and Elinor Carne. Not Rectory Fields. I've spent so long this week trusting my gut, working on the alternatives and nudging people in Seren's direction that it has never once occurred to me what would happen if the vote went Brotherson's way.

I've won. But it feels like the worst defeat.

I can't believe it.

Instinctively, I look across to Seren and our eyes meet. She smiles but is she just hiding her own disappointment?

Lou Helmsworth takes the microphone. He looks visibly shaken – while he's been a fair and objective host for these town meetings, I know he's poured his heart and soul into winning this battle. He looks how I imagine Seren must feel, although I can't read her expression as easily as I can his.

'Ladies and gentlemen, thank you for your time and careful consideration. I think it only fair we hear from Jack Dixon as the spokesman for the winning campaign.' And suddenly, the microphone is thrust in my face and the room stills. This is supposed to be a victory speech, but I don't know what to say. It *is* good news, and I will see the plans and dreams I've had for Rectory Fields happen in real life. But I expected Seren to win.

At the back of the hall, the door opens and Bill Brotherson appears. He has the smile of a lottery winner and several people nearby are shaking his hand. Now I *have* to say something. But where do I begin?

'Um, just – thank you to everyone who voted for Rectory Fields. I want to promise you again that I will make sure the site is honoured and its history preserved for the future. I think the plans we have made will do that and I hope you are pleased with the result.'

'He's a legend!' Brotherson shouts from the back of the room, as every head turns.

I see Lou's expression darken, but he beckons my new employer to the stage. A rumble of reaction shudders through the crowd as Brotherson strolls to the front.

Now Seren's smile slips and I can't help watching her as Lou takes the microphone from me, passing it to Brotherson. There is so much I want to say, but the words stick in my throat. I wanted Nessie and me to have a secure future, and now we have one. But I didn't want that to be at Seren's expense. She has lost everything – and I'm the one who caused it. Whatever might have happened outside means nothing now. I've lost any chance I might have had of getting to know her beyond this vote.

How could I let this happen?

'Now, I know Mark MacArthur wanted to save the parsonage and many of you supported him and his daughter. Like Jack says, we heard you. Rectory Fields will be a nod to the past with one foot in the future.' He looks pleased with his soundbite. Seren looks sick at his mention of her father. Lou sees it too, taking the microphone from Brotherson a little too forcefully and closing the meeting.

As the people in the hall noisily stand, Seren smiles at me and walks over. I should have known what to say, but I feel completely embarrassed, not least by my employer's casual reference to her dad. I panic, any words I might have snatched from the ether deserting me.

She holds out her hand. 'Congratulations.'

'Thanks,' I mumble, making as quick a contact as I can. I want to hold on to her forever but this wasn't how I expected tonight to turn out. What I planned to say was that I wanted her to win, that I thought she would be a better custodian of her father's dream than Brotherson or me.

'Actually, can we have a chat somewhere? The very least I should do is buy the victor a drink. I hear from a good

334

source that Harbour Fish and Chips do a cracking late-night tea . . .'

I'm about to reply when a huge slap stings my shoulders and Bill Brotherson's head fills the space between Seren and me.

'Didn't he do well, eh?'

Seren's smile tightens. 'He did. Congratulations.'

'And, hey, sorry about your old man. I guess he'll be haunting me from now on, eh?'

Horrified, I jump in before my employer says any more. 'We should be going, actually.'

Her eyes flick to me, a crease appearing between her eyebrows. 'But I thought . . . ?'

Brotherson looks like he's gearing up for another wise-crack and I just can't let that happen. So I make a decision to get us out of there as quickly as possible. Seren's suffered enough; she doesn't need to be insulted on top of everything else. 'Yeah, sorry, we've got a lot to do, you know? Now we have the vote we need to set the wheels in motion.'

'Yeah, bring the diggers in and start demolishing the place.'

Bill Brotherson did *not* just say that. I try to push him away but Seren steps into our path.

'Hang on, I thought you were salvaging the parsonage building as part of the development?'

'We wanted to, but . . .' I begin.

'But that ruin is *knackered*, girl. Seriously. Best to rip it all out and start again.'

'Then you lied – to everyone?' I can't tell if her question

335

is directed at Brotherson or me but it feels like a slap across my face.

'We didn't, Seren. The fact is . . .'

She shakes her head, her eyes full of fury. 'Save it, Jack. I might have known you'd say anything to win the vote. Well, you did it. I hope you're happy.'

And then she's pushing past us, blazing a trail off the stage and out of the Guildhall.

And in that moment, I know I've lost her.

Chapter Fifty-Five

Seren

He lied.

Jack Dixon promised he would look after the site and honour its history. But he didn't mean a word of it. The town believed him.

Worst of all, *I* believed him.

And now what's left of Elinor's home is due to be pulled down. I've lost the place Dad cared about, and I'm about to sell the shop he loved. All his work, his passion, gone. It's all my fault.

All week, I've been working for this outcome. I've won, in a way. But as soon as Jack admitted they're demolishing Bethel Parsonage, I realised what I'd lost. I didn't win for Dad. Or Elinor. I did it for Jack Dixon, who made me believe he was a good guy. I don't know what's the biggest offence – that he chooses to align himself with an arrogant rat like Brotherson, or that he could so blatantly lie about preserving the building Dad fought so hard for. Or that I believed him.

And what about earlier? I almost kissed him. What's worse, I *wanted* to kiss him. Was that all part of his plan, too?

I can't stay in the Guildhall and I can't face the others yet. I saw Aggie's shock and Kieran and Cerrie's disbelief when the result was announced. I was supposed to lead them to victory in Dad's name. Everything I thought I wanted has been turned on its head and I've been left with nothing.

When the parsonage is demolished and MacArthur's is finally sold, what will be left to show St Ives that Mark MacArthur ever walked its streets? One initial carved into a single brick in the wall of our house isn't much of a legacy. I'll be responsible for the two things he cared most about being lost. My decisions. My mistakes.

I've turned my back on Dad. I've lost Elinor Carne's home. And for what? For a man I never really knew. I was swept along by the magic of the seaglass stars and forgot myself, believing that what I saw on Gwithian Beach was a sign of what could be possible. I don't even believe in signs!

Even though it's dark outside and my friends will be looking for me, I walk up the hill, past the station and across the road that leads to Carbis Bay. I can't stop the tears falling but the streets are empty and I don't care any more. Within ten minutes I'm at The Maidens, crossing the empty car park and walking through the long grass to the middle stone.

When I reach it, I let the full force of what I've done hit me.

I've lost everything, and for what? I thought Jack needed to win and that when he did – and when I'd told him I was the other starmaker – we might have a chance together. But my hope was as based on fantasy as these blocks of stone, no more the stuff of legend than the concrete car park or the faux-gothic house beside it. Someone's idea of a romantic story, set into the ground to fool holidaymakers. I let myself believe a fairy tale and found an empty façade instead.

Sinking down to the cool grass at the foot of the middle Maiden, I close my eyes and wish I could become stone, too.

Until I heard the result I didn't realise what it would mean to lose the parsonage. I thought I could let it go because Jack and his daughter needed the work more than I needed to remember Dad. I wasn't prepared for the reality of it.

Now it feels like losing Dad all over again.

The night we found him, he was in his favourite place in the world, doing what he loved best. He'd worked a long day at the shop and said he needed to hang out with the stars for a while. Mum and I understood – he'd been looking tired lately, but watching the night skies always seemed to re-energise him. So we had tea together and he headed outside, blanket and thermos flask in hand, with Molly's excited paws tap-dancing across the kitchen tiles beside him.

I'd promised to join them in a while, but I went to my room and ended up getting preoccupied with a seaglass bracelet I was making for Aggie's birthday. The silver wire wasn't sitting right across the seaglass pieces and I had to unwind and rewind several of them in an attempt to make the design work. When I eventually solved the problem and glanced at my watch it was almost midnight. I rose stiffly from my workbench and peered out of the attic window to see if Dad was still in the Shedservatory. The hatch window was open, so I grabbed my coat and hurried downstairs to join him.

Molly met me at the Shedservatory door, unusually alert; her blanket box bed, where she would normally snooze until Dad had finished, abandoned.

'Hey, Dad,' I called, seeing his blanket-swathed frame up on the mezzanine bench. Clarabell's pink Dralon cover was draped at his back, the beloved telescope pointing through the hatch towards the stars.

Patting Molly's head, I climbed the ladder, noticing how bright the constellations appeared through the open hatch.

I was chilly but it didn't matter: I would steal half of Dad's blanket and snuggle up beside him, just like I had always done. He would pretend to be annoyed, but his warm chuckle would rise into the night as he wrapped his arm around me.

'Sorry I'm late,' I said, reaching the edge of the bench and sliding alongside him. 'I lost track of time. Stars look amazing tonight, don't they? Give us some of your blanket . . .'

He didn't answer, his eyes trained on the night sky.

It was only when he didn't move that I realised he wasn't there.

After the shock and the emergency call, the ambulance and the defibrillator, the race to hospital and the countless anguished, urgent prayers in corridors, waiting rooms and a relatives' room with sympathetic looks and whispered conversation, we knew. The cold, stark, awful reality dawned that we were in the first minutes of our lives without him.

A heart attack, the emergency doctor said as he sat opposite us. Sudden, catastrophic – it was far too much for his body to recover from. *It's likely he knew nothing about it*, he assured us. *Take comfort from that, if you can. He wouldn't have been in pain . . .*

But I don't know that for certain, do I? Because I wasn't with him, where I should have been. I was too preoccupied with making my own dream happen.

And it's happened again, hasn't it?

I let my attention be drawn by what I thought the sea-glass stars could bring me. But I can't make that happen, any more than I could make a living from my jewellery. It was all an illusion: I've traded Dad's beautiful memory for a handful of old, shattered glass on a deserted beach.

The shop is finished. Dad's campaign is over. And Jack Dixon was no more mine than the stars in the sky.

What have I done?

Chapter Fifty-Six

Jack

'Jack Dixon, you bloody legend!'

Bill Brotherson raises the just-opened magnum of champagne to a chorus of cheers from the build team. *My* team – I can hardly believe the job is mine and the build will happen. The project team mingles with Brotherson Developments' executives, looking awkward in suits and ties with bright yellow hard hats and pristine green wellington boots.

Brotherson poses with a gleaming silver spade for the eager gaggle of photographers. The shell of Bethel Parsonage watches us and waits as my new employer breaks ground on the next chapter of its life.

I'm proud to be here and excited by the prospect of what we will build on this windswept old site, but I can't shake the memory of Seren MacArthur as she left the meeting last week. So I smile, shake hands and accept the congratulations of my colleagues – the very model of a professional project manager – but inside I'm battling doubt.

I should have gone after her. Or visited her shop next

day. I should have told her about the crack in the foundations of the parsonage, warned her that our plans were about to change, reassured her that I would save every piece of stone it was possible to salvage and build Elinor Carne's legacy into the building that rose from the ashes of her former home. I could have left a message with Lou Helmsworth, or Aggie, or the tall blond bloke I saw going into her shop. I could have walked around St Ives until I bumped into her – anything would have been better than what I've actually done. Which is none of the above. I've told myself I'm busy, that she wouldn't want to see me, but the truth is I don't know what on earth I would say to her. Several times, driving out to the Rectory Fields site, I've seen the sign to St Ives and almost changed direction. A ten-minute detour would be all it would take: park in the station car park, walk down the hill, turn left into Fore Street and carry on until I reach the courtyard. In my mind I've imagined walking that route, going into Seren's shop and refusing to leave until she listens to me.

I almost kissed her. That has to count for something.

But what would I say?

'This is so good, Stink.' Owen grins as he joins me. Nessie is giggling with her cousins, the too-big hard hats provided by Bill Brotherson slipping over their eyes. Sarah does her best to herd them close, giving me a warm smile when she sees me. 'A great job, good money . . . I knew you'd come out of this okay.'

I have, haven't I? This is what I longed for during the sleepless nights when the precariousness of our lives threatened everything. Despite my regrets over Seren MacArthur, *this* is what matters. I have a job to do. That's all I can think of for now, putting the rest of it aside.

'I'm just glad Ness and I have some security. And I think I can build something great here.'

'If Brotherson lets you.'

That remains to be seen, but I'm prepared to give him the benefit of the doubt. 'He will. There are too many people watching him on this one. Plus, he has his eye on another old building at Trevalgan so he'll want to keep the community on side.' I'm counting on the glow of positive publicity to speed Bill Brotherson through all the decisions I want him to make.

With work secured for the foreseeable future, I finally took the risk and asked Jeb about the chalet last night. We're scarily close to the main holiday season and I wanted everything in place before I begin the Rectory Fields build.

'I was sort of hopin' you'd stay on a bit,' Jeb said, surprisingly downcast. 'But I'll understand if you need somewhere better.'

'That's not why I'm asking. I thought you'd need it for the holidays. To rent out.'

He'd instantly brightened. 'What, that old place? Not likely. I've only just managed to get my TripAdvisor ratin' back up after the last person stayed in it. Figure I'm best doin' the vans for the moment. The shack's been better since you and Nessie have been there. Wenna and me have got used to you bein' around, too. So you stay as long as you like.'

It isn't forever – and as soon as I have a decent amount saved, I'll look to rent somewhere better for us. But I like the idea of Nessie having the beach on her doorstep for the summer. We've both been better for spending time on Gwithian every evening.

The only sadness is that our seaglass stars stopped being completed a few days ago. Nessie and I found our star from the previous evening exactly as we'd left it. I suppose it had to end eventually, but it was still sad to mark the end of the adventure. Nessie was understandably upset, but after a disturbed night she emerged with a typically philosophical response.

'Maybe the mermaids decided that we know what we're doing now. So we should carry on, but finish the stars ourselves. And they'll be watching, won't they, Dad?'

'I'm sure they will.'

So we've made a star every night, completing the last point ourselves. Nessie has taken to wearing the seaglass bracelet when we're making them, just in case the mermaids are watching. It's our thing now, in our new home, on the beach that has come to mean the world to both of us.

Whatever brought about the game, or whoever it was that joined us in it, I will always be grateful to those stars. They appeared when we needed magic most, something beyond where we found ourselves, something that gave us hope. They became a sign of better things ahead: everything good in our lives began when they arrived. I hope the other starmaker realises what they did for us. I hope they are happy.

Chapter Fifty-Seven

Seren

This morning I walked on Porthmeor Beach as the sun rose. For the last few days I've stayed in St Ives for my walks, visiting the lovely beaches every morning – Porthgwidden, Porthmeor, Bamaluz, Porthminster, Lambeth Walk and Harbour Beach. Each has its own character, and you can categorise locals in the town by which beach they prefer. My favourite is Porthmeor, with its dramatic surf, crops of black rocks filled with pools and the Island rising majestically from the sand; Mum's is Porthminster, wide and warm, with its beautiful view. Dad loved tiny Bamaluz and Lambeth Walk beaches, where he first took me seaglass-hunting. Molly is happy to pad her paws on any of them, if she gets the chance. Bamaluz is where we usually walk her these days, largely because dogs are allowed on it all year round. We are blessed with beaches in this beautiful part of the world, and I feel like I've neglected the gems on my doorstep in recent weeks.

I haven't been to Gwithian Beach since the vote, and I

don't know when I'll return. I didn't go there to complete the star that would have been waiting for me the morning after the vote. Part of me wanted to, just one last time, to end what was a magical adventure before I lost everything. But what would have been the point? All day, I sat in the stillness of MacArthur's and thought about Jack and Nessie heading to the beach that evening, finding the star still unfinished. I didn't want to let Nessie down, but I just couldn't carry on, knowing what I know.

I'm glad I didn't tell Jack I was his starmaker. I might have made a complete fool of myself, but that would have been an admission too far. Let him wonder who played the seaglass stars with him. It should stay magical and elusive. Tainting the game with the mess of the vote would diminish it, I think. That can be my gift to him and Nessie: a tiny mystery for a time now passed.

I still need the sea's calming presence before I start my day, even if I leave its treasure untouched in the sand. I try not to notice the seaglass when I walk, even though it calls to me. I just can't bring myself to do that yet.

Mum asked last night about the seaglass jewellery. She'd brought fresh towels to my room and noticed my workbench empty.

'You're not working on anything?'

'No.'

'But – what about your online shop?'

'I'm just taking a break, that's all.'

I think of the announcement I've posted on my Etsy shop:

347

Stargirl Gems is closing for a while.
At this point I have no plans for new designs.
Thank you for your valued custom.

My heart just isn't in it any more. I can't think of my jewellery without thinking of Dad, or Jack, or Nessie. I tried to make something the evening after the vote but my fingers turned clumsy, the seaglass dulling in my hands. It might change, when it doesn't hurt so much. I have more pressing concerns to attend to.

The sky behind the Island chapel on the hill turns a strengthening gold, sending armies of sunbeams sparkling across the sea. Facing the horizon, the chill of sea breeze in my face, I let the sunrise soothe me. Today I need the strength I find on the beach to help me.

MacArthur's is eerily still when I enter, the sound from outside deadened by the silence inside. It's as if the shop knows I'm about to abandon it. I don't know if Dad is watching, but I hope he knows why I have to do this, and why I have no choice.

I called the estate agent yesterday, after days of soul-searching. I knew before the vote, back when everything seemed like an opportunity and I thought I could easily let go. I've known for a long time that MacArthur's can't continue. We're haemorrhaging money, and if we don't act soon we might be too deep in debt to save ourselves. So I had the conversation I'd been dreading with Mum and didn't hide any of the horrors. She was shocked and upset, but I think deep down she'd expected it.

I can't save Dad's business, as I've tried so hard to do.

But I can sell it before the bank forecloses. It's the only decision I am able to make, our last bit of control in a situation that has been spiralling dangerously towards oblivion. Dad might not be remembered for being a roaring success, but at least he won't go down as someone forced out of business by a bank's decision.

The estate agent arrives at nine a.m. and I recognise him immediately. It's Nick Boleyn, the adjudicator for the St Ives vote, who is part of the volunteer crew at the local RNLI Lifeboat Station. Fitting, I think, as I pour coffee from the machine. He's become part of this story, and now he'll help me finish it.

'How are you doing, after the vote?' Nick asks.

'Well, it was a shock, obviously,' I reply, handing him a mug. 'But Lou and Aggie already have ideas of how to build on the support we received. The vote was close, so we're taking comfort from that.'

'You know, if you need ongoing financial support I'm sure my boss would swing some more your way. We were happy to help before and it would be good to make it a more permanent thing. Whatever you decide to do for Elinor Carne will be worth supporting.'

'Thanks. I appreciate that.'

Nick scans the shop as he drinks his coffee. I hope he can see potential, not the faded paintwork, splintered shelves and patches of damp. We need enough to clear Dad's debt from the sale of the shop – and until I know what price it might be able to fetch, I'm nervous it won't cover what we owe.

'Right. I'll just get on with measuring up, take some notes and see what we can do for you.'

'I suppose everyone says this, but the more you can get for the shop the better. We're in quite a lot of debt . . .'

'It's okay.' Nick has a warm, reassuring smile that stops me before I say any more. 'I understand. Trust me, Seren, this is a good thing.'

It doesn't feel good. It feels like admitting defeat.

Mum's gone to stay with a friend in Porthleven for a couple of nights and Molly's gone too, so I'm on my own again. I don't blame her – she's taken the result of the vote hard and even though she knows selling the shop is our only option, she doesn't want to be there to see the sign go up. The house is too quiet without them, which is why I headed for the beach as soon as I woke up. Aggie is coming over later and has insisted on cooking us dinner. I might persuade her to stay overnight, just so that I'm not alone.

Nick takes half an hour to survey the shop, pausing to ask questions as he takes notes on a clipboard. Although he's respectful and polite, it's hard to discuss Dad's shop in such clinical detail. I know it's necessary, but it hurts.

'So, working on what we've sold similar commercial premises for in the area, plus the current state of the shop, this is what I'm thinking we can expect to achieve.' He pulls a wad of yellow sticky notes from his jacket pocket, writes a figure, peels the note from the pad and hands it to me.

I take a breath, praying for good news.

It is good – not as much as I'd hoped, but definitely enough to cover what we owe.

'Oh, that's a relief,' I say, tears flooding my eyes unexpectedly.

Nick nods, his hand briefly brushing my shoulder. 'Tough too, though, eh? It's hard to keep in business in this town. Trust me, I know. But the good news is that there are plenty of people willing to have a go. A shop the size and age of this place might struggle to make its asking price anywhere else. I'm confident the location will sell this shop, quickly and at a good return. Now, where do you think it's best to put the For Sale sign?'

Aggie is clearly on a mission when she arrives at Mum's house that evening, insisting on sitting me down with a large glass of red wine in the kitchen while she works her magic on dinner. To be honest, I'm not hungry and haven't been for over a week, but it's so lovely to have someone fuss over me that I'm determined to eat every last mouthful of Aggie's meal.

'Bird, you've got to see this as a sign from the universe to start takin' care of yourself.'

'I don't believe in signs, Ag.'

She snorts. 'Well, I do, and it's about time you started. You've done everythin' you could, but now it's time to think of you. What do you want to do when the shop closes? Find another job? Go travellin'?' She jabs at me with her wooden spoon. 'Sit and mope around your mother's house all day lookin' like bleddy Eeyore?'

'If I'm Eeyore then you're most definitely Tigger.' The comparison makes me smile, despite my mood. 'I haven't

351

decided what I want to do yet. I'll need to start looking for a job initially, to help Mum out.'

'Well, I reckon Becca would give you more shifts, if you asked. And you know I can always find you bits to do at mine.'

'I'll bear that in mind.'

'Make sure you do. Oh, I expect you didn't hear Lou's latest news, did you?'

To be honest, I've avoided Lou since the vote. He was so invested in the campaign – and so certain we'd win – that I haven't been able to face him yet. 'No, what's happened?'

'He's got three major local companies supporting the Foundation. Two came to see him after we lost the vote, and they brought a third bloke in afterwards. I think a lot of folk assumed we'd win. When we didn't, it gave them the kick up the bum they needed to get more involved. They're helping us plan a mobile exhibition we can take to schools, clubs, town centres and so on, to spread the news.'

'That's fantastic. He must be so pleased.'

'He's over the moon, as you can imagine. And very concerned about you . . . No, bird, you need to hear it. I know you blame yourself for the vote, but it was always goin' to be the town that decided. And like you said before that meetin', we never really needed the parsonage to spread the word about Elinor Carne.'

I still believe that, even after everything else I mistaken-ly did. Cerrie's class proved that Elinor's story has the power to inspire people regardless of where it's told. Maybe the great lady herself would be amused that an exhibition dedicated to her life and work wasn't confined to the location she could never leave.

Aggie's meal is delicious, and afterwards we sprawl on the two saggy sofas in the living room. Like most of the furniture in this house, they have been here forever, but they are so comfortable and reassuring that replacing them has never been an option.

'I reckon you could do anythin' next, you know,' Aggie says, her half-full wine glass sloshing as she raises her hand. 'Be anyone. Go anywhere.'

'That's not how it works, though. We still have to find a buyer for the shop.'

'Which you will. Easy.'

'And clear Dad's debt.'

'That'll happen. With any luck, the next poor sap who buys that shop will fall in love and pay over the odds.'

I drain my glass. 'Maybe.'

'Your mum says you haven't made any jewellery. Why?' Aggie doesn't flinch when I stare at her.

'When did you speak to Mum about me?'

'Yesterday. She came into the hut for coffee. She's worried about you, Ser.'

'She doesn't need to be.'

Aggie raises an eyebrow. 'Doesn't she? Bird, it's a mistake to throw out everythin' just because stuff hasn't gone your way.'

'It's a bit more than me not getting my own way,' I reply, sitting up. I love Aggie, but I didn't ask her over for a lecture. And she doesn't know the full picture. I've told nobody about Jack or the seaglass stars, even now. It hurts too much to think about him or the thoughts I'd entertained before. 'I don't have the time or energy to try to make anything new. Until the shop sells and Dad's affairs are in order, I can't even think about it.'

'You could sell those bracelets in my hut,' my friend offers, putting her empty glass down on the old grey carpet. 'Or put flyers for them on the counter. Sharon might sell some in her shop if you ask. You can reopen your Etsy shop, we can even hunt out some craft fairs and storm 'em. You can finally put the time in to make this the business you've wanted. You *have* options, Ser. You just need to be brave enough to try them.'

I know she means well, but this feels like an attack. I'm not brave – the last time I was brave I threw away everything I cared about for someone who didn't care about me. 'Can we change the subject, please?'

Aggie has known me well enough to recognise when I've had enough. 'Your call. Anyway, we have puddin' to attend to.'

'I'm stuffed from dinner, Ag.'

'Listen, you, I never said you had a choice in this. We have ice cream and it demands an audience. You can't deny ice cream.'

So even though I doubt I'll be hungry again for a week, I let her bustle back into the kitchen. Dad's photo grins at me from the mantelpiece, catching my heart up in a well of emotion. I don't know what he would make of everything in my life, but ice cream was one of his favourite things, and he would definitely have agreed with Aggie on that.

I can't think of the future yet, I whisper to him in my mind. I need to see this season through. Maybe when it's all over I'll be able to see a way forward.

Chapter Fifty-Eight

Jack

It has been raining for ten days now and the Rectory Fields site is a quagmire. I'm huddled up in the Portakabin with the build team, waiting for the break in the clouds that forecasters have promised for today. I'll believe it when I see it. The stubborn army of thick grey clouds above us doesn't look as if it'll move any time soon.

We can't even call it a day: Brotherson Developments' schedules won't allow for delays. It took longer than we anticipated dismantling what was left of the parsonage, so the new schedules drawn up are scary. It's been a shock to the system to work on a project at this level but the challenge is as invigorating as it is terrifying. I'm just so glad to be working at last, the months of uncertainty now a fading memory. So I go over plans and shore up arrangements for material deliveries, talk over the specifics of each part of the build with my team and keep our minds as full of the development as I can.

While the weather might not be co-operating, other

areas of my life are decidedly brighter. I had worried that Rectory Fields getting the green light might cause problems for Ness at school, when St Piran's Primary had made such a stand for the opposition. But nothing's been said. One of the school gate mums told me the school is supporting a mobile exhibition about Elinor Carne that the Foundation is putting together. I wonder if Seren is part of this. It wasn't the outcome I'd hoped to see her get, but maybe in time it might be a good alternative. Nessie has made me promise to take her to see it when the exhibition starts to tour the local area. I've said yes, but I'm hoping she'll forget. Either that or I'll persuade Uncle Owen and Auntie Sarah to take her instead. I should just man up and face Seren MacArthur, but I'm still in wuss mode. I guess I'll face that hurdle when I get there.

Leaving the team to their fifth mugs of tea of the morning, I put my Brotherson Developments jacket on and brave the rain to inspect the site. Jeb mocked my new corporate clothing when he saw it, but it's a NorthFace jacket worth a good couple of hundred quid, and infinitely warmer and drier than my old yacht waterproof. I'm an employee of Brotherson Developments now; as long as everything remains on an even keel, I plan to stay so for a long time.

I've been looking at places to rent in the area, to give me an idea of what money I need to put by. I already have a bank account further from the red than it ever has been, and I've been able to buy a few bits for the chalet to make our stay there more comfortable. It means Nessie and I will be warm, well fed and secure. I never pictured myself working for Brotherson, given his fearsome reputation, but the reality is far better than I could ever have imagined.

The foundations for the development are going in and as I walk the site I can see the beginnings of Rectory Fields. We're incorporating into the design the stone bricks from two walls of the original Bethel Parsonage, which we painstakingly removed piece by piece. It's a bold decision and Bill Brotherson took some persuading, but to give him credit, he agreed. It doesn't hurt that a large part of his proposal for the development up the road at Trevalgan is based on this approach. Baby steps for the big bad developer, but I believe he'll do it.

Rain beats relentlessly down on me as I check the boundary markers and retie a length of white tape the wind has worked free. This build is going to be a triumph over the elements for sure. I wipe rainwater from my cheek where it's dripped down from my hood, and notice a small pile of stones by the edge of the foundation trench. Bending down to clear them, I spot a deep blue round of glass in the centre. It looks like it was once the base of a small bottle, its shattered edges smoothed by the elements over years. As I feel the weight of it in my hands, I suddenly think of Seren MacArthur.

It stops me in my tracks.

Is she okay, now the dust has settled? I've been so busy looking at the logistics of my new job that I haven't thought about how she might be doing, three weeks on from *that night*. I hope she's found some peace. Last Monday was May Day, the unofficial start of the holiday season in Cornwall. I hope the fresh influx of visitors has been good for her shop. Things always look bleakest in the winter and spring here; maybe the summer will bring the trade she needs to keep in business.

Does she know how much of this building we're salvaging? There have been countless reports in the local papers, as journalists are keen to keep an eye on Bill Brotherson. Has she read any of them?

When Tash died, it made local news for a week, the tragic and sudden circumstances of her death perfect for papers that usually focus on lifeboat shouts and local council cuts. I stopped reading the *Western Morning News* for a month; the free papers delivered to our house went straight in the recycling. I couldn't risk Nessie seeing her mother's photograph plastered over the news or the specific circumstances of Tash's death being revealed to her. It was hard enough explaining why her mum, who had been so vociferously and ferociously alive at breakfast that morning, wasn't coming home again. Tash had yelled at Nessie for getting felt pen on the cream carpet she'd insisted on having in the living room, and for a while Ness thought her mother had left home because she was still angry about it. As far as I know, Nessie doesn't know the full details of how Tash died – and that's good for now. If she ever asks me, I'll tell her, but I want to let her make her own memories of her mum until then.

Maybe I should go to St Ives at the weekend. I haven't taken Nessie for ice cream for a while and I know she'd love a visit to Moomaid of Zennor. I might glance up the courtyard towards Seren's shop as I pass by on Fore Street. If it looks busy, I might even risk a look in the window . . .

'Jack!'

I look back to see Ray, the splendidly bearded build team foreman, waving to me from the Portakabin door. 'Brotherson on the phone.'

I give him the thumbs up. 'On my way.' Pocketing the blue glass disc, I hurry out of the rain.

Chapter Fifty-Nine

Seren

Four people view the shop in its first week on sale. I don't know what I was expecting potential buyers to look like, but the only defining feature they all share is the exaggerated smiles and eyebrows raised too high. The photos Nick Boleyn took of MacArthur's made the space look enormous and even though the exact square footage has been listed in the property details, actually standing in it makes you realise how small it is. As I show the buyers around, I can see their smiles tightening, their questions becoming less specific, and I watch them hurry away when the viewing ends.

'It's early days,' Nick assures me when he calls to see how the latest viewing went. 'You generally get casual viewers first. Newly listed properties always catch attention.'

The bank's deadline is a fortnight away. Serious buyers need to start visiting soon – I don't want to consider what happens if they don't. A firm accepted offer would be enough to call off the bank's bloodhounds. I'm not about to give John Trevelyan and his beak-featured small business manager the pleasure of foreclosing on our loans. There *has* to be someone who will see the potential of this space. Dad did; he can't be the only one.

Completely unexpectedly, Mum has found herself a job. I didn't even know she was looking, so it was a huge surprise yesterday evening when she announced it. I was grooming Molly after her unscheduled bath on the kitchen floor, wishing I hadn't taken her on Bamaluz straight after work where she'd found a large pile of stinking seaweed to roll in, when Mum calmly told me.

'So, I have a full-time job.'

'What? When did this happen?'

She shrugged, unable to hide her delight. 'This morning. I met Sam and Mary Lyons from my drama group for breakfast at Porthmeor Beach Cafe and I told them the shop's for sale. We got talking and I said I was thinking of finding a job, with our finances being what they are. Anyway, it turns out Mary is looking for supply teachers, especially in Art and English. So I mentioned my English MA and that I used to teach Art before I had you. They've signed me up!'

'That's brilliant, well done!'

'I have to do a refresher course and have all the checks and so on, but St Ives School in Carbis Bay needs an Art teacher to cover maternity leave from September. Looks like it's going to be me!'

I hugged her, immeasurably proud of her bravery for getting back out into the world so soon after losing Dad. 'And this is what you want to do?'

'It is. Your dad was such an old fuddy-duddy about not wanting me to work. He thought he should support both of us so that I could paint and sell my work in the shop. It never really worked out the way we'd hoped, but I loved him for trying to facilitate my dream. Since he died I've been feeling itchy, like I want to do something with my life. This is the perfect opportunity.'

The brass bell above the shop door rings out as a young woman walks in, an older man following in her wake. She can't be more than twenty-one, but she has the confident air of someone much older.

'Miss MacArthur? I'm Mhairi Peters, here to look at the shop?'

I rise to shake her hand. 'Welcome. Can I get you a coffee before we start?'

'I won't, but Dad probably will.' She shares a knowing grin with the older man and my heart contracts.

'Notice she doesn't introduce me,' he laughs, offering his hand. 'Luke Peters, silent partner and not-so-secret moneybags.'

Mhairi glares at her father and I remember countless conversations where Dad embarrassed me. I miss that strange mix of frustration and fun you feel as a kid when your parent makes you cringe. 'Dad's going to fund my business for the first five years. That's the plan.'

'What business are you looking to start?'

She beams and it's the kind of smile Dad always wore whenever anyone asked him about MacArthur's. 'A boutique. I design and make my own line of dresses, hats and bags. It's only small, but I have big plans.'

Mhairi and Luke are noticeably different from the previous viewers, from their questions about the premises to their willingness to discuss both pros and cons of running a business here. I can't afford to like anyone who can't buy the shop, but I really like these two. They leave over an hour later and I'm left feeling hopeful that even if they aren't the eventual buyers, they represent the kind of people Nick promised would view the shop.

At Becca's Bar that evening, I bite the bullet and ask Becca for more shifts. I'm inspired by Mum's example and cheered by the viewing today – and while I haven't yet considered what the future might hold for me, lining up work for after the shop sells is a good place to start.

'Thought you'd never ask,' Becca grins, her new ruby-set front tooth catching light from the festoon of fairy lights looped over the bar canopy. 'You tell me how many nights you'd like to do, and then we can add day shifts when the shop sells. Sound all right?'

'Sounds great. Thank you.'

'My pleasure, bird. You're the best worker I have – and the others think the world of you. I'd be nuts not to use you more.'

Aggie and Kieran meet me on the back steps of the bar when my shift ends and we walk down the narrow alley to Harbour Beach. The tide is in, but a narrow sliver of sand is still accessible, so we head down the slipway opposite the Italian restaurant and carefully step over mooring ropes until we find a place to sit.

'Haven't done this in a while,' Aggie says, cranking the

metal caps off three cider bottles and handing them out. 'Remember our last week of school when we came down here and Kieran got off his tits on Jägermeister?'

Even in the low light reflected from the town across the harbour, I can see Kieran turn green. 'Ugh, don't remind me. How come so many of our memories involve me getting smashed and chucking my guts up?'

'Oh, I don't know, maybe because you're a lightweight?' I say. Aggie and I giggle.

'Oh cheers, Seren MacArthur! That'll teach me to feel sorry for you.'

Aggie nudges me with her elbow. 'Good to have you back, babe. You always had the best one-line comebacks.'

It feels good to be laughing again, and I wonder if the shop selling might be key to finding myself again. Like it is for Mum.

I look at my friends, who have been by my side most of my life, and decide to start as I mean to go on. 'Talking of me being myself again, I want a word with you two.'

Their smiles vanish in sync, but I won't stop now. It's all very well them lecturing me about my life, but they've been failing to address the huge issue between them for weeks. Even though it's the most obvious thing.

'When are you going to just admit you're in love?'

Kieran swears and drops his brow. Aggie stares at me. 'Seren!'

'No, I've had enough of being the middlewoman between you two. So you got together and it was unexpected, but it was also wonderful and you both realised – at last – how you feel about each other. So what? Why let it scare you away from making the best decision of your lives?'

'You don't understand . . .'

I fold my arms and stare them down. 'I do. Because I've heard from both of you how frustrated you are with each other, how neither of you wants to say anything but you wish the other would. So, here we are on a beautiful night in a beautiful town. Say it.'

They look at me, then at each other. Nobody speaks, the sounds of St Ives filling the gaps where the words should be.

'*Say* it!'

In that moment, I'm furious with them. I jab my cider bottle in the sand and stand up.

'You know what? Do what you want. I'm going home.'

'Seren, sit down. You can't force us to do this . . .' Kieran begins but I've heard enough.

'Not everybody gets the chance to find happiness with someone else. Some people wait a lifetime to meet the right person. Some put their faith in someone only to realise it could never work. You have the chance of love – real love – the kind that everyone else is looking for. Are you going to let that go, just because you're too stubborn to admit it?'

'It isn't your job to sort us out, Ser.'

'Maybe not. Do what you want – but leave me out of the constant agonising over each other, okay? I have more important things to worry about than your stupid pride.'

I regret it as soon as I get home and hurry out to the Shedservatory, not even checking to see if Mum is still up first. Molly is already waiting by the back door, so she comes too. I don't mind her company – she's unlikely to demand an explanation for my mood or expect anything other than treats, so that's fine by me.

I shouldn't have yelled at Kieran and Aggie. And even though this thing between them has been going on far too long, it wasn't my place to tell them to sort it out. They are my best friends. Whatever lies in wait for me in the future, I'm going to need their love and support, no matter what.

I'm such an idiot.

I push open the hatch windows and stare up at the stars, barely visible through the passing veils of dark clouds. Dad's blanket is warm around my shoulders and I know he would have called out the real reason for my outburst as soon as I'd told him about it. I wasn't really shouting at my friends about their almost-relationship. This wasn't ever about Kieran and Aggie.

It was all Jack.

The truth is, I keep thinking about him. Most of what he did was to win the vote, I'm convinced. But that moment on the Guildhall steps as we waited for the vote; was any of that real? It may have only lasted a few seconds, but I can't shake the memory of us moving towards each other, or the feeling of being suddenly certain of him . . .

I'm furious with Jack Dixon. But more than that, I'm furious with myself. I didn't tell him about the seaglass stars, or seek him out after the vote. I was hurt and angry, too blinded by my own loss and fear to even give him an opportunity to speak. I'm still not sure how I feel. But he won't leave my head, and I have no way of going back to that night to discover the possibilities if I'd talked to him.

People keep telling me I have to decide what I want for my life, now that the shop is closing. I have no idea what waits for me when I hand over the keys. One thing's for certain – if I'm ever in a situation like I was with Jack Dixon again, I won't make the same mistake.

'I wish I knew what to do,' I whisper into the indigo night, hoping Dad is somewhere out there, listening.

From the floor below me, Molly whimpers in her sleep.

Chapter Sixty

Jack

'Dad, why are you nervous?'

I look down at my daughter as we queue by the cash-point. 'I'm not nervous.'

'You *so* are. You only ever jiggle your keys like that when you're nervous.'

As soon as she says it I'm aware of the telltale sound of shaking car keys in my hand. I shove them in my pocket. Since when did Nessie become so observant? 'There. Happy?'

She shakes her head. 'Now you're tapping your foot. You do that when you're nervous, too.'

'Okay, thank you for noticing.' The queue moves forward and we follow it. 'I'm fine. It's a lovely day, we're going to have a nice walk and an ice cream at the Moomaid, and then we'll walk over to Porthmeor Beach and make sand-castles. Nothing to be nervous about whatsoever.'

'There's your squeaky voice.'

'My voice doesn't squeak.'

'It does when you're nervous.'

'Ness, can we drop this?'

I have no need to be nervous. But my insides have been like funfair waltzers since I woke. St Ives is busy today, with noticeably more people than the last time I was here. Weekends are a mix of locals and holidaymakers and this time of year, still early in the main season, it's comfortably busy with a laid-back vibe. Which is even more reason for me *not* to be nervous.

Except that I'm not just here for the ice cream and the atmosphere. I'm going to talk to Seren MacArthur.

I've thought it through, and I have to try to make amends. Nessie will probably be overjoyed to see her, as she hasn't stopped talking about 'Ellie's friend the nice lady' since Seren's visit to St Piran's. Maybe the sight of my daughter will stop Seren slamming the door in my face.

What am I going to say to her? I have no idea. I tried rehearsing potential speeches last night after Ness had gone to bed, but they all sounded crass and insincere. Best to trust my instincts, such as they are, and just go with the flow.

That's *if* she talks to me.

Bill Brotherson hasn't offered any more gossip about Seren's business, which I'd hoped he might. Satisfied by his victory, he's forgotten she exists. I can't approach Lou Helmsworth or try to contact her friends because they'll likely tell me where to go. So trying to talk to her is my only option. I have to give it a go. She's taken up residence in my head; that won't change until I see her again.

'Can we look in the bookshop?' Nessie asks as I collect my money from the cashpoint and we cross the street.

370

'Of course we can, noodle.'

'*You're* the noodle.'

We walk along Market Place and reach the junction with Fore Street. Nessie races ahead into the bookshop. I stop and watch people walking along the street, knowing that at the other end of it is the courtyard and the conversation I've been thinking about for a long time. Will I say the right thing? And what *is* the right thing anyway?

I can't say I'm sorry about the vote going our way, even though I wanted it to be different. Weeks on from the vote, I've fallen in love with the site and the challenge of building something special there. It's given me financial stability and professional recognition – more than that, it's made me believe anything is possible for my building skills. I had lost sight of that belief long before Tash died. I'm no longer apologising for my job, like I did so often when my wife was alive. It was never enough; she saw building work as a lack of ambition and in the end I stopped trying to persuade her otherwise. Having the St Ives community's backing and Brotherson's apparent faith in me has helped me change that. However bad I feel about Seren, I can't say I wish it hadn't happened.

But what I want her to know is how important her friendship was to me, during the campaign. I appreciate what she shared with me when she didn't have to, and I found her inspiring. And beautiful. And so much stronger than she thinks she is . . .

My life, this is really happening, isn't it?

Nessie spends almost forty-five minutes in St Ives Bookseller, which is no mean feat considering the compact nature of the shop. It's a treasure trove for her and I don't try to chivvy her to make a decision. Several times I have to back out onto the street to allow more people to go in, and each time I do I think I almost catch sight of Seren in the early May Saturday crowds.

I'm losing the plot. Why did I even think this was a good idea?

My daughter emerges from the bookshop with three new books, a smile as wide as St Ives Bay illuminating her face. Grandad Dave gave her money to spend today and she's invested it wisely. Tash wouldn't have approved. Her idea of bookshelves was as minimalist display areas for strange bits of ceramics and glass. No books. But Nessie loves books and so do I. When we have a place of our own, I think, we'll have bookshelves everywhere. If I ask Jeb, I reckon I can probably put up some shelves in the chalet for the time being. I make a mental note to seek out books to display wherever possible.

'Where now, Dad?'

'Let's just walk along this street and see what takes your fancy.'

We buy fudge for Dad at the Cornish fudge shop and some beautiful yellow courgettes at the deli. Nessie giggles while trying on waterproof jackets far too big for her in the outdoor shop and insists we stop at the Baptist church to buy homemade cakes from their Spring Fayre. I appreciate every stop that puts time between now and reaching Seren's shop, but eventually we're out of reasons to delay our progress along Fore Street. I can see the Poppy Treffry shop, James King Jewellery and the crazy shop that sells everything from postcards to watches and pocket knives – and beyond that, the entrance to the courtyard.

'What's up here?' Nessie asks, when I slow a little. 'Can we see?'

This is it.

'Sure.' I watch my daughter race beneath the archway and stop abruptly by MacArthur's. I follow, steeling myself for what's to come.

Just speak from your heart, Jack. The words will come. I hope they do. I've thought about it enough this week. I just hope she listens . . .

'Oh.'

Nessie's smile has gone and she is looking above the shop. 'That's a shame.'

I follow her pointing finger and see it.

A SOLD sign.

Spotlights light the single display window, but the sign on the door confirms the shop is closed.

I'm too late. I can't believe it.

Brotherson was right: Seren MacArthur's business has folded, and I've missed my chance to speak to her. Again.

'Never mind,' I say, the heavy thud of disappointment landing on my shoulders. 'Come on.'

'Ice cream?' Nessie asks, brightening immediately.

I manage a smile. 'Absolutely.'

We walk down the rest of the cobbled street, Nessie babbling about the ice cream flavours she wants to try today. I feel like a complete failure. Part of me hopes we might bump into Seren anyway – St Ives is a small town and it's where she lives, so it's possible, right?

Deep down, though, I know I've lost my last opportunity to talk to her.

Nice one, Jack.

We climb the grey stone steps to Moomaid of Zennor's tiny ice cream parlour and score a table by the window, despite the queue leading out of the door. Good things are happening, I remind myself, watching Nessie's utter joy at being in her favourite cafe, the delicious scent of sweet ice cream and smoky coffee filling my lungs. Two months ago I couldn't have justified spending money on anything but the bare essentials; being here with Ness now represents just how far I've come. I made this happen. I *have* to be happy with that.

I just wish I felt more like celebrating.

Chapter Sixty-One

Seren

The sign went up today. And even though it means Mum and I can pay off our loans and maybe even have some money left over, after the generous offer we've accepted from Mhairi Peters and her father, I couldn't stand to watch the banner across the estate agents' board being changed.

SOLD.

It feels so final.

I told Nick Boleyn I wasn't opening today. He understood. They wouldn't need me to open up anyway; the sign over the shop can be changed whether I'm there or not. It seems his faith in the location of the shop paid off, which is a good thing. But it's strange to think that in a few weeks' time Dad's gallery will be a clothing boutique.

Not wanting to be anywhere near MacArthur's, I called Aggie. I was worried that she wouldn't want to see me, but she immediately invited me over to the coffee hut. I'm glad she's still talking to me after the night on the beach.

All the same, I've brought flowers and a bottle of her favourite beer as a peace offering.

As soon as I arrive she receives the gifts with a smile and bats away my apology.

'Don't mention it, okay? It's done and forgotten.'

'All the same, I'm sorry, Ag.'

She shrugs. 'You just care about us. I appreciate that. You've an odd way of showin' it, mind. Anyway, turns out you were right.'

I look up from the large cappuccino she's just made me. 'How do you mean?'

Her huge smile breaks like surf over rocks. 'Me and Kieran. We're officially a *Thing*.'

'No! When?'

'After you left. We were proper angry with you, but when we'd calmed down Kieran said you had a point. So we told each other how we really felt and – you can probably guess the rest.'

'That's amazing!' I grab her across the counter for a hug.

'Get off, woman! Seriously, though, you did okay.'

'Just be happy. That's all I want for the pair of you.'

'No idea what'll happen, but it's started well.' She giggles and leans towards me so the regulars at the counter can't hear. 'Left him sleepin' happily in my room this mornin', actually.'

I love this news, more than I could ever express to Aggie. More than the actual fact of them finally being together, I love knowing good things are happening to my dearest friends. It gives me hope.

'So, the big red sign is up, then?' Aggie gives me a sympathetic smile and squeezes my hand.

'It will be by now. I probably should have been there . . .'

'No need, Ser. You don't have to see that happening. It's tough, even though it's what you want.'

My emotions are difficult to pin down today – a mix of relief, defeat, resignation and a smattering of hope. 'I'm staying closed till Monday. And Garvey's covering my shift at Becca's tonight. I just need some time . . .'

'Yes, you do. Been sayin' that for a while. Do you have any plans for the weekend?'

'Not really.'

'Right. Beers at mine, yeah? I'll get Cerrie to come over, too. Kieran will already be there, of course,' she grins again. '*Recoverin'* . . .'

I spend the rest of the day walking along the coast path, across beaches and up over cliffs, with the breeze in my lungs and the tingle of salt on my skin. The weight of responsibility I've carried for months drifts away and I focus on just *being*. The power of the sea and the heart-stopping majesty of the landscape are all I need: where I've come from and who I am. I could be anywhere in the world in a year's time, but I hope I'll still be in Cornwall. This is where I feel most free: and I can't believe I've lost sight of it with everything I tried to carry in Dad's name.

No, wait . . . I didn't completely lose sight of it. Before the night of the vote there was one place I knew I could reconnect with that feeling . . .

On the top of the cliffs I look back towards St Ives, far in the distance, and let my eyes trace the sweep of St Ives Bay to Godrevy Lighthouse – so small I can only just make out its white outline rising from the small, rocky island in the perfect blue sea.

I found my freedom again at Gwithian Beach as the lighthouse looked on. I thought it had died when Dad passed away, but it was there waiting: the everyday magic Dad always promised me I'd find.

Magic is everywhere, Seren, if you look hard enough for it. Life is extraordinary, if you let it be . . .

Even though he'll never know it, Jack Dixon and his daughter *were* my everyday magic.

Is he still going to Gwithian Beach? Has he forgotten the other starmaker?

If only I had told him . . .

My heart plummets like a diving seabird as the beach I loved seems to stretch further away in the distance. Until I knew Jack was making the stars, I was happy. Why should knowing have made such a difference?

It's still playing on my mind when I arrive at Aggie's that evening. My walk home wasn't easy; the closer I got to my hometown, the larger the loss loomed. Loss of the shop, loss of my dream, loss of the seaglass stars and the freedom I'd rediscovered making them. But I don't want to think about it tonight. I am so *done* with thinking. My whole life has been picked apart, prodded and studied in a petri dish. Tonight, I don't want to think about anything.

'Steady on, Ser,' Aggie says, as I drain my second bottle

and reach for a third. 'You don't normally leave me for dust in the drinking department.'

'I'm fine,' I reassure her, but I'm not numb enough yet. I haven't been drunk for over a year, but I reckon today counts as extraordinary circumstances. I watch my friends relax around the lounge – Kieran daring to snuggle on the sofa with his now-official girlfriend, and the grins he and Aggie keep getting from Cerrie, who is curled up on an oversized beanbag that only she is able to make look comfortable. I sink into the old wing-backed armchair, hugging a cushion like a shield in front of me.

In this room, gathered as we are, it's as if the years melt away and we are teenagers again. Back before I realised that real life isn't made of the wildly fanciful assumptions you entertain when you're young; that bad stuff can happen which blasts your dreams off-course; and that the people you love don't last forever. In this moment, we are as we were then. I close my eyes and relax into it, their conversation washing over me like a summer wave. Here I can relax and be myself, without worrying about anyone or anything else.

But the illusion doesn't last. I can't relax – and beer isn't helping, either. Blood courses through my veins at a hundred miles an hour, like a shot of adrenalin without the thrill. It could be stress: I've noticed buzzing in my ears at night and recall it being a symptom. Being within it makes me feel as if I'm standing on sand that's receding with the tide, my foundations shaken and everything I know being pulled from under me . . .

'Seren? Lovely, are you all right?'

I blink as Cerrie's face fills my view. She pushes hair from my forehead, concern etched into her expression. And the compassion and gentleness hits a switch within me. Suddenly I'm sobbing and I can't stop.

They are all around me now. Cerrie and Kieran and Aggie, merging together through my tears, their soothing words becoming a warm flood of noise surrounding my head.

'Just let it out, girl . . .' 'Shh, now . . .' 'This has been comin' on a while, hasn't it?' . . . 'Breathe, lovely, it's okay . . .' 'Oh Seren, you poor thing . . .'

'I'm sorry—' I manage, my apology sharp-edged against the softness of their voices.

'You don't need to apologise . . .'

'Shh, bird.'

'No,' I insist, needing them to understand. 'It's important . . . I've ruined everything. I didn't *say* . . .'

'You haven't ruined anything. You faced an impossible task.'

'Cerrie's right, Ser. Nobody could've done more than you.'

I shake my head, the pain gripping my stomach and all comfort from the alcohol gone. 'Not the shop. Not the campaign. *Jack* . . .'

I've said too much: I realise it straight away. But his name is out there and the rest follows like a rollercoaster behind it.

'Jack who?'

'*Jack* . . . My Jack . . . Jack with the stars and the kiss and . . . and . . .'

380

'Oh my life, I think she's talkin' about Jack *Dixon*.'

'No, not that Jack . . .' Kieran shakes his head and turns to me, but his confidence fades the moment our eyes meet. I can't hide this any more. I have to tell someone about the stars and the seaglass, about Gwithian Beach and the mermaids, the bracelet Nessie Dixon loves so much and the tiny driftwood house I can't bear to throw away . . . So I tell them everything. The words crash their way out of me; I couldn't halt them even if I tried. I've carried this secret for too long; it's burning inside me like acid and I need to let it go. If I'm ever going to move on from this, I have to talk about it with the people who love me most. They listen, and although I can't tell what they're thinking, I'm vaguely aware of them exchanging glances. I should be mortified admitting all of this, but I'm just relieved to finally talk about it.

'And he kissed you?'

'No. Almost. I don't really know. I should have told him about the stars . . .'

Aggie squeezes my arm. 'Perhaps it's better you didn't. I don't think he could have made you happy, Ser . . .'

'No! Don't say that!'

'I'm only sayin' – that man was our opposition. And pleasin' to the eye though he might have been, he was still a Brotherson pawn. And he got the result he wanted, didn't he?'

It's time to be honest about the result. 'I might have helped him.'

My friends stare at me – and immediately I'm ashamed. They worked so hard for the campaign, daring to believe that we could win. But the person who should have been leading the charge was working against them.

'Please don't hate me,' I sob, the last of my strength ebbing away. I'm dog-tired, exhausted from carrying this on my own along with everything else.

'We don't hate you . . .' Kieran says. But he isn't smiling. 'Why would you do that?'

'I thought Jack needed it more. I'd met his little girl and I realised he wasn't working for Brotherson for his own greed; he was doing it for her.'

'Just like you always say your dad did for you – working extra jobs to get you what you needed, making ends meet even when the business was in trouble . . .' Cerrie says – and there it is. I saw the qualities I loved about Dad in Jack. It's a classic case of seeing what I wanted to see.

'I can't believe you'd do that, Ser. What were you thinkin'?'

'I thought I was doing the right thing . . . That's all I've ever tried to do . . . But I've hurt you and I've screwed it all up. I hate myself . . .'

Aggie's frown disappears. 'You had your reasons. That site would've bankrupted us all in the long run – that much we learned from the town debate. We always knew it was a tall order to save it. Even your dad, bless 'im, who believed a wing and a prayer could make anythin' happen. No, love, don't try to say any more. Close your eyes now. We all love you, daft beggar, so you just try to get some rest now.'

Cerrie makes strong coffee while Kieran and Aggie settle me on the sofa. Within minutes I'm asleep.

It's twelve hours before I wake again. My hangover is threatening to crush my head, but I feel a little lighter for confessing to my friends about Jack. My cheeks hurt from where the salt marks have dried and it will be a very long time before I consume that much alcohol again.

But as I stumble into the kitchen in search of tea and toast, bright May sunshine bursts in through the window. I'm dazzled for a moment, the shock of the light making my eye sockets throb. But I'm warmed by it, and underneath the pain I feel hopeful.

Last night hurt, but it was necessary. I've faced everything that was holding me back, all the secrets I've been carrying for weeks that bound my heart and chained my feet – and I've emerged into a new day.

From now on, I promise myself, *I'm going to seek my own magic.*

I don't need anyone else to conjure magic for me. I'm going to throw myself into the uncertain future and believe that life is extraordinary if I dare to let it be.

Just like Dad told me.

Chapter Sixty-Two

Jack

I've been trying to think of a way I can encourage the great community support we've enjoyed for Rectory Fields to keep going. The build is a quarter complete and pretty soon the old resentments towards Bill Brotherson will resurface, especially as he's just secured the old buildings in nearby Trevalgan village for his next project and is rumoured to have earmarked a third site already. Doing something that involves people in the building's construction will give them a tangible link to the past – and demonstrate Brotherson Developments' new ethical responsibility policy in action.

When St Ives voted in our favour, I was concerned that Nessie might be bullied for her link to me. But it appears my fears were unfounded. Nessie hasn't told me of any problems, which is encouraging. Certainly she talks of her entire class as her best friends these days. So when her teacher calls and asks to meet me urgently, alarm bells ring. When she suggests meeting on a Saturday morning in a beachfront cafe, I'm downright confused.

With Nessie happily on her way to the farm with Uncle Owen and her cousins, I drive a couple of miles along the coast to Hayle Towans beach – part of the long stretch of golden sand that reaches around St Ives Bay to Gwithian and Godrevy. It's a glorious day, the sunlight so bright it causes a haze over everything, like you are viewing it all through fine gauze. Summer isn't far away and the season has begun in earnest – there is a sense of expectation in the air and everyone is looking forward to longer days and brighter times ahead.

I won't let anyone spoil it. Not when Nessie and I are doing so well.

Miss Austin is waiting for me when I arrive, an already half-drunk mug of hot chocolate in front of her. From the cafe windows I can see the sweep of Hayle Towans beach below and an army of surfers making the most of the huge waves rolling in. I order a strong coffee to steady my nerves and do my best to look nonchalant about it. Teachers can smell your fear, I think. If she's here to challenge my daughter, or my parenting style, I don't want her thinking she has an instant advantage.

'Thanks for meeting me,' she says, shaking my hand. 'I'm sorry it was late notice.'

'And out of school.'

Her smile fades a little. 'I thought it might be best . . . Is Nessie with you?'

'She's with my brother and his family today. I didn't think she was invited.' Realising I sound far too defensive, I rein myself in. Time to hit her with the idea I've had for Rectory Fields. Driving here I decided to strike first, show willing and support for the school and hopefully diffuse any tension before it's allowed to manifest. 'Actually, I'm glad you wanted to meet. I have an idea I'd like to run past you, if you don't mind?'

'Yes – erm – fine.'

Good, she wasn't expecting that. Round one, Jack Dixon . . .

'Given the school's support of the Elinor Carne Foundation, I've been thinking of ways we could translate that to the site,' I say, watching Nessie's teacher carefully. Things are okay at the moment, but like I said to Bill Brotherson when he visited the site last week, we need to be seen to be considering the local community, even if ultimately they won't benefit from our building. 'We could create a lasting reminder of Bethel Parsonage's past. I was thinking perhaps the school could create a mural to go on the entrance wall? It would be along the lines of the tile mural on the shelter on Smeaton's Pier in St Ives. Have you seen it?'

'Yes, I know it well.'

'We could use a whole-school design, so that all the children feel involved. Each class could design a row of a picture, which Brotherson Developments will then have made into tiles. The kids can decide what they want the picture to include – maybe scenes from Elinor Carne's life, or the stars she studied.'

'It's good. I like that idea.'

'Could you put it to the head and the staff, to see if they think it's achievable? The turnaround would have to be pretty quick, though. We anticipate the build completing in six to eight weeks' time.'

Miss Austin agrees again and is certainly making the right noises. But she seems preoccupied and I can't work out what I'm missing.

'Of course, if you think it isn't workable . . .'

'Oh, it will be,' she says quickly. 'It's just . . . Look, Mr Dixon – can I call you Jack?'

'Um, sure . . .'

She takes a breath. Is she nervous? 'Okay – Jack – I'm Cerrie, by the way.'

'Hi, Cerrie.'

'Hi. Jack, I didn't come here to talk about Rectory Fields. Or Nessie.'

The clink of coffee cups and hiss of steaming milk fill the space where my response should be. Is this an official visit or not? And if not, then why on earth are we here? 'You didn't?'

'No. Although I really like your mural idea and I'm sure the school will do you proud.' She spreads her hands on the red-and-white polka-dot tablecloth and I notice her nails have been painted in alternating rainbow colours – red, yellow, green, blue, violet, from thumb to little finger. Nessie's mentioned Miss Austin's brightly coloured nails many times before – she longs to be let loose with nail varnish and I know it won't be long before she's doing her own. 'I'm sorry if I gave you the impression this was an official meeting. I just didn't know how else to get to talk to you.'

'Miss Austin – Cerrie – why are we here?'

She gives an apologetic smile. 'Forgive me. In my head

this was a lot more straightforward than it's turning out. Tom said this was a bad idea.'

Now I'm completely lost. 'Tom?'

'My boyfriend. It doesn't matter. The thing is, I'm here on personal business.'

'Oh?'

'It's about the stars.'

'Which stars?'

'On the beach. The seaglass stars you've been making with Nessie. And the bracelet you found there that she brought into school . . .'

I'm not sure which revelation to react to first. How on earth Nessie's teacher knows about the seaglass stars is mystery enough, but did Ness really take the mermaids' bracelet to school when I'd told her not to? 'She brought the bracelet in? When?'

'A few weeks ago. The day Seren MacArthur visited, actually.'

That explains Nessie's suspicious behaviour when I picked her up from school and the thing she'd shoved in her pocket in the playground that afternoon. But what do that and the beach stars have to do with Cerrie Austin?

Unless . . . Oh *man*, this could be awkward . . .

'Wait – was it you? Did you finish the stars for us?'

Horror drains her face chalk white. 'Me? Oh goodness no, it wasn't me.'

I'm embarrassed by how relieved I am about this. Miss Austin seems lovely, but I can't picture her as our star-maker. Besides, she has a boyfriend. Not that it's important. My head hurts. I'm tired and uneasy about where the discussion might be going next. 'Then how do you know about it?'

'I know who finished the stars. And who made the bracelet Nessie brought into school.'

'Who was it?'

'Seren MacArthur.'

I know my mouth has dropped open but I can't do anything about it. 'Seren made the stars?'

'Yes. And she'll kill me for telling you, but I think you need to know.'

Seren finished the stars. She made the stunning bracelet Nessie treasures and she helped set us on course for all the good things that have happened. She is the missing piece in the mystery, the kind soul who made my daughter believe in magic again. But I took away everything she ever cared about . . .

'Are you all right, Jack?'

'Just give me a minute. It's a bit of a shock.'

'I thought it might be.' She waits and watches me, her rainbow-tipped fingers fidgeting on the tablecloth. Her voice is lower, softer when she speaks again. 'I wasn't going to say anything because Seren is my dear friend and she's been doing so much better now the shop is sold. But she told us – me – last night and she was so upset that she never got to tell you.'

'Does she know she was making the stars with me and Ness?'

'She worked it out when I showed her the bracelet Nessie had brought into school. And then she went to the beach and saw the two of you down there. We didn't know anything about it until she confessed it all yesterday. I think she was going to tell you after the vote, but—'

'But I was an idiot when I won. I was trying to protect her from my employer but I stuffed it up. I think I hurt her.'

Cerrie bows her head.

'I don't think she's over you, Jack.'

'What?'

'The way she talked last night – I think she'd started to fall for you before the vote. She admitted she'd spent the last week of the campaign trying to swing the vote your way. I know – it goes against everything she said she believed in. But that's what she told us.' She looks directly at me. 'I don't think she would have done that for you – for Nessie, too – risking losing her friends in the event, if she didn't care about you.'

'Wow.'

'I'm glad you were sitting down when I told you.'

'Me too.' My world has shifted on its axis, all the certainties I'd accepted now turned on their heads. What am I supposed to believe now? 'What made you decide to tell me?'

She blushes a little and picks at a cake crumb on the tablecloth with a rainbow nail. 'I feel bad about ambushing Nessie. I invited Seren to speak to my class because I thought the kids would love Elinor Carne's story – but I also knew Nessie was your daughter, and I thought she might persuade you to give up the parsonage job. I'm sorry, Jack. I got caught up in the campaign and it was only afterwards that I realised what a position I'd potentially put Nessie in. And how unprofessional of me it was. Not to mention unethical.'

'It could have caused major problems. She's already had to defend herself in school over unkind comments about her mum.'

'I know. Nessie deserved better. I'm so sorry.'

Given everything else I've learned in this tiny cafe with its view of the sea, I'm not going to make an issue of Cerrie's mistake. 'I appreciate your honesty, thank you. It's been a crazy time. That debate swept everyone up in it.'

'It did. But out of all of us I think Seren was thinking the clearest. She really liked you, Jack.'

I stare at her. 'I don't know what to do with this.'

'Do you feel the same way?' She shakes her head. 'No, sorry, you don't have to answer that. It's none of my business. I just thought you should know what she did for you and why. What you choose to do with that is totally up to you.'

'I don't think she'll ever speak to me again.' I'm surprised by the words sounding in front of me, but I realise I need to talk about this. Cerrie Austin is the very last person I'd expect to say it to, but I need to work out what to do, and my mind is blank. 'When the vote result was announced she came to congratulate me, but I was too busy feeling guilty about her losing. I just dismissed her, and when she left she looked like she hated me. I didn't want that to happen. I –' I stop myself; but why conceal anything now? 'Okay, here's the truth: I spent the last week of campaigning trying to throw the job. I wanted Seren to win because I could see what it meant to her.'

Cerrie's eyes become as wide as Nessie's when she's trying to persuade me to agree to a treat she wants. 'No way! That's incredible. Look, I can't tell you what to do, or even if you should do anything at all, but you *know* now. Seren is a remarkable woman. I'm completely in awe of what she's done to keep everything going since she lost her dad. This is what I know about Seren MacArthur: she never does anything without really considering it first. If she was prepared to give up the parsonage for your sake, you must mean something to her. That's all.'

When I leave the cafe I walk to the edge of the dunes, the push of the oncoming wind strong against my chest. I thought I'd lost my chance to know Seren better. I might still have blown it. But she gave up so much to benefit my daughter and me. I have to find a way of repaying that kindness.

I unfurl the crumpled serviette that Cerrie scribbled her mobile number on before she left. Holding it steady to enter the numbers into my phone, I type a text:

Cerrie – thanks for today.
    I want to do something to thank Seren. Can you help me?
    Jack ☺

Chapter Sixty-Three

Seren

Today is one of my favourite weekends of the year in St Ives. And for the first time, I'm not just a visitor.

The vibe of the St Ives Food Festival is laid-back and fun, with crowds gathering on Porthminster Beach from all over the world for a weekend of food, music and a great time. I look forward to it every year, but this year more than ever. I need a weekend where I don't have to think about anything other than eating, dancing and hanging out with my friends.

So when Becca asked me to man the beer tent she's running, I jumped at the chance.

Garvey, Shep and I set up the bar on the beach as the sunrise paints everything in gorgeous pale blue and gold. Even though the first visitors won't be here for a few hours yet, there's a decidedly festive atmosphere already. I know most of the food stallholders and several of the acts performing at the music festival tonight. This is the weekend when the people of St Ives come out to play and party, whether they are working here or not.

Positivity seems to rise from the sand beneath our feet and seep into everyone. I've seen nothing but smiles since we arrived, and it's only going to get better. Added to this, Molly has been given special dispensation to be an honorary member of Becca's bar staff for the day. She's happily snuggled into the warm sand just inside the marquee tent, her nose being warmed by the early morning sun as she snoozes. She's the picture of peace and contentment.

I know exactly how she feels.

'It's going to be nuts today,' Shep grins, lugging a barrel of beer from the trailer at the back of the tent and ducking under the temporary bar to hook up the beer pull pipe. 'Garvey's on the pull, too, so we'd better keep our eyes on him.'

'What happened to his last girlfriend?'

Shep grimaces. 'She tried to change him, he reckons. Nasty business. Didn't like his clothes, apparently. I mean, what did she think she was going out with? I can't see Garvey in a suit, can you?'

'That's a shame. He seemed settled with her.'

'Well, he is officially the terror of St Ives' single ladies once more.' He chuckles as Garvey strides in, a huge box of bar snacks in his enormous hands.

'Who is?'

'You are, Romeo Jones.'

'Guilty *as*, m'lud.' He winks at me as he walks behind the bar. 'Don't mind him, Mum, he's only jealous.'

At the sound of Garvey's voice my dog sits up, tail

beating a welcome on the cream canvas. He gave her a handful of crisps a few months ago and she never forgets bringers of food. Garvey, who's a bit of a softie underneath all the brag and bravado, kneels down in the sand to tickle her ear and sneak a dog biscuit to her from his jeans pocket.

'I can't believe you brought dog treats,' I say. 'You don't even own a dog.'

'Knew old Moll was coming down, didn't I? Gotta keep my fellow staff sweet.'

'See that? Blatant favouritism,' Shep says, laughing when Garvey tosses him a bone-shaped biscuit in reply.

I need this today. When the crowds descend the work will be full-on until sun down, but I don't mind. It's so markedly different from working during the death throes of a business. There's nothing joyful or uplifting about that.

Many of the paintings are gone from the walls in MacArthur's now, a steady stream of artists and crafts-people coming into the shop to claim their work. It's a sad, rapidly emptying shell of its former self and already the ghosts of the past are reappearing. I found a note in Dad's handwriting stuffed between the driftwood counter and the chipboard carcass upon which it sits. It's only a list of long-defunct phone numbers, but it was like Dad trying to make his voice heard in the shop again. I've begun to notice small details of the shop's fabric as its stock has been taken away – the nail Dad hammered into the wall over the corner of the stockroom that sufficed as a kitchen, that irrevocably bent when the hammer slipped, so he declared it a tea-towel holder; a line of measurements pencilled onto the inside of a cupboard door, their original purpose lost in time; the chip of paint on the doorframe Dad refused to paint over because he thought it looked like a highwayman on horseback. There are countless marks and dents and scratches whose stories will be patched up and painted over when the shop is no longer ours.

Since the SOLD sign went up it's been a dark, sad, cold place to work, shrouded in shadow despite the spotlights burning all day. I think the building knows. Even Molly hasn't wanted to be there with me this week. I watch her now, rolling onto her back and warming her paws in the strengthening sun as the beach comes alive with the first flush of visitors, and it makes me strangely hopeful. Neither of us should be cooped up in a sad, dying place. Out here on Porthminster Beach there is life, and light and laughter. Whatever happens next for me, I want to pursue this feeling of hope.

By lunchtime the festival is a loud, exciting bustle of bodies and noise. Unsurprisingly the bar is busy, a long good-natured queue stretching out through the entrance onto the sun-soaked beach. On a day like today, nobody minds waiting much.

'Alright, bird?' Aggie's huge grin looms over my shoulder behind the bar.

'I'm good, thanks. But the queue is *that* side.'

Aggie slaps a hand to her heart. 'I'm wounded. Here was I just poppin' in to see how my best friend was getting on and I'm *accused*!'

'My mistake,' I grin, handing two plastic pint glasses of beer to my waiting customer. 'How's the coffee stall?'

'Busy. Kieran's runnin' the thing like a military operation. He's driving me insane.'

'Aww, lucky you, getting to work with the love of your life.'

'If he carries on the way he's going I might turn celibate.'

'Two beers, thanks,' says a bearded guy in a Breton T-shirt, cut-off skinny jeans and straw trilby, handing me a twenty-pound note. 'And whatever Aggie's having.'

Delighted, my friend lets out a whoop and for a horrible moment I think she might dive over the bar to hug him. 'Guy Trennack, I bleddy love you! Pint of Doom Bar, ta.'

Things in my life will come and go, but my best friend's ability to scrounge free alcohol is one sparkling constant I can always rely on. I'm still a little careful of what I say to her and my friends since my drunken confession, but I think they've forgiven me for railroading the parsonage campaign. Cerrie has gone out of her way to check up on me every day and Aggie is never more than a phone call away. She's asked me to revamp the design for the coffee hut's website when MacArthur's closes, and she was talking about a new logo too. I haven't attempted much visual design work since Grafyx folded last year, but I'm excited by the prospect of doing it again. With so many people rallying around to look after me, the future isn't as bleak as it looked a few weeks ago.

'I love your bracelet,' says a young woman in a bikini top and long, African-print skirt, pushing a pair of enormous sunglasses onto the top of her head as she studies my wrist. 'Where did you get it?'

The blue-and-green drop bracelet was one of the first I made, the silver-wired seaglass gems suspended from an aqua leather thong instead of my usual silver chains. Even though I haven't made any jewellery since the vote, I've taken to wearing this one. It's comforting and I remember Dad's surprise when I showed it to him. Dismantling his shop has left me needing tangible reminders of him to get through the necessary tasks.

'I made it.'

'It's gorgeous. Do you sell them anywhere?'

'No,' I say quickly, handing over her change.

'You should. I'd buy that.'

I watch her weave out of the packed beer tent into the sunshine, suddenly uneasy.

'Why did you say no?' Shep is crouched beside me, pulling bags of crisps from the box under the bar. 'I thought you had an online shop.'

'I'm not doing that at the moment.'

'Why not?' he asks. 'They're good.'

I don't have a good reason why. Seaglass reminds me of Dad, and Gwithian Beach, and Jack. It's too painful to go there right now. 'Just taking a break. I've more important things to think about.'

Shep holds up two packets of cheese and onion crisps in surrender. 'Fair enough. Would you ever make a necklace, though? For a bloke?'

'I've never thought about it.'

'Could you make me one? I'd pay. Black leather with

398

one of those seaglass drops. Blue, if you had it. It'd be like a sea charm.'

'I don't know . . .'

'Think about it. Let me know.'

'Okay. Thanks.'

'Oh, and me and Garvey are good for half an hour if you fancy a break?' He nods at the queue that has lulled a little. 'They'll all be back after they've eaten. Food stalls are packed right now.'

It's been a long and busy morning and I'm glad of the chance to get out for a while. Molly plods beside me and I stop to take my flip-flops off. The sand feels good between my toes as we walk around the festival site.

The most incredible aroma fills the air – sea salt and sand, warm spices and cool herbs mingle with roasting meat, lemon, frying fish, pungent cheeses and the irresistible scent of freshly made chips and doughnuts. All around me people are lounging in the sand, enjoying a multi-ethnic feast and locally made beer, cider and wine. It feels like a huge party to which everyone is invited. On Porthminster Beach people from all walks of life and all parts of the globe meet as one, locals and tourists, children and adults, old and young. St Ives has that air, especially during the summer, but the festival is where it feels magnified. Our town belongs to everyone; if I wasn't lucky enough to live here, I don't think I could visit without its beautiful beaches and quaint streets calling me back time after time. St Ives gets under your skin and into your soul. It's what draws people back every year, and what makes those of us who live here year-round stay when times are tough and the sun isn't shining.

I feel at peace with the world, despite my aching calves and back from working in the beer tent. I feel *alive*.

Whatever else happens, I have to pursue this feeling. I won't be cooped up or hemmed in by expectations again. Once MacArthur's closes for good, I will draw a line under that chapter of my life.

'Come on, girl,' I say to Molly. 'Let's get a bag of doughnuts, shall we?'

Molly has already turned in the direction of the doughnut stall and is way ahead of me.

Chapter Sixty-Four

Jack

Persuading Brotherson was always going to be a tough sell. Without his support, my plan is dead in the water. So even though it risks rocking the calm working relationship I've so far enjoyed with him – not to mention potentially annoying the man who currently pays our bills – I make an appointment to meet him in Plymouth.

I'm armed with an impressive report of the work my team has completed on Rectory Fields. We are officially four weeks ahead of schedule – something unheard of on previous Brotherson builds, according to my colleagues – and within budget, having been able to repurpose so much of the original parsonage stone. The team he's assembled are brilliant, easily the best I've ever worked with. And the incentive for St Piran's school to contribute to the building has gone a long way to keep local support on our side. I'm in the strongest position possible to ask a favour. I just hope it doesn't mean I'm at a higher point from which to fall . . .

He's in a typically bullish mood when he greets me at the door to his office, a suspicious whiff of whisky on his breath from an earlier brunch meeting.

'*Jaaack*, my favourite construction manager,' he exclaims, slapping my back. 'Take a seat. I hear you bring good news from Rectory Fields?'

I run him through the latest developments and, to my relief, see delight register on his flushed face. It's always good to keep your boss happy – even more so when you're about to severely test it. 'All in all, we're on course for an early finish. I reckon we'll be ready for the sales centre on site within the next three weeks.'

'Good work, boy,' he says, rubbing his hands together. 'Stroke of genius with the school kids, too. We'll get local press on that ASAP, push the good news story for all its worth. That should shut the beggars up in Botallack.'

'Problems there?'

He shrugs. 'No more than usual. Great site there, Jack. Bigger than Rectory Fields or Trevalgan, with much more scope. I'm thinking cottages as well as the main apartment building. Views there are incredible. We'll have folks falling over themselves to buy them. Trouble is, Botallack people got wind of it before we'd pushed the St Ives vote story through the local papers. They're gunning for us despite there being no moral covenant this time.' He gives an over-dramatic sigh. 'What can you do, eh? Short of us doling out random acts of kindness for the next five years, we've just got to put up with the backlash.'

That's my cue. I'd hoped for an open door somewhere in the conversation, and it's the best one I'm likely to get.

'Actually, I might have an idea that could help . . .'

The chalet is deserted when I get home, tired and aching from two and a half hours in heavy traffic on the congested A30 and A38. It's been a hell of a day. I wonder if Owen might have taken Nessie back to the farm after she finished school. Looking back outside where my car is parked, my heart sinks at the prospect of getting in it again to drive to Helston. But just as I'm resigned to making the journey, I notice the sheet of paper propped up against the tea-cosied teapot in the middle of the table. It's covered in Nessie's large, happy handwriting:

Dad
We are on the beach.
Bring pop.
Love Nessie xx

Owen, Ellis, Arthur and Seth are being schooled in Nessie's latest dance routine when I join them on the beach. The sun has hidden itself behind a thick band of cloud blowing in from the sea, and I can feel the air temperature beginning to drop. My brother sees me and excuses himself from my daughter's beachside dance class, red-faced and chuckling.

'Hey, Stink, glad you found us.'

'Nice moves, Reekie.'

'Glad you approve. I'm getting better at it, apparently.'

'Dad! Come and join in!' Nessie yells, flinging her arms above her head and spinning in the sand.

403

'In a minute,' I call back, grimacing at Owen. 'How long has she had you all dancing?'

'About ten minutes. We were running, star-jumping and being disco-monkeys before that.' He laughs. 'And I thought *I* had too much energy. At least the boys will sleep tonight, so Sarah will be pleased.'

'Faster!'

'I hope the boys forgive her,' I say, watching my nephews collapse one by one in the sand, leaving Nessie still twirling and jumping.

'They'll survive. As far as they're concerned she can do no wrong.' He takes a can of Coke from the bag I've brought down to the beach at Nessie's command. 'So, how did it go with Brotherson?'

I let myself smile for the first time since leaving Plymouth. 'He went for it.'

My brother gawps. 'All of it?'

'Mm-hmm. Turns out good PR comes in all shapes and sizes.'

'Cost too?'

'All in. It's tax deductible, apparently, so he's not being completely selfless. But it's probably the closest to a philanthropic gesture he's ever likely to make.'

Even now I can't quite believe Bill Brotherson agreed to help me. I wasn't going to mention Seren, but I found myself admitting it anyway. Unexpectedly, my boss found it highly amusing.

'Like *that*, is it, Jacky-boy? I see. Well, far be it from me to stand in the way of true love.'

'Wow – um – thanks, Bill.'

'Don't mention it. You wait till I tell Mrs B about this. I'll be in her good books from now till Christmas!'

'So, a tax break and getting brownie points from his missus, eh?' Owen laughs. 'No wonder you're his favourite employee.'

Now there's a mental picture I won't be able to shift in a hurry . . .

We finally drag Nessie and her exhausted cousins away from the beach and enjoy fish and chips from the mobile van that will visit Jeb's caravan park three times a week until the end of the holiday season. It's a treat for all of us and Nessie is delighted. We're celebrating – but I know that the challenge that lies ahead is going to need both Nessie and Owen's blessing, too.

'How often will you be away, Dad?' Ness asks, piling chips onto a buttered slice of bread and rolling it into a cylindrical chip butty.

'During the week Uncle Owen and Auntie Sarah will pick you up on Wednesdays and Fridays, so you'll have tea at the farm. Uncle Jeb and Grandad Dave might look after you a bit at weekends. If it goes the way I've planned it, this should only last a few weeks. Are you okay with that?'

'No problemo, Dad-o,' she grins, and I suspect this is another phrase in her vocabulary I have Jeb to thank for.

'I'll have a job for you to do, too, when it's almost ready. Think you can help me?'

'Er, *yeah*. Because I'm brilliant at helping. Auntie Sarah says so. So does Grandad Dave. And Miss Austin at school. She calls me her Superstar.'

I hide my smile. Cerrie Austin said she was going to make it up to Nessie. I have her to thank for making this happen.

Now all I have to do is bring our plans into being . . .

Chapter Sixty-Five

Seren

We're supposed to be selling Dad's business to make money, but all I seem to be doing at the moment is writing cheques and handing over cash. Everything costs – from settling up with our departing artists to buying huge tins of white paint, brushes and rollers to prepare the shop for handing over to Mhairi Peters. It's something I could have avoided, but painting the shop feels like my last gift to the place Dad worked so hard in and loved so much. It's a chance to wipe the slate clean, removing the dirt and dust just as we are removing the debt that crippled MacArthur's.

There's another reason, too: I want to walk away from the shop knowing it isn't ours any more. For all of its life as an art and craft gallery, it's never been painted white. *Too clinical*, Dad always said, disliking the colour scheme of choice of every other art shop in St Ives. The pale blue and pale yellow scheme he chose is faded now beyond recognition. Nobody paints shop walls those colours any more. Like so much in the shop he created, the coloured walls are from a different time, when trade was more forthcoming and banks less ready to withdraw their support. It's time to consign the colours to history.

I've always considered the shop unit tiny, but with most of its stock gone and only me to paint its interior, I'm realising just how much space it has. The pale blue Dad chose might have seen better days but it's stubborn – I've painted two coats of white over it already but it refuses to disappear. I'm so sick of painting, but it's going to need at least another coat, if not two.

I put my roller down in the paint tray balanced on the top of the rickety wooden stepladder I've borrowed from Sharon at Wax-a-Daisy, and climb down for a break. The ladder creaks as I descend, but I can't say for certain whether it's the old wood complaining or my limbs protesting.

I'm so tired. But knowing I'm nearing the end of this is keeping me going.

Mum has been studying for her teaching refresher course, so all of the final work on the shop has fallen to me. I just want it done now, and for the day I hand over the keys to arrive. My plans for afterwards are still sketchy, but I'm optimistic that they will fall into place once the shop is no more. So far I have three jobs secured: shifts at Becca's, redesigning Aggie's website – and, most recently, a day a week doing design work for Alistair, a former colleague from Grafyx who's set up his own business, after I dared to call him a few days ago. I'm willing to do more if it means I can provide for myself. I can't afford a place of my own yet, but I've decided that will be my first goal –

finding somewhere to rent and the money to cover it each month. Mum's happy for me to stay as long as I want to, but I like the idea of striking out on my own.

Cerrie was talking about moving from her one-bedroomed flat in Lelant to somewhere bigger, taking on a lodger, and I have to admit I'm tempted to ask her to bear me in mind. But I can't and won't do that until I'm confident I can pay rent. I've had enough of being in debt to last me a lifetime.

The shop is still officially open for another two weeks, but so much of our stock has gone that there was little point in waiting to repaint. When I think customers might venture in I can push the ladder and paint pots to a corner I've cleared and throw a dustsheet over it. Kieran joked last week that an art fan might see it as an avant-garde installation and attempt to buy it. I told him they were welcome to. Any money we can make in the last fortnight of trading will be a bonus.

In truth, I've had no customers in for a week. The SOLD sign has warded them off. I don't mind really. A sudden rush would have been heartbreaking. I've watched other businesses fold in St Ives over the years, and that last-minute onslaught of bargain hunters picking over the remains of a shop always horrified me. It must be the biggest kick in the gut, delivering an unwanted shot of last-minute hope when it can achieve nothing.

Molly lifts her head as I pass her basket on my way to the kettle.

'Yes, there's biscuits,' I say, hearing the excited flak-flak-flak of her coat shaking as she rises to follow me into the back room. The wooden shelves where our stock was stored are largely empty; it's strange to see light getting in where it was always trapped between muslin-wrapped canvasses and brown boxes of ceramics and glassware tied with string. I've brought two Kilner jars from home, one filled with chocolate biscuits, one containing Molly's favourite bone-shaped treats, and my dog knows which one is hers. She stands by the folding table where the kettle and tea things sit, her nose inches away from the dog biscuit jar, keeping guard. No biscuit will be able to escape the jar without Molly noticing.

I make tea in a large RNLI mug Dad had for years and toss a dog biscuit to my ever-vigilant canine companion, slipping another into my pocket to surprise her with later. Although it's never really a surprise to Detective Molly, it's her favourite game. I love it almost as much as she does.

Grunting happily, she follows me back to the main shop and flops back into her basket as I sit cross-legged beside her.

'All a bit weird, isn't it?' I stroke her head and she pushes her nose up under my hand. 'But we're doing the right thing. I just wish I didn't have to do it on my own – no offence.'

My dog grumbles a little and shifts so that her nose is pointing towards my jeans pocket. *Give me a treat and you can say what you like . . .*

There are three missed calls and a splatter of white paint on my phone when I pull it from under the corner of a dustsheet. Kieran has called twice, Aggie once. It's lovely to know they are checking on me, but I'm so tired

410

and have so much left to do that I can't lose time returning calls. I know they won't be offended, so I make a note to ring them later tonight – if I'm done before midnight, that is.

Most days this week I haven't made it to bed until the early hours. Each job I've had to do has taken far longer than planned, so much so that I'm beginning to wonder if the shop is deliberately setting roadblocks and delays in my way to put off our inevitable parting. There isn't long to get it all finished, and no money to pay someone else to do it. Once again I have no choice but to work until everything is complete.

Molly huffs against the corner of her basket, her chocolate eyes observing me with disappointment.

'Okay, you've been very patient. Here you go.' I give her the dog biscuit from my pocket, drain the last of my tea and struggle back to my feet.

I'm rearranging dustsheets on the floor when a sharp rap on the window startles me. When I turn, I see a familiar grin peeking through the glass. It appears that one of my friends isn't willing to wait for a return call.

Kieran is all smiles when I open the door, clearly pleased with himself for taking the initiative. 'Evening, ma'am,' he says, striding in, planting a kiss on my head and plonking a carrier bag in the middle of the floor. My dog forgets she is a doddery old lady and is out of her basket like a boisterous puppy, bouncing around Kieran's feet and joyfully flinging herself on the dustsheets for a belly rub. 'And hello *you*, Molly May.'

Lovely though this scene is, I can't stop to watch it. 'This is a surprise.'

'Thought it might be. How are you getting on?'

I daren't even look for fear of spotting more unfinished tasks to add to my ever-growing list. 'Slowly. Sorry, Kieran, I'd offer you a drink but I need to get on. You're welcome to help yourself, if you like.'

'I might just do that.' He waggles a finger at me. '*You* didn't return my calls.'

I know he thinks he's being funny, but this evening his tone irritates me. I look around at the half-painted shop, the boxes that still need sealing and labelling, the piles of stuff that still need to be sorted. 'I'm a little busy, in case you hadn't noticed. I was going to call you later, when I was finished.'

'You said that last time I phoned you.' His grin grates on me.

'Well, the *last* time I talked to you, I was dealing with this, too. And the time before that. I have an entire shop to paint, every fitting to dismantle, tons of rubbish to remove . . .'

'And your best friends to be rude to when they come to see you. Because you *won't call them back* . . .'

I love Kieran Macklin with all my heart, but he has no filter when it comes to joking around. He doesn't know when to stop; and either can't read the signs when people have had enough, or is so caught up in his own enjoyment he simply doesn't see them. I am too tired to deal with this now and my emotions are so close to the surface, I know

I'm likely to dissolve into tears or scream at him to leave. Neither option is appealing.

'I'm sorry if I've offended you, but I really have to get back to work. I'd like to be in bed before midnight tonight.' I return to smoothing the dustsheets back across the carpet where the legs of the stepladder have pulled them back.

'Oh come on, Ser, you need to lighten up with this. Your buyer's bought the place *as seen* – you don't have to do anything other than pack boxes and hand over the keys.'

I stare at him. 'Yes, I do. Have you seen this place? It's not in any state to pass on yet.'

'Or maybe you're coming up with reasons not to let it go.'

'Don't try to pretend you know what I think about this shop, okay? This is necessary. That's all.'

'I thought you'd end up doing something like this.'

'Right, that's enough.' I stand and face him, ready for a fight. 'Thank you for visiting, but as you can see, I'm fine. I just need to get this done – by myself, like everything I've had to do lately – in the way I want to do it.'

'Listen, Ser . . .'

'And you know what? If you really wanted to help me you wouldn't bombard me with calls and come here late at night to attack me for not answering; you'd be turning up with a brush and old clothes and bloody well offering to help.'

He reaches down and scoops the carrier bag from the floor.

'You mean like these?' He opens the bag to reveal a paint-splattered red checked shirt and two paintbrushes.

'Oh.' I don't know what to say. I stare at the bag's contents, feeling like the biggest fool on the planet.

'I'm not a completely heartless moron, girl. I figured you'd like real help more than moral support. So, here I am.'

Mortified for yelling at him, I accept his hug and burst into tears against his warm chest. 'I'm sorry.'

'Don't be daft. I'm sorry it's taken so long for us all to realise how much you had to do. Aggie'll be here in half an hour and Cerrie's on her way over, too. She's bringing that big strapping Aussie of hers, too. You shouldn't have to do this alone. It's time we stepped up and helped you.'

True to his word, my friends duly arrive and suddenly the shop is filled with love and laughter and light. Aggie brings bottles and Cerrie brings homemade caramel apple cake. Her boyfriend Tom brings his surprising skill for painting woodwork, and Kieran brings jokes all night. Molly is in seventh heaven with so many minions to attend to her fussing needs and I stand in the middle of it all, amazed and loved.

It might not be as romantic as seaglass stars on a beach, but this evening I've found the magic I need in this tiny shop. With my friends by my side, anything is possible.

Chapter Sixty-Six

Jack

I'm tired, but there's no way I'm missing being on the beach with Ness. She's been so good about being looked after by Owen, Dad, Jeb and Wenna while I've been working on the side project, but I want to give her every scrap of time I can.

Gwithian Beach is stunning tonight. It seems to glow in the late afternoon sun as we head down the wooden steps, and we glow with it. I can see threads of warm gold in Nessie's dark hair where the sunlight catches it. On days like these I am beyond grateful to live in such an amazing place.

'I'm going to make a bunch of stars tonight,' Nessie says, swinging her bucket filled with seaglass from our stash in the chalet. I'll let her, too, the lightening evenings giving us more time for starmaking.

Every part of me aches but I'm almost finished. I just hope it's enough.

I've thought about Seren a lot since Cerrie Austin told

me. It's perfect that she was our secret starmaker and if I ever tell Nessie I reckon she'll love it, too. I don't know why Seren didn't tell me. I wish she had. If the vote hadn't been between us, would we have found out sooner?

She might not talk to me. She looked pretty angry the last time I saw her and so much has happened in her life since then. That's why I've been doing what I know best: building. It's harder to ignore a physical structure. I hope, anyway. She might hate it, or assume I have a hidden agenda for getting Brotherson back in her good books. I hope she sees it for what it really is. It's my best and only shot and I'm banking everything on making it work.

'Dad!'

Nessie is perched on the bottom step, pointing at the beach. I wonder why she hasn't run straight down on the sand. It's not like Ness to waste a second of potential beach time.

'What is it?'

She turns back to me, eyes wide with wonder. 'The mermaids. They came back!'

I hurry down the steps, my heart in my mouth. Has Seren come back to Gwithian? Could she have made another star for us?

But then I see it. And my breath deserts me.

The beach has been strewn with blue jewels as far as we can see. On every rock, laced between the ribbons of seaweed marking the high tide line and dotted across the ridged sand leading to the sea, sparkles of blue catch the early evening sun. It's stunning.

'What are they, Dad?' Nessie asks in a squeaky whisper.

'I don't know. Let's go and see.'

Gwithian Beach is littered with hundreds of tiny, electric blue discs. They're delicate and ringed with tiny concentric lines, like the rings in the middle of a tree. In the centre of each is a transparent triangle, rising like a catamaran sail. They're not moving, but it looks as if they might have once. Each one is a work of art but the sheer volume of them is overwhelming. I've never seen anything like it before. We pick our way slowly over them until we reach our starmaking site. Our star from yesterday evening is still there, free from the strange blue discs. Ness and I pause and look back. People have come down onto the sand to see the spectacle and are dotted over the length of Gwithian Beach. Even some of the die-hard surfers have ventured onto dry land to look. There's a sense of reverence, like you would expect in an ancient cathedral.

'Do you think the mermaids sent them?' Nessie asks.

'I don't know. Maybe.'

Her frown-wrinkle appears again. 'Even if they didn't, it's like it rained jewels on the beach. I think that means we're meant to be here, Dad.'

I stare at her. I've seen how at home in Gwithian she is but I've never actually heard her say it. I'm struck by how quickly my baby girl is growing up. She's confident and unafraid and I adore that she is her own person. I love being with her on the beach, our only concern to make a better seaglass star than the evening before. But, like the passing days on the beach, I know it's fleeting.

'I think we're meant to be here too, ladybird. Are you happy?'

417

She regards me carefully. 'Are you?'

I blink away my surprise. 'I am with you.'

'I want you to be happy with everything. And don't work so hard.'

'Sorry?'

'You work really hard and that's very good of you. But you don't need to worry and work *all* the time. We're going to be okay, Dad.'

When Nessie says it like that, I can believe we will be.

Later that evening we carefully retrace our steps and climb back up over the dunes to the caravan park. I managed to find one of the bright blue, triangular-backed discs marooned on a small rock that we could take with us. Nessie carries it beside me like she's bearing the crown jewels. I can hear her whispering to it as we walk along the sand-strewn path towards home.

I figure Jeb might know what the strange object is, so instead of going straight back to the chalet, we head for his bungalow by the entrance to the site.

'Alright, birds?' he grins at the door, ushering us into his home. 'Wenna's just made biscuits and she's popped out for more sugar. We can probably scoff most of 'em before she gets back!'

Jeb and Wenna's bungalow is a shrine to the weird and wonderful. My theory is that Jeb was denied the chance to collect things as a child; as soon as he had a home of his own he unleashed his passion for all things collectible. We pass a coffee table in the hall with two Samurai helmets and a group of battered Smurf figurines, who look like a post-apocalyptic tour group viewing a museum exhibit; beyond that a stuffed toy tiger lurks by a hatstand draped in long, striped woollen scarves Dr Who would be proud of. There are film posters and framed, faded classic LPs on the walls, and a random collection of old milk bottles randomly advertising Hovis, Kellogg's Cornflakes and Bisto gravy line a shelf above the kitchen door. It's a grotto of ephemera, and magical in a dented, dusty and decrepit way.

But even Jeb's eclectic collection can't boast the treasure we have brought. As he pours tea into three mugs that don't match, Nessie slides the rock carefully onto the vinyl kitchen table top.

'Uncle Jeb, do you know what this is?'

Jeb puts the teapot down and leans closer. 'Where did you find that?'

'On the beach. There's millions of them.'

'That's a jellyfish.'

Nessie wrinkles her nose. 'It doesn't look like a jellyfish. It's not . . . jelly-ish.'

Jeb grins at her and then at me. 'It is so. That's a By-the-Wind Sailor. Get them on Gwithian every now and again. But you say there were lots?'

I nod. 'The beach is covered in them.'

'Ah, see I heard of that happenin' a few years back. They float on the water, see? An' that bit on their backs is like a sail. But sometimes they get blown off-course and end up beachin' themselves.'

'That's so sad,' Nessie says.

'It is and it isn't. They follow the wind, so wherever it

419

takes them they go. Quite romantic, if you think about it. It'd be nice not to be tied to one place all the time.' He chuckles. 'But don't you let on to Wenna I said that. She likes limpets better – stickin' fast to one place!'

Nessie is a bit subdued when we get home, cradling the rock with its deceased jellyfish resident. It's only when she's in her PJs and climbing into bed that she answers my question.

'I'm all right, Dad. Just a bit sad.'

'Things don't last forever, ladybird. I wish they did . . .'

She fixes me with a look. 'I don't mean *that*. I know stuff dies.'

'Ah. So what are you . . . ?'

'The mermaids. They didn't send the blue things as a gift, did they?'

'No, but . . .'

'Because that game is over, isn't it? We do the stars ourselves now. That's what we decided. And we're good at making them, so it doesn't matter. I just think it's sad that things have to change. But it's okay to miss them, right?'

'Of course it is.' I pull the duvet up and tuck it under her chin. 'You have the right to feel whatever you want to about it. There's no right or wrong reaction. Just what's best for you.'

'Like you and Mum.'

I don't even know where to begin to respond to that.

'You shouted at each other. A *lot*.'

'Wow, Ness, I—'

'And you weren't happy. Well, you were sometimes, but you shouted more. It wasn't fun when Mum yelled. She

420

yelled at me, too. And she hardly ever wanted to play games, or read stories, not like you did. I liked her hugs, though, even if she usually yelled first.' Her hand finds mine. 'But it's okay to feel sad that she isn't here any more, isn't it? Like the person who finished our stars? Even if the memories aren't always good, it's okay to miss the good bits, right?'

I don't want to cry in front of her. So I swallow hard and force a smile. 'Yes, it's okay. If you miss Mum, it's okay. If you don't miss the bad bits, that's okay, too. And don't ever let anyone tell you any different.'

I'm completely shaken when I leave her room. I don't know if I ever thought I'd have a conversation like that with my daughter, and definitely not this soon after Tash's death. I need alcohol.

There are no bottles in the fridge – I've worked so much recently that I haven't had either the time to buy beer, or the inclination to drink it after long days on both sites. In desperation, I raid the sideboard stash of thank-you-whisky. Not liking the spirit and knowing virtually nothing about it, I pick a bottle at random and take it out on the veranda.

The light has almost gone and here at the top of the cliff the stars burn brightly. My eye catches the sight as I slug a mouthful of whisky, shuddering as the heat sears back up my throat. This stuff really tastes disgusting, but it provides the warm buzz I need.

I didn't know Ness was so aware of how it was with Tash and me. You assume kids are so caught up in their own worlds they don't see yours. Especially being so young. But I should have known: Nessie misses nothing, so why would she miss this?

In truth, I don't know how to feel about it. I'm heartbroken she has adverse memories of her life with two parents, but would ignoring them be good for her in the long run? I want her to have good memories of her mum, but I want them to be real, too. It doesn't work to build an idealistic, rose-tinted picture of someone you've lost, because ultimately you lose the very essence of who they were.

I can't experience this for her, or save her from it. She has to work her own way through her grief.

If Ness needs to remember the Tash who yelled frustration with her life out at her six-year-old daughter, so be it. If she needs to remember the bedtime stories not read, the hugs not given, that has to be her prerogative. I have no right to stop that or suggest it be somehow edited out of the bunch of contradictions she knew as 'Mum'.

My throat burns where the whisky has scoured it and from the anger I've buried just to keep going. Maybe I need to remember everything about Tash, too. It's been too easy to be angry with her for dying and not think of the times we were happy, or the dreams we once shared.

She was passionate and antagonistic, soft and jagged; her beauty became ugly when she was angry, returning to beauty when she got her own way. And I must have loved her, before all the complications and recriminations clouded my view. I loved her enough to start a family and endure her many late-night lamentations over what she swore she'd lost as a result. There were times I was poleaxed by her spirit and determination; where she could kill my strongest argument just by looking at me the way she did when we first met. She had the ability to floor me with her beauty and passion. Even at the end, when battles were all that remained, I still caught glimpses of the woman I'd married. That was what kept me going through the rest.

The By-the-Wind Sailor is on its rock at the top of the veranda steps, its blue still vivid, even in the dim porch light. 'Blown by the wind, wherever it goes,' Jeb had said. He could have been describing Natasha Lucy Dixon. There were times when her actions confused me. I couldn't understand why some things mattered to her so much – the way she obsessed over small details nobody else would notice. Maybe she focused on the insignificant things as a way of avoiding the big issues, like our crumbling marriage or her frustration with life in general. But she was wired to act like that. Tash stuck out her sail and let herself be blown along by her need to have what she wanted. And while she was following that powerful breeze, she ended up beached, her life suddenly over.

She was hell to live with. But I must have loved her once.

I take another slug of bitter-tasting liquor.

I *did* love her.

I've been avoiding the truth, too angry and scared to even look at it. I loved my wife, but I was going to leave her and then she died on the day I'd planned to go. For months I've carried so much guilt for not trying to talk to her the night before, when I had the chance. I should have used the unusually calm evening to make one last bid to save us. There had been a moment then, with her curled up on the sofa and me in my armchair, where I looked across at her and thought how beautiful she looked. The blue-white light from the television dancing across her face, her newly washed dark hair curling over one shoulder, the gentle rise and fall of her chest as she relaxed. I should have told her I loved her then. I should have left my chair and crossed the invisible wall across the living room carpet to take her in my arms and remind her why she loved me.

But I didn't. I hunkered down and wished the time away, my head filled with plans and contingencies for walking out of her life next day. And then she never came home.

Above me, the stars are brighter now. From my very limited knowledge of them I can make out the Plough and Orion, but frustratingly the rest remains a jumble of tiny lights. I have a sudden memory of sitting close to Seren MacArthur, looking up at the blue screen of her phone as it revealed all the constellations. I wonder if she is watching the stars tonight; if she sees what I can see.

I want Seren in my future. But first, I have to acknowledge Tash in my past.

So on the cold front step of the chalet, I finally allow the tangle of emotions inside me to tumble out. Tomorrow I'll blame the whisky and exhaustion for this, but for now I just cry. Great big, unattractive tears of hurt, frustration, guilt and every fear I've hidden punch their way out of me, until my throat is on fire and my eyes sting from the flood of saltwater. I am emptied out, finally shedding what has weighed me down for so very long. Out here with nothing but the stars and the distant rumble of surf for company, I am on the edge of the world, the questions I haven't dared ask myself finding their answers at last. Everything aches. Everything hurts. But I know what I want.

I don't know what time I finally drag myself inside, but the first glimpse of morning light glows through the gap in the curtains as I pull the duvet over my head.

In two days, the project will end. I have to be ready.

Chapter Sixty-Seven

Seren

The shop is mine till midday. And even though I don't need to be here, I am sitting in the middle of the white, empty space on a folding chair, waiting with the shop that's meant the world to my family, as if keeping a beloved relative company before a journey that will part us forever.

I've already taken the keys from my key ring, putting them with Mum's spare keys and Dad's set from the pocket of his jacket that still hangs in the hall at home. The keys lie together in my right hand, joined by a length of yellow ribbon I found while clearing out the storeroom. Their weight in my palm is both comforting and intensely sad. I may have willed this day to arrive since accepting the offer, but the reality of it is only now sinking in.

At midday today, MacArthur's will cease to exist.

It feels like an execution date.

Time of death: twelve noon.

I've told myself not to be sentimental, but suddenly it's too soon, too close to the day we lost Dad. I haven't had time to say goodbye, I argue with myself – except that's all I've been doing lately, isn't it? I've bid a slow farewell to this tiny shop unit tucked in a corner of a Cornish court-yard with every brushstroke, every roll of the white-paint roller. I've whispered goodbye with each shelf dismantled, each nail pulled out, each scar in the plaster filled smooth. Step by step, I've been letting go, setting it free.

I'm going to be okay. This is the last link chaining me to debt: once I hand over the keys I'm handing myself the freedom I've longed for since Dad died.

But knowing that doesn't stop it hurting.

Last night I sat on the bench in the Shedservatory, look-ing out across St Ives. A heavy fog rested over the town, but instead of frustrating my view, it felt as if St Ives was being enveloped in a cool, white embrace. The air was so still; and I remembered that feeling of holding my breath whenever Dad gave me a hug. As a child, I wanted to always stay close to him, his reassuring arm around me; the steady, sure beat of his heart sounding through his dark blue fish-erman's sweater.

I don't know where Dad is, but I think if he could have seen me last night he would have told me it was okay. The peace I felt was as close to a hug from him as I'll ever experience again. He would be asking about my next adventure, not demanding an explanation. I took on his business because I had no choice, but I think Dad would have fought me over it. He wasn't one for being hemmed in; the last thing he would have wanted was to impose that on me.

Painting the shop white was the best idea. It's different

enough to be at odds already with the wealth of memories I've accrued here. I'm sitting with a friend who bears only a passing resemblance to someone I've loved before. That's how I'll be able to hand the keys to Mhairi when she and her father arrive.

And then what?

I've thought about today a great deal as I've been preparing the shop for handover. I can't go straight home – that would be too much like scurrying away to lick my wounds. Do I wander down to the harbour, where life goes on and I can lose myself in the crowds? Or walk over to Porthgwidden and the familiar welcome of Aggie's coffee hut? Do I get in the car and visit Gwithian again, or go a little further up the road and walk around the headland at Godrevy? The skylarks might be flying there now, and seals could be bobbing in the coves far below the cliff path. Or do I escape St Ives for a while, to follow my heart and find space to just *be* . . . ?

I think about the note I've left for Mum on the yellow-gingham-covered kitchen table; the small holdall packed and waiting in the boot of my car. The map on the passenger seat, already marked with possibilities; the list of B&Bs where I might call in en route . . .

It's time to find my freedom. Wherever that might be. I can't do that here, with all its memories, all the links with my life. My friends will understand. Everybody needs to get away once in a while. I've saved a little money working at Becca's Bar, enough to sustain me for a couple of weeks. It won't be forever: I just need to breathe, to let everything I've loved and lost wash over me and to find my peace.

At five minutes to midday, I see Mhairi and Luke Peters walk into the courtyard. I'm tempted to keep the door locked until the last moment, but I know it's time.

Rising slowly and folding up the chair, I take a final look around the shop and walk over to the storeroom doorway. My fingers find the deep scratch shaped like an 'S' just above the door strike plate on the architrave. I trace the serpent-like shape, tears filling my eyes. I can almost feel Dad holding my young hands over a bradawl as we carved the first initial of my name into the wood.

'There. You're part of history now, sweetheart. "S" for Seren. This shop will always remember you.'

With all the strength I can find, I pull my hand away.

'Goodnight, sweet one,' I whisper, the words Dad always said before locking up the shop for the night leaving my own lips for the last time.

Mhairi meets me at the door, two minutes early. Her face shines with every dream she has dared to imagine for when this place is hers, every hope she has for its future. I hand her the keys.

'Congratulations. I hope you find happiness and success here.'

'I will.' She gives me a hug and whispers, 'I'll take care of it for you.'

And then I am out in the courtyard, empty-handed, seeing two new business owners celebrating the beginning of their adventure through a door that has just closed on Dad's dream.

My mobile buzzes in my hand. I knew Aggie would be first to contact me.

Hope it went well. You did great. Onwards, lovely! Beer at The Maidens to toast the shop? K and Cerrie coming too. Pick you up at 6pm! A xxx

I haven't told them I'm going away. Walking out of the courtyard into the warm sunshine on Fore Street, I pocket my phone and decide to call Aggie from wherever I decide to stay tonight. If I leave within the next hour or so, I can be there long before she arrives to pick me up at Mum's. I don't want to discuss it, just get to my car and go as soon as I can . . .

Chapter Sixty-Eight

Jack

Everything is ready.

I stand back to look at the final element Nessie helped me complete and realise how nervous I am. For the last three weeks this project has consumed my thoughts – even while working on Rectory Fields and spending time with Ness, my mind has been working overtime. I don't think I've ever been so tired, but neither have I believed so strongly I'm doing the right thing before. This *has* to work. It has to be enough.

I have poured everything into making this happen. Not just my time and physical effort, but every word I've wanted to say, every thanks I've wanted to give. My brother would rib me for eternity for even thinking this, but I almost believe if you put your hand against the reclaimed stone you'll feel the beat of my heart. It's the structure I've dreamed of creating; on a small scale, admittedly, but it represents my hope for the future. Just like the tiny driftwood and moss house we left with the seaglass star on Gwithian Beach weeks ago.

The house we left for Seren.

Last night, I told Nessie the real reason I've been working so much. I wasn't sure what to say or how to frame it: after all, it's just a gesture for now; she might refuse. But Ness lit up like the horizon when the sun emerges from the sea.

'That's amazing!'

'You think so?'

She nodded emphatically and hugged me for a long time. 'It's the best, Dad. Even better than the marshmallows.'

That's all I needed to hear.

Brotherson called me yesterday on Skype unexpectedly and I gave him a probably very wobbly video tour. From his grainy image in the inset box on screen, he seemed genuinely impressed. I'm so grateful for all his help, getting planning permission granted so quickly by the council because of the purpose of the build and the amount of sustainable material we were using. Without him gifting it to the community, I doubt the project would ever have got off the ground.

'So this is it, eh?'

'It is. What do you think, Bill?'

He nodded his approval. 'You did good. *We* did good. Never thought I'd hear myself saying that. I hope it's worth it, Jack.'

So do I.

I can't worry about that now. It's all been arranged for

432

this evening, so I have to wait. I check my mobile again but there aren't any new messages.

Stop it, Jack!

It's almost three p.m. I have to go and pick Nessie up from school. With a final look, I take a breath to push the nerves away and head for my car.

Cerrie meets me at the school gate as Nessie dashes to my side for an extra-large hug.

'Everything's ready,' I say.

As soon as she smiles, I know something is wrong.

'She isn't answering her phone. Aggie and Kieran have been calling and texting her since midday.'

'Well, where is she?'

'I don't know. Nobody seems to.'

'She's just sold her shop. Perhaps she needed some time alone.'

Cerrie chews a rose-gold nail. 'Possibly.'

My nerves begin to twist. 'You're worried, aren't you?'

'No. I'm trying not to be. Look, maybe it's like you said: she's gone somewhere for a bit to have some time on her own. Why don't you take Nessie home and I'll call you when I hear anything?'

Owen, Sarah and the kids are waiting at the chalet and have promised to look after Ness while I go to the site. My brother thinks I'm a hero for finally admitting how I feel; Sarah was less demonstrative, but I think even she can see what it means for me. But all of that will be academic if Seren doesn't show.

'I'll take Nessie home and then I'll come back here. You might have heard from her by then, yeah?'

'I hope so. I'll be here for another hour at least, so, sure, come back if you haven't heard from me.'

I can see Nessie observing me from the rear-view mirror as we drive. It's too quiet in the car but my head is whirring too much to make small talk. I find the dance music radio station Ness likes and turn the volume up a little. She settles back in her seat, but her eyes remain on me.

'You don't like this music.'

'But you do.'

She nods along with the music as if considering her next move. Sure enough: 'You're being weird, Dad.'

'Am I? Sorry, ladybird. Working too hard.'

'Grown-ups always say that. But you work hard all the time, so that can't be why.'

'Leave it, Ness. Enjoy your music.'

She gives a loud groan and stares out of the window, while I breathe an inward sigh of relief. I can't even explain what's going on in my head, so I have no chance of making my daughter understand it.

It never occurred to me that Seren wouldn't be there. For the last three weeks all I've thought about is *that* moment, when I can finally show her the project. I still don't have a clue what I'll actually say, but her reaction, her opinion are what matters.

If she turns up.

Part of me understands completely why she wants to go away. If I hadn't had Nessie when Tash died, I might have done the same. So much crowds in on you: so many people

434

wanting your time – meaning well, but becoming another pressure adding to the weight already on your head. If I could have packed a bag and set off on my own for a while, I don't think I would've hesitated.

I know I'm being selfish, but I want to see her this evening. Not just to show her what I've done and explain why, but because I've missed her. I've missed the stars on the beach and I've missed being on the opposite side of a debating table. I just didn't realise what missing someone could feel like.

But I didn't know Seren had to hand over the keys to her dad's former shop today – no wonder escape was her first priority. I'd assumed she'd closed the shop earlier this week and that Cerrie and Aggie had chosen Friday as a good day to commemorate its passing. I wish I'd known. This is too much for her to have to bear. And how conceited must I appear to demand that she come to the site on such a difficult day? Maybe I don't deserve her time after all. I've ploughed ahead with this project because I thought I was doing the right thing, but is it what Seren would want? I'm a fool for only asking myself this now.

I park next to Owen's battered Land Rover Discovery beside the chalet and walk round to Nessie's door, but she is already clambering out. She shuts the door and folds her arms.

'Dad.'

'What?'

'Why are you so quiet?'

I sigh. 'I don't think Seren is going to come and see what we made for her.'

'Why?'

'It's hard to say. She's had a very sad day today and I don't know if she wants to see people.'

Nessie's frown softens. 'But she'll want to see this. It's lovely.'

'Thanks, kid.'

She wraps her arms around my waist. 'I think you just need to learn to believe more.'

'Sorry?'

'You didn't think we'd see any more stars but we did. I knew we would. That's because grown-ups always have too much *other stuff* in their heads.'

'Oh Ness, you are funny.'

She looks up at me, pleased she's made me smile. 'It's true, though, isn't it? I can believe in magic because I'm supposed to. I don't worry about what other people think. But grown-ups worry about that all the time. You only get to play like I do when you're playing with me. So, if I say it's okay to believe things will turn out okay, you have an excuse to believe it.'

I reach down and cup her face. 'How did you get so wise?' There's something I haven't told her yet, and I think now is the time. 'Ness, I know who made the stars with us.'

She looks up at me. 'How do you know?'

'I found out.'

'Who was it?' There's just a hint of caution in her question, as if she isn't sure she'll like the answer. I know we've joked about mermaids and for a while Nessie wanted to believe they were really responsible, but the moment I tell her I can't take it back. A wash of nerves passes over me.

'It was Seren.'

Her mouth drops open. 'Is that why you made her the round building?'

I nod. 'What do you think?'

She lets go of me and stares out across the caravan park towards the beach she adores. Is she picturing Seren there, completing our stars? I'm tempted to prompt her for a reply, but she needs to work out her own response. This is as much her discovery as it was mine, and Seren's before that. All three of us are now joined by this knowledge, and while I don't know what Nessie's reaction will be, it's comforting that all of us know the truth at last.

'Do you like Seren?' It isn't the reply I was expecting.

'Yes, I do. Very much.'

'And does she like you?'

I wish I knew. I don't want Ness to experience any more uncertainty, but that's real life, isn't it? I can't protect her from it. All I can do is be honest. And even though I never thought I'd be discussing matters of the heart with my seven-year-old daughter, I answer her honestly. 'I don't know. I hoped she might but – I just don't know for sure.'

'Then you have to tell her. Maybe you were meant to be together because you both loved the stars on the beach.'

'She might not want to be with me, Ness.'

She crosses her arms again. 'It doesn't matter. You *have* to tell her, Dad.'

I should ask her how she feels about her dad possibly being with someone else and have all the grown-up conversations I'm meant to have with my child about a prospective Other Person coming into our lives. But I get the feeling

Nessie is happy with what she knows so far – if anything else happens, we can talk more then.

We go inside to find Owen and Sarah setting up their Xbox on our small TV. Their boys are bouncing excitedly on the sofa and Ness goes to join them as they await their latest game battle.

'All set?' my brother grins, leaving Sarah to finish the job. It's long been a source of amusement to me that Owen is a complete technophobe, despite giving all the outward fuss and bluster of a man who knows everything about it. If you didn't know him you'd assume he was a whizz with anything technical; in truth he has problems making a call from his iPhone, let alone anything else.

'They can't get hold of her,' I say, lowering my voice as we move away to the kitchen. 'Cerrie's trying, but so far no joy.'

Owen pulls a face. 'Ah. Not good.'

'Nope.'

'So, what's Plan B?'

'There isn't one.'

'Bro, that's tough.'

There's a loud cheer from the living room as Sarah raises her hands in triumph and the kids all crowd around the games controller.

I look at Owen, fear rising in my gut. 'What if she doesn't come?'

'Then you find another way to tell her. She doesn't know what she's meant to be going to the site for. She has no idea you're going to be there, or that her friends have told you about the stars and everything. If she doesn't

438

come it means she'd rather not see anyone this evening. You can't take it personally.'

I know he's right. But I can't escape the feeling that it has to happen tonight. Once Brotherson launches it tomorrow, it becomes everyone's property. To show Seren after the event would take something fundamental away. 'It feels personal,' I say, holding up my hands when he chuckles. 'I know it doesn't make sense.'

'You're in love, Stink,' he grins, the Owen Dixon Hair Ruffle a heartfelt gesture in the circumstances. 'It's not supposed to make sense.'

Chapter Sixty-Nine

Seren

It's good to be on the road. I have the radio on and the windows open, the smell of the sea filling the car and the beautiful haze of sun painting the road ahead of me pale gold. It's been so long since I last went away that I'd forgotten the huge sense of relief that comes with finally being on my way. This must be how every visitor to St Ives feels when their cars are packed, work is done for a week or a weekend and all that lies ahead is a journey towards the sea and time in one of the most beautiful places on the planet. No wonder people return year after year. This place calls you home even if you weren't born here. It becomes part of you even if you've only spent a few days in it.

Before I left I had a call from Lou, who wanted to meet me for coffee. I'd just visited Becca to tell her I was going away for a while, and all I wanted to do was get on the road. I almost didn't agree to see Lou, but I'm so glad I did.

We met at Porthmeor Beach Cafe, where the view was

so stunning it was hard not to just sit in amiable silence with our coffee and cake and drink it all in. Lou offered his condolences for the loss of the shop, which I appreciated. He lost his own bait and tackle business in the town fifteen years ago, and it took him years to recover. His wife owns a small clothing store now, which he helps to run, and I think they've finally managed to reclaim much of the money they lost. But it's been a struggle, like it is for many business owners in St Ives.

'You still made your dad proud,' he assured me, the loss and experience in his eyes giving his words weight. 'Mark wouldn't have wanted you to carry on as it was.'

'I hope I did the right thing.'

'You did.' He fell silent for a while, fiddling with a paper napkin. 'I was aware of the mess he left you, you know.'

The revelation surprised me. Dad was generous with his time and his enthusiasm for everyone else, but intensely private about his own affairs. 'Did he tell you?'

'I guessed and he told me the rest. We were talkin' about the campaign, not long before he died. I was worried about him – he'd got so thin and tired and I didn't think he was lookin' after himself. My brother went the same way before his heart attack. I saw the signs and I told him. I just didn't know how close he was to – well, you know.'

'None of us did, Lou.'

He nodded but his eyes reddened. 'He was a good man.'

'He was.'

'You've done us proud, girl. Kept your dad's memory alive. Fought for Elinor Carne.'

'But the vote . . .'

He batted this away. 'Aggie told me. You did us a favour, I reckon. It would have been difficult to make that site work for us. I was just too concerned with stoppin' Brotherson to see it. Better that we got the town fired up about Elinor. This mobile exhibition is a much better option. Folks are gettin' behind it now because they can see something for their money straight away.' He smiled. 'Jack Dixon is a good bloke. Just supportin' his family, like your dad wanted to.'

'It doesn't matter now,' I said, not wanting to think about Jack. He was just one more thing I wanted to put at a distance to myself. Another thing I was about to drive away from.

'I have somethin' for you,' Lou said, taking an object wrapped in a carrier bag from the seat beside him. 'Lady got in touch with me after we'd had the announcement about the mobile exhibition in the paper. Turns out she's the great-niece of the woman who gave your dad Elinor Carne's journals. The old lady passed away last year and this was among her things. She thought we could have it for the exhibition, but I think you should have it.'

I took out a tissue-paper-wrapped parcel and cleared a space on the table to set it down. Pulling the crumpled paper aside, I found a small roll of midnight-blue velvet. 'What is it?'

'Open it and you'll see.'

The fabric was old and patches were beginning to fray at the ends. I unrolled it slowly, taking care to support the material. As the last section rested open against the table, I saw the stitching and gasped.

'It's a star map.'

'It's *Elinor's* star map,' Lou said, his voice a reverential whisper.

Across the velvet were tiny stitches of silver, remarkably vivid given their age. The constellations of the night sky, stitched in perfect place by the woman who loved the stars. It was the most stunningly beautiful thing I'd ever seen. But to know Elinor Carne created it made it precious beyond price.

'I can't have this, Lou.'

'Yes, you can. Elinor was denied the chance to show us what she was capable of. But it didn't stop her doin' what she loved, where she was. She used what she had to do what she most wanted to do.' Lou placed a hand on mine. 'Plans change, girl. Doors close. But dreams come in many forms. You can find what you were always meant to have, if you look hard enough for it.'

It's in my bag in the boot of my car now, the most wonderful gift as I set off to rediscover my life. I imagine Elinor in the parsonage she was to live in all her life, stitching stars into the scrap of fabric – fixing her dreams into material. She never stopped gazing at the stars or recording what she found. I'm sure it frustrated her that someone else claimed credit for her discovery, but she didn't give up her passion. Her journals charted her stargazing right up until the week of her death, aged just fifty-six. She carried on, making her dream happen in the best way she could.

I didn't expect to find myself here, having taken on and then relinquished Dad's concerns. I didn't think I'd be looking at a future I hadn't planned, or be considering how I want my life to be. I didn't think I would be driving away for a while on my own. And yet, here I am. What happens next is up to me.

I'm already twenty miles from St Ives when I suddenly remember I didn't leave any water for Molly. I pull over into a layby and try Mum's phone, but it goes straight to voicemail. A call to our neighbour goes unanswered, too. I'm furious with myself, but I don't know when Mum will get back and I can't risk leaving my dog without water all day.

Reluctantly, I turn the car around and head back towards St Ives.

As soon as I get to Hayle, the road congestion begins. It's a Friday and glorious weather, so in addition to the usual traffic heading home for the weekend, opportunistic holidaymakers are driving along the coast for a long weekend break. Plus, a lorry has decided to overtake a tractor going up the hill on the bypass, blocking the road completely. All I can do is sit in the slow-moving queue and be part of the snail-like procession.

My mobile rings again from its cradle on the dashboard.

AGGIE – 4 missed calls

With nothing better to do, I hit the speaker button.

'I've been callin' you all afternoon. No answer. And then I just saw Becca and she said you'd gone. Wasson, Ser?'

Aggie sounds out of breath and I can hear the angry dig of her boots as she walks.

'I just need some time out, Ag. I was going to ring you . . .'

'What about your mum? Does she know where you are?'

444

I sigh. Why can't she just accept I need some time for myself? 'I've left her a note. She'll be fine anyway.'

'But you might not be. You've had a hell of a day – and one hell of a six months before it.'

'Which is why I need to escape for a bit. Please, Ag, try to understand.'

'You need to get back here. We said we'd toast the shop this evenin'. That was a date, right?'

I know she means well, but I feel under attack. I sweep a line of dust from the dashboard stereo with my finger. 'I know we said we'd meet and honestly, it's a lovely idea. But I just don't think I can deal with it today. We'll do it when I get back.'

'And when's that likely to be?'

'Couple of weeks? I don't know for sure.'

'No. Come back now, do the toast, set off tomorrow. It's one day, Seren. Won't make no difference.'

I stare at the almost stationary line of cars and vans ahead of me. In my rear-view mirror it stretches back as far as I can see. I'm trapped. 'I just want to get away, Ag. I wasn't prepared for how hard it would be to give up the shop. I need time to get my head around it.'

'And you can, but . . . You shouldn't be on your own tonight. We know what you've lost, okay? So, who better to be with than your friends who know it all?'

Why can't she let me be? I'm torn: talking about it has made me wonder if I really can just drive away from this huge loss. Would marking it make my journey easier? Would I find closure drinking beer with my friends at The Maidens? Part of me is scared that if I stay in St Ives I'll talk myself out of leaving at all. I think I need this: time to make sense of everything that's happened; time to finally grieve for Dad without all the other concerns getting in my way. I want a wide, open space to feel whatever I need to feel. It's my first chance to make a choice about what I want to do and I'm reluctant to let anything stop me. But would postponing it by a day really make any difference?

'I don't know.'

'Where are you now?'

'On the road. Stuck in traffic.'

'Maybe the traffic is a sign . . .'

'A sign of weekend traffic, maybe.'

'Seren, come on.'

'I don't believe in signs.'

'Please. I think you'll regret it if you don't. Sayin' goodbye is important. You need it to close the door and move on.'

'I'll think about it,' I say, seeking an end to our conversation.

'Promise me you'll come back. Just for a few hours?'

'I'll think about it. That's all I can promise.'

I end the call and lean my head back against my seat. Ahead of me the stubborn line of red lights refuses to budge. At this rate it could be too late to set off again once I've visited Molly. Should I wait for one more day?

Chapter Seventy

Jack

It's almost four forty-five p.m. when I return to Nessie's school. I've told myself I can't worry about Seren not showing. Her friends know her better than I do and they won't give up trying to get her there. Owen was right: she doesn't know what's really happening. It isn't personal and she isn't avoiding me because she doesn't even know I'm going to be there.

While I've been building the new structure, I've thought about all the chances I had to talk to her after the vote. I'm an idiot for not taking them. I should have gone to see her next day. I definitely should have tried to see her before she lost the shop. I *should* have sought her out and apologised for how I was the night we won.

Can I really expect her to feel anything for me now?

I can't think like that. Everything I've done in the last three weeks has been my attempt to make amends. When she sees the building, I hope she'll see apology in every stone.

If she sees the building . . .

Cerrie is waiting for me in St Piran's school car park. She greets me with a wave – but my heart sinks when I see how quickly her smile fades.

'What's happening?' I ask, leaving the car and walking over to her. 'Is she coming?'

Cerrie shrugs. 'I'm so sorry, Jack. I've heard nothing.'

I stare at her. 'What has Aggie said?'

'She's keeping on trying Seren's mobile. There isn't anything else she can do.'

I turn away, run a hand through my hair, trying to think. 'What happens if she doesn't answer at all? It's all ready for the public launch tomorrow. I need Seren to see it.'

'I wish I could tell you different, but I think Seren might have decided to be on her own tonight—' She breaks off as her mobile rings and I spin back. 'Hang on, Jack . . . Ag? Have you . . . ? And what did she . . . ? Oh.' She smiles but I can tell the news she's received isn't what she was hoping for.

I watch helplessly, her side of the conversation not giving me enough clues. After too long waiting, she puts her hand over the receiver.

'She isn't coming.'

I stare at Cerrie. 'What do you mean?'

She looks as lost as I feel. 'She just spoke to Aggie . . .'

'Tell Aggie to persuade her.'

'She can't.'

'But she just spoke to her . . .'

'On the phone. I think she's gone . . .'

448

No, this can't be happening! She has to see it today. Tomorrow is the big public launch Brotherson has planned, and after that it will be splashed across the local newspapers and TV news. It will be too late for me to show her first, to explain why I made it and who it's really for. I hold my hand out. 'Let me talk to Aggie.'

'Jack, I don't think it'll do any good . . .'

'Please? Just – let me have the phone.'

She passes it to me, folds her arms and watches with concern.

'Aggie? It's Jack. What's happening?'

'Hey Jack. I've been callin' and textin' her since midday. No answer. Then she just answered. She says she's going away for a while.'

'Where has she gone?'

I can hear Aggie's breath in quick, rhythmic bursts against the receiver. 'I don't know, but she mentioned leavin' a note for her mum. I'm headin' over to her house now. I don't think she can have gone far. Becca saw her about two hours ago.'

'Who's Becca?'

'Owns a bar here where Seren works sometimes.'

Yet another bit of Seren's life I know nothing about. How is it possible to feel so connected to someone you hardly know? 'Please, do whatever you can to find her. We need her to see this before everyone else. I need her to see it.'

'Just tell me one thing, Jack Dixon: why? Why does it matter to you now?'

Cerrie is watching me closely. I haven't spoken about

this out loud, but I can't bear to miss the chance to see Seren today. Aggie is her best friend and it's clear from the tone of her voice that she doesn't trust me. If I stand any chance of finding Seren, I have to convince Aggie.

'Because I think I'm in love with her.'

Cerrie gasps and claps an apologetic hand to her mouth. But I can see the beginnings of a smile underneath and it gives me hope that at least one member of Seren's close circle likes me.

There is a long pause on the other end of the call. The footsteps have slowed. I wonder if Aggie even believes me.

'You do?'

I close my eyes, wishing I didn't have an audience. 'Yes, I do. I've been falling in love with her since we first met, before I knew she was on your committee, or leading the campaign. I just didn't realise what was happening. It's been a long time since I felt like that.'

The footsteps stop. I hear seagulls in the background and a distant rumble of the sea. 'Go on.'

What more does she want me to say? 'Cerrie told me about Seren making stars with me and my daughter and it all finally fell into place. What she did on the beach meant the world to us. I think I was already falling for whoever was helping us: when I knew it was Seren everything made sense.'

Cerrie is grinning at me and her eyes have misted a little. 'So what if she doesn't feel the same?'

I don't even want to consider that possibility. 'Then at least I'll have had a chance to thank her. And make amends for winning the vote.'

The warmth of Aggie's chuckle takes me by surprise. 'Bleddy Nora, boy, only you would apologise for winnin'. Right, hold tight. You and Cerrie get over to the place and I'll get her there. Somehow.'

I hand the phone back to Cerrie. 'Aggie says we should head over to the site.'

'Has she found out where Seren's gone?'

'Not yet. She thinks Seren's mum might know.'

'What happens if she can't find her?'

'I don't know. I can't even think straight. Let's just get over there and wait.'

Cerrie flaps a hand in front of her face as if trying to shoo impending tears away. 'Oh my *life*, Jack, you totally love her, don't you?'

Until I said it out loud I didn't know if I loved her yet, only that I was falling. But I do love her. That's what's been gnawing away at the inside of me as I've worked on the project. It's pushed me to use every last minute to get it right and kept me going through torrential rain, high winds and every other hurdle I've encountered.

I can't escape it. I'm completely out of control and it scares me. But I've gone too far down this road to back out. All I can do is wait. And hope I haven't set myself up for the biggest fall of my life . . .

Chapter Seventy-One

Seren

When I arrive home, there's a text message on my phone from Aggie:

Called by your house but nobody home. We're going to The Maidens anyway, so just know we'll be raising a beer to your dad and his shop regardless. We love you. Do whatever makes you happy tonight xxx

I can't do this now. Losing the shop has become impossibly entangled with everything else – losing Dad, losing the vote, losing the stars, all the ideas I wrongly entertained about Jack. It's too much to deal with. But I love that my friends are honouring today whether I'm there or not. Aggie won't be happy that I'm not there, even though she understands. I know she prides herself on us sharing every high and low point of our lives. And we have. This will be the first one she'll miss.

Molly is snoozing happily in her basket and appears

unconcerned that her water bowl is empty. I take it to the tap and watch the water swirling into its silver base. The stream from the tap catches light from the late afternoon glow, gold dancing through blue. I glance at the kitchen clock. Five twenty-five p.m. If I go now, I can still make Port Isaac before dark. I checked with the B&B there and the owner said they have three rooms free. Should I call and book it now?

I think of the traffic that ensnared me earlier and decide against it. I'll chance there being room when I get there. I can always sleep a night in my car if it's fully booked. I plan to be up with the dawn anyway.

I put Molly's water bowl down quietly but her nose appears over the edge of the basket with a whimper.

'Hey girl, it's only me. Don't get up,' I say, stroking her warm snout. She replies with a long lick across my hand and snuggles back down.

With a final look around the kitchen, I slip quietly out. But as I reach the front door, I have an idea. Racing up to my room, I pull out the box I'd stashed in the back of my wardrobe when we lost the vote. Being given Elinor's star map this afternoon made me think about my own dream – my jewellery. I'd assumed because of all that had happened with the last bracelet I made that I wouldn't be able to make anything else. As if the bad experience with Jack and the choices I'd made because of him had cursed my ability to create.

The distance from St Ives and all it means to me might help me to focus again. Designing jewellery has been part

453

of me for so long, but I let myself lose sight of that. Maybe it's time to try again while I'm away.

The thought gives me a shot of excitement. This trip is no longer about escaping: it's about discovering who I want to be. I've heard other people talking about going away to 'find' themselves and always assumed it to be a bit of an indulgence. But that's exactly what I'm doing and it feels like a vital next step. I'd shelved so many of my own ambitions when Dad died that I don't know what I want to be now the responsibility for his things has been lifted from my shoulders.

Out in my car, I check my phone. No more calls. Good. Patting the box of my jewellery-making things on the passenger seat, I start the engine. Time to find out what I want the next chapter of my life to look like . . .

Chapter Seventy-Two

Jack

I'm here.

Alone.

Cerrie has gone to pick up Aggie from St Ives. She said they'd be back by five thirty, but it's already five forty p.m. and my nerves are kicking in.

There's still no word from Seren beyond that conversation she had with Aggie. I don't know if Aggie has managed to change her mind, or if Seren will be in the car with them all when they return. Maybe that's the reason for the delay. Perhaps they're still convincing her to come . . .

I stand at the door of the new building and look out across the hill to the shimmering sea beyond. I know every stone of this place. I put each one in place with my own hands. After months of doing odd jobs for other people to make ends meet I'd all but forgotten the surge of joy I get from building whole structures from the ground up. Even with Rectory Fields I've supervised others putting the build together. With my hand resting against stone that once formed Elinor Carne's home, I realise that during the three weeks I've toiled putting this place together I've felt alive again. This is *my* design, the work of my hands, the building that grew in my mind long before it rose from its new foundations. And the reason for it all was Seren. Without realising it, *she* made this happen. It's my response to what she did for Ness and me, not just with the stars on Gwithian Beach, but also the vote she pushed in our favour. She's given me the gift of a chance to build something entirely on my own terms.

Watching the early evening sun stretch across the long grass towards me, I face the possibility that she might never know what she's done for me. Or how I feel about her.

Fearing she might not be here has made me understand how deep my feelings run. I don't find it easy to admit how I feel to anyone, least of all myself, but I didn't think I'd ever fall in love like this. I'd assumed this was the stuff of soppy films and fiction. But it's as real inside me as the blood racing through my veins or the heavy beat of my heart. I love Seren MacArthur. And I don't know what I'll do if she doesn't feel the same.

I lean against the open doorway, the reclaimed oak frame warmed by the sun soothing against my back. At the end of the path leading to this place are the three standing stones falsely claimed to be three heartbroken maidens doomed to await forever their lost lovers' return. Turned to stone by their tears. I have no fear of still being here hundreds of years from now, but maybe this place will prove a more significant location for my building than I thought.

Have they convinced her to come here? And even if she knew the real reason, would she want to see it? I've assumed an awful lot based upon what Cerrie told me, but at the end of the day it's Seren's decision. And nobody knows what that is. This entire project might have been built on false pretences or misplaced hope, as shaky a foundation as you can get.

Not that it will entirely be in vain, of course. Tomorrow it will become everybody's. I just wanted it to be Seren's tonight . . .

I reach into my jacket pocket and pull out the seaglass bracelet I picked up from Nessie's bedside table this afternoon. Turning it over in my fingers, I let the motion calm me. Nessie was right. Making the seaglass stars on the beach with Seren restored my faith in magic. I *have* to believe I can find it again . . .

A car swings into the car park. From where I am, I can't see who is inside. I quickly pocket the bracelet and walk down the new path. Is Seren there? Have they found her?

I slow as I get closer, then stop.

I can only see three people. The moment I see Cerrie's expression, I know the worst has happened.

I've lost her. Before we even began.

'What happened?'

'I'm so sorry, Jack.'

Aggie and the tall blond guy who I recognise from when I almost went into Seren's shop follow Cerrie from the car towards me, their eyes wide as they see what I've built.

'You did this for her?' Aggie shakes her head as if the mirage might disappear. 'Wow, Jack.'

'Man – respect.' The guy holds out his hand and I shake it. I know my smile doesn't sit well. I'm gutted.

'I told you it was special,' Cerrie says as she passes them, coming straight up to me and giving me a hug. I'm so surprised I can't even react to it. 'Jack, I'm so sorry. I think she just needs time. This might have been too much for her.'

I notice the bloke put his arm around Aggie. Ah, well, that clears *that* mystery up.

'Have you heard from her again?'

'No. Aggie left a text and Kieran's left some, too.'

It's time to admit defeat. She isn't coming. But this is still hers, no matter what. I wish it could be different, but if I were in her place, would I have come here? I've always worked out problems on my own – the thought of bringing a group of friends into the equation makes me queasy. I have no right to expect Seren to be any different, especially not on my account.

'Can we look inside?' Aggie asks, her hand touching my arm as she heads up the path.

'Be my guest.'

I'd wanted Seren to be the first to see it, but it doesn't matter now. Kieran gives me a sympathetic smile and we stand in awkward silence as Aggie swears loudly from inside the building.

'Aggie's impressed,' Cerrie offers with a smile.

At least that's something.

'I probably should go,' I say, suddenly tired and keen to return to Nessie.

'No, mate, stay,' Kieran says. 'We have beer.'

'I'm driving.'

'Cerrie has a bottle of water in her car,' he insists. 'Come on, we need to give this place a proper welcome. Stay with us for a bit, eh?'

'For Seren,' Cerrie says. 'We promised her we'd toast her dad and his shop even if she didn't want to come. We're all part of this now.'

I don't want to stay. But when she puts it like that, how can I refuse?

Aggie spreads a blanket across the thick grass and we sit down. Kieran passes out beers; I sit like a child with Cerrie's bottle of water. A gentle breeze shivers across the grass around us, the metal wind chime Cerrie insisted on hanging above the doorway to the new building ringing out. It's a cluster of hammered tin stars suspended at intervals from silver wire; her boyfriend Tom made it for us. A craft thing he does, apparently. It's lovely, if an odd addition, but I appreciate the thought. We sit with our backs to the building but I feel its presence behind me, strong and proud. It will be here long after me, and there's reassurance in that.

Seren's friends are making the best they can of the situation, their soft laughter and good-natured chatter swirling around me. But her absence is like a shadow between us.

'So how's the parsonage coming on?' Kieran asks, pulling me back into the conversation.

'Good. We'll be ready ahead of schedule. And the mural

by your kids looks great, Cerrie. You're all welcome to come and see how we're getting on.'

'That'd be good,' Kieran says, looking to his friends for their support. 'Maybe we should arrange something.'

We exchange smiles and fall back into silence. I'll give it another ten minutes, then make my excuses. It's after six now; there's no point hanging around. They're being kind, but I can't cope with much more of this.

'Lou was saying he has a whole month of venues confirmed for the Elinor Carne exhibition,' Cerrie says as the others make too-forced murmurs of approval. 'You know, I think it worked out for the best for everyone. The vote, I mean.'

'I reckon so, too,' Aggie says. 'Took me a while to get there, but I think we all won in the end.'

'I hope you like what we've done with Rectory Fields,' I say. 'We salvaged a lot of the original stone like I'd hoped we could, and I've tried to emulate elements of the original building to hint at its history.'

'Is that where you got the stone for this place?' Kieran asks.

'Most of it, yes. Other bits we found in neighbouring fields, and some from a small artisan quarry that's opened not far from the place the stone was originally mined.' Talking about the building warms me a little. This is still my achievement; still my dream in physical form. I'm proud of it no matter what.

'It's stunnin', Jack,' Aggie says, and for the first time I see real regard in her face. 'You did a beautiful thing. We all think so.'

'Thank you.' I chance a glance at my watch. 'I probably should get going.'

'What *is* this?'

Confused, I look at Aggie, but she's no longer looking at me. Like Cerrie and Kieran her face is turned to the left, surprise filling her eyes. I follow the line of their gaze – and see a fifth person by the standing stones, her body thrown into silhouette by the bright sky behind.

Seren MacArthur is staring past us at the building I made for her. And suddenly all my words disappear like skylarks rising into the blue . . .

Chapter Seventy-Three

Seren

I don't know what made me turn back from the main road and come to The Maidens. I was happy driving away from St Ives, leaving everyone else behind while I chased myself. I thought I knew what I wanted at last. But when I passed the familiar small road leading up to the car park, I somehow couldn't drive past.

I knew my friends would be here. But I wasn't expecting this.

I'm here in the place I said I wouldn't be, and Jack Dixon is with them. But what I can't take my eyes off is the new building next to the standing stones. A perfect replica of the driftwood and moss house Jack made for me – which nestles in my jacket pocket, where it's been since the morning I found it. I've tried to forget what it meant to me, but I haven't been able to put it away. Even after everything went wrong and my visits to Gwithian ceased, the little house still gave me hope. The new building has old stone where the tiny one has driftwood, and a

462

grass-covered roof where its tiny predecessor has moss and bark. It's beautiful – but confusing.

'What is this?' I ask again, seeing Jack scramble to his feet. He looks shocked, but there's something else; something I can't quite put my finger on.

'You came! I knew you would!' Aggie is at my side quickly, pulling me into a hug. 'Sit down! Grab a beer!'

'Why is he here?'

Cerrie smiles as she joins us. 'Jack is – um . . . Jack?'

Jack Dixon reddens. 'I'll give you a moment. I'll just be in there . . .' He turns and hurries away from us, into the building.

'Classy move,' Kieran mutters, shaking his head at Aggie.

I stare at my friends, hardly believing they've all colluded with Jack. 'What's going on?'

'This was Jack's idea,' Cerrie says, her soothing voice warm against the nerves shaking me. 'You need to talk to him.'

'Why didn't you tell me he'd be here?'

'Because—' Cerrie begins, but Aggie raises her hand.

'Shh, don't. Seren, you need to talk to him. He made this for you.' She ushers me to follow Jack, stepping back with Cerrie and Kieran.

I look towards the building. It's new but familiar, looking as though it's risen from the ground and has always been here. I don't want to see Jack, not when I'd decided to leave him in the past. But I want to know why the building is here and if what Aggie says is true.

So I walk away from my friends and the standing stones. The breeze makes my hair dance around my face, the dipping sun casting long shadows as I walk. When I reach the new path leading to the building, my breath catches.

Set into the path are four stars made of row upon row of seaglass. The path is the colour of sand and the glass sparkles in the early evening light, just as the dawn caught the Gwithian stars every morning I found them. I know my friends are watching, but in this moment I am only aware of my own breath and the steady pulse of my heartbeat. Why would Jack build something like this, here?

I reach the door, which Jack closed behind him as he disappeared inside. Resting against it is a small wind chime made of a waterfall of tin stars on silver wire. But it is an engraved slate plaque set into the stone of the round building that draws my attention.

STAR OBSERVATORY
A GIFT TO ST IVES
IN LOVING MEMORY OF
ELINOR CARNE (1801–1857)
and MARK MACARTHUR (1956–2017)

'*The stars are my friends, the heavens my home.*'

It's too much.

How did Jack know this place was special to me? Or that Dad's dearest dream was to establish an observatory in Elinor Carne's name? How did he know to place the stars from our game to lead people to the observatory – and why do all this now, when I've heard nothing from him since the night of the vote? I bite back tears, determined to walk into the building with my head held high.

When I open the door, Jack Dixon is waiting for me . . .

Chapter Seventy-Four

Jack

She's here.

Framed in the old oak doorway, Seren MacArthur is the most beautiful woman I've ever seen.

She also looks like she wants to attack me.

Have I offended her? Was it wrong to dedicate the observatory to her father as well as Elinor Carne? My back finds the safety of the rounded stone wall as I try to look calm.

'Hi.'

'What is this?' she asks again, slowly. There's the faintest quiver in her voice that could be emotion or simmering rage. At this point, I can't tell which.

'It's an observatory.' I point up to the small mezzanine floor above me, where a brand new, state-of-the-art telescope has been installed.

It's amazing the strings Bill Brotherson can pull when he puts his mind to it. The roof is designed on a hydraulic system, too, so that it effortlessly parts to allow the telescope through. There are hidden solar panels at the back of the roof, invisible from the entry, and the plan is to link with schools and universities across the southwest to ensure that a generation of astronomers can have access to this place, furthering the research Elinor Carne longed to be recognised for. Nessie's school will be the first to visit, and Cerrie is planning a year of astronomy-themed activities to promote the observatory and Elinor's legacy.

All of this will be loudly announced by Brotherson at the official opening tomorrow, as he smiles benevolently for a barrage of press flashbulbs and I maintain a respectful distance, standing by the structure I designed and built from my heart.

But none of that matters as much as what I say next.

'I built it for you. For your father and for Elinor too. But mostly just for you.'

She frowns and is about to speak, but I've played out this moment so many times preparing for today, and I just want to say it all before she has a chance to shoot me down in flames.

'Please, just listen. I know you were the one finishing our seaglass stars at Gwithian. Cerrie told me. I can't believe I didn't work it out. And I now know what you did with the town vote. What you did for Nessie and me. I couldn't believe it. Worst of all, I couldn't believe how cowardly I was towards you that night. I'm so sorry, Seren. I should have gone for that drink with you, like you asked, not been embarrassed by Brotherson and dismissive of you. For what it's worth, I spent the last week of the campaign trying to persuade people to vote for your side.

As if I ever had any influence to bear on that. I should have realised the town would vote whichever way you asked them to. So thank you. You offered me grace to take on the parsonage and you put your faith in me. That was a huge gift . . .'

'But I didn't . . .'

'It was a gift. But nowhere near as much of a gift as the stars you completed. That gave us back our belief in good things. It brought my daughter and me closer than ever.' She still isn't smiling and I can feel the hole around my feet being dug deeper as I speak. 'So I built this. To say thank you. To show you what it meant to me – what it *means* to me.'

She says nothing. The only sound is the wind moving through the observatory, the creaks and clicks of the new building, still unfamiliar to my ears. I wanted Seren to see the observatory first – and against all odds, she has. I have to be happy with that. And I can't expect anything more. I want to tell her I love her; that I've been falling for her since we met. But it feels like too much to load her with. And judging by her expression, I don't think she feels the same. So I stuff the last part of my well-rehearsed speech away, before I make the biggest fool of myself.

'How long have you known about the stars?'

For a moment I'm thrown: does she mean the stars the observatory is designed to watch, or our game on the beach? 'Which stars?'

'On Gwithian Beach. How long have you known I was making them?'

'Not as long as you've known about Ness and me.'

She looks away. Damn, I've blown it.

'I'm sorry. Look, I'll go. Leave you to look around. Check out the telescope, it's pretty cool. It cost Brotherson a small fortune, by the way. So you get the last laugh there. I think – I *hope* – your father would have liked that.' I pick up my phone and car keys from one of the oak benches set into the wall and begin to cross the flagstone floor. I'm almost level with Seren when her hand reaches out and touches my chest. It's like a jolt of static and I stop, unable to move, as our eyes meet . . .

Chapter Seventy-Five

Seren

I don't know what I'm doing. Or why I stopped him. I just know it can't end yet.

'You tried to influence the vote for me?'

He nods. His eyes become very still and I'm suddenly aware of the rise and fall of his chest against my hand. I want to pull away but it feels . . . *safe*.

'Thank you.'

'I'm sorry. I should have followed you out after the result, or come to see you weeks ago. Earlier that night . . .'

My shoulders tense. He remembers that, too? 'Jack, don't . . .'

'I wanted to kiss you.'

I stare up at him. I could deny how I felt but now the truth is out there, why even try?

'So did I.'

His fingers close gently over my hand, his heartbeat padding away against my palm. 'I have no answers. I don't

470

know what's going on or what's possible. But I think I love you . . .'

'I'm going away.'

The words are out like jagged knives before I realise I've said them. I'm shocked and in shock, so close to telling him everything yet terrified it will break me apart if I do. I was going to leave St Ives tonight – I was planning time for myself, to work out what I wanted. I want Jack – amazingly, astoundingly, so powerfully it steals my breath. But being with him won't answer every question or set my course for the future. And yet even as I say it, I see his smile fading. This isn't what I wanted for the day I said goodbye to Dad's shop. I didn't expect to break anyone's heart but my own.

'I know,' he says. 'Aggie told me.'

'I have to. I need time – for me. So much has changed this year. I feel like I don't even know myself. It isn't forever, just for a few weeks.'

He closes his eyes but his hand still holds mine. If I'm going to start believing in signs, this is a good place to begin.

'Would you wait for me, Jack?'

As his eyes open, I reach up and touch his cheek. I don't know if I even have the right to ask, but if I'm going away to find answers I need to start here.

His kiss is immediate, soft and strong. I melt into his embrace and we rise and fall like a sea tide, moving closer, pulled together towards a new shore. And like Gwithian's seaglass stars, we find what we were missing, completing each other piece by piece.

When we walk out of the observatory, hand in hand, the stars are starting to appear in the deepening blue evening. As my friends cheer and rush over to join us, I take a look over Jack's shoulder and smile. My ageless celestial friends above gaze down at us and I wonder what they see – how short a pinprick of light our lives together will appear to them in the long stretch of eternity. Somewhere, I think Elinor Carne and Dad might be watching us, too.

I'm still going away for a while. But not this evening. For now, I have the whole world in one tiny corner of Cornwall: the sunset-painted sea, the wide sweep of St Ives Bay, my dearest friends – and Jack.

My Jack.

Dad used to say that magic is everywhere, if you look hard enough for it. I went looking for treasure on Gwithian Beach and found more than I ever expected. And as the night begins and the stars claim the sky, I am no longer fearful of what lies ahead. Jack's arms around me – and the promise of what I'll find for my future – are all I need to know.

THE END

Acknowledgements

I'll let you into a secret: this is one of the best bits about writing a book. It's also the *scariest*, because I might miss someone. So I'm giving you *all* a hug right now, just in case I forget later!

First of all, my deepest thanks to *you*, lovely reader. All my life I've dreamed of writing stories people wanted to read. By reading this book, you've made that little girl in Kingswinford Library's dream come true. Thank you. Hope you enjoy Seren and Jack's story – I wrote it for you xx

Next, my lovely Dad, Brian Harvey Dickinson: actor, raconteur, runner, ultimate sweetie and Best Dad Ever. Writing this book has been strange because it's the first one without him here to chat about it. But if you look closely, you'll see him running through these pages (doing his *best times*, of course). I reckon he would have been chuffed with that. Miss you, Dad. Secret sign xx

Huge thanks to my brilliant agent, Hannah: chief cheer-leader, confidante, consoler, fierce advocate and friend. Big thanks also to my editor, Caroline Hogg, and the fab team at Pan Macmillan, including Jayne Osborne, Kate Tolley, Camilla Rockwood and Kathryn Wolfendale.

All my love to my fabulous writer friends, for constantly inspiring me, cheering me up and *woop-woop*ing me onwards: Cathy Bramley, Julie Cohen, Rowan Coleman, Kim Curran, Jo Eustace, Kate Harrison, Rachael Lucas, Tamsyn Murray, A. G. Smith and Cally Taylor. Thanks also to the Dreamers, my writing group, and Anna Mansell, for our regular St Ives chats in The Hub and on Twitter! You all rock! xx

My Twitter, Instagram, Facebook and YouTube lovelies. You are fab! Huge thanks to everyone who has contacted me about my books, chatted with me on social media and been so excited about my writing. As usual, I've sneaked a couple into the story: Sharon Thomas – @Starflower68 – appears as Sharon, owner of Wax-a-Daisy candle shop and member of the Save the Parsonage Committee (she named her shop, too!), and Anthony Lee @Holland4La appears as Lee, the young writer who visits MacArthur's.

Thanks to my family and friends, for their love, understanding and enough cups of tea and coffee to fill St Ives Harbour. I love you all xx

Huge thanks to Emma Stevens, whose gorgeous song 'The Star That Guides You Home' inspired the very beginnings of this story. Thanks also to Seth Lakeman, Cara Dillon, Sam Kelly & The Lost Boys, Ed Sheeran and Kate Rusby, whose music has kept me company and created a perfect atmosphere through every stage of this novel's life. Thanks also to Charlie Bowater, whose beautiful painting 'The Old Astronomer' inspired the character of Elinor Carne.

Much love to Kat Stallard aka @saltyseakat on Instagram – her beautiful beachcombed seaglass photos and handmade crafts inspired Seren's passion. Love also to Laura Evans, the real-life St Ives Mermaid, for inspiring Nessie's mermaids in the story (and appearing in a flashback!).

And lastly, my gorgeous Bob and beautiful Flo. You are my sky, my stars and my sea. I love you more than all the seaglass on all the beaches of the world xxx

St Ives stole my heart and inspired this story you hold in your hands. I found magic there, and I hope I've done this amazing place justice in *Somewhere Beyond the Sea*. Magic *is* everywhere, if we look hard enough for it. I hope this story inspires you to find the magic you're looking for.

Brightest wishes
Miranda xx

Bibliography

While writing *Somewhere Beyond the Sea*, I found these books incredibly helpful for researching stargazing, observatories and the history of female astronomers for Elinor Carne's story.

An Astronomer's Tale: A Bricklayer's Guide to the Galaxy by Gary Fildes, published by Century, Penguin Random House, 2016. This fabulous book inspired the character of Seren's father, Mark MacArthur, and his Shedservatory – it's a brilliant true story of one man's passion to build an observatory, and reads like a Hollywood movie!

Memoir and Correspondence of Caroline Herschel by Mrs John Herschel, published by Palala Press, 2015.

Queen of Science: Personal Recollections of Mary Somerville by Mary Somerville (with Introduction by Dorothy McMillan), published by Canongate Books Ltd, 2001.

Miranda's Favourite Sea-gazing Instagram Accounts

Living in the landlocked West Midlands, I needed lots of seaside inspiration while writing *Somewhere Beyond the Sea* when I couldn't be in St Ives. I love Instagram (I'm **@wurdsmyth** there) and found it to be an Aladdin's cave of Cornish gorgeousness. Here are my favourite seaside-y IG accounts:

@porthmeorcafe – lovely food and gorgeous views of Porthmeor Beach.

@kernow_shots – Lee's stunning photos capture Cornwall at its most beautiful.

@saltyseakat – follow Kat's beachcombing adventures with gorgeous seaglass finds, beautiful beach photos and her wonderful handmade seaglass crafts.

@tidelinetreasure – Jo makes amazing jewellery from pieces of found seaglass – she'll even make a necklace from your own seaglass finds.

@loving_stives – almost as good as being there! Lovely photos of St Ives through the year. Their online magazine at www.lovingstives.co.uk is a great source of information for events and the best places to visit.

@lovecornwalluk – Visit Cornwall's IG account is a treasure trove of amazing places in Cornwall and their website is fab, too.

@walkingcornwall – this account is a collection of photos of Cornwall taken by visitors, and is a great source of other Cornwall-loving IG accounts to follow.

@aspects_holidays – gorgeous photos of St Ives and Cornwall from the lovely team at this local holiday let company. I stay in their properties when I go to St Ives, and I *may* have spent a few hours gazing lovingly at the webcams on their website while researching my book . . .

Miranda's Favourite
Sea- and Star-loving Artists

A book about St Ives wouldn't be complete without a nod to amazing artists, artisans and craftspeople. In the spirit of MacArthur's, here are some wonderful artists you should check out:

Charlie Bowater (www.charliebowater.net) I adore Charlie's artwork. It's sweeping, romantic and breathtakingly beautiful. Her painting, 'The Old Astronomer', hangs in my office, and when I was dreaming up the story of *Somewhere Beyond the Sea*, this painting inspired the character of Elinor Carne. I mention it in the story, too. You can buy her work from **www.society6.com/CharlieBowater** and on **Etsy.com/uk/shop/CharlieBowater**

Poppy Treffry (www.poppytreffry.co.uk) Poppy draws gorgeous pictures using a sewing machine and her designs are made into a lovely range of art, home furnishings, accessories and more. A visit to St Ives isn't complete without going into her cute shop (42 Fore Street). I have several of her cushions and a rather fabulous tea cosy, which kept my teapot toasty for the many, many cups of tea it took to write this book!

Kat Stallard (www.etsy.com/uk/shop/SaltySeaStudio) As I've already mentioned, Kat's Instagram account inspired Seren's seaglass hunting. I have several of her beautiful seaglass-decorated shapes in my home, and a lovely seaglass-covered starfish sits on my desk to inspire me.

Cliffside Gallery (www.cliffsidegallery.com) This gallery in picturesque Port Isaac is the home of Katie Childs' beautiful and evocative art. I love her work! Her seaside and harbour paintings are stunning and also feature on cushions, blinds and lampshades – and Katie is a lovely lady to chat to, too!

Miranda's Guide to St Ives (and Beyond)

As you may have gathered, I adore St Ives and the surrounding area. There are so many wonderful things to see, do and visit – far too many to list here. Everyone has their favourite places to visit on holiday, so here are mine, Bob's and Flo's.

Porthmeor Beach

Gorgeous at any time of year, Porthmeor Beach is wild and wide and completely wonderful. I stayed in a house overlooking the beach while I was writing *Somewhere Beyond the Sea*, and was amazed by how quickly the seascape and colours changed through the day. It's Flo's favourite beach, too. She's been known to insist on making sandcastles and sand-angels in January here!

Porthgwidden Beach

A short walk round The Island headland brings you to this small, perfectly formed beach with its cafe (the setting for Aggie's coffee hut in *Somewhere Beyond the Sea*). When we were in Cornwall two Septembers ago, Bob got up early on the morning of our wedding anniversary to make a gorgeous heart on the beach for me using seaglass, mussel shells, seaweed and bits of driftwood – it was this that sparked the idea for the seaglass stars being made on Gwithian Beach, which began the whole story of *Somewhere Beyond the Sea*.

Fore Street

It gets very busy in the summer, but this famous cobbled street in St Ives is one of my favourites, because it's always our main route into town when we stay there. There are lots of gorgeous shops and cafes, galleries and foodie places and Flo's favourite Post Office, which sells toys, art supplies and Cornish goodies.

St Ives Bookseller (2 Fore Street, www.stives-bookseller.co.uk)

A tiny bookshop at the entrance to Fore Street that packs a mighty punch. This is my go-to place for holiday books and Flo adores choosing stories from the well-stocked kids' section. Lots of local authors, signed books and unusual titles alongside favourite authors and, if you don't mind a bit of a squeeze, you can while away a happy half-hour inside.

Seasalt St Ives shop (4 Fore Street, www.seasaltcornwall.co.uk)

Friendly staff, gorgeous clothes and window displays you want to take home. I love this shop!

Ebb and Flow (25 Wharf Road)

My favourite shop in St Ives. It's a fabulous ethical boutique right on the harbour front packed to the rafters with gorgeous clothes, jewellery, treats and gifts, many sourced in Cornwall. Stay for a chat with lovely owner Karen and say hello to Domino, the shop dog. Also has the best playlist of any shop in the town! **www.facebook. com/EbbandFlowStIves**

Further afield . . .
Gwithian Beach is a very special place for my family and me. Gloriously wide and windswept, with huge skies above, this fudge-coloured sandy beach is a favourite with surfers and families, and when I was writing *Somewhere Beyond the Sea* it was the only choice for the beach where Seren, Jack and Nessie make their seaglass stars.

Visible from Gwithian Beach is the tall, proud, white tower of **Godrevy Lighthouse** on a tiny island, just off-shore. If you park at Godrevy National Trust car park, you can walk right around the headland on a stunning cliff path. In the summer, skylarks wheel high up in the sky and you can spot cheeky seals in the tiny, rocky bays far below most of the year round. Godrevy is one of the first places I visited with Bob's family, also one of the first places we took Flo.

The pretty towns of **Carbis Bay** and **Hayle** are well worth a visit. **Carbis Bay** has the most wonderful beach (which is where Flo first discovered the joy of wriggling her toes in the sand). **Hayle** is on a tidal estuary and is a bustling little town with lots of lovely shops and cafes.

St Michael's Mount – the famous castle on its own island separated from the mainland by a causeway – is a must-visit. But make sure you also head into the lovely little town of **Marazion**, with its quirky shops, restaurants and the utterly brilliant **Marazion Museum** on the ground floor of the Town Hall (2 Market Place), which is a uniquely Cornish treasure trove of curiosities.

Miranda's Top Ten Favourite Foods in St Ives

Any visit to St Ives should definitely involve gorgeous local food. These are the must-have treats for Bob, Flo and me whenever we visit:

1. **Ice cream from Moomaid of Zennor Ice Cream Parlour, 1 Wharf Road** Quite simply the best ice cream in St Ives, produced locally in nearby Zennor with a dizzying array of delicious flavours. The coffee is great, too. You can even sit outside on the tiny covered terrace, snuggled up in red fleecy blankets watching the bustle of the harbour. And yes, we've had ice cream there in January. Why not!
2. **Enormous cinnamon rolls at The Hub, 4 Wharf Road** Overlooking St Ives Harbour and offering a fantastic menu all day and evening. We love The Hub for its atmosphere and family-friendliness. The cakes are amazing – and huge – too!

3. **Stew, bread, cakes from St Ives Bakery, 52 Fore Street** Known for its daily bakes, on our winter visits we've also adored their homemade stew and rosemary bread.

4. **Pasties from The Cornish Bakery, 9 Fore Street** A huge range, and every one freshly cooked and gorgeous.

5. **Fish and chips from The Balancing Eel, 10 Back Lane** for a takeaway treat – or eat in at **Harbour Fish and Chips, Wharf Road**. Both offer the freshest, tastiest fish you'll ever have.

6. **Crêpes at Pels of St Ives, The Wharf** I *may* have had a few jam crêpes here when I visited to write *Somewhere Beyond the Sea* in May last year. A tiny cafe overlooking the harbour with a huge menu of crêpes and pizza.

7. **Anything at Porthmeor Beach Cafe, Porthmeor Beach** All the food here is absolutely delicious and you have *that* view . . .

8. **Breakfast at Sky's Diner, 43 Fore Street** Flo's favourite cafe in St Ives. Very family-friendly and lovely food. Their breakfasts are a staple of our visits to St Ives.

9. **Hot chocolate at Porthminster Beach Cafe, Porthminster Beach** The food and the views are glorious here, but it's their lovely hot chocolate that we love best.

10. **Cream teas from The Yellow Canary Cafe, 12 Fore Street** The freshly made scones, clouds of clotted cream and scoops of local strawberry jam are heaven. You can even send a cream tea home by post. Also try their fruit and lemon tarts, which are delicious.

Somewhere Beyond the Sea
Book Soundtrack Playlist

I make a soundtrack playlist for every book I write, to create the right atmosphere and capture the characters' journeys in the story. Here is the playlist I compiled for *Somewhere Beyond the Sea*:

1. 'The Star That Guides You Home', Emma Stevens (*Waves*)
2. 'Tinseltown in the Rain', The Blue Nile (*A Walk Across the Rooftops*)
3. 'Going Nowhere', Sally J. Johnson (*The Beacon Field*)
4. 'Symphony' (feat. Zara Larsson), Clean Bandit ('Symphony' – single)
5. 'A Sky Full of Stars', Coldplay (*Ghost Stories*)
6. 'The Bold Knight', Seth Lakeman (*Kitty Jay*)
7. 'Nebraska', Lucy Rose (*Nebraska – Remixes*)
8. 'Glow', Ella Henderson ('Glow' – single)

9. 'If I Could Change Your Mind', HAIM (*Days Are Gone*)

10. 'I Wish You Well', Cara Dillon (*After the Morning*)

11. 'Chasing Shadows', Sam Kelly & The Lost Boys (*Pretty Peggy*)

12. 'The Greatest' (feat. Kendrick Lamar), Sia (*This Is Acting*)

13. 'Stop Crying Your Heart Out', Oasis (*Time Flies . . . 1994–2009*)

14. 'Breathe Me In', Jared & The Mill ('Breathe Me In' – single)

15. 'We Are Stars', Callum Beattie ('We Are Stars' EP)

16. 'What Do I Know?' Ed Sheeran (*Divide*)

Plan Your Own
St Ives Adventure

All of the places in *Somewhere Beyond the Sea* are real and can be visited (apart from The Maidens and Bethel Parsonage, although both are inspired by real places in Cornwall and Bodmin Moor). So if you fancy treading in Seren, Jack and Nessie's footsteps, these websites will help you plan your perfect Cornish adventure:

www.aspects-holidays.co.uk – a friendly, locally run self-catering cottage company offering lots of lovely places to stay right across Cornwall.

www.visitcornwall.com – the official Tourist Board website for Cornwall, packed with places to visit, events, guides and accommodation.

www.stayincornwall.co.uk – lots of information about visiting Cornwall, offers, events and accommodation listings.